Under the Golden Sicilian Sun

ROBERT ADAM

ISBN 978-1-00522-690-9 (ebook)

ISBN 979-8-59893-651-1 (paperback)

240121

CONTENTS

Preface

'Nel riconsegnare nelle vostre mani il glorioso tricolore, vi invitiamo a gridare il nostro prorompente inno all'amore: ITALIA, ITALIA, VIVA L'ITALIA!'

'In placing the glorious tricolour in your hands again, we invite you to raise your voices in our overwhelming chorus of love: ITALY! ITALY! LONG LIVE ITALY!'

Chapter One

Brussels - Friday-Saturday, 4-5th September 1970

It was almost midnight by the luminous green dial of my watch. The days were cooling as summer drew near its end and the clear skies of the past two weeks promised a chilly night.

I raised my arm and called forward a taxi from the rank at the end of the street. The driver started his engine, swung out, and cruised the short distance up to the reception venue's entrance in low gear. I turned to face the steps leading down from the double swing doors and shook out a cigarette from my pack, cupping my hands over my mouth as if lighting it.

The young woman I was waiting for emerged and I dropped the unlit cigarette into my side pocket. She hurried down the steps and I reached for the handle of the rear passenger door, holding it open for her as she got in. Looking over the roof of the taxi to the pavement opposite, my other companion for tonight was already on his way over, stepping smartly out of the shadows and remembering my warning not to run.

As I'd left the reception venue, I'd slipped on a pair of black leather gloves and what would look like a black woollen hat to a casual passer-by - not that I expected there to be many about. Now as Pavel reached the car, he pulled down his rolled-up ski mask and wrenched open the far passenger door. I unrolled my mask too, reached behind my back for the Makarov pistol tucked into my waistband and got in the front, next to the driver.

'Drive to the lorry park just past Zaventem on the A3

autoroute. Move,' I rasped at him, pointing the Makarov at his groin, holding the gun well below the level of the windscreen.

Pavel had already grabbed Sophie von Barten by the neck and shoved her face down onto the rear seat, yanking the thin formal jacket she was wearing off her shoulders and down her back to restrict her freedom of movement. Now, as the taxi moved off, I glanced across to see him pulling her arms tightly together, gripping both wrists in one meaty hand while he cuffed them with the other. As I turned back to watch the driver again, she was being gagged with her own pashmina shawl.

The whole manoeuvre, from her appearance at the top of the steps had taken less than thirty seconds. But now the clock was ticking, and we had to get our prisoner across two countries by tomorrow morning.

The streets of Brussels were clear at this time of night and after twenty minutes we had sailed through onto the autoroute. Five minutes further on, I waggled my gun with intent and the driver pulled off into the rest area. I directed him to the far corner, where Pavel's twin-axle heavy-duty truck was parked nose-first close alongside a high-sided Volvo articulated unit with the name of a Danish haulage firm printed on its tarpaulin.

I kept my gun trained on the driver as Pavel got out, dragging Sophie backwards by the cuffs before forcing her out of sight down the narrow gap between his truck and its neighbour.

I ripped the taxi's registration plate from where it was attached above the glove box and thrust it in front of the driver's face as he sat staring straight ahead, hands still gripping the wheel.

'You breathe a word of this, to anyone, and we will find you and kill you.'

He swallowed, knuckles white.

'She won't be hurt, but you will.'

I ground the Makarov into his temple, just so he got the message, then dry-fired it for good measure too. At the sound of the soft click as the firing pin was released, he lost control of his bladder, a dark stain spreading down his legs as he soaked his trousers.

'Now get out of here, fast,' I said to him, his eyes filling with shame.

I got out of the car myself, slamming the door and thumping the roof with my fist to get him moving.

I watched him drive off, presumably glad to be gone. But I wondered how long it would be before his conscience troubled him, he cleaned himself up, and he reported the abduction of a blonde-haired girl in a long green satin evening gown. If so, hopefully by men in a Danish truck.

In the meantime, Pavel had turned Sophie to stand facing the side of his own vehicle, head bent down towards the tarmac. I took over, holding her by the neck and pressing my gun firmly in her back, as he stripped off his ski mask and went to unbolt the heavy rear doors to the Mercedes' cargo area.

When he was done and had stepped up inside, I prodded her from behind, directing her down the gap between the trucks again to stand by the open doors. Her clutch bag dragged over the ground as she stumbled along, its long gold-coloured shoulder strap caught up in the coat pulled down around her wrists.

My accomplice reached down, grabbed Sophie under the arms and unceremoniously pulled her straight up into the truck. One of her shoes fell off and I picked it up to toss inside after her, before quickly climbing in myself.

While Pavel held her, I took the steel chain which we had attached earlier to a cargo lashing point on the floor of the truck bed and threaded it around her cuffs. Then the Pole pushed her down onto the slats and jumped out, closing the doors behind us.

After a few seconds, the engine roared into life and he

pulled slowly out of the lorry park onto the autoroute. We had a long drive ahead of us, a good eight or nine hours to the border crossing from West into East Germany just outside Lübeck.

Before he picked up speed, I stood over Sophie for a moment to undo the roughly tied gag. Then I reached up to switch on a battery lantern hanging from another lashing point up by the roof, before sitting down myself to lean back against the opposite wall.

'Your hand must be hurting under those gloves, Oskar,' she said coldly.

I unpeeled the balaclava and returned her stare measure for measure, our mouths set in the same grim line.

At some point, the left-hand strap of her evening dress had slipped down from her shoulder to her elbow. I got up again and squatted before her, reaching into my side pocket for the pistol. I carefully hooked the strap with the Makarov's stubby foresight, holding her stare as I slowly raised my arm, gently pulling the material back into place. She flinched at the initial touch of the cold metal, then parted her lips as I ran the gun up over her skin. In her eyes something else was mixed along with the rage, perhaps a genuine fear, and perhaps something else again, underneath all that too.

She quickly collected herself, furrowing her brow in anger. 'What's your game?' she demanded, as I sat back down again on my side of the truck.

'And who put you up to this?' she asked more suspiciously now.

'What did you think would happen when you threatened me last month?'

I let the question hang.

'I told you back then I was sorry for what I'd have to do next,' she replied.

I glowered at her. 'So because I wouldn't help your boyfriend with his family trouble in Italy, you thought you'd write to my East German cousin and encourage her to try to flee to the West? Knowing that even sending your letters would compromise her? Your letters which resulted in her arrest three weeks ago.'

I remembered the awe in which the teenage Karin had been of Sophie when they'd met in 'sixty-nine. Sophie in her Chanel suit was the sophisticated, stylish Western woman who the socialist schoolgirl aspired to be. Earlier this summer, Karin was still looking up to her, asking me if I could arrange for them to be fashion pen-pals. How I regretted renewing their connection now.

In the uncertain light of the lamp I thought I saw the faintest, the very faintest of smiles crossing her face at hearing the news that Karin was in custody. She must have already guessed, though, that her plan had worked, given the situation she now found herself in.

'Now that you know what I meant, it proves you should have listened to my warning,' she replied, unrepentant again and somehow making it my responsibility for what she'd done.

I lowered my voice to a growl. 'Have you no shame? Do you have any idea, any idea at all, of the trouble you've got her into? Her and her whole family? You've screwed up her entire life. She's only seventeen. And all for what? To satisfy your petty vindictiveness?'

The girl chained to the grimy floor of the truck was luckier than she knew. I'd smashed some furniture when I had first found out what she'd done. Right now, she was completely at my mercy, should I get to the point where I needed to take out my frustration again. But I also needed her cooperation to improve my chances of making this work.

'Your cousin's arrest doesn't even begin to compensate for what happened to my family, after you got yourself involved in affairs beyond your depth,' she said.

'I'm not going to dignify that claim with an answer. However, you are going to admit your guilt to the East German police and undo the mess you got her into.'

'So this is a freelance operation after all? Good luck then,' she retorted contemptuously.

'I thought it was odd, the way you offered to find a taxi home for me,' she added, admonishing herself now and still seemingly uninterested in Karin's plight.

I reached inside my jacket again and leant across to drop a typewritten sheet onto her lap, upside down for me, the right way up for her.

'If you don't sign this statement, the truck keeps rolling all the way to the border.'

'What will you do when we get there and I still haven't signed?' she asked, unimpressed by my apparent naivety.

'Why do you think you're in handcuffs? I'll ask for the officer who interviewed me when we were over there together last spring and I'll hand you into him, even if I have to go back to jail with you myself.'

'When we were over there together last spring?' she echoed mockingly. 'You mean, when my uncle lumbered me with you on an assignment which I could easily have done myself.'

'Yes, it was so easy, you managed to get us caught by barging into that apartment in Rostock. The one with a dead body in the bath.'

'You're the one who lost us half a day beforehand, so it was really your fault they arrested us.'

For a final answer, she shrugged the page off her lap onto the floor. I hadn't seriously expected anything else. Of course, even if she had signed the statement, she was still going over the border because I had to know I'd tried everything.

'I didn't really expect you to go to all this effort for your cousin,' Sophie said evenly, as if reading my mind.

'She's my cousin, one of the only two I have. How would you like to be sitting in juvenile prison in some forgotten corner of the Republic at this very minute? Wondering if tonight was the night you were going to be picked out by the predatory warder, the one whom all the girls whisper about?'

That did seem to make Sophie pause to think, but only for a second or two.

'Did you bring any clothes for me? I'm freezing here. As you can no doubt see,' she said, glancing down at her chest.

I had brought a pullover and overalls - they were stuffed into a holdall next to me on the floor of the truck. But her complete lack of remorse at Karin's situation, or even any slight verbal acknowledgment of the danger she'd put my cousin in, disgusted me once more.

I got back to my feet and loomed over her hesitantly. I wanted to slap her face but was worried it might tempt me to take things further and perhaps even further than that. But ultimately I wasn't my father - whoever he was.

Instead, I dragged her to her feet, turned her around to face the side of the truck and undid the cuffs. I grabbed the collar of her linen jacket and pulled it back up over her exposed shoulders. Finally, I shoved her against the wall, causing her to reach out to steady herself as I went to unzip the holdall.

'Here,' I said, tossing the clothes over to her. 'I won't look if you want to change.'

'No need. This dress is going in the dustbin. I won't wear it again, not after tonight.'

She slipped off her jacket, pulled the jersey over her head and rolled back the cuffs. The hem came down a few centimetres below her waist.

'Give me your jacket, it's warmer than mine,' she said brazenly, as she put back on the shoe which had fallen off when Pavel hauled her up into the truck.

I shook my head. I wasn't going to play her mind games. Instead, I picked up my walkie-talkie, its sibling hanging from the dashboard in Pavel's cab, and spoke with the smuggler.

I looked over at Sophie. 'You're in luck. In a quarter of an hour there's another rest area, then you can come into the front with us. Any nonsense, though, and you'll be back here on your own, sitting in the dark.'

As we sat in silence, waiting on Pavel to pull off and park, I began to worry at the lack of fresh threats coming from Sophie. There wasn't even the acid observation that I would never get away with it. In my recent experience, this suggested she was either cooking up or had already prepared some new devilment. I wondered if she'd signed the same false confession last year in Rostock that I had, the one in which I admitted we were both spying for the West and had murdered an East German citizen into the bargain. Perhaps she'd done a deal with the other side too and had some secret influence with the Ministry that I didn't know about.

'Before the truck stops, tell me - this family trouble of your boyfriend Rizzo, that I refused outright to get involved with. How serious is it that it made you want to subvert my cousin in revenge?'

She pursed her lips. 'You keep calling him my "boyfriend,"' she hissed. She paused for a moment. 'And it is serious. It's Mafia trouble. Giovanni's father is being forced to transport some goods to Sicily for them.'

'Why didn't you say?' I replied mockingly. 'Look, we have a truck and a driver. Let's go there now.'

She stared back at me.

'But instead of explaining this,' I continued, 'your first thought was that you'd get my family into trouble with an even bigger Mafia organisation, the one on the other side of inner-German border.'

She frowned at me. 'Who's your accomplice then?'

'He's just someone recommended to me by a former police buddy from Hamburg.'

'I'm sure he is. I bet your friend is another corrupt *Bulle* too, as you probably were. Not that we should expect anything better from your type.'

I chose to ignore the class insult.

'So what are these "goods" that are too risky for even

the Mafia to move? And what is Rizzo to you, anyway, that you're getting yourself caught up in this? Is he really so special?'

'You know exactly what he is,' she snapped. 'Nothing more, nothing less.'

I raised an eyebrow.

'Don't be so prudish,' she said disapprovingly. 'It's the nineteen seventies and I'm still human after all. No matter what you thought of my uncle or what you still probably think of me and the rest of my family.'

We felt the truck slow, turn off the road and come to a stop. The bolts were undone and Pavel appeared, silhouetted in the glare from the headlights of the vehicles roaring down the autoroute a few metres away across the grass verge.

Sophie got down by herself under the Pole's watchful eye. She went round to the cab's passenger door without fuss and clambered up inside, going to sit on the neatly made-up sleeping berth behind the two front seats.

We got in after her. Pavel twisted around to give her a proper look as he switched on the ignition and got ready to pull back into the traffic stream.

'You're the best-dressed hooker I've ever had in this truck,' he said in heavily accented German. 'What is she? Special delivery to some general in the East?' he asked - jokingly I thought, but it was hard to tell with him.

Given that he was driving, and she didn't want to die, she leant forward and slapped me in the face instead.

'Feel better for that?' I asked.

She ignored me and turned to Pavel. 'Crawl back under the stone where Lenkeit found you, you stupid Polack.'

'Told you earlier, Pavel,' I said, 'Tonight, we're taking a charming, well-spoken lady of real quality to the fairy-tale republic in the East.'

'I've never heard of anyone trying to escape there,' he replied thoughtfully. 'I've been made offers by people in the West, to transport people coming out the other way. Never agreed to it though, no matter how much they offered.'

He sucked his teeth. 'The Stasi are no saints.'

'Sit still, woman, and be grateful for the warmth,' I said, as she made to offer her opinion.

I rummaged in the holdall I'd brought with me from the cargo area.

'Coffee?' I offered, finding the flask.

'No. This is a kidnapping in case you hadn't remembered, not a picnic,' she retorted.

'Suit yourself,' I said, sipping the black nectar. She didn't deserve it anyway.

We crossed the border into West Germany without incident. Either the taxi driver had taken my death threat seriously or they were still searching for a Danish truck.

At three in the morning, I suggested I take over the driving.

'I drove a lorry a couple of times in the army,' I said to Pavel. Sophie was asleep, having laid down just after Cologne, fussing until I gave her my heavy twill jacket in the end after all.

The stop and start motion must have woken her though, or maybe it was the grinding of the unfamiliar gears, for after I'd pulled back on to the main carriageway, she leant forward between the seats and eyed me suspiciously.

'Are you qualified to drive this thing?' she asked.

'It's amazing what you can teach yourself, if you have to,' I said, glancing to look at her as she sat back again. She'd fastened all the buttons on my jacket, all the way up to the collar and was sitting with her arms wrapped tightly around herself, even though it wasn't that cold, I thought.

'What if the police stop us and ask for your license?' she demanded.

'You sound concerned that we won't make it, almost as

if you're looking forward to us visiting our East German comrades again. Anyway, both Pavel and I need to drive if we're to get to the border before someone starts looking for you.'

Despite my nonchalant tone, the longer that time passed, the less confident I was that we'd carry on avoiding detection.

She didn't comment again and remained silent as I drove on through Westphalia. As we passed Bremen, the morning sun began to peep over the eastern horizon, but I kept going - if nothing else, it was an excuse not to have to speak with her.

Three-quarters of an hour before we reached Lübeck and the crossing point into East Germany proper at Selmsdorf, I pulled off the autobahn into the Buddikate rest area.

'Time for you and I to get in the back again,' I said, prodding Pavel awake. If he was a normal businessman, I'd be asking for a discount at this point for all the hours of slumber he'd enjoyed whilst I'd been doing his work for him.

I brought the truck to a stop with a hiss of brakes in an empty space by the boundary of the parking lot, well before the filling station proper.

Pavel cuffed Sophie again, hands in front so as to be less obvious to any casual onlookers once she was outside the cab. He gagged her again too, pulling the shawl up over her head, as if she was a headscarved Russian babushka. Not that they tended to wear shooting jackets and fishermen's jerseys over ankle-length satin dresses, as far as I knew. When she was ready, he made her get out of the driver's door, on the side shielded from view from the other vehicles, then held her tightly under one arm as he marched her down to the back of the truck and up into the cargo area.

'I need to piss,' I announced loudly, as I watched him push her into a battered airline cargo container, up at the cab end of the load area. 'I'll be back in five minutes.'

Pavel jumped down beside me and closed the rear doors almost to.

'I need to make some final arrangements,' I said softly. He nodded at me as he lit up, taking a long drag on a foul-smelling cigarette. Maybe he was feeling apprehensive too.

The morning sun wasn't strong, but I put on my sunglasses anyway, hoping to distract the other customers inside the cafe from the distinctive scar on my cheek running down from the corner of my eye.

Even as I'd been walking across the tarmac, I was in two minds on how to approach what came next. For I was bringing Sophie over the border against my Stasi handler's express instructions, not to put any kind of pressure on the Ministry over Karin's case.

I needed to create enough of a stink at the Normannenstrasse headquarters to make them want to let Karin go as the path of least resistance to keeping me on side. But I had to judge it carefully such that they didn't lose patience, decide I was a loose cannon, and get rid of me through deliberate exposure to the West German BND. Throwing away the key to Karin's cell at the same time, of course.

There was another reason to get things moving quickly on the other side today. First prize for this manoeuvre would be to get something agreed on Karin's charges and get Sophie back in Brussels in time for work on Monday morning. Before she was missed and the police started asking questions about the girl in the green dress, who'd last been seen at midnight on Friday leaving the Agricultural Directorate's reception honouring the new members of the Malfatti Commission.

As for myself, if I did end up being absent from the office for a few days, I knew my political sponsor at the Berlaymont would have a word with my actual direct boss there and get me excused after the event.

Major Johannes, my East German handler, had given

me a duty emergency line I could call - a West Berlin number where messages were relayed across the Wall to a Stasi communications centre in the East.

There were code phrases for certain emergencies, such as if you suspected imminent arrest by Western counter-intelligence and had to cross the border fast. However, having a platoon of East German border guards, the Volksarmee's Grenztruppen, stand to with heavy machine guns and a couple of armoured personnel carriers to stop the other traffic coming through the crossing point would hardly be keeping a low profile.

There was no queue for the phone at this time of day. I fished for the right coins and dialled the number.

'This is Thomas Hofmann. I'm delivering a package from Wismar to Rostock today and need directions.'

It was no code that would be found in any Stasi manual. 'Thomas' was supposedly my cover name and coincidentally also the name of Karin's brother. 'Hofmann' was my cousins' surname and Wismar was where they lived. Hopefully I'd dropped enough hints to be identified and hopefully someone would realise we were coming through the wire at Selmsdorf.

There was a pause of a few seconds. 'Repeat please.'

I did so, feeling even more foolish as I said the words again. 'Any other message?' came the disembodied female voice again.

'No, that's all. I need directions in the next hour,' I added as an afterthought.

I didn't expect they had many joke callers on that line. I wondered what kind of reception party there'd be on the other side and if Major Johannes would turn up in person based on their deductions.

I tapped the top of the phone with a couple of ten-*pfennig* pieces, weighing up whether there was time for a second call. Without pausing, in case I changed my mind, I dropped in the coins and called my mother's flat in Hamburg.

She wasn't working at the hospital this morning and answered after a couple of rings - the flat was so small it didn't take long to get to the phone.

'Mother, I'm going East, maybe for a few days. I want to see what can be done for Karin.'

'What's prompted this? Why now?'

'I've had an idea. Of trying to speak to someone.'

'Who do you plan to see?'

I wasn't going to lie to my mother.

'I'm going to the police over there. I want to make it very clear to them that she's not solely at fault.'

'How are you going to persuade them of that? What new information do you have on her case?'

'I can't say over the phone. It's a long shot, but I need to try it.'

There was a pause for a couple of seconds while she collected her thoughts. The traffic on the autobahn was getting heavier as the morning wore on.

'Be careful over there. You should know that the church has been praying for her release,' she said cautiously.

Spiritually speaking, I'd only recently turned over a new leaf myself - in August, on the last day of my Irish trip. But I hadn't said anything to her about that yet.

'That's good,' I replied encouragingly, trying to sound sincere. I sensed the surprise and perhaps the hope at the other end of the line.

'I need to go now. I'll call you when I get back.'

'Goodbye then, son.'

I walked back to the truck in increasing trepidation, for I'd committed myself with those two phone calls. Up until that point I could have changed my mind and just about got away with it, if we'd turned around and raced straight back to Brussels. Now I even said a little prayer for myself, not that I was confident that kidnapping a woman was morally justified - even if it was done to try to help someone else worse off.

But if I was in trouble with Sophie for taking her on an involuntary weekend excursion to East Germany, she hardly knew the half of what I'd done. For there was another thing that had been hanging over me since the thirty-first of March, nineteen sixty-nine. And now that I had started to reform and to confess my sins, at some point that one had to come out into the open too.

It had to, if I ever wanted to go after her with a clear conscience. And much as I resisted admitting it to myself, I knew that deep down, I did. That despite how she'd misled my cousin, I'd always done.

The airline container was partially angled on one side so it could fit snugly in the curved fuselage of an aircraft. Sophie was half-lying on the sloped side, feet pressed against the opposite wall. A thin light came down through the skylight in the roof of the truck body and leaked into the container past its canvas side opening.

I closed the flap and arranged myself beside her, but sitting facing the opposite direction, head to toe. I was careful to try not to touch her but did so once by accident before quickly shuffling away. Her eyes gleamed fiercely in the half-light as she finally realised that last night wasn't a bad joke after all and that I really was going through with my threat to deliver her to the police on the wrong side of the border.

'We're crossing from the West in secret, there won't be any record of us having left. If you and I can't convince them today to show some leniency to my cousin, then we'll both disappear into the East for the next few weeks. Maybe longer. You'll have to work with me, whether you like it or not.'

I couldn't see her face properly, but I knew she'd heard me because I got a half-kick, half-stab in the ribs with her heel. Whether she'd understood was another matter.

The truck lurched into motion and we started the final stage of the journey. Despite the cramped angle I was sitting at, what with the dark and the low rumble of the tyres, after half a night's driving I drifted off, fatigue overcoming my attempts to stay awake.

It was the clang of the bolts on the doors which brought me to my senses, just before Pavel stuck his head in through the canvas side of the container.

'I've told them that you're political activists seeking asylum in the Republic,' he announced without ceremony. 'It's up to you now to make sure I get away from here smoothly.'

I rubbed my eyes and quickly turned Sophie onto her side to unlock the handcuffs, before undoing the gag.

'We're parked out of sight of the guards on the Western side,' he continued. 'Their side of the checkpoint is half a kilometre away.'

He rolled up the canvas curtain to reveal two East German border guards in rain pattern camouflage peering in from the road, one with an assault rifle slung behind his shoulder, the other with his weapon held at the alert.

'I've been kidnapped,' exclaimed Sophie, holding out her wrists to show where the cuffs had rubbed. 'I shouldn't be here. I need to go to the West immediately.'

'Words that I'm sure these gentlemen have heard before.'

'Shut your mouth, both of you,' said the corporal. 'Get down from there and no tricks.'

They seemed confused as to what to do next. We were probably the first asylum seekers either of the two soldiers had ever encountered, so they fell back on their default assumption that any people they couldn't safely pigeonhole were Western spies or agitators, until proven otherwise.

Now it was my turn to be patted down and restrained. 'I can explain that,' I said, as the Makarov was fished out.

'Now do you understand?' asked Sophie. 'I was brought here under duress.'

'With an empty pistol?' replied the sergeant.

'Call your duty officer,' I said. 'She's here to confess to helping an East German citizen try to flee to the West. I can explain everything.'

'Don't worry, you will,' he smirked.

The border crossing post was a mean collection of low-rise concrete buildings. It didn't have any proper holding facilities for I presumed anyone trying to escape from East to West would be shot. I also suspected that no one, until today, had tried it in the other direction.

We were made to sit in the unit ready room, under the watchful eyes of the guards coming on and off shift. Sophie certainly got more than her fair share of glances. Forget Pavel's female companions in the back of his cab, from what the soldiers could see of Sophie underneath the male clothes - and they tried - she was also the most elegantly dressed escapee from either direction to have passed through Selmsdorf.

After around three-quarters of an hour, a lieutenant wearing the green cuff-band of the Grenztruppen on the sleeve of his tunic appeared in the open doorway. He beckoned me to my feet and out of the room, then led me down a couple of short corridors to a small, stuffy office in a different part of the building.

He shut the door tightly behind us before speaking.

'The pistol you were caught with is one that was issued to our foreign intelligence service.'

'It was issued to me,' I replied. 'I need to speak to Major Johannes of the HVA, Department III.'

He looked at me appraisingly for a moment. 'Okay, let me try to reach him. I doubt he's on duty on a Saturday, though.'

He went to undo the cuffs.

'No,' I said, stopping him. 'The person I came over with mustn't know I work for the Comrade Major.'

'As you wish.'

'When he comes, or when he sends for me, your men

need to act as if she and I are both in trouble with the Ministry.'

'Don't worry,' he said, grinning broadly. 'We always assume that, no matter whom people claim to be.'

Chapter Two

Just before noon, the Grenztruppen lieutenant strode into the duty room again, followed closely by Major Johannes in his Saturday casual wear. I needn't have worried about him pretending that Sophie and I were in trouble with the Ministry. From the look on his face as he stared at me, I was - or at least, if not in trouble with the Ministry as such, I was with him personally.

But it was Sophie who bore the initial brunt of his anger.

'You!' he shouted at her. 'What are you doing here? Come to join Lenkeit's cousin in the women's prison? I suspect you'd like that, wouldn't you?'

Sophie blushed red. I was nonplussed.

'Okay, bring them along,' he said impatiently to the lieutenant.

We filed out to Johannes' Wartburg. Another plain-clothed officer was standing by the car, his elbows leaning on its roof, smoking as he gazed across the ripe cornfields beyond the chain-link fence. I wondered if he also minded working on a Saturday, but maybe the Ministry paid overtime.

Before Sophie's natural suspicion kicked in, I thought it was high time that Johannes and I started playing the part of us being strangers.

'Where are you taking us?' I asked him, trying to inject the right note of uncertainty into my voice. 'I've brought her here to confess to her involvement in the Karin Hofmann affair.'

'Oh, you have, have you?' Johannes replied dryly, acknowledging me for the first time. 'I'm meant to be taking my son to watch a football match this afternoon in Berlin. That's not going to happen either, is it?'

That was the end of the pleasantries for the next half hour as we drove through several villages of varying sizes, before reaching a largish town that was somehow familiar. Johannes pulled up at the back of a four storey red-brick building with a jab of the Wartburg's brakes, alongside another couple of small cars. It looked more like a town council office built in the time of the Kaiser than anything else. A regional headquarters of the Stasi, for instance.

'Recognise where we are?' asked Johannes.

'Wismar?' I hazarded, based on the direction we'd travelled and the time it had taken us to get here.

'Yes. Appropriate, isn't it? To be brought back to the town from where your cousin tried to flee the Republic. We caught her at the train station just a few hundred metres from here.'

'It looks just as much of a dump as the last time I was here,' commented Sophie.

'Well, some straight answers are needed, or you'll be spending a lot more time here or hereabouts,' he replied shortly. 'I understand that no one in the West knows you're this side. That's handy.'

'I need to be back in Brussels for work on Monday morning,' insisted Sophie.

'You do, do you? Well, we'll see about that too. You can both go to the cells to cool off for a while until I get some more instructions,' he announced, as we trooped inside. 'Use the time to think about why you're here and give me a story I can buy. And it had better be a good one, if I'm going to sell it to my boss,' he said to no one in particular.

There was a short corridor of cells in the basement - not one of the building's original features, I was guessing. Sophie watched me being locked up first, before she was taken away. From inside my cell I could hear Johannes thumping each door as he went past, causing a shout to come from somewhere near the far end of the row.

When she was finally put away, he came back, rattling the doors again. My cell was quietly unlocked to reveal him framed in the doorway, glowering. With a jerk of his head, he summoned me out and back up the stairs to an office on the ground floor.

He sat down slowly behind the desk, then swivelled the chair round so he could stare out at the car park through the dusty window.

'Are you deaf?' he asked my reflection.

I didn't reply. He turned back around to look me full in the eye, shaking his head impatiently.

'Are you unable to grasp simple instructions in German?' he carefully enunciated, as if to someone feeble-minded.

'Which words in the sentence, "Leave your cousin's case for me to deal with," were too difficult for you to understand?'

Now it was my turn to flush.

'You can't put people in jail for receiving letters from the West, even if you do catch them with packed bags at the station. Prayer meetings for Karin's release are happening across the Western church right now,' I exaggerated, then instantly regretting the lie.

He balled his hands into fists, knuckles white. 'We run our country as we see fit, you know that. You don't get to lecture us. You get to tell us what's going on in Brussels so we can assure Germany's friends in the Kremlin that the EEC won't one day turn into a Fourth Reich. Your most important job right now is to support the faction in Moscow that's not neurotically paranoid, for all of our sakes.'

'She's my cousin and she's only seventeen. Don't you people have any awareness of that? There's nothing I won't do to protect my family. That's why I brought you the real culprit.'

'There's nothing that you won't do, is there? Except to trust me, of course,' he growled through gritted teeth. 'I was on the point of getting your cousin released. Not that she deserved it and not entirely free of criminal taint either, but close enough, for all practical purposes.'

He stopped, waiting on my response. 'Are you going to ask how, or why? No? I'll tell you, you amateur. Because I had managed to convince my boss that charging her would do you, me and him no good in the long-term. That we should show some actual mercy to her and prove to everyone else that we're the good guys, the opposite of the fascists in the West.'

He tilted his chair forward and leant over the desk, waiting on my reaction.

'You were really just going to let her go?' I asked faintly. I didn't believe his story for a minute about them doing it from the goodness of their hearts, though.

'I told you in Berlin I'd manage it, even if I had to use my own reserves of goodwill with the Ministry. But your visit here changes that. Because of the way you announced your arrival here today, I can't very well hush it up now, can I?'

He sighed, the first flood of his anger on the ebb.

'One point of view at the Normannenstrasse these past couple of weeks was that we think up some new demand from you, in exchange for her release. A different set of people wanted to find her guilty but suspend the sentence with the implied threat to you that she still might go to jail.'

He looked at me for some acknowledgement of the minefield he'd been navigating on both my cousin's and my behalf.

I'd known I was straying over the line by abducting Sophie and now I'd just heard that all of my planning and effort might have been for nothing. A secret, dangerous part of me was even annoyed at my mother's church praying for Karin's release, somehow blaming them for today's outcome.

'Do you think there'll be any new conditions attached to her freedom now?'

He shrugged.

'What's Fiedler's view?'

Fiedler was the general I'd been introduced to earlier in the summer. Someone very high up in the Ministry and well-connected to the KGB, or so I had been told.

'Thankfully, for you and your cousin, Fiedler's instincts are to trust the handler. After all, he spends enough time carefully selecting us.'

He drummed his fingers. 'But now you come along with your prisoner, like a cat bringing a dead mouse to its human owner. Who has no idea what to do with it. Or with you,' he said, narrowing his eyes again.

'You realise that right now we don't want any new Western hostages? If you've read any newspapers recently you might have heard of this thing called "détente"? Or as your pretend socialist chancellor calls it, "Ostpolitik". Where the two Germanies acknowledge each other's existence and we try to persuade the Americans and the Soviets to take their fight with each other elsewhere.'

'Vietnam proves that Ostpolitik is already working, then. Sophie von Barten's being here won't change that.'

'Whatever you say, Henry Kissinger. Now we have to carry out a charade of a police interview with your girlfriend, so that the pair of you can travel back to Brussels this afternoon. All without letting her know that you and I are working together. That's going to take some performance, some real acting. Like on a Babelsburg film set, going for the Grand Prix at the Karlovy Vary Film Festival,' he looked at me narrowly. 'Think you can pull that off?'

Whilst I thought about it, he proceeded to bring up something else, something that I'd much rather he'd forgotten about.

'It's been one problem after another with you lately, ever since you got back from Ireland.'

He leaned forward again, arms folded now, his expression stern.

'I already had to talk my daughter down from using her Ministry connections to try to find you again. After what you and she got up to together on that course in the summer.'

I was sure I felt my face go redder than ever before in my entire life. Even the scar on my cheek seemed to be burning in a thin, hot line of fire. There was nothing I could say just now to make the situation any better.

For hand on heart, it was Sigrid, the daughter from his first marriage, who had started things at the Stasi college in Bad Belzig where she was a staff instructor. But I couldn't tell her father the full truth, that she hung around the student bar most evenings to pick up a different man for the night. She'd come back to my room two nights in a row, so maybe for her it meant something more.

'Anyway,' he said, bringing me back to the present. 'We've spent enough time up here already. What are we going to do with your woman? Why did she decide to target your cousin? Was it revenge? Some kind of lovers' tiff?'

'She wanted me to help her Italian male friend, I suppose you would call him. His family are mixed up in a Mafia affair of some kind. But I didn't ask for the details at the time, I just refused point blank because I know she's trouble.'

'That makes two of you then. At least you made the right decision for once.'

'I brought her here with the idea that if you could extract a confession it would help my cousin.'

He pursed his lips.

'But the Mafia angle is news to me, I only learnt about it today. I need to know what mischief she's planning because now that she's started, she won't give up trying to drag me into it,' I said.

I also wanted to know for her sake, even though she didn't warrant my concern right now.

Johannes drummed his fingers on the table a couple of times.

'I'm not that bothered about the favour she wanted done for the other guy. But this is a chance for me to test if she might be amenable to working for us, or at least try to push her along in that direction.'

He glanced out the window, thinking.

'Oh yes. And I know how I'm going to do it. I'm going to enjoy this. You - not so much,' he said, smirking at me and clicking his fingers with anticipation.

We went through the rigmarole of me being locked back in my basement cell. Then Sophie's cell being opened and her being brought down the corridor to watch me being unlocked again. Once more, Johannes banged on the other cell doors as he collected Sophie, continuing the game he'd played earlier to distract her from my comings and goings.

Back up again we went to the office I'd just come from. Johannes went over to a grey metal document cabinet, withdrew a fat folder and reinstalled himself behind the desk.

'I've missed the football match I was going to with my son - an Oberliga pre-season friendly between the Ministry's team and the army's: Dynamo Berlin versus Vorwärts.'

He leaned in confidentially.

'Erich Mielke, the head of the Ministry is a football fanatic. Each year he becomes more and more obsessed with Dynamo winning their first Oberliga title. The mark of the man, I suppose. That's why pre-season matches are the fairest ones that we get to watch. For some strange reason, when it counts towards the championship, referees tend to miss obvious handballs and vicious tackles by the Stasi team. But now that that simple proletarian pleasure has been denied to me today, I've got the rest of the weekend for you pair and longer too, if I need it.'

He straightened up, looking at both of us in turn, staring hard.

'First things first. What did you really hope to achieve by bringing Fräulein von Barten here, Lenkeit? Against her will, I might add.'

I glanced at Sophie. Aside from a slight, momentary pursing of her lips at the form of the address, already archaic in the West, she looked pleased. Like her team had scored an early goal, back of the net two minutes after kick-off.

Johannes didn't wait on my reply. Instead, he tapped the folder lying in front of him.

'I've had the Ministry file pulled on the case of Lenkeit's cousin. We're almost ready to take Karin Hofmann to trial. It's a clear case of *Republikflucht*, encouraged, admittedly, from the West,' he said, looking darkly at Sophie as he did so.

He opened the folder and threw a bundle of letters bound with tape between us on the desk.

'You don't need to open them. They've been typed up and put on permanent record. Oh yes, they have. For everyone with the right clearance to look at. Let's see what they say.'

He thumbed through the file now, picking out a sheet which he held up to read, before stretching his arm to reposition it slightly further away from himself.

'Encouragement from the West,' he said, looking down his nose at Sophie, 'This kind of encouragement. *"If you come to Brussels, I have a spare bedroom in my apartment. We can be special friends together."* And the word "special" has been underlined twice. I'll spare Lenkeit the embarrassment of hearing the details in some of the later letters.'

Did you really have no idea, Fräulein von Barten, of

our view on these things?

She shuffled her feet, the heels of her shoes clicking on the linoleum.

He wrinkled his nose. 'Even if, for women, it's never actually been a criminal offence here, it's still a sign of Western moral corruption. So not only have you got Fräulein Hofmann into trouble over her betrayal of socialism you've doubly-damned her with something even harder to shake off.'

I remembered Karin's tear-streaked face through the cell door in Hohenschönhausen and Johannes involuntary spasm of fear at what might happen to her in a juvenile institution. Doubly a target for abuse, too.

Finally, Sophie had the grace to blush in embarrassment at something she'd done. But part of me had died inside. I turned to her solemnly, 'Did you know? Or were you so determined to bring her down you didn't care?'

She flushed some more.

'And even if you didn't mean what you wrote, those kinds of thoughts went through your head,' I added, maybe a little primly this time.

For a couple of seconds her eyes widened slightly, as if in alarm at losing a hold over me. Then the contemptuous look came back as I carried on.

'I thought perhaps that if von Barten here confessed to being a Western agitator, you might show leniency to my cousin,' I said to Johannes, before turning to look disapprovingly at Sophie. 'I didn't know what form the subversion had taken, though. She's only a schoolkid,' I added grimly.

'"Von Barten"?' she spat back. 'What right do you have to speak about me in that way? You're the one who chained me up in the back of your criminal friend's truck.'

'I did it for your own safety, to stop you trying something crazy, like jumping out in the middle of the autoroute. Anyway, in the end we let you come up front into the cab and annoy us there.'

'Listen to you two,' exclaimed Johannes, shaking his head. 'I've been married twice and had a child with each woman. You pair will either end up with one of you on an assault charge, or it will be the other thing.'

'What do you mean, "the other thing"?' I asked sharply. Johannes rolled his eyes.

I glanced at Sophie, who'd just finished doing the same.

'There's no way in hell that's happening,' she snarled.

'I've heard that said before too,' Johannes said smugly to the room. 'But you must have picked on Lenkeit for some reason, known only to you. However, if you want any encouragement to stay away from him, let me explain to you both the trouble his family is in.'

Johannes focussed on Sophie. 'You do understand that Karin Hofmann's problems won't stop once she's out of prison? She'll lose the apprenticeship at the Fashion Institute in Berlin she was going to take up, of course. The closest she'll get to that world in future will be sewing on buttons on workmen's overalls at a textile factory.'

Sophie gave a little frown as Johannes continued.

'And then who knows what else might happen? Her father might get passed over for promotion at the shipyard. Rumours might be planted about an affair between her mother and their church pastor.'

He paused, waiting for a reaction, but she simply stared back silently, expressionless now.

'We call it *Zersetzung*, persecution as payment for treachery, persecution that lasts for years. A living prison without walls. And for the people that we practice *Zersetzung* on, the worst of it is that they're never quite sure why the younger man became factory leader, or who denounced the pastor to the church's regional synod. They end up in a state of constant suspicion, destroying all hope of normal relations with others in society.'

Sophie broke his gaze and looked down at her feet, another first for her, as far as I knew.

'And what we can do to our own citizens we can also do to people in other countries, Fräulein von Barten.'

'You wouldn't dare,' she said.

'Try me,' Johannes replied stonily. 'I can do a lot with your letters.'

They stared hard at one another.

'So, Fräulein von Barten. How do you propose to make recompense for what you did?' he asked.

She opened and closed her mouth, beaten into silence. Finally, someone had asked her a question she couldn't give an immediate answer to. Someone who was not her uncle, the senior EEC *fonctionnaire* who'd sent us to Rostock last year, not her immediate boss, and not even the Agriculture Commissioner himself

'What if I give you some information in exchange for my release?' she hazarded after a few seconds.

'Your uncle paid a ransom when we caught Lenkeit and you over here last year. Seems like we could ask the same of him again.'

'My uncle is dead. He committed suicide in the aftermath of that trip,' she said tightly.

Johannes held her gaze.

'I tried to put pressure on Lenkeit, because... because one of my acquaintances, one of my supporters at the EEC asked for my help to find some discreet people. His family in Italy is in difficulties.'

'Why is this of interest to East Germany?'

'Because they're being forced to raid stocks of weapons set aside by NATO for their stay-behind resistance organisation. The partisans, if you like, who will fight on behind the lines after a Soviet invasion of Western Europe.'

My jaw dropped. She was a certifiable lunatic. No wonder the Rizzos and their West German helper only wanted to use people on this job whom they had a close hold over. They had to, if they were intending to rob the Italian Republic of its emergency stores of arms for a last-ditch defence.

'And why would your other boyfriend's family do that, even under duress?' Johannes asked without breaking stride, professional that he was.

She frowned at Johannes' presumption as to Rizzo's and my status. But her confidence was snapping back as she started to lead the conversation.

'They've done a deal with the Mafia in Sicily, to supply them with weapons. A deal they now can't get out of.'

'Serves them right. Typical Western capitalists, no loyalty to their country or their society,' Johannes replied contemptuously. 'No morals,' he added, looking sharply at Sophie again.

'Lenkeit now, he's not as clever as you, but he understands loyalty, loyalty to family. That's why he came up with the fetchingly quaint, but stupid idea of knocking you over the head and dragging you here.'

'That's because he was sired by a Russian peasant soldier during the war.' Her natural arrogance had let her tongue run away with her. The colour drained from her face as she realised what she'd said.

A slow anger started inside me, but I was learning to recognise the danger signs better these days. I bit my lip and slowly shook my head instead. She looked down at her feet again while Johannes watched the both of us bemusedly.

But then the realisation came that maybe this was my opportunity after all, the right time to finally confront the past and say what needed to be said. Forget digging into the Rizzos' treachery for the time being. We were both stuck here on the wrong side of the border and when she heard what I was going to tell her, she would have no one to run off to such as her family, or worse, the Belgian police. It was as good a place and as good a time as I'd ever get.

The voice of my conscience grew louder inside, commanding me to speak regardless of the consequences.

'So you did say something like that to your uncle last year, after we got back from East Germany?' I said solemnly. 'About me being Russian scum?'

I stared at her closely for a moment, seeing the shame in her eyes. I flicked a glance at Johannes.

'He told me so. He told me that he agreed with you too,' I said tonelessly.

I took a breath and then the words slipped out in blessed relief.

'That's why I snapped, put a gun to his head, and shot him.'

There was a long second of stunned silence. In the distance, I heard the slam of a door.

'Jesus,' said Johannes softly.

Tears started in Sophie's eyes. She got up, came over, and slapped me hard in the face. First the left side, full on my scar, then the right.

She strode out of the room in distress. Johannes got to his feet, came round from behind the desk and followed her out the door, glancing back at me with a cold look of wonderment.

I heard sobs in the corridor, fading as he took her into another room somewhere on the same floor.

He let me sit there for ten minutes as I played and replayed in my mind the conversation leading up to the point of my confession. But ultimately, the only part of me that regretted it was the part that worried about Karin. To get her away from juvenile prison, I'd do anything Johannes demanded of me now.

He returned to the room and looked at me appraisingly. Underneath, I sensed deflation, too.

Over the past year or so we'd got to know one another as real people. You could even say we were colleagues of a kind, given that his success was bound together with mine. But ensnaring his daughter, the events in Ireland, and then Karin's arrest had changed all that. During today his attitude had reverted to something approximating to that of our first meeting in 'sixty-nine, the afternoon when he'd forced the false confession out of me.

'What made you do it? Not the shooting, we'll come to that later, I suppose. But then he was a Nazi functionary masquerading as a reformed character, so I'm shedding no tears.'

'He was more nuanced than that. The history there wasn't as straightforward as you make out,' I interjected.

'It was to us. We only meant you to smear the old fascist, not execute him. But why did you tell her now after a year? What did you hope to gain from it?'

'Where is she now?'

'She's with a female comrade. They're going to look through the disguise wardrobe and find something more practical for her to wear.'

'Tears are their secret weapon, the one we have little or no defence against.'

'Yes, and not murdering their uncles is one of ours. Anyway, weeping women aren't news to me, as I suggested earlier. So why tell her now?'

I sighed. 'It's no mystery. Getting it off my chest has been on my mind since that day in March last year. Von Barten provoked me, he insulted my mother. But you need a genuine reason to do what I did.'

'You've had a year to think about it already. What changed?' he asked disdainfully.

'It was the last day of my Irish trip. I finally gave in, I finally confessed to God what I'd done. From then on I knew I couldn't put off telling her eventually - whatever the consequences.'

'And you chose today? Your sense of timing is different to everyone else's, that's for sure.'

He shook his head.

'As it happens, right now my colleague Sergeant Riesner and I are her sympathetic friends. We're showing her the human face of the Ministry in contrast to you, whatever your religion is.'

He folded his arms. 'I don't understand all that guilt before God stuff either, so don't try it on me. My father might have understood. He was a church deacon before the war, but he's no longer with us.'

His voice dropped a notch. 'I'm wary of idealists. Some of the Ministry's Western colleagues end up more purist in their socialist beliefs than us. They become fanatics, as opposed to the practical people we originally started out working with. And I'm especially wary of people who kidnap women one day and want to be all holy the next. Don't tell me it's because you've been practising at compartmentalising your thoughts.'

I shifted uneasily on my chair, for I had way more locked rooms in my head than I cared to share with him.

He looked up as Sophie returned, dressed in a navy synthetic fibre skirt suit and carefully avoiding my eye. She deliberately shifted her chair away from mine before sitting down.

Johannes opened with an offer. 'Here's the deal, Fräulein von Barten, we'll force Lenkeit here,' he grimaced at my name, 'to take part in the action that you're planning in Italy. On pain of his cousin going to trial, being found guilty, and spending the next three years in Hoheneck, the jail for female political prisoners.'

Good of Johannes to warn me of his change of mind.

'And in exchange?' she asked warily.

'We get to send some of our people to Italy instead of the ones you meant him to hire. They'll be instructed to come back with photographs, inventories and samples of the weapons that are being sold to the Mafia. We especially want to take a look at any anti-aircraft surface-to-air missiles and anti-tank guided missiles that might be in the consignment for Sicily.'

'It seems like most of the long-term benefits in this deal are on yours and his side.'

'Very few secret deals of this nature end up perfectly balanced. But Lenkeit is liable for our success. No data on the weapons, no homecoming for his cousin before nineteen seventy-three or seventy-four,' he said, scowling at me.

'And if we're not satisfied with what comes back, he'll have gone to all this trouble in abducting you,' here Johannes grimaced again, 'for nothing, but you'll still have got the job you wanted done in Italy.'

How had Sophie ended up on top, yet again? Had she somehow planned for this all along? Maybe her relative docility on the truck ride had been suspicious after all.

Johannes was right about what he'd said just after we arrived. He was enjoying making me look a fool. If he was acting, then he really should have got the prize he'd mentioned earlier, because there was no falseness in his tone or expression that I could detect.

'Any last questions Fräulein von Barten?' Now Johannes' voice did stray over the line, just a touch too unctuous.

Upset as she may have been, her antennae remained very sensitive.

'Yes,' she said reflectively, folding her hands on her lap. I watched her cautiously, sensing that quiet Sophie was way more dangerous than when she was throwing out spur-of-the-moment insults.

'The last time we were over here together, when we left to return to the West, you gave Lenkeit the document we'd originally come to Rostock to collect. Why was that?'

It was the worst question she could have asked, because what Johannes didn't know was that Sophie had stolen the file from my luggage while I slept, just before our train arrived in Brussels at six that morning. She and I had never, ever talked about that. My fear, both at the time and still today, was that she would guess the Stasi had given the document to me because I'd signed up to work for them.

Johannes surprised me with his answer. 'We gave it to him because it was part of the deal with your uncle. He paid the ransom for you and the document, not Lenkeit. We threw him in for free anyway, because he wasn't worth anything. No one was going to ransom him. He was just the courier.'

All of this Johannes said quite naturally. My own eyes widened, as I realised his matter-of-fact tone might have been because the report of his conversation with von Barten was completely accurate.

'Why did you let the document go West?' she asked.

'It was of historical interest, nothing more.'

Sophie frowned. She half-turned her face but didn't actually look at me. 'What did they tell you back then? What were your instructions?' she asked me, still speaking in Johannes' general direction.

'Just what the Major said. To take it back to the West.'

She frowned again. Now I'd just effectively told her that her theft and the events it triggered had been unnecessary, that she would have got the document anyway.

'They told me to get it safely to Brussels. When we got on the train, I didn't think you were in any fit state to be responsible for it.'

She looked sharply at Johannes. She'd told me they had tried to extract a confession from her through sleep deprivation. I hadn't been sure at the time if it was true, but maybe it had been.

She left her line of questioning for now. I suspected there'd be more once we were on our own again.

'I'm going to Italy on Monday. Lenkeit will have to come along too, in order to hear what's to be done,' she said in a disgusted voice. 'Your people need to be ready to get out there within the next few weeks.'

'Okay, I'll see who we know in the West that we can trust. We have fixers connected to the arms trade who work for us from time to time,' he said, giving her all his attention.

'We'll make sure Lenkeit hears from us by the end of next week. But now I think it's time for you and him to get out of here and back to Brussels. You didn't have passports, did you?'

'No. Lenkeit snatched me directly outside a drinks reception at midnight, then stashed me inside some kind of container once we got near the border to make sure no one knew we'd crossed.'

Johannes raised his eyebrows. I ought to earn at least some marks for initiative today, even if it had been misguided.

'Well, we'll give you some East German passports. Quick fakes, good enough for the West Germans to glance at and stamp once. But not good enough for you to get back in here again,' he warned.

'They'll have no real authentic history,' he explained, 'it's highly unlikely that people of your age would be allowed to travel to the West, unless as part of an organised group.'

'How long will this take?' she demanded.

'We can do it in under an hour, but we'll need your photograph first. I'll make up some names - Herr and Frau Hofmann, perhaps? You pretended something like that once before, didn't you?'

By the way she glowered at him, Sophie hadn't forgotten his earlier prediction. 'Maybe not, then,' he grinned faintly.

He picked up the phone, dialled a number and asked for someone, the duty photographer presumably.

As he spoke, I stole a glance at Sophie, but her eyes were still fixed firmly on Johannes. He replaced the handset and began to wrap up with us.

'As I said, we'll make the arrangements with Lenkeit, Fräulein von Barten. You won't be connected to us in this affair.' he assured her. 'However, my apologies, but I am bound to remind you that when you're with us you never know which conversations we've recorded.'

He looked at her seriously now. 'We're very good at cutting and recutting audio tapes so they say whatever we want them to. As I hinted at earlier, we're also very skilful at placing manufactured evidence in the West German press for the exact degree of effect which we're trying to achieve.'

'So what you're saying is, I don't let anyone find out that Lenkeit is going to betray NATO's secrets and nothing comes back to me?'

It was one way to describe her arms dealing.

'If you do, we'll make sure the people in Bonn believe that Lenkeit was your decoy, and that you were the real brains behind the scheme which no one will find hard to believe.'

They were starting to coo at one another like doves now, even as the threats went back and forth. Part of me was left wondering again whether she really hadn't had any contact with Johannes since last year.

The photographer arrived with a genuine Polaroid and an encouraging smile for Sophie. I guessed she was the female comrade that Johannes had referred to, the one who had lent Sophie a sympathetic ear and helped her pick out the least-unflattering set of new East German clothes.

She positioned each of us in turn against a blank wall, Sophie first, gently tilting her chin this way and that so as to get the angle she wanted for the photograph, avoiding shadows.

I wasn't welcomed into the bosom of the Party in the same way. A jerk of the head accompanied by a terse '*Dort drüben*,' the camera pointed quickly, and the shot snapped off. It was unlikely the photographer had been told exactly what had upset Sophie, but then when women got together as sisters, all men were bastards. In my case, literally so.

While we waited on the documents being made up, another Stasi colleague brought in a late lunch: rolls wrapped in plastic film, bottles of water and Vita-Cola - East Germany's own take on Coke. We ate with Johannes at the conference table in the corner of the room.

I was suddenly overcome with fatigue after half a night spent driving and worrying about getting caught as we left West Germany. On top of the trouble I'd gone to beforehand as well, planning the abduction and finding an accomplice from the Hamburg underworld.

Unsurprisingly, there was little small talk at the table. How many meaningless pleasantries could you exchange in a regional office of the East German secret police anyway? Especially when two of the three people were pretending in front of the third that they didn't work with each other?

To smooth over the awkwardness, Johannes flicked on the transistor radio standing on top of the file cabinet next to the door.

'There,' he said, after briefly fiddling with the dial. 'West German radio news, just to show you how open-minded and ready for détente we are over here.'

We caught the tail end of a news bulletin, the sports section. My eyes widened in shock as in sombre tones the newsreader announced the death of Jochen Rindt in a practice lap for this weekend's Italian Formula One Grand Prix.

'There goes Germany's chance of winning a first Driver's Championship,' I said laconically.

'He's Austrian, no?' asked Johannes.

'Born in Germany, grew up with grandparents in Austria. Parents were killed in an air raid on Hamburg,' I explained.

'Well, I was going to propose a toast to the success of your trip to Italy, but it doesn't seem quite the right moment now,' he replied.

'Today wasn't a victory,' Sophie said dully, events catching up with her too.

I wouldn't have used that phrase just then. It was just the kind of interjection which might make the Stasi suspicious, experts at misdirection as they were.

For if I was to think like them, I'd be starting to wonder if Sophie and I had just laid on an elaborate show to get them to send some of their agents to Italy and then either expose or entrap them. But my confession couldn't have been scripted, Johannes must have understood that.

And what came next back in Brussels wasn't scripted either. For even if I wasn't intending to, Sophie might decide to confess von Barten's murder to the Gendarmerie on my behalf.

Johannes drove us back to the border, to the rail crossing point at Herrnburg, a few kilometres along from Selmsdorf where we'd come through this morning.

Our train was already there, but Johannes checked his watch and didn't see the need to rush.

'It's only just arrived. It'll be another forty minutes before it leaves. They need to check every passenger, and under the train too.'

He shook his head. 'There's no way your cousin could have tricked us with her mother's exit papers by using a dash of make-up to make herself look older.' As he said it, he frowned to himself as something came to mind, but he didn't share what it was.

Instead, he left us on the platform for a few minutes as he took our new passports with him into the Grenztruppen post to get them stamped and to pick up freshly issued exit visas.

When he returned, he handed me my passport but kept hold of Sophie's for a moment.

'Before we part ways, I have one last question for you, Fräulein von Barten,' he said. 'How did you think getting Lenkeit's cousin into trouble here would help your associates in Italy. Or was it simple revenge?'

She didn't answer, but raised her eyebrows instead.

'Oh, you thought there was a chance that something like this might happen, did you? You thought you might be able to manipulate us into forcing him to help you?' Now Johannes mirrored her expression, but in subdued admiration.

There was the faintest hint of smugness in the play of her lips.

'But why pick Lenkeit for this task?' he asked.

'Because I've told you how illegal this thing is. We need to use someone we know. And I don't know any other criminals,' she added sarcastically.

'I don't believe that. I'm coming round to the opinion that you chose him because you know he'll do anything for you, even if he doesn't know it himself. As for his criminal nature, he tells me he's a new man. I think you'll be safe enough with him on the journey back. There's no bullets in his gun today.'

She composed her face again and addressed him more seriously.

'Once your people have had a good look at the arms cache and examined the weapons, and once you eventually let his cousin go, tell her that Lenkeit had nothing to do with the letters. Make sure she knows that it was all my idea and that he tried his best to secure her release,' she said.

That surprised me. More than Rindt's death in Monza earlier. Johannes finally decided to make his pitch.

'I want to make a request in return. You should come and work for us as one of our Western political advisers. We're always looking for up-and-coming people in different areas of European public life, but especially now to help make détente a success for all of us.'

But with the carrot came the stick.

'However, we are serious about smearing you in the press if this Italian business goes wrong for us. Or we can even go beyond that,' he added more darkly. 'Lenkeit snatched you once, we can do it again ourselves, pretend you've defected to East Germany. Something like that might have happened to Otto John in 'fifty-four.'

Sophie shrugged.

'He was the head of the West German counter-intelligence organisation,' he explained. 'Shame that we're unlikely to meet again anytime soon, I could tell you some stories.'

Johannes had planted the seed. For him that was enough for now. With a half-wave of his hand he saw us into the train, turned on his heel, and left.

We found a compartment near the front and sat silently waiting on the border guards to release the train. There was a jolt followed by the creak of the couplings taking the strain, then we glided through the high-sided barbed wire cage which marked the border proper.

We kept studiously saying nothing, avoiding eye contact until after the West German border guards had made their rounds, taking only a cursory look at our new passports. As soon as the compartment door had closed behind them, she turned and fixed me with a stare, waiting for me to start.

I looked back at her equally solemnly.

'I am truly sorry for what I did to your uncle and for the disrespect shown to your family,' I said. 'I ask for your forgiveness and theirs.'

She kept looking at me, her expression unchanging.

'I've confessed my sins to God and repented of them. I am not the person I was then.' My voice deepened as I said the awkward words.

'When we return to Brussels, my fate is in your hands, whatever you decide to do next,' I said, trying to convey genuine sincerity.

She didn't reply, but instead turned away to look out of the window for a long minute.

She turned back to face me with a sigh. She re-crossed her legs and smoothed her new navy nylon skirt over her knee.

'No one else I know would have done for me what you did for your cousin. I don't inspire that kind of loyalty in anyone,' she said flatly.

I stared back, waiting, giving her the space to say more. Part of me wondered for the very first time if she was actually lonely underneath the confident exterior, despite the gaggle of *fonctionnaires* on heat around her back in Brussels. Maybe that was why she had picked out Rizzo to use. Compared to the rest of them, he wasn't as hard and aggressive. Still overweeningly ambitious though, at a guess. Maybe he was better suited to her than she realised herself, despite what she said he merely was.

Now the habitual gleam in her eyes died and she surprised me again.

'I apologise for what I've said about you in the past, and also for what I said again today. I regret if my words provoked you to do what you did, wrong as it was.'

Now I broke my gaze, glancing at the outskirts of Lübeck just beyond the dirty carriage window. It was like we'd both aged a decade since Johannes picked us up this morning.

She spoke up again. 'I have something I want to tell today, too. Something I haven't told anyone else before, apart from my own parents.' She gave a deeper sigh, 'Do you promise never to speak of it, if I share it with you?'

I nodded, 'I promise.'

I was relieved too. Mutual secrets suggested that once back in Brussels she wasn't about to call on Lieutenant Bonfils of the Gendarmerie who'd tried to trick me into admitting to von Barten's murder last year.

'When I first moved to Brussels from Bruges after graduating from the College of Europe, I stayed for a few weeks with my uncle and aunt at their place in the Forêt de Soignes.'

It was the house where I had shot her uncle that day. It was also the place where I'd first met Sophie at a dinner party. I would never forget it.

'One evening, when his wife Anne was out, he made some inappropriate remarks to me after supper. Although I showed my displeasure, he still followed me upstairs when I went to turn in. He stood in the open doorway of my bedroom, making small talk, but with an edge, testing the boundaries and refusing to go away until I closed the door right in his face. I locked it that night, too.'

I clasped my hands on my lap, the right covering the left, the one which was the more badly scarred of the two.

'After that evening I soon found my own place to stay. I didn't say anything, of course, I needed his sponsorship for my career. But the day I moved out, I mentioned to my aunt that almost none of the upstairs bathrooms at their place had locks.'

I frowned, sensing that despite the build-up she'd given, this was still really only a story about a story.

'Anne had no compunction in telling me why, in fact, she may have been glad to. During the war they, like other households of officials in the regime, were sent foreign labourers as domestic staff. But somehow, the only ones sent by the Sauckel Organisation to cook and clean for Anne were fourteen- and fifteen-year-old Polish and Ukrainian girls. She thought some of them might have been younger than that.'

I nodded my head, but more in sympathy for the Ukrainians than for the moral predicament Anne von Barten had found herself in with her husband.

'Who knows what he got a taste for during the war,' she speculated. 'When you are surrounded by, or surround yourself with foreign girls who no one will believe if they complain about you. Not that they would hardly have dared to, I imagine.'

'I suppose, with the position he had in the administration of the war economy, he could have had his pick of the slaves?' I suggested neutrally.

'I don't want to say much more. They never had

children of their own as I think I told you once, but that might have just been the way things were. Not every woman can conceive.'

I wondered what had prompted the story when she had no need to tell it. Exposing a vulnerability didn't chime with her natural defensiveness. Then again, it wasn't the first such confidence she'd shared with me. When I first met her back in 'sixty-nine, she'd told me that Anne von Barten had stopped living full-time with her husband in Brussels that year and had effectively returned permanently to West Germany. I now supposed that story and the one of Sophie being tentatively importuned might be linked.

And there was another piece of the unfinished Brussels jigsaw puzzle from last year that might now fit, too.

'I wonder...,' I began to say.

'What?'

I grimaced. 'I'm sorry. I don't really want to say it.'

She frowned and shrugged impatiently. 'You've told me everything else today, what more is there to know?'

I wrinkled my brow in reluctance. 'That first time we met, at dinner, Rizzo spoke to me at one point in the evening.'

'Go on,' she said, suspicious now.

'He tried to warn me off you. He said there was a false rumour about you that I should ignore.'

'What was it?' she asked sharply.

'Okay, I'm just the messenger. He said the rumour was that when young up-and-coming *fonctionnaires* joined von Barten's circle of intimates, they would get favours from...'

'The bastard. The absolute bastard,' she spat.

'Who? Rizzo?'

'No, *Dummkopf*. But yes, I'm annoyed at Giovanni. And at you too, for remembering the story and for not putting it out of your head.'

'Well, now you know. Ask Rizzo if you don't believe me.'

'Oh I do. You're very careful in certain areas.'

She explained some more, just to make sure I knew I wasn't being complimented.

'You covered your tracks well at my uncle's house. We - the family, that is - paid someone in the police to make sure his death was treated as murder and to tell us how the investigation was going. The family even had your background checked out too, from the time when you were in the police in Hamburg.'

I should have known that Lieutenant Bonfils' diligence hadn't been for real.

'I was a probationer - a cadet. I never completed the three years' training. I came to work for EEC Internal Affairs instead. There would have been nothing to find out.'

'You're a man with a completely unremarkable past, up until nineteen sixty-nine. But what other things have you been covering up since last March I wonder?' she asked with a harder edge to her voice. I sensed that détente was over, and the Cold War was about to recommence.

'I was desperate that day,' I said. 'I was in horror at what I'd done. But I was determined not to be discovered, that's all. It was only natural.'

'But you were discovered, in the end. You just told me back there in Wismar, and you told the Stasi too. That seems particularly stupid of you, Oskar.'

She was back onto one of her favourite topics when we met, my manifold failings. At least she'd pointed out this particular error in her schoolteacher voice, the one which indicated disappointment at some unfulfilled potential, rather than an outright scold.

'If they can threaten to blackmail me, Oskar, they can do the same to you as well. Although I suppose your family is in big enough trouble with them as it is,' she said, seemingly forgetting that the trouble was largely down to her.

'Did your conscience make you confess back there?'

she added. Now that she'd properly found her tongue again, she was hard to stop.

'Yes.' It was the simplest answer and also the true one.

I asked my own question, my confidence growing that von Barten's murder had been put to one side for now.

'So what's the real story in Italy? I'd have thought that stealing ancient rifles stored in grease from NATO's secret long-term arms dumps wasn't your lot's sort of thing.'

'My lot?' she asked, jutting her jaw forward in instant annoyance.

'You know what I mean - aristocrats, landowners, industrialists.'

'I don't care if you dislike us or dislike me. You now have a job to do, which you need to do well,' she said tetchily.

'I'm still waiting to be told what's actually going on in Italy.'

She sighed impatiently. 'Very well then. There's another dimension to this, certain factions, which Giovanni's family are linked to, are trying to recruit the Sicilian Mafia to work for them on the mainland. His family are stuck in the middle between the two, trying to keep both sides happy.'

'What connection do Rizzo's people have with the Mafia?'

'Family connections. His grandmother was from a prominent clan. Giovanni has cousins of different degrees who live on the island and who are still involved.'

'And these factions you mention?'

'Some people that Giovanni's father knows. Old comrades from the war whom he has obligations to. But none of that gets back to the East Germans when they next contact you. Otherwise we'll have a reception party from the Italian secret services waiting for their people in Sicily and that really will be the end of the road for your cousin.'

'So what's happening in Italy next week that we need to

go out there? Conference of former Italian fascists?'

She raised her eyebrows. 'I'm trying to get you to take this seriously Oskar. Goodness knows, you have enough reason to.'

She shook her head in annoyance now. 'It's the seventy-fifth birthday of Giovanni's grandfather.'

'So that's why you were desperate to get back to the West?' I bit my tongue, holding back a sour comment about her being more interested in partying with Rizzo at his family estate in Apulia than helping my cousin whom she'd led astray.

'You need to get yourself onto the first flight from Brussels to Rome on Monday. Then we change for the evening flight to Bari. *Capisce?*'

'*Alles klar*,' I replied tersely.

'Why didn't the Major ask you about your injuries? They're prominent enough,' she pointed to my cheek and my hands.

'I told him about the fight in the bar in Dublin when you were getting changed.'

But I felt awkward as I said it. What was the future for a confidential agent who was squeamish about lying?

I looked at her gravely, wondering. What if I took a risk and told her everything? That in Rostock in 'sixty-nine, unlike her, I had agreed to work for the Stasi. Or that today in Brussels, my Internal Affairs job was only a cover for my work for the EEC's own embryonic intelligence gathering agency. How would she react to honesty?

I'd already owned up to the murder of her uncle, wherever that left us now. I narrowed my eyes as I gazed at her, the moment passing.

She spread her arms out wide to each side, palms pressing down onto the seat.

'I want to sit on my own for the rest of the journey. I've had a lot to take in this weekend,' she said evenly. 'I still haven't decided what I think about it all.'

I nodded, got to my feet and pulled my holdall down

from the overhead rack. I unzipped it to rummage inside for her clutch bag. It had gone in there with our other possessions, including my Makarov - but not her long green dress which I guessed she'd donated to her new friend, Sergeant Riesner.

As I handed over the bag, I asked her if she had enough money to get home from Brussels Central. She half-smiled and shook her head, faintly amused at the notion that she might need to borrow money from me. But she watched shrewdly as I reached behind me to slip the Makarov back into my waistband.

When we'd left Brussels in the early hours of this morning, my cousin was on her way to being released, if Johannes was to be believed. Now I'd put the brakes on that and who knew what I'd end up having to do in order to get things moving again. I should have known that in any affair where Sophie was involved, there was usually only ever one winner.

I found my own compartment and pondered a while as to why Johannes had been so ready to send me to Italy.

I couldn't imagine that anything we might find in the shipment would be that interesting to the Warsaw Pact. In fact, it seemed rather reckless to risk an asset placed deep within the EEC for some technical data they could surely find elsewhere. Unless Johannes was prepared to risk sacrificing me for the prize of obtaining even more blackmail material on Sophie. Angling to catch a bigger fish.

Today though, I had achieved something which they couldn't take away from me. I'd laid the demon of guilt over her uncle's death properly to rest. And that was something, regardless of whatever else might come my way over the next few weeks.

Chapter Three

If I was to fly out to Italy tomorrow, I had to get up to speed fast with what was happening in the EEC's poorest member state. Especially if I was getting mixed up in some ill-defined alliance between the Sicilian Mafia and Rizzo's father's wartime comrades.

The problem was that I didn't know much about the real Italy at all. The Belgian newspapers carried the odd story about elections, strikes and earthquakes, but Rizzo was the only Italian at the EEC I had even a passing acquaintance with. '*Macaronifresser*' was what some people called them back in Hamburg; bombastic little people who'd tried unsuccessfully to ride on the coattails of bigger nations for years.

But there was someone in Brussels I did know: a left-wing lecturer friend at the Free University, who might be able to help me see below the surface. My drinking buddy, Jan Stapel.

Jan and I were an unlikely pair. We'd met by chance in a pub in 'sixty-eight in the centre of the old town and had got talking. He had a curiosity for everyday life and work outside academia - he liked to put on a man of the people act for his students and I supposed he was always on the lookout for new material. In that respect Jan had been in luck on our first meeting, for I'd been out drinking with my other close friend, Bernd, the ex-policeman from Hamburg who'd originally recruited me into the EEC and my first job in Internal Affairs.

Since late 'sixty-eight, the three of us had kept up our

acquaintance. Jan had even helped me out professionally last year too, when I was trying to navigate my way through the political minefields laid by von Barten. Afterwards though, he'd tried to extract payment for his advice by inviting me to join the left-wing political group he belonged to in his spare time. To my faint amusement he was too late, as I was already working for the Comrade Major by then.

This Sunday, following my epiphany in Ireland, I supposed I ought to have been in church. The bigger moral question of whether I should be involved in arms-trafficking as a follow-on to the abduction I'd just carried out, I'd leave to a later date. One thing was leading to another, thanks to my good intentions of helping Karin. But instead of being admonished by the preacher at one of Brussels' fringe Protestant churches, I was sitting with Jan at a corner table in a cafe near to the Cimetière d'Ixelles.

This surprised me a little. Not the location, which was near to the Free University and Jan's apartment, but the fact that it wasn't a smoky bar some time after midnight. For Jan was a good-time socialist, happy to make the most of everything which capitalist society had to offer, including the string of impressionable undergraduate girlfriends he seemed to be able to get through at a rapid rate. It was probably the combination of his impish good looks, suggestive beatnik protest poetry, and supplies of weed that did it for them.

We started with the usual pleasantries. He glanced at the scar on my cheek, which I'd explained away the last time we'd met.

'So?' he asked. 'Where's Bernd hiding these days? I haven't seen him for weeks.'

'I haven't seen him myself since the start of the summer,' I said. 'He's got his eye on a promotion at Internal Affairs, he's been putting in extra hours to impress his boss.'

That position wasn't Bernd's first choice though. Over a year ago, when my political sponsor set up the confidential department I worked for within Internal Affairs, it was the job given to me which Bernd had wanted for himself. From his guarded comments over the past year, he still hankered after it.

'Any new women, then?' Jan asked, switching to his joint-favourite topic of conversation alongside politics.

'Only old ones, of a kind. A gentleman never tells.'

'You sly dog.'

I paused before replying, for I'd only meant it as a quick aside. If my very first trip with Sophie to the East had been a disaster in the romance department, then the second one just now had been even worse, if that were possible.

'But maybe you can help me there, to make an impression,' I suggested, telling myself I was simply sustaining the story for Jan, as opposed to allowing treacherous hope to take root in my heart.

He grinned. Not only had he introduced me to my first serious girlfriend in Brussels - one of his students - he'd also effectively dumped her for me when she turned out to be an obsessive. She would pester me with constant phone calls at work and always seemed to find some reason, which was only ever my fault, to make a scene in public when we were out together. The pestering started early on and soon became serious, quickly outweighing the other benefits from our relationship, especially as those were only erratically granted after the first couple of weeks.

Still, it provided an entry to talking about Italy.

'I need to know where the hidden fracture lines in Italian politics are. It's for this girl at work who's trying to stay on the right side of some people out there. I want to give her a helping hand,' I said.

He smirked. 'I bet you want to give her more than that.'

Once again, I was slightly taken aback. Strangely,

despite his success at attracting girlfriends, or perhaps because of it and with nothing to prove, banter about women wasn't really his style. Something had changed in him. But working part time for the Stasi was changing me too. I was becoming extra-sensitive to anything and everything out of the ordinary these days. I wondered, at what point did professional competence become paranoia?

'Well, if you help me to help her, I'm sure I'll get an appropriate level of gratitude.'

That was one way to cover the range of likely outcomes given Sophie's natural selfishness.

'Okay then. Fire away,' he said, grinning, eager for the chance to show off his knowledge. He always enjoyed the opportunity to remind me that I hadn't been to university - his socialist sympathy for the lower classes only extended so far.

I drummed my fingers on the table for a second or two, thinking where to start.

'The things that are happening in Italy today, the bombs and political unrest we hear of from time to time, aren't they simply a continuation of sorts of the nineteen sixty-eight student protests in France, or what your lot got up to here in Brussels that same year?'

'"From time to time?"' he retorted. 'It's the worst political violence anywhere in Europe right now. Didn't you hear about the Piazza Fontana bombing in Milan last year? When seventeen people died?'

I nodded vaguely.

'And it's completely different to 'sixty-eight in France,' he said, shocked, angry even. 'It's a chance for a genuine, full-blown workers' revolt.'

Anger could work too. I wanted the facts raw.

'Nineteen sixty-eight in Italy was triggered by true hardship - for both students and workers alike.'

I frowned, not really understanding how students as a group could be hard up.

'Italy has seen massive internal migration during the

past two decades. From south to north, millions of people have been on the move. When the southerners arrive in the North they get treated like foreign immigrants, forced into low-wage jobs by the gangmasters. They don't even always speak proper Italian when they take jobs on the production lines. Instead, they have to make themselves understood in their southern dialects, almost separate languages.'

But he wasn't done.

'It's also hard for them to find housing, which isn't made any easier when some landlords refuse to rent to southerners. They end up crammed together in impoverished neighbourhoods, or in shanty towns when they can't find anywhere else to live.'

I raised my eyebrows. He seemed to be describing somewhere in South America rather than southern Europe.

'Really, in nineteen seventy?'

'Well, maybe it's not quite so bad these days, but earlier, yes. And when they bring their families, they find that the school system and hospitals haven't been able to cope with the earlier influx of migrants. There are no comparable conditions elsewhere in Western Europe. No one cares for their plight.'

I wasn't so sure about his tale of woe. I knew he wanted to make a point, but eventually governments in a democracy sorted these things out. I wondered if Rizzo's family employed southerners. His father was some kind of industrialist in Milan.

'When was all this?' I asked. 'This movement off the land, I'm guessing?'

Jan looked at me narrowly, as if surprised by my question.

'It started in the late fifties. There was an export boom when Italy joined the Common Market, driven by the gradual reduction of customs tariffs and the exploitation of cheap southern labour. Italian ingenuity helped too, in designing products which Europeans wanted to buy - from Candy washing machines and Olivetti typewriters to cars.'

'And exactly how bad were things in the rural areas of the South? To make a shanty town a more attractive option.'

'Near feudal employment conditions. Labourers locked inside their barracks at night by the landowners. In Calabria, the mainland province across the Messina Straits from Sicily, half the population was still illiterate only twenty years ago.' he said grimly.

I looked back at him in shock, but he wasn't done.

'Given that historic level of deprivation it's no wonder that Calabria's regional capital exploded into armed revolt in July this year. You remember the Italian express train that derailed earlier this summer, when six people died? It happened just outside Reggio Calabria and now there's talk that it wasn't an accident after all but might have been a bomb.'

'Who's behind all this?'

Sophie blithely talked about supplying arms to the underworld, but somehow I doubted that she and Rizzo had stopped to think much about human cost when people actually used them.

'Who knows exactly? People are angry,' he replied.

'How about the communists? Have they been secretly stirring the pot? Isn't the Italian Communist Party the biggest in Western Europe or something?'

This had been de Gaulle's fear for France, that unless the farmers could be persuaded to remain on the land, they'd move to the cities and turn to communism. It was the original justification for the Common Agricultural Policy. Of course, the main reason for French enthusiasm today was that they'd since found they could get other people to pay for it. West Germany right now and in a couple of years' time, the British would take on the strain of funding the ever-growing subsidies.

'The PCI has one-and-a-half million members. In fact,

they're not just the biggest western communist party, they're the biggest political party in Western Europe overall. But I doubt they've been planting bombs under trains. They haven't threatened the political establishment in Italy since nineteen forty-eight and they only had tangential involvement in 'sixty-eight.'

I grunted.

'What's the point in a communist party that can't or won't take advantage of revolutionary conditions?'

'You forget how they got to where they are today. Only a couple of years after they were founded, the PCI had to go into hiding because the fascists came to power. They only properly emerged on the scene when Mussolini fled Rome in 'forty-three and the country was divided into Allied and German occupation zones.

'I know. The British and Americans thought they would quickly roll up Italy, but we held them off in the north almost until the end.' I said the words automatically, without thinking.

Jan raised his eyebrows. 'The PCI have always played a long game. Even after Mussolini was deposed, they had no choice in the southern occupation zone because it was the British who dictated political policy to the Allied Military Government there.'

'Why did they get to decide things? What did the Americans have to say?'

'The real question is "what did Moscow say?" At the Yalta conference, Stalin agreed with Churchill that Italy would remain outside the Soviet sphere of influence after the war.'

I wished they'd agreed the same for Germany, but I couldn't say it out loud. Not if I wanted to stay on Jan's good side.

'The British were determined to avoid a re-run in Italy of the Greek debacle, when the liberation movement turned on itself and a civil war ensued between left and right. So the PCI trimmed their sails and joined the provisional Italian government in the southern zone for the sake of the greater cause of anti-fascism. They tried to enact some limited land reform in the South before the war's end, but even that was too much too soon for their coalition partners.'

'What happened in the North?'

'In the northern zone it was an Italian civil war with the PCI's partisans leading the resistance against Mussolini's puppet regime. But after the liberation, the communists had little choice but to lay down arms. They would have had to anyway, even if Stalin hadn't done his deal with Churchill. Although the British left after the war, the Americans still effectively occupied the whole country militarily until nineteen forty-seven. Any attempt at armed insurrection would have been quickly put down and the party banned once more.'

'So the PCI prioritised their long-term survival, like they did in the twenties? How did that work out for them?' I asked.

'The first national elections after fascism didn't take place until nineteen forty-eight. The Americans spent millions of dollars to ensure an outright win for their favoured political party, the Christian Democrats - the DC. After the election, the DC kicked the PCI out of the coalition and have kept them out since 'forty-eight. But despite that, there still remains a hard core of PCI support - about a third of the popular vote.'

'But what good has a third of the vote done them so far? You're suggesting that they were asleep when nineteen sixty-eight blew up? They'd become part of the established political system by then? Captured by the salaries and pensions paid to deputies?'

'It's the challenge all the traditional left-wing parties faced when the protests started - and the long-established trade unions too. Some became more radical and adopted the demands of the activists. That's what the unions were trying to do in Italy last year - regain control of the movement. Which meant that they had to become more militant themselves. The "Hot Autumn" they called it. Remember the Fiat strike in Turin at their factory in Mirafiori? The one which ended with running street battles and barricades across the Corso Traiano?'

I vaguely recalled seeing something on TV, but there had been so many demonstrations, marches, and riots across Europe the past two years that they all tended to run into one another in my memory.

'Did you take up arms during the protests, so to speak?' I asked instead. 'Were you part of the sit-in at the university here?'

'Of course I was. I wanted to see history being made. I supervised the erection of Roger Somville's giant canvas in our main assembly hall. Roger Somville, the Marxist painter?' he asked.

I shook my head politely. 'I'm sure it had a message.'

'It took him ten days to paint it, section by section,' Jan concluded, disappointed in my lack of enthusiasm for revolution by paintbrush.

'Did you think "this is it"? That 'sixty-eight was the moment to strike a blow?'

I'd bet he'd had no such intention. The life that capitalism provided him was much too comfortable to want to overturn completely, let alone to risk injury doing so.

'We have other longer-term plans in place. And anyway, it wasn't all just days holed up behind barricaded doors and late-night debates on second-wave feminism. The atmosphere made it easy to get girls to say "yes" to individual acts of revolution against convention too.'

I shuffled my feet under the table. The clumsy insinuation didn't suit him.

'So why did the 'sixty-eight protests in France and Belgium fade away but carry on in Italy?'

'Momentum was lost across the West because just enough of the demands were met by the established political parties. And although the New Left were impatient with the traditional left parties and trade unions, those entities had something the newcomers didn't - organisation. It's difficult for new parties to overcome the inertia in the system.'

'Which implies that the PCI aren't going away anytime soon?' I volunteered. 'They won't lose one-and-a-half million members that quickly?'

Jan tilted his chair back slightly as he finished his coffee, then clicked his fingers for another one. Lecturing was thirsty work.

'So where does the revolution go from here?' I asked. 'If the traditional communist parties aren't the agents of popular change and if it turns out that the militant New Left can't overthrow the system with violence either, what do you do next? Wait for the Soviet Army to arrive and do the job for you?'.

'The Italians aren't stupid you know. People look down on them because they're the poorest of the six EEC countries. But even if people have forgotten the Renaissance, Italian innovation is there for everyone to see today when Ferrari wins a Grand Prix race. Olivetti makes personal electronic calculators as advanced as anything the Japanese can produce.'

I shrugged, suspecting that West Germany wouldn't be far behind.

'But they're clever politically too. There was an Italian communist politician called Antonio Gramsci, one of the early leaders of the PCI who was imprisoned by Mussolini for his trouble. He invented a concept known as the "War of Position", whereby the proletariat would found their own cultural institutions - in education, the arts, the press - to provide an alternative to those of capitalist society.'

'What's new about that?'

'Because he realised that these institutions needed to be more than workers' self-help societies. He realised that the workers needed their own cultural identity and values, distinct from the social norms of the bourgeoisie.'

It still didn't seem that radical so far.

'And what came after that?' I asked, now regretting that I'd taken him down this side path.

The waitress brought over our drinks. Jan dropped a couple of sugars into his, slowly stirring them in as he spoke.

'Gramsci understood that the capitalist states' coercive organs on their own - the police, courts, and prisons - couldn't successfully control a population of millions. Not without the people's sheep-like willingness to comply with the establishment and the values they stood for – respect for the nation, respect for property and so forth. Only once the people had learnt to reject bourgeois morality, only then would they have the willpower for violent revolution - his so-called "War of Manoeuvre."'

It was sounding a little more plausible to me now.

'Has any Marxist revolution ever occurred that way?' I asked.

'Not quite in that way. Not yet,' he admitted.

'But Gramsci's ideas inspired Rudi Dutschke, the student protest leader from your country. He's recently evolved Gramsci's strategy of creating new cultural institutions from the ground up. He believes the left can bring about change far more powerfully and effectively by taking control of the structures that already exist in society - a so-called "Long March Through the Institutions."'

'You people always need to give names to everything.'

Jan ignored my disparagement as he got up to speed on describing his new pet theory.

'Dutschke's "Long March" is a patient, decades-long takeover, first of the education system and then the mass media. All to choke off the messages of the right at source and change the very nature of a country without anyone realising it.'

As excitement took hold, he began to speak even faster.

'We'll bring about change without the need for armed revolution. And in the very long-term, without even needing to win any elections,' he added, smirking.

'Is that your plan, then? To take over the Free University so you can run society for the greater good of the people?'

'I'm doing it already. I only give high grades to students who write essays supporting the left-wing point of view. I make sure that my doctorate students only get their degrees for the same reason. Any selection committees for professorships that I get to sit on, I only vote for socialists. Once we control the faculties and the running of the university, we'll shut down the right-wing student groups, ban their newsletters, and finally squeeze out all wrong thinking from the campus.'

He said all this quite casually. I had no idea that academic life could be so brutal, or so biased. I'd always assumed they sought objective truths. As for the unfortunates who didn't realise why they'd failed their exams or hadn't been given a research position, he could have taught the Stasi a thing or two about silent persecution, about academic *Zersetzung*. It all seemed a bit far-fetched for the West.

'Within thirty years, regardless of what happens between the USSR and America, we'll have quietly built up our power base. We'll make academia a fortress and hold it secure against our enemies. We'll encourage our graduates to infiltrate the media and once we own the press, we'll eventually own politics. It will be inevitable. And we'll have done it all so gradually that no one will realise what's happened.'

It was the secret nature of the takeover he kept referring to which seemed to excite him more than anything else.

'But where are the workers in all this? Do they get a say in this revolution? And will the students have the patience for a decades-long plan? They want results now, don't they?' I asked.

'This the only way that will guarantee us success. There'll no longer be any need for people to risk going to jail for starting a riot or risk being blown up if a home-made bomb goes off prematurely. We won't need to risk the vagaries of parliamentary debate either. We'll sit above politics.'

Jan had got really carried away. The people he mixed with were more dangerous than the gun-toting left-wing revolutionary fanatics across the world who aped Che Guevara. It was the crass cynicism which jarred the most.

'Who needs politicians anyway, once your educated class control everything from behind the scenes?' I challenged him.

He frowned at the suggestion. 'What do you mean? Politicians won't become defunct.'

'Look at Italy,' I said, steering the conversation back to the original topic of our meeting. 'They manage to survive even with a change in government every nine months. Or so it seems from the newspapers.'

'No, in Italy it's different. Sure, they have an election, and then the politicians immediately start arguing amongst themselves for weeks or months to try to form a stable coalition. And it's always been a coalition, right since nineteen forty-eight. But it's the shadow state: the managers of the nationalised combines in sectors like electricity, oil and steel - backed up by the police and the courts - who really run the country.'

It sounded like Dutschke's Long March had already taken place – but by the right.

'You can see why Togliatti, the leader of the PCI after Gramsci, thought that alongside building a cultural power base, it was just as important to capture the institutions of power, the mechanics of government rule. Almost as important as winning elections to become the actual government itself.'

Maybe the Italians thought permanent coalition

government made so little practical difference to their lives that there was no point in taking elections seriously and they should just let the real managers of the country get on with it.

'But the constant turnover of governments in Rome only proves my point,' I asserted. 'In Italy, when you remove politicians from the equation, life still carries on.'

'But you misunderstand,' he said impatiently. 'A shadow state can only be a shadow state if it remains hidden. Politicians in a bourgeois democracy are necessary to give the ordinary people the illusion that they have a say in appointing their rulers.'

Just then, Jan looked up and over my shoulder. Despite myself, I couldn't help turning around to look too. A group of three girls had just come into the cafe, all wearing barely-there miniskirts. The middle one of the group had stopped and was staring at Jan. She pursed her lips and with a toss of long silken hair, turned around and marched out again, dragging one of her companions by the hand.

'Someone you know?' I asked Jan.

He muttered something under his breath, and I wondered just how many girls in Brussels he'd been through and if it actually made him happy.

The morning was drawing on so I pressed him again. 'But if the Italian political system is so chaotic, why haven't the PCI been able to negotiate their way back into government, even if they're communists? A third of the votes must go a long way in forming a coalition?

'The DC have run Italy with their chosen partners since 'forty-eight. They and their cronies have manipulated the system to stay continuously in charge for twenty-two years.'

'No wonder people want to change things.'

'The electoral system doesn't help. It's a very pure proportional representation system, notionally highly democratic. But their system also requires voters to express preferences within the party lists, which means they're effectively voting for individual candidates anyway. All the horse-trading for votes gets very complicated at election time.'

'But despite all that, Italy still somehow works, in spite of the Italians. Is that what you're saying?'

'It the way the country's always been. A remote government in Rome, ruling a state which only came into being a hundred years ago when the northern Kingdom of Savoy imposed their authority on the rest of Italy at the point of a gun. And because of those origins, a sclerotic one, too. Rome was fearful that radical social and economic reforms forced on the South would damage the consensus for unification, such as it was. But it's resulted in long periods of stagnation in national life over the years. Which in turn has led to clientelism in politics and corruption in public administration as the only way to get things done quickly.'

'Wasn't Mussolini's chief claim that he was going to make a difference, rejuvenate Italy? Remake it in the image of the Roman empire?'

'For all his bluster, clientelism and corruption were how the fascists ran Italy too. Right now, there's a veneer of liberal democracy which makes the country appear modern and progressive, just like the rest of the Six. But ten years ago, a study showed that sixty-two of Italy's sixty-four regional prefects were former fascist regime officials. Same proportion for the police chiefs.'

'Isn't that all a little cynical? Once democracy comes to a country, people start to change. West Germans did. Italy just needs to be given time.'

He shook his head impatiently. I guessed that stealthily undermining societies was more enjoyable than giving them the chance to fix themselves.

'Sure, on the surface they have all the outward democratic forms and procedures you'd expect, but the real Italy endures underneath. Clientelism means DC politicians have influence over who gets jobs at state enterprises and in the municipalities. And as surely as night follows day, that means continual growth in public sector employment, so the DC can hand jobs out to their supporters, even if it's only meaningless menial work on offer.'

I glanced up at the bar, the bartender polishing glasses, the waitress perched on a stool checking her nails as she waited for the next customer to call her over.

Jan finished his coffee and lit a cigarette. He waved one at me, but I declined. I usually only smoked after a lot of alcohol.

'If there's so much inefficiency in Italy,' I said, 'how does the economy keep going? Momentum from the previous decade of economic boom?'

'It's only inefficient from a northern European point of view. Politically, it's very efficient. The DC have organised themselves into a pyramid of patronage franchises. Minor DC activists control blocks of votes and ensure these are cast for their own patrons higher up within the DC, such as deputies in the national parliament and city mayors. A hierarchical system, like the Catholic Church or the Mafia.'

It all still sounded too foreign for my liking. Whatever Rizzo's family had got themselves into, the players they were mixed up with intimately understood the exercise of power.

'How do you know all this stuff? Aren't you meant to be a historian, kings and emperors, dates of treaties, that kind of thing?'

'I work at a university. I speak to the other professors here,' he said, just to remind me again that I was only a high school graduate.

And that was his problem. He looked down on the DC, but they were the smart ones. They'd presumably been lining their pockets as they milked an entire country over two decades. But no one was rarely that successful without outside help.

'Where does Italy stand with America? And vice versa?

Are people still resentful about the interference in the 'forty-eight election because it led to two decades of DC cronyism?'

'Italy is one of America's closest allies, a founder member of NATO. Hardly surprising, as the DC was in the pocket of the CIA from the start. As for the interference in the 'forty-eight election, the US unashamedly propagandised Marshall Aid to help the first leader of the DC, Alcide De Gasperi. Newsreels of ships arriving laden with American grain for Italy's hungry with the implicit suggestion that they'd stop arriving if the PCI won. That kind of thing.'

'Was the CIA genuinely fearful of a communist takeover in Italy in the late forties?'

'It was a crazy time, who knew what to expect back then? I suspect the Americans are still suspicious of the PCI, even after all these years, which is short-sighted. Putting myself in their shoes, if they were smart and played their cards right, they could perhaps peel the Italians away from the other European communist parties. Especially after the violent suppression of the Prague Spring two years ago.'

'How come?'

'The guy tipped to be the PCI's next leader publicly rebuked the Soviets over the invasion of Czechoslovakia at an international conference in Moscow last year. He wouldn't have dared do that if Stalin or even Khrushchev had still been in charge. The PCI could be the vanguard of a moderate movement within communism.'

It was my turn to speculate. 'Maybe the Americans are suspicious because the public face of the PCI isn't fanatical. Maybe they believe they're playing a deep game of deception and will one day burst forth brandishing AK-47s from secret arms dumps.'

I spoke more and more slowly as I reached the end of my sentence. Maybe Sophie and Rizzo were more aware of what they were doing than I was giving them credit for.

'And the Mafia connection between America and Italy?' I asked, trying my luck. He seemed to know everything else about Italy.

'Okay, let's walk,' he said. 'I have to go to my office at the university to pick up a couple of reports of proceedings before giving tomorrow's lecture.'

We settled up and ambled along the hazy late summer streets. As we walked, I repeated my question about the Mafia.

He turned it around. 'What do you know about those guys?' he asked instead.

'Just what's in the movies. Prohibition and Al Capone, the Saint Valentine's Day Massacre - that sort of thing.'

'It goes back to land reform, or rather the lack of it. The Sicilian Mafia were originally the local enforcers for the managers who ran the estates of aristocratic absentee landlords. They ensured that labour contracts were honoured and organised the workers. Over time some of them became landowners, became dons themselves.

'And the American Mafia?'

'I'm not sure. The Italian-American diaspora has a strong network on both sides of the Atlantic. What the links between the criminal fraternities might be, I don't know. America is a land of bigger opportunities in every sense.

We arrived at his office and waited in the corridor outside while he fumbled in his pocket for the keys. He finally produced them in triumph and unlocked the door.

The last time I was here over a year ago, his office was a mess with papers covering every conceivable surface. It might have looked messy to me, but he had his system and was able to retrieve papers he hadn't seen for months.

But when he opened the door now I was surprised. The wild jungle of books had been severely hacked back. Instead of tottering piles of papers, his desk and tutorial table were now clear and the books were on the shelves where they belonged. There was even an in- and out-tray on his desk with opened, unfolded letters in the former. To be sure, they weren't squared off very neatly, but still.

I turned to him with raised eyebrows.

'I have a new secretary,' he mumbled.

'Oh really? Because getting your office into order I would have thought went well beyond the call of duty. More like a labour of love.'

He went slightly red and waved his hands about helplessly.

'So it is an act of love. She likes you. And if you've tried to keep your room tidy… you like her, don't you? The world is upended. How can this be?' I asked brusquely.

That explained his crude comments earlier. He was at sea without a compass.

I frowned at him. 'Just how serious is it with this girl?'

He opened and closed his mouth.

'You're not actually thinking of turning this into a domestic arrangement? With your flat also neat and tidy, and one day little Stapels running in and out of the nursery?'

'What can I say? It's always a danger once you really get to know someone. Sometimes it's just the way things turn out. You can't always stop it happening.'

'And does she want to make an honest man out of you? Does she know what you're like?' I asked dubiously. 'I thought that true socialists believe marriage is a construct of the patriarchy or something?'

'We do. But women generally don't. Even socialist women, over time.'

For all his talk of a long march and subverting the Western political system, someone had instead breached his defences and taken charge.

'I'm thirty-five. It's not unheard of, you know,' he said, more indignantly now.

'No, no. My best wishes. I hope it ends up the way you

want.'

'We'll see. Anyway, enough about me. How are you going to impress your mystery woman? You should meet up with my radical friends. Some girls like the air of danger that hangs around men who take risks for a cause.'

He found the papers he was looking for. It had taken him at least five minutes, pulling files in and out of cabinets, while he got ever more frantic.

'At last,' he sighed, looking around at the mess he'd made. Then he shrugged. 'She'll help me get it back into order by Monday lunchtime. I think she enjoys it, secretly.'

If that's how he got his kicks these days, then the worm had indeed turned.

'By the way,' he said casually, in conclusion. 'Speaking of Italy and Italian politicians, have you ever come across someone called Altiero Spinelli?'

'Who is he?'

'He was appointed as EEC Commissioner for Industrial Policy only this summer. He's one of us.'

'How do you mean?'

'He also believes in the "Long March Through the Institutions" in the cause of social justice.'

'What institutions? He's in the EEC, not in academia or the media. Or are you trying to take over the Commission too?' I asked sharply. 'And why should I have heard of him?'

'He was imprisoned by the fascists for sixteen years. But when Mussolini fell, Spinelli returned to politics and founded one of the first pan-European federalist movements on the back of his credentials as a prisoner of the former regime.'

'There were a few of those opportunists about at the time,' I commented.

'Well, when it came to European federalism, Spinelli and his followers were able to influence De Gasperi into doing something unique - although to be fair, the DC leader was already one of their sympathisers. On their prompting, De Gasperi wrote a clause into the country's new post-war constitution explicitly permitting the transfer of Italian sovereignty to future, yet to be established supranational institutions. That was in nineteen forty-seven. Eleven years before the founding of the EEC.'

'I had no idea the Italians were so keen. So Spinelli was a socialist too? Imprisoned by the fascists alongside the PCI leaders, Gramsci and Togliatti?'

'Gramsci died the year before Spinelli went to jail. Togliatti never went to prison. He resisted fascism from exile in Moscow.'

I rolled my eyes.

'Enough. There's a long political tradition in Italy of agitating from abroad, dating from the time of the unification movement. In Moscow, Togliatti had access to copies of Gramsci's prison notebooks and refined the Party's thinking. And you could say that while he was in prison, Spinelli was in internal exile in a way, too.'

'And what flavour of left-wing political philosophy did Spinelli agitate for? Or was it just European federation?'

'Oh, mainly that. Nothing much else. He was quite monomaniacal about it. He spent the last couple of years of the war in Switzerland waiting for the British and Americans to liberate Italy. While he was there, he organised a conference of resistance leaders from across occupied Europe. He persuaded them to adopt his manifesto for a single European state, which he and his collaborators hoped would be established after the war. They thought there would be a revolutionary situation, like after the First World War and in the chaos they wanted to impose a new European order.'

'What manifesto? Something like the document I was trying to find last year?'

'No, that one was a manual for economic administration. Spinelli's was purely political, at a high conceptual level.'

'But the same idea, people making plans for a post-war

Europe.'

'In outline. But you can take a look yourself, if I can find it,' he said, suddenly doubtful.

He got up to run his finger along the shelves. 'Reference texts by minor authors sorted alphabetically now,' he muttered to himself.

He pulled out a slim pamphlet, no more than thirty pages or so long.

'Here you are, *"For a Free and United Europe."* Take a read, you'll appreciate the socialist sentiments,' he said, once more assuming too much.

He leant back in his chair.

'Have you heard enough now? Are you any more open to the idea of joining us? After all, you complained we're not taking the voice of the workers into account. This is your opportunity to have a say.'

'Not everyone is suited to that work.'

'It doesn't matter. As I said, the Long March might take thirty years, we need all kinds of people at all levels of society to support us on the way.'

I deflected. 'Should I meet Spinelli? He must know some inside stories about Italian politics.'

He looked at me a little impatiently now. 'Read the manifesto first. Maybe I can set something up with him.'

'Privately, away from the Commission?'

'If you like. He might convince you to join us.'

'What? To advance the Red Banner and trample the class enemy underfoot?' I retorted mockingly.

If only he really knew who was sending me to Italy.

On the way back to my flat, I tried to put my finger on something which had been bothering me the longer I listened to Jan talking about Italy. He knew lots of facts, he was righteously indignant about the workers' plight at times. But it had felt like the concern of the theorist, remote and somehow detached. Or the frustration of the zoologist, that the animals he had under observation weren't behaving as he thought they ought to.

As for myself, it seemed that the Italians as long-time enthusiasts for the EEC project were exactly the type of people that Brussels ought to be nurturing. Set against that, in the EEC's eyes, they were enthusiasts who refused to take formal government seriously, masters at private deals and playing the system as they were.

Incubators of the Red menace in Western Europe, too. Mutating and transmitting the virus to West German radicals but managing not to catch it themselves.

People, not just from Hamburg, underestimated the *Macaronifresser* at their own risk.

Chapter Four

Brussels - Monday, 7th September 1970

I arrived at the airport later than planned and made it to the gate just as boarding started. From the back of the queue, I searched the line in front of me for my travelling companions.

After a gaggle of businessmen in suits I saw them, just ahead of a family with small children. When I looked closer, they were holding hands, or rather, Rizzo seemed to be holding Sophie's hand. They didn't turn around and I didn't make myself known to them.

I was surprised. Rizzo wasn't meant to be a proper boyfriend, just a companion on the Brussels dinner circuit. In the back of the truck on the way to Selmsdorf, Sophie had alluded to what his other duties were, but in public they weren't intimate - just a friendly linking of arms at most.

I pursed my lips. Even going on the little I'd seen of them together so far, I suspected that in private Rizzo might be taking things a lot more seriously than she was. I knew the hold she had and still had over me, after only a limited time spent in her company. One dinner, a seven-day trip to East Germany in spring 'sixty-nine, two meetings this summer before Ireland, one afterwards, and then a second trip to the East. If that's how I felt, what must Rizzo's addiction be like? Especially if after all these months with her he thought it might be the real thing?

They had seats at the front of the plane, so I had to walk past them on my way to the back row, next to the toilets.

Rizzo's amiable face lit up when he saw me, then the brightness faded, as if he'd remembered he was with someone who'd disapprove of his cheerfulness. When Sophie saw who Rizzo was looking at, she reached over and took his hand on to her lap, then watched me from under lidded eyes as I walked past with a casual nod of the head.

Either she'd lied to me in the truck and she was serious about Rizzo, or she'd had a think on the train after I'd left her, decided I wasn't forgiven, and was going to make certain I knew it. Not that I presumed she'd do anything about it until after the arms had safely reached Sicily.

Although I knew I'd be cutting it fine at the gate, I searched for an Italian primer in the bookshop at departures to read on the plane. They only sold an Italian-English one and I wondered what other foreign languages they spoke south of the Alps. Presumably following the American occupation of Italy and with a long history of emigration to the States I should come across enough people who knew English to get by. I'd spent enough time speaking it in Ireland, after all.

I gave the book a go for the first forty-five minutes of the flight, mouthing the words silently to myself. It turned out I was sitting next to the mother of the family ahead of me in the boarding queue. Out of the corner of my eye I glimpsed her looking in my direction from time to time, especially when my finger stopped at the longer words on the page.

I closed the book with a snap and glanced across at her myself. I guessed she was in her mid to late thirties, short with a full figure and wearing a sleeveless polka-dot blouse. The children were sitting in the row ahead of her, along with her husband.

She must have been bored, because she struck up a conversation in heavily accented English.

'How do you find learning Italian?' she asked.

'I speak French at work, so that helps,' I replied

guardedly, as was my second nature with strangers now.

'Where's work?'

'The EEC,' I said, even more unwillingly.

'My husband has just finished a secondment there from the Italian Ministry of Agriculture,' she added in a huskier voice. 'He was a member of a task force on the creation of a new regional development fund to help the poorer areas of the Community.'

'Did you come with him to Brussels?'

'Yes, we hired a house near to La Cambre.'

'And how long were you out here for?' I asked, more to deflect further questions about myself than out of interest.

'Six months. We're on our way back now, before the new school year starts properly. We brought the children along to get the experience of living abroad. Also, because I would have gone crazy if I'd stayed at home with my husband's mother around all the time.'

'Where's home? In Rome?'

'No, Sicily. Alfredo was a local DC party official, but he also worked part-time as a consultant to the Ministry in Rome when the Sicilian parliament was in recess. He resigned to take on the secondment with the promise of a permanent position in the capital afterwards.'

That seemed like a cosy arrangement. I presumed I was hearing a first-hand account of the DC's patronage networks which Jan had talked about yesterday.

'How did your children find Brussels?'

'They went to the European School. Lots of ambitious parents. Ambitious children, too. My daughter's best friend there was German.'

Her daughter must have heard, because she turned around in the row in front of us and spoke to her mother between the gap in the seats.

'Ursula wasn't my best friend. She just told everyone that.'

'Do you miss Sicily?' I asked the child - whose English pronunciation sounded the most authentic of all of us.

'I miss *nanna*.'

'Grandmother,' explained her mother.

I nodded. 'So, is it true what people say about Sicily, about the bad guys?' I asked the woman, as her daughter turned away again.

She furrowed her brow. 'What do you mean?' she asked coldly. 'The Mafia? That's all people ever want to know about our region.'

I reddened. 'My apologies. I don't know any Sicilians.'

'It's not what people think. They're just another set of community leaders, like the priests. My husband used to deal with them. He had no choice, not if he wanted the votes they controlled.'

I decided not to push it any further. Instead, I remembered what Jan had said about the dialects spoken by the southern migrants.

'Do you know any Sicilian? Is it much different to Italian?' I asked, tapping the primer lying on the seat tray in front of me.

That seemed to mollify her. 'My parents and grandparents spoke it at home, so I grew up around it. We use some dialect words in everyday speech with our own children, like "*nanna*." I could still probably speak it if I had to.'

She picked up the book and flicked through it.

'Keep making your way through this and you should stay out of trouble. Are you on vacation?'

'I'm with friends. We're only passing through Rome on the way to Apulia.'

'Don't let me stop you from reading your book then.'

So I didn't, until we landed an hour later at Fiumicino.

I met Rizzo and Sophie at the baggage carousel.

'Good flight, Giovanni?' I asked, still thinking in English.

'First class on Sabena isn't the best,' Rizzo replied in French. I darted a glance at Sophie, wondering if he'd switched back for her benefit. Maybe she didn't speak English as well as I'd assumed.

'We're going to drop our bags at left luggage and then go into town until the next flight,' Sophie said, but not in a way that suggested I was invited too.

Rizzo ignored her. 'Is this your first time in Italy, Oskar?' he asked.

'The summer after conscription finished, I went camping in the Italian Alps with friends I'd made in the army. We hiked up around the Gran Paradiso. There was still snow on the peaks there, even in August.'

My mind went back to days of brilliant blue on the roof of Europe. Hard trekking followed by hard drinking in the evenings.

'We're going right down to the far south, no snow there. It should be quite pleasant now after the heat of high summer.'

He looked at his watch and glanced at Sophie, who'd retrieved their bags from the conveyor belt herself.

'Come with us into the centre of Rome for lunch,' he offered. 'If you haven't seen it yet, we can eat on the square outside the Pantheon.' His voice went up a notch as the mask of the suave Brussels bureaucrat slipped, eager that I should see one of the ancient marvels of his country.

'Sophie tells me you like military stuff, weapons and things. Marcus Aurelius' Column is near to the Pantheon. You can take a look at that afterwards too.'

I was bewildered, for I'd never talked to Sophie about my time in the army, not even once. Maybe she'd been referring to my Makarov in conversation with him. But I was annoyed too, that she and Rizzo had been discussing my likes and dislikes behind my back.

'Well let's go then, if you're coming,' she said impatiently.

The ride into the centre of Rome took three-quarters of an hour but our connecting flight wasn't until seven in the evening so the Germans in the taxi should have been relaxing. But by now, Rizzo had picked up on the tension between Sophie and me. It seemed to have spoilt his excitement at showing me Rome, for an uneasy silence opened up in the car.

Outside, the sky was overcast and the atmosphere muggy. It felt five degrees warmer than Brussels. There had been rain earlier and I caught the smell of wet concrete as the moisture was driven out by the ambient heat, for above the low cloud, the sun still shone down on Italy.

We were definitely in southern Europe by other clues as well, such as the cars and bikes passing us haphazardly without regard to traffic rules. Noticeably cheaper and smaller cars too. Our driver was no better than the others, as he weaved past comical three-wheeled vans and overladen trucks straining on their way into the Eternal City.

As we neared our destination, high rise public housing on either side of the highway gave way to elegant apartment blocks and grand office buildings from the last century. Not quite so imperial in style as Berlin or Vienna, or even back home in Brussels, but still a reminder that there was money to be made in Italy. After all, with fifty-or-so million people it was the third-biggest country in Europe, just ahead of France.

I decided the awkwardness had gone on for long enough and twisted around in the front passenger seat to quiz Rizzo about the reaction of the woman on the plane to my Mafia comment.

'Yes, Sicilians don't like to be reminded of it. But there you go, it's the price they pay for all their luck. The volcanic soil from Etna makes the east of the island very fertile. Long growing season and the perfect climate for citrus. Right in the middle of the Mediterranean, too - at the crossroads of the trading routes of the Greeks and everyone else from antiquity. There's a saying in our family that God blessed Sicily so much He had to balance things out by creating the Sicilians.'

'Your grandmother's from there?' I asked.

'Sophie told you?'

'Yes, the other day. She said your *nanna* was a Mafia princess.'

Rizzo chuckled at Sophie's description and slapped her on the knee, leaving his hand there.

I kept my eyes on him as he replied, hoping for his sake he wouldn't be tempted to make a quick aside about Sophie being his royalty.

'It's the great love story in our family. Her family were wealthy dons in south-eastern Sicily, but they had a house in Rome and spent time there. My grandfather met her socially once or twice before the First World War. Then the fighting started, and they didn't see one another for three years. After it was all over, he went down to Sicily and demanded to be allowed to marry her. When her family refused, he broke into her father's house and carried her off to Syracuse. By the morning it was too late for anyone to do anything about it. *Matrimonio riparatore.*'

'Sounds like he had a death wish to do that to the Mafia.'

'He was Arditi. They didn't know the meaning of fear.'

I shook my head in ignorance.

'Storm troops. They attacked with daggers and other trench weapons ahead of the regular formations. Sometimes they even wore armour plate, which made them look like medieval knights. My grandfather has photographs somewhere in the house we're going to.'

'Your grandfather's house?' All told, *nonno* sounded like he'd had a bad case of shell shock.

'Our family's summer house. The former main house on our family's old estate actually. We sold off the land during the fifties and sixties to our farm workers under the land reforms.'

I deflated a little inside. Sophie had warned me last

year, the very first time we'd met, that the circle of young up-and-coming *fonctionnaires* around the now dead von Barten weren't my kind of people. Rizzo's landowner talk had just reminded me why.

'Are your grandmother's family still in their old line of work?' I asked, fishing for something to make me feel better.

He laughed again. 'They're basically property developers in Catania and Syracuse now. I'm sure they make payments to get the land rezoned for development, but that's fairly normal in Italy.' He frowned to himself as he said it.

'But we're going to change all that over time through the EEC,' he continued more determinedly.

'I want us to show Italians that political systems can work if they follow the rules. But to convince people, the regulations need to be equitable. We at the EEC have a duty to set an example where we can. Right now, we can't even agree on agricultural subsidies that are fair to everyone. They're skewed to support northern European farms - dairy products rather than citrus fruit.'

He lifted his hand from Sophie's knee. I flicked a glance at her, but she was looking out the window, disinterested in our conversation. Lunch was going to be fun.

Rizzo found us a table at the top of the gently inclined square. We sat and watched the tourists go in and out of the Pantheon at the bottom as we waited on our food.

I couldn't tell if Sophie was more annoyed at me for having accepted Rizzo's invitation or at him for having extended it. I'd seen her in an almighty sulk once before, during our first trip to East Germany, and now it seemed she was building up to it again. It was probably all a delayed reaction to what I'd done to her at the weekend and what I'd told her in Johannes' office on Saturday too.

However, her mood was Rizzo's problem today. I

probed him some more about the Mafia.

'If you say your grandmother's family are merely property developers with menaces, why do the Mafia have the reputation they do?'

'It's not just the violence. It's the secrecy that goes with it. The shootings get into the newspapers, but there's a mystery as to how they decide these things, how they organise themselves and settle disputes. *Omertà* is a real thing.'

He topped up our glasses from the carafe.

'Do the police ever solve much Mafia crime, then,' I asked.

'You were in the police for a time. How did you get things done in Hamburg?'

'Paid informers were the fastest way to find out what was happening on the street. That and a little coercion of suspects in the cells when the duty sergeant wasn't looking.'

'There you go. As long as *omertà* remains intact, the Mafia are safe.' He took a sip of wine.

'Or unless someone has a mental crisis and confesses to a crime.' Sophie spoke up now, looking at me carefully as she did so. Like a cat watching a mouse.

'Or unless someone confesses, *cara*,' he said, lingering over the last word.

Forget his grandfather. Now Rizzo was the one with the death wish. I held my breath, but there was no explosion. Sophie gave me a nasty, secret look, as if enjoying my disappointment.

'It's not unknown, though,' continued Rizzo, still oblivious. 'In America, one of their members called Joey Valachi turned federal evidence a few years back. The state always has the ultimate power to deal with these guys if they really want to.'

'What happened to Valachi in the end?'

'I don't know exactly. He's famous because he was the first of them to even acknowledge the existence of the

Mafia.'

'Does the American version have much to do with the one over here, down south?' I asked.

'You're going to meet someone at the party who's been in both. My second cousin. He's a "Giovanni" too, but the family call him "Gianni." His grandmother and mine were sisters.'

'His grandmother being the respectable one?' I suggested with a half-smile.

Rizzo grinned at this. It would take a lot of sourness from Sophie to drag down his naturally buoyant mood, whatever the circumstances he found himself in.

'Gianni went to America eight years ago to avoid the draft in Italy and make his fortune. Spent time with his cousins over there and helped out in their family businesses. But he's back now.'

'What would he have done to a Valachi?'

'Shown no mercy, I expect. These guys know what they're getting themselves into when they join. They can't expect any forgiveness if they have an attack of conscience and change their minds.'

I glanced involuntarily at Sophie. Her mask was up again.

Rizzo concluded. 'But if they do confess, knowing what's likely in store for them, then that's a rare form of courage.'

Our food arrived and Sophie brought us back to the task in hand.

'Tell him some more about what needs moving,' she told Rizzo. 'The goods.'

'The people my father has an obligation to are arranging for the items to be collected together from a couple of different places across the South. Then you're taking them to a house we own in Sicily, up in the hills around Ragusa, where we have a secure place to store them.'

'What happens after that?'

'That's the limit of your involvement. Gianni's family, the Di Lucas, will take care of the shipment from then on.'

'How many goods?'

Rizzo looked at Sophie, then up at the writing on the facade of the Pantheon, pondering.

'A truckload I guess.'

'Heavy truck, medium truck? Two-axle, three-axle? An articulated unit?'

'Like an Italian Army truck.'

That wasn't very helpful. I wondered about suggesting to Johannes that I hire Pavel again and just leave behind whatever his truck couldn't carry.

'And you want me to take care of the whole move? From loading to unloading?'

'We need you for complete deniability. Tomorrow we'll show you where you'll pick up the crates. When you arrive in Sicily, Gianni Di Luca will meet you and show you where they're to be hidden. I'll travel separately and come out the day after once everything's safe and secure.'

'What happens if something goes wrong and we get caught on the way?'

'You'll get well paid,' said Sophie contemptuously.

'We'll have to send a second consignment, I suppose,' Rizzo said with a shrug.

'How does your family have access to these kinds of goods in the first place?'

'That's not your concern,' he said coldly.

It was the first time I'd ever had a sharp word from him. Not even when he was warning me off Sophie that first evening I'd met them both.

She pouted at me in sympathy with him. I ignored her.

'Have all the details been agreed? Will tomorrow be the final discussion? I want to leave Italy with enough information to make a plan,' I told Rizzo.

'Yes. A couple of the other key players are coming out to Apulia tomorrow too. We'll tell you all you need to know after they arrive. The next time you come back here, it will be for real.'

We finished our meal in silence, Sophie glancing across to Rizzo from time to time with a speculative look.

He called for the bill and settled it, but the pair of them didn't give any signal they were ready to leave just yet.

Eventually, Rizzo cleared his throat. He indicated the Pantheon on the other side of the square.

'It's definitely worth a look. Go and get yourself a city map too. The column I mentioned is a couple of streets away in that direction,' he pointed over his shoulder. 'If you keep going, you'll come to the presidential palace, the Quirinale. And further south of that there's another column, Trajan's Column, with more military depictions.'

I took the hint and left them to get up to whatever they'd planned next. Just inside the entrance of the Pantheon I turned around and looked back, concealed by the dark interior. They had got to their feet and it seemed like they were about to leave the table. I saw them speaking and Rizzo glancing at his watch before they moved off, walking together up one of the side streets leading off the square, but not hand in hand this time.

Even with its original interior stripped out and the building repurposed as a Catholic church, the Pantheon was still a marvel of Roman engineering, the Italian ingenuity which Jan Stapel had talked about yesterday. An unsupported concrete dome soared high above the marble floor, illuminated by the grey light coming in through the hole at the top. For me, it wasn't so much the design that impressed me as the sophistication of the society which had made it all happen - bringing together labour and capital to construct something which had lasted until now.

A quarter of the way round from the altar, someone had placed candles and a couple of small flags of the old Royal Italy by the tomb of Victor Emmanuel the Second. Jan might not think much of either the current or the former Italian regimes, but some people still did.

Later, standing in the Piazza Colonna, I looked up to follow the march of stone-carved legionnaires around Marcus Aurelius' Column and thought again about the genius of the former inhabitants of the peninsula for administration. They'd run an empire of millions with no more technology than handwritten letters and post horses. No mainframes, satellite communications or undersea telephone cables for them.

A light summer rain began to fall on my upturned face as I stood there, transfixed. As a German of the post-war generation I didn't much hold with excessive admiration for politicians, but the sense of confidence and triumph of the old emperor was still there to be felt across two thousand years. His soldiers looked confident too, as they bridged rivers, formed a shield wall to assault the barbarians and marched their prisoners from the conquered lands off into slavery.

Jan had said the modern Italian state was only around a hundred years old, as Kaiser Wilhelm's unified Germany would have been if not for a couple of wars. No wonder Mussolini had tried to clothe himself with legitimacy by harking back to the glory days of the only true European empire. A feat of conquest and unification attempted on more than one occasion since, but never equalled. The USSR was having a good go in the East, though, with its own shield wall of vassal states.

Whatever Jan said about a patient takeover of the institutions of society, only war ever truly shook established states to their foundations and got the pieces on the chessboard into motion. I wondered what Spinelli's manifesto on European federation had to say about it all and about the revolutionary situation he'd expected to arise as a result.

The Quirinale was next on the circuit which Rizzo had recommended. Truthfully, there wasn't much to look at from the outside. A wide piazza opened out in front of the main entrance for dignitaries, a high porticoed doorway surrounded by low bollards and flanked by a couple of ceremonial guards. The palace area itself covered several city blocks, but it appeared to be walled by high buildings on all sides, as far as I could see anyway.

I took in Trajan's column next and more spiral relief carvings of Roman military might. I left in good time to get to the taxi rank on the northern side of the Largo di Torre Argentina, where I'd agreed to meet the others and waited at a cafe across the street.

According to the key of the city map I'd picked up after leaving the Pantheon, the ruins I could see in the square marked the remains of the Senate building where Julius Caesar had been assassinated, stabbed by the defenders of the Republic. Germans liked to talk about the verdict of history these days - thinking of the past fifty years - but the Italians counted the passage of time in centuries. And they were reminded of it simply by walking down the street.

But I'd had enough sightseeing for today. The time passed for our rendezvous, but it was no hardship to wait some more, sipping espresso whilst watching the Roman girls buzz past on their Vespas.

Sitting there, it was difficult to imagine the chaotic, decadent Italy that Fellini had captured when he filmed 'La Dolce Vita', as a land of factory riots and bombs on trains. I didn't care how enthusiastic Jan Stapel was about overthrowing governments - Rizzo and his father's arms dealing wasn't the sort of thing decent people got themselves involved with, if they could help it. As for Sophie, goodness knew what she and her own clan were getting out of it.

Forty minutes after the time when Rizzo had suggested we should be leaving by, the pair of them casually ambled up to the taxi rank, hand in hand. Rizzo glanced away when he caught sight of me sitting at the table, letting go of Sophie to negotiate the fare, or possibly even the route, with the driver at the head of the queue.

Her hair had been in braids when they left the square where we'd had lunch. Now it was gathered back into a loose ponytail with her sunglasses pushed up over her head. The top couple of buttons of her dress were undone too, when I thought only one had been before. She eyed me with an insolent look as I stood up, left some coins for a tip, and walked across to them.

Rizzo was still avoiding my eye as I took the front seat next to the driver. He asked me in a desultory way how my walk had been, and then we all sat quietly for the rest of the trip.

The silence in the back felt deliberate, for Rizzo said a couple of things to her which she ignored. I flicked them the odd glance from time to time in the driver's rear-view mirror. She stared impudently back at me in the reflection, as if she was sitting there waiting for me to pay her attention.

What a bitch she was. Daring me to believe they'd paid for a cheap hotel by the hour in the backstreets off the piazza and done it there. If she'd really just wanted to let off steam, she only had to wait until this evening, for I was sure they'd be sharing a room in Apulia. Unless Rizzo's family was extra-religious, which he'd given me no indication they were.

Either I was paranoid, reading way too much into the signals or she was deliberately needling me with her unavailability as some kind of punishment. Not that I'd ever made a move on her. I had shot her uncle, though.

I stopped speculating. This trip needed delicate handling as it was, without encouraging my latent obsession for her any further. And anyway, right now she was Rizzo's woman, and it was him I was working for, in order to spring my cousin from jail. Rizzo himself hadn't done anything against me, as far as I knew. The mess with Karin was on Sophie's account.

And even if she was simply just being a bitch, then I

felt sorry for her in a way too, that she should be so consumed by nastiness. Or revenge.

For the flight to Bari, I was allocated a window seat on the same row as the pair of them, but on the opposite side of the aircraft. The plane was half-full and apart from the three of us, there was no one else in our part of the cabin. I turned to speak to Rizzo across the narrow aisle of the turboprop, reckoning to get him to open up more about his family and fill me in about what his father did these days.

'It's complicated,' he said, sipping his scotch on ice. 'My great-grandfather was from a land-owning family in Apulia, youngest of two brothers and likely only to inherit a minority share of the estate. So he went north to Milan to try his luck in business there. He fell on his feet, got apprenticed to an engineering firm owned by a family friend and eventually opened his own factory manufacturing scientific optical equipment. He luck held, because during the First World War he made a fortune by switching to components for artillery rangefinders.'

'And you're still in that line of work, I understand?'

'Yes, we produce miniaturised gyroscopes for gunsights and navigation systems - high value items. My father runs the firm on his own now. My grandfather retired five years ago. He's not as well as he was,' he said a little sadly.

'How did your grandfather's branch of the family end up owning the main estate house then?'

'My great-grandfather's brother didn't marry, so all the land in Apulia eventually came to us anyway.'

'And your family kept up the connection to Sicily too, despite the history there? How well do you know your second cousin, if he spent time in America?'

'As adults, not well at all,' he said distastefully. 'He's a necessary evil on this job.'

I left it and swirled my own scotch for a while, trying to frame a question about Rizzo's father's wartime activities as tactfully as possible.

'What did your family do during the liberation?'

Instead of answering right away, he waved me to move closer, over to the next seat along on my row. On his other side, Sophie was staring out of the window into the gloom of the gathering night.

He leant towards me across the aisle. 'How much do you know about Italy towards the end of the war?' he asked.

'I know that the country was divided for the last couple of years.'

'Our family's factories were in the North, in what became the rump fascist state after the Allied invasion - the so-called Italian Social Republic. My father had been with the Italian Army in Africa. He escaped on one of the last boats to leave Tunis, in May 'forty-three. In July he was still at home on leave in Milan when Mussolini was deposed and imprisoned by his own fascist government.'

So much for being a dictatorship, I thought. Italy couldn't even get that right.

'The new government tried to change sides and even declared war on Germany. But the Germans moved in troops to secure the northern cities, rescued Mussolini from captivity and formed a new state governed by his loyalists. My father was drafted into the anti-partisan force there because of his prior service in the army.'

The battalions raised from the German police who'd carried out anti-partisan operations behind the front line on the Eastern Front were some of the most vicious and brutal of all the units attached to the Wehrmacht. The year before I joined the Hamburg police, some former officers had been arrested for war crimes committed in Poland. The trials had still been going on when I left in 'sixty-six.

'Did he fight right to the very end?' I asked.

'It was a difficult time for our family. We had to gradually unwind our connections to the regime as it collapsed around us. There were awkward compromises.

Secret support under the noses of the Germans for the Liberation Committee organised by the workers at our main factory. My father elsewhere in the zone, fighting for the Germans against communist partisans, both Italian and Yugoslav.'

I looked over at Sophie, for her uncle had danced that same dance in Germany at the end of the war too. She'd turned to listen to Rizzo's story and was staring back at me coldly. I was the only one in this row of seats whose family didn't own several factories. The Lenkeits didn't even own part of one factory.

Now she placed a hand on the inside of Rizzo's thigh as she sat beside him - high up his leg too, just to make sure I knew my worth as a man compared to the heir to industrial wealth.

Rizzo ignored the distraction of her fingers and carried on with his story.

'But my grandfather performed that balancing act well. He paid off the local Socialists who nationally were the junior left-wing partners of the PCI, and our factories weren't attacked in the last week of the war when the workers rose up against Mussolini. The same arrangement allowed him to lay off workers to survive the immediate post-war slump and give him time to rebuild his business. Then he transferred his allegiance to the DC when they won the first election after the war. Someone once said that Italian businessmen use politicians in the way you and I take a taxi. Whoever's available will do.'

'And since those early post-war years? Did your family benefit from the export boom?'

He raised his eyebrows at this question. Maybe he didn't expect me to be aware of the economic side of things. Sometimes a lack of higher education was an advantage, because people underestimated me.

'Everyone did. My father started traveling extensively in Europe and beyond. He now speaks better English than me, even though he didn't learn it at school like I did.'

'We can speak English now if you like.'

He glanced to see if Sophie was still listening. 'No, it's okay. French is fine.'

'But what's happened now? Has the past caught up with him, somehow?'

'The country's not in great shape. The DC has been in power too long and each year the students and workers become ever more militant. The economy needs to keep growing to meet people's increasing expectations for quality of life and to smooth out social inequalities. But the situation is fragile and strikes and riots are undermining business to the detriment of everyone, at all levels of society.'

Before his speech earlier on the way into Rome, about making the CAP fair to all, I'd never have put him down as having a social conscience.

'The public sector is an increasing drag too. The political settlement with industry was that they would get cheap labour, no planning laws, and minimal corporation taxes. In exchange there would be no opposition to the DC creating ever more public sector positions to be dispensed to their supporters.'

'Because your electoral system encourages clientelism? With the votes for individuals on the party lists?'

He frowned again. 'Who told you all this?'

'It's my job to be informed.'

'So I can see,' he said, now switching to English after all.

I carried on in the same language, hoping it would annoy Sophie. 'What does your father think? Is he worried about how things are going?'

'Not particularly, but longer-term I imagine he might be,' he said guardedly.

'How did he get mixed up in the affair with your cousin's family in Sicily?'

'We'll say more when we arrive at my family's place. He's under an obligation to help some people.'

'Some of the people from his past?' I asked, even though Sophie had already told me this on the way back from Wismar.

Sophie squeezed his thigh a little tighter. '*En français s'il vous plaît*,' she said.

Rizzo obliged her and switched back. 'What did your family do during the war, Oskar?'

Sophie withdrew her hand and folded it with the other, laying them on her lap as she awaited my answer.

'My mother served as a nurse but was pregnant with me at the war's end. My father was gone by then. She ended up in Hamburg, but her sister stayed behind in the Soviet occupation zone. That's it, really.'

'What do your family do in the East? Are they political?'

'No, not at all. My uncle is a foreman in a shipyard and my aunt a secretary to a trade union official. They go to church, so they're not in favour with the regime.'

'Catholic church?'

'No, East Germany is almost entirely Protestant.'

He gave a kind of jerk with his chin, like a shrug but without using his shoulders.

'My sister is very Catholic. She volunteers with the Vatican social relief organisation, the POA. Leaves copies of her magazine, Famiglia Cristiana, lying around the house in the hope that we'll pick it up and read it.'

I wasn't sure how to respond to this. 'Has she tried to convert Sophie?' I asked lightly.

'Sophie's only met her once,' he said in a slightly strained voice. 'I did well to get her to come down here for this party.'

Yes, Rizzo, I thought to myself - because she's got no intention of getting close to your family unless she has to.

I couldn't help myself now, she'd been provoking me all day.

'I'm sure there'll be time enough in the years to come,' I suggested innocently.

Now she folded her arms tightly across her chest and I could feel the chill running between the occupants of the two seats next to me, although maybe it was more from the air conditioning nozzle she'd just angled in my face.

'Yes, I expect there will,' said Rizzo lamely.

I thought back to the time when she and I had to pretend to be engaged in front of my aunt's family, during that first trip to East Germany. And about how much Sophie had hated the fake stories I made up for them, of how we met and fell for each other. No man possessed her. Of that she was very clear, both then and now.

When Rizzo had warned me off Sophie that first evening, he said it was to spare me from frustration. But I suspected the moth had spent too long fluttering before the flame. I didn't know how often she let him into her bed, but I suspected that was a drug which only the strongest-minded could take without becoming entirely enslaved to her will. Even as all these things passed through my head, I half-consciously brushed my temple where she'd kissed me once.

Rizzo misinterpreted the gesture, thinking I was touching the scar on my cheek just below my eye.

'Does it still hurt?' he asked.

'No, it's healed,' I said, a little too curtly for politeness.

The pilot dipped a wing to turn the plane onto a new course and I returned to my window seat for the final approach to Bari.

By the time we'd retrieved our bags it was well past nine and Sophie's temper was even shorter than before. It wasn't improved when the driver who Rizzo had assured her would be there to pick us up didn't show.

'What do we do now?' she snapped.

Rizzo looked helpless.

'Giovanni,' I said, 'Over there.'

I pointed to the car rental clerk who'd just switched off the light in her kiosk and was now standing outside locking up.

He went up to her and began jabbering away in voluble Italian. Several shrugs, raised eyebrows, and flicks of the fingers were part of the performance as well. Eventually, she went back inside and the kiosk lit up again.

When he came out with the car keys, I suggested I did the driving as the least awkward arrangement for everyone.

'You sit in the back with Sophie,' I told him. 'You said it's about forty kilometres away? Just point me in the right direction when we get near.'

He havered, his Italian male pride no doubt torn between wanting to show off to Sophie how fast he could cover the distance on the back roads in the dark, against not wanting to play chauffeur.

'Let me drive,' I insisted again. 'If I'm to come back this way with a truck, I need to learn the roads.'

'Yes, Giovanni, let him. He needs all the practice he can get. He's not a very good lorry driver,' Sophie said sneeringly. 'Here, you don't have much baggage, Oskar. Carry some of mine to the car as well.'

'It wouldn't do to leave any behind, would it, Sophia?' I replied frostily, trying to remind her of that morning in 'sixty-nine, arriving in Brussels Central on the train from East Germany when she'd first betrayed me, rushing out of the station with only half her luggage and a stolen document. I hoped she'd be irritated by the use of the formal variant of her name, too.

For a moment Rizzo gave the impression he thought he was the fifth wheel today.

'Lenkeit Spedition, satisfaction guaranteed,' I said as I slung a bag over each shoulder by their straps and picked up another with my right hand. I still didn't like to put too much strain on my left one yet.

Sophie just had to have the last word. 'I wouldn't trust them. They tend to take people to places they don't want to go.'

The air had been heavy in Rome, but it was slightly cooler down here. Still warm enough, though, even at this time of night. Rizzo grinned as he saw me wipe a trace of sweat from my brow after I'd dumped the bags in the boot of the hire car.

'Welcome to Apulia. I told you this was the best time of year to visit.'

After the spat at the airport, the rest of the journey from the coastal plain up into the Murgian Hills behind Bari was uneventful. We made the final turning onto Rizzo's family's property and approached the house down a long dusty lane, lined by what looked like poplars in the car headlights, waving gracefully in the light breeze and suggesting a cooler night.

The lane widened out and became a gravel drive just by the house. The Rizzo place was built in grey stone and looked like it was a couple of centuries old at least. I got the impression it had originally been a large farmhouse which had been extended over the decades into something grander as the family's prosperity had grown.

The front door opened into a terracotta-tiled hallway, overlooked by the busts of a couple of Roman senator types and an elegantly hand-drawn family tree hanging in a frame on the wall. After we dumped our bags by the stairs, Rizzo took us through to the covered terrace at the rear.

His father was already there, sitting at a low table in the gloom. He was staring out over the grounds, which were bounded on their eastern edge by a belt of trees silhouetted in the starlight. Above the treetops, studded in the inky blackness of the country sky by night, shone constellation upon constellation and the odd planet too. Creation in all its breath-taking glory.

Rizzo's father got to his feet and stepped forward into the lamplight spilling from the house. He was an older version of Rizzo, his skin more weather-beaten and a splash of grey at his temples. He kissed his son on both cheeks, Italian style. Sophie was similarly embraced, but thankfully he only offered me his hand.

He led Rizzo to the seat next to him, an arm around his waist. I watched them, coldly jealous. Sophie crassness in Wismar had opened up my oldest wound again. I'd trade all the factories in Italy for a father.

Rizzo's father showed me to a chair positioned facing the house. I sat with my back to the stars, under three watchful pairs of eyes.

He explained something in Italian to Rizzo, who translated into French for Sophie and me.

'My father apologises for the lack of a driver at the airport. We sent the usual servants away for the next couple of days because we have caterers coming in for the party. A message should have been left for us at the terminal before we landed.'

While Rizzo was relaying this, his father got up again to fetch glasses and a bottle of yellow liqueur from somewhere just inside the house through another set of double doors leading off the terrace.

'*Strega*,' he explained, pouring me a slightly more generous measure than the others. '*Bevi, bevi.*'

I obliged and he poured me another.

Rizzo half-turned to Sophie. 'We're going to speak English with Oskar now. Just for a minute or two.'

His father dove straight in.

'I'm told you know some professionals who can help our family with our problem.'

'I have contacts in Hamburg from when I was with the police there a few years ago,' I improvised. 'I used them the other week on another job,' I added as an afterthought.

Sophie's English wasn't that bad, because she darted me a look of poison at this.

'How long have you known him, Giovanni?' his father asked.

'Since the spring of last year. Then Sophie and I met him again at the start of the summer.'

'Have you done this kind of thing before?' he asked me

now.

'What, transport weapons? I was in the army before the police.'

'You mean in the army as *coscritti*?'

'Yes, fifteen months service for my year class.'

Rizzo's father turned to his son and shrugged, unconvinced. I glanced at Sophie and wondered reluctantly about making an appeal to her. This was all her idea, after all. She knew back in August why she wanted to hire me, so she could help seal the deal now.

'Tell them how you got your scar,' she said in halting English. I was sure she hated having to reveal a lesser ability at something compared to me, or to anyone else for that matter.

Rizzo's father looked at her sharply.

The words for a story fell into place. But I in turn now hated having to give away even a slight approximation of the truth.

'I was in Ireland this summer. Some people asked me about importing arms from Hamburg. I got jumped on in a bar.'

'*Ci ha detto che era in una rissa da bar*,' said Rizzo to his father, forgetting to speak in English for a moment.

'You told Sophie and I that you were in a bar fight. Is that what it was about?' he asked warily.

'I didn't give them the offer they wanted. They didn't like it.'

'Okay,' said Rizzo's father slowly, looking at the scars on my hand now.

I could tell that Rizzo himself was still dubious that I had a parallel career outside the EEC as an international arms dealer, but he said nothing.

Sophie spoke up again, in both French and English to make sure there was no confusion.

'*Ma famille se porte garante de lui.* My family guarantees him. We have personal debts to each other.'

Rizzo frowned. But he could hardly be expected to

know this, because Sophie had only found out for herself on Saturday the full extent of what she'd done to Karin and what I'd done to her uncle before that.

Rizzo's father shrugged again and spoke to me in English.

'Tomorrow you're going to meet some other people who are coming to the party. They'll want to speak to you as well, to check you out. I've been asked to make arrangements to move the goods, but they have the final say.'

'Do they have the same background as you?' I asked.

'Yes, we know each other from the war. What has Giovanni told you about payment?'

'We haven't discussed it yet.' I hadn't given it much thought, for the Stasi were supplying free labour on this job.

'I need to know the quantities that are to be moved,' I said. 'Your son wasn't sure. And when you need it done by. Once I know that, I'll speak to my guys in Hamburg and tell you how much they want.'

'How are you involved in this kind of thing if you work at the EEC in… what did he say?' Rizzo's father turned to ask his son.

'Internal Affairs,' he replied. 'In one of the special departments, or Sophie tells me.'

She was too good at guessing for my liking.

'Some other people from the Hamburg police were recruited to work there too,' I obfuscated. 'We keep up our connections with home and give them tips from time to time from what we hear in Brussels. In exchange, they assist us on special jobs like this one.'

It was a mishmash of half-truths and inferences and I suspected it wouldn't stand up to hard scrutiny. But tomorrow was another day.

'Giovanni's girlfriend might vouch for you but if you want this job, you need to be convincing,' said Rizzo's father. 'His cousin from Sicily is coming to the party too.

He'll have his own questions for you.' He grimaced slightly.

As for myself, I wondered how highly the Sicilians thought of the Apulian side of the family, given how the split had originally come about.

Rizzo took me upstairs to a bedroom at the back of the house with a balcony.

'The bathroom is through there. They've left towels.'

I wondered if all the guests were given an ensuite room.

'We're on the ground floor,' he said, quite casually. 'There's breakfast things in the kitchen - off the hallway, opposite the door to the terrace. You might see my grandfather out in the garden in the morning. He's an early riser, even in retirement.'

When he'd gone, I opened the full-length louvred door onto the balcony and stood for a moment listening to the cicadas and gazing at the stars.

Why did Sophie think I was the person to help Rizzo? She knew that I had done confidential work for her uncle and she suspected I still did it for someone else at the EEC. Would she have gone elsewhere if she'd had the choice? At least she knew the Stasi were planning to be part of this affair now, so there was only so much mischief she could get up to, even if she wanted to change her mind.

A light went on in the room below mine. Through the vines arching over the terrace I saw shadows cast on the flagstones by people moving about inside. There was a snatch of French as the room's outside doors were closed and the curtains drawn.

They were sleeping directly underneath me then. I realised that I'd never asked myself why she didn't speak Italian nor why he hadn't learned German.

I left my own balcony door open and went to bed too.

I listened out with half an ear for what was going on in the room below, but no sounds came through the floor.

Maybe Rizzo really had got lucky in Rome. She always seemed to.

Chapter Five

I woke at half-past six. The stars had gone and the sun was peeping in through the open door to the balcony. I padded to the rail and looked out. The house was set on a gentle rise of broken rock, surrounded by grassy gardens interspersed with shrubs and small trees. A modern swimming pool had been built at the foot of the outcrop, a little way from the house. The line of trees at the eastern boundary of the grounds, which I'd seen silhouetted last night, seemed to mark the start of a slope, back down towards the plain and Bari beyond, I supposed.

I had started sleeping better after Dublin and my conscience was certainly feeling better for having confessed to Sophie in Wismar, no matter how she was reacting now. But I wasn't going back to sleep, so I thought I'd wander down to the tree line and see how far I could see beyond it.

As I made my way along the path, I caught sight of an elderly man under the smaller trees dotted about the roughly-mown lawn. He was bending down to pick something off the dewy grass, moving from trunk to trunk. Rizzo's grandfather perhaps, or some kind of gardener. I didn't think gardeners wore crisp white linen shirts, though. Out of curiosity I went across to him, greeting him with a tentative '*Ciao*'.

'*Eh? Sei in ritardo.*'

We both looked at one another, a little confused. He beckoned me closer and opened the flap of a cloth bag hanging from his shoulder. Inside, it was half full of shiny hazelnuts.

I pointed at them. '*Haselnüsse*,' I said helpfully.

'*Si, si. Nocciole. Per mangiare*,' he pointed to his mouth. '*Per colazione.*'

Now he mimed picking them up from the ground and then tugged at my sleeve, which left me confused again. Maybe he had a big order to complete before breakfast.

I quite liked hazelnuts, so thought why not? If he was Rizzo's grandfather, it couldn't hurt to make friends. He made the decision for me by handing over a second cloth shoulder bag and I got to work collecting.

We passed the next ten minutes sociably enough together as we made our way on up to the trees next to the swimming pool.

For someone in his seventies he didn't seem to have many problems bending down to harvest the nuts, maybe the exercise kept him supple. As we worked, from behind the rattan screen around the pool, I heard fast even strokes as another early morning riser got in some lengths.

Once both bags were full to the old man's satisfaction, we turned to go back up to the house. But now as we climbed the steps, he leaned on my arm for support. I motioned for him to hand over his bag of nuts and hung it from my other shoulder, the straps criss-crossed over my chest.

We heard the slap of flip-flops on the steps behind us as the swimmer climbed up too. My companion stopped and turned to look.

'*Ciao bella!*' he cried, as Sophie came up towards us.

She was wearing a black high-necked swimsuit, the taut fabric glistening wet in the strengthening sun, and a thin cotton sarong wrapped around her damp legs. She stopped on the step below us to exchange kisses on each cheek with Rizzo's grandfather. I didn't get an Italian morning greeting though.

She avoided my eye as the smacking of lips took place.

'You're busy this morning,' she said neutrally, after they

were done.

I'd expected a comment more along the lines of me being usefully employed at last, but she held back.

'We're collecting nuts. For breakfast, I believe.'

I even got a faint smile now. The ghost of the charm she'd used on me the first time we'd met.

Rizzo's grandfather looked appraisingly from Sophie to me and back again.

The wrinkles at the corners of his eyes deepened as he tried to work out the connection between us. Good luck to him because I didn't understand it either.

'*Tedesco e tedesca*,' he finally muttered to himself.

I'd read enough of the primer on the plane to recognise the Italian male and female forms for 'German.' I guessed he in turn had recognised the language of the words that she and I had exchanged.

She strode on up ahead of us and disappeared through the double doors off the terrace back to her room. Rizzo's grandfather took me through the end doors to the terrace I'd come in by last night and into the kitchen across the passageway.

With a wave of his hand he motioned me to sit at the large wooden table in the middle of the room, while he fetched a bowl and nutcrackers laid out on a side table by the freestanding refrigerator. Next to that stood a Candy automatic dishwasher, presumably another of Italy's export successes.

But there was no time to look around properly, because I was set to work shelling the nuts. He'd had more practice, because my bag was only half empty by the time he'd finished. He got up again to go to the fridge and came back with a bowl of yoghurt. Then he pointed vaguely at the cupboards and I guessed I was to fetch dishes. As I opened and closed the doors with a clatter, out of the corner of my eye someone appeared in the doorway to the kitchen.

I turned round and saw a young woman standing there,

looking at me and then at Rizzo's grandfather with concern.

'Who are you?' she asked in Italian and then in English.

'I'm one of Giovanni's friends from Brussels. We came last night.'

'I'm his sister.'

'I guessed so.'

Unlike Rizzo's black curls, her hair was chestnut brown and perfectly straight. As she bent down to kiss her grandfather, I could see it hung halfway to her waist. She was wearing a black calf-length skirt and a white blouse, a demure Catholic girl going for the lay sister look rather than full nun. She'd be wasted as a nun though. I guessed she was barely out of her teens, her glowing skin clear and unblemished. And the skirt didn't much disguise the lithe form underneath, somehow it managed to be more revealing than Sophie's sarong.

'Are you helping *nonno* with breakfast?' she asked curiously.

'Yes, we bumped into each other in the garden a short while ago. I like hazelnuts too.'

She gave me a swift smile and tucked some strands of hair behind her right ear.

'I'm just making sure he... he has everything he needs,' she explained.

I placed the bowls on the table and her grandfather began carefully spooning out yoghurt for the two of us.

'Will you join us?' I asked. 'We collected extra nuts.'

'He's done that most mornings so far this month. We'll have to put them in the garbage again before tomorrow.'

Now the man himself spoke up and said something in insistent Italian. I smiled politely and glanced questioningly at Rizzo's sister. She blushed red.

'You can tell me. Little shocks me,' I assured her.

Her grandfather repeated what he'd just said, in a more distressed tone at my lack of reaction.

She blushed again. 'My grandfather says, if you love a

woman you must be bold and go after her and take hold of her.'

Now it was my turn to be embarrassed. 'Sorry. I wasn't expecting that piece of advice.'

I looked at *nonno* with what I hoped was the right combination of admiration at his wise words and gratefulness to him for sharing them.

'*Grazie, signor.*' I clasped my hand over my heart so he got the message that way too.

She left us to our meal but looked in after a few minutes to clear the dishes.

'My father has asked me to ask you to join him in his study,' she reported.

'What's your name? *Sono Oskar,*' I said as I held out my hand.

She took it somewhat bemusedly with a light, dry grip. Maybe she expected me to come in close and say 'hello' in the Italian way.

'Caterina. Nice to meet you, too. Are you staying for the party?'

I resisted the temptation to quip about how I'd looked forward to nothing else all summer.

'Yes. But we're leaving tomorrow.'

Rizzo's father was sitting behind his desk when I knocked on the open door to his study, but he didn't invite me to take a seat.

'Did you drive here last night? Do you know the way back to the airport?'

'Yes.'

'I need you to go back there this morning and pick up two people off the half past nine, *halb zehn,* flight from Rome. I sent our usual man away, as Giovanni explained to you yesterday.'

'Okay. Who are they?'

He looked at me in silence for a moment as I stood there before him. He was a much harder man than his son.

In Brussels, Rizzo was the genial, happy-go-lucky friend to all. Based on personality alone, you wouldn't have made a connection between him and his father. Maybe he got his softer side from his mother.

'One of them was my commanding officer during the last couple of years of the war. Big guy, heavily built. Black hair, but bald on top. The other guy is younger, has receding hair too. Angular face with a hooked nose. You'll know them when you see them.'

'Okay. How do I introduce myself?'

He looked at me with narrowed eyes for a moment. 'Say that Vincenzo from the Tenth sent you. Say it to them in German. But that's all. You don't ask their business or why they're here.'

I nodded slightly.

'One last thing. Giovanni's cousin is staying for the celebration tonight too. He's also a guarantee of your silence in this affair. He had a vicious reputation in New York. He cut out someone's tongue once, which I can tell you from what I saw during the war isn't an easy thing to do.'

'I've no desire for anyone in Brussels to find out that I've been here either,' I replied. Some people in Berlin might, though.

'Okay. To prove this isn't personal, I'm going to trust you with a private matter which is much more important to me just now. I want you to stay close to Di Luca tonight and keep him away from my daughter. Discreetly, because that's what you've suggested is your speciality. Giovanni has invited some party girls from Bari that he knows as a distraction for his cousin.'

'Okay.'

A no-nonsense attitude and getting things done without fuss was fine by me. My own cousin Karin was relying on it. I wondered if Sophie cared about the other women. Probably not. They were surely long in his past, now that he'd met her.

The men's plane landed and fifteen minutes later they were through arrivals with their hand luggage. Rizzo's father was correct, they were easy enough to spot. They both still had that presence that came from having been in the military. Rizzo didn't have it. I wondered if he'd wangled an exemption from conscription to the Italian Army. His cousin had simply ran away to New York.

I offered to carry the former commanding officer's bag, just as a colonel's driver would have done in the Bundeswehr, but he waved me away.

In fact, after making my slightly ridiculous introduction, they pretty much ignored me for the rest of the journey. I looked a couple of times in the rear-view mirror on the way back to the house but they were deep in conversation. Very few gesticulations, just earnest Italian spoken in low voices.

Rizzo's father must have been watching the lane, for he came outside to meet us on the gravel drive. After the greetings, he told me to come to the study in an hour's time and to bring Rizzo too. He didn't mention Sophie in the invitation - Rizzo could have the pleasure of explaining that to her himself.

I left the three of them to make their own way into the house and went to what I'd guessed last night was Rizzo and Sophie's room, wondering if she was there. Rizzo answered the knock, opening the door wide. Although there was no sign of her, I couldn't help but glance at the double bed with its rumpled sheets and their things on each of the bedside tables.

'Your father has asked you and I to meet him with his guests in an hour's time.' I said it extra loud, in case she was sitting out of sight on the terrace past the open double doors.

He acknowledged me with a nod, then closed the door again.

I wandered around the grounds for a while, kicking my

heels, and being stalked by a black cat who slunk in and out of the dense shrubs. Only a short distance through the belt of pine trees at the bottom of the garden, the ground did indeed drop away suddenly to a long wooded slope running into the distance. There was a low wall marking the end of the path and a little way back from it, looking east, a stone bench covered with a dusting of dry pine needles. At the edge of vision, in the blue haze towards Bari I thought I saw the line of the sea, thirty kilometres away.

I was completing my circuit at the front of the house when another Fiat hire car raced up the drive and braked hard at the front door. Out got a tanned, good-looking guy of roughly my age, maybe a couple of years younger than Rizzo. He grabbed a suit carrier bag from the back seat of the car and strode inside like he'd been here before. If he was Rizzo's second cousin, I could see why his father was wary about him getting close to Caterina.

The hour passed and I presented myself at the study door at the due time. All of them, including Rizzo, looked up as I walked in. Not Sophie though. She hadn't pulled it off this time.

There were some muttered words among which I caught '*ritardo*' and then chuckles from different parts of the room.

Rizzo's father was sitting behind his desk again but got up to introduce me properly to each of them in turn. Borghese and De Mauro were the men I'd picked up at the airport. Borghese was Rizzo's father's old commanding officer and was now apparently a businessman and occasional consultant to foreign militaries on special forces techniques. De Mauro was another former comrade, also introduced as a consultant. I wasn't sure how he fitted into the picture. As I'd guessed, the guy who'd arrived in the hire car was Di Luca. In his patterned open-necked shirt and flares he looked even more out of place than I did.

Rizzo's father motioned me to a seat and launched straight in.

'We're going to deal with your task first Signor Lenkeit, then you can leave. We have some other matters to discuss in private after you're gone.'

'*D'accordo.*'

'I've just finished building a factory in one of the new industrial zones on the outskirts of Bari. It's not been commissioned yet, it's still a bare shell. Under the factory floor is a concealed chamber where several crates of supplies have been cached by the Italian Ministry of Defence in the event of a Soviet invasion.'

He waited for me to respond but I was giving nothing away.

'You're going to go there and take them all. It should be easy. Your men can drive right inside the building and load up hidden from sight. The goods have to be manhandled up a narrow single flight of stairs, but otherwise shouldn't present any problems.'

I raised a finger and Di Luca looked at me sceptically.

'What state are they in?' I asked.

'They've been made ready for long-term storage. They're safe to handle.'

'How many crates?'

He thought for a moment. 'About sixteen pallets, loaded to the same height as the pallet width. A large truck should do it.'

'What? Like a Mercedes LP?'

'I don't know. Here.' He picked up a business magazine and flicked through the pages. 'Like this one.'

I approached the desk to take a closer look at the advertisement for what was labelled as a Fiat 619. It wasn't much bigger than Pavel's vehicle.

'Okay.'

I glanced around the room. The others were watching us with interest. Trying to make their minds up about just what kind of a professional Signor Rizzo had found.

'Okay,' I said again. 'How long is the journey to Sicily. What's the timetable for the move?'

Now Di Luca spoke up. He had a harsh American accent, from somewhere on the East Coast I reckoned.

'With a fully-laden truck it'll take a good seven or eight hours to get to the Messina ferry from Bari. Once across, you'll have to drive down almost to the southern coast of Sicily. About twelve hours in total from loading to unloading.'

'And where exactly is my crew going to in Sicily?'

'There's a house there in a secluded valley which is owned by our family,' said Rizzo's father.

'You mean his family?' I asked, pointing at Di Luca.

'No. Our own bolthole if the Reds come or if there's a nuclear war. There's a cave running into the side of the hill where the goods are to be left.'

De Mauro looked impressed, and a little jealous, I thought.

'You'll get the precise directions nearer the time.'

'So we arrive, stay in Bari one night, pick the goods up first thing and deliver them the same day?'

'No,' said Rizzo's father. 'Pick them up in the middle of the night, cross on the first ferry in the morning. Then you can take the ferry back the same afternoon and get away up north.'

There was silence in the room for a moment. I heard the black cat mewing outside, just under the window.

Borghese hadn't spoken yet. Now he had his say.

'Who are you?' he asked in English with a heavy Italian accent.

I looked him full in the face now. A strong-featured, arrogant one. He reminded more than a little of Otto Skorzeny, the former Nazi commando who I'd met earlier in the summer, just before going to Ireland.

Just as on that occasion, I guessed Borghese was more interested in my motivation than my criminal history. Sophie had talked about 'factions' being involved on the train back from Wismar and given all the unrest in Italy right now, this caper had to have a political angle. I thought I had a good idea of what I needed to say.

'My family were refugees from the east of Germany, driven out by the Russians. I do what I have to, in order to get by. But one day I'll pay them back for what they did.'

Di Luca raised his eyebrows and pouted with his lower lip, nodding silently in agreement.

'How did you get those?' Borghese asked, pointing at my cheek and hands. I tried to remember the exact form of words I'd used with Rizzo's father last night.

'A deal that went wrong. But I got my revenge in the end.'

'Did you kill someone?' Di Luca asked.

I shook my head in refusal at the question.

'Who was the first person you killed then?' he insisted, giving the clear impression he'd done his fair share of murder.

All three of the older men looked at him with contempt. If Rizzo's father, De Mauro, and Borghese had been anti-partisan fighters, then they had every professional right to. For whatever Di Luca's body count was, theirs was certainly higher.

I gave an impatient sigh as if it was an everyday occurrence for me too.

'Someone who disrespected my mother,' I replied.

'How did you do it?'

Now he really was trying my patience.

'I put my gun to his mouth and pulled the trigger. Why? Is there any other way?' I retorted.

'Okay. Enough,' said Rizzo's father waving his hands to the sides to lower the temperature.

It was a good thing Sophie hadn't been present. But I'd forgotten all about Rizzo and I looked at him now. His eyes were as wide as saucers and his normally olive skin was pale by the light coming in past the half-closed shutters. What kind of business did he think he and his father were involved in here?

'Any more questions? From anyone?' he asked, looking around the room.

'No? Then find your crew. Tell Giovanni how much it will cost and when you're ready to move. Don't gouge us with your mark-up because we'll know if you are.'

'The price will depend on how soon you need this done.'

'We're going to discuss that after you leave.' He glanced at his watch. 'Lunch will be served in an hour's time. Giovanni will take you to the factory afterwards. Then dinner is at eight. You need to hang around in case we need to call you back for further questions.'

Lunch was a rolling affair, a buffet set out on the terrace by Caterina and her mother, working as a pair. As they carried the dishes in and out of the kitchen, I got the odd glance from them. Maybe none of their other house guests to date had been press-ganged into collecting nuts first thing in the morning.

The Italians were still conferring in Rizzo's father's study as Sophie came out of her room a little further down the terrace to join us. I'd expected her to be angry at not having been invited, but maybe I'd misjudged her. Maybe she already knew what the old fascists were getting up to beyond stealing weapons - the political side to the operation that they'd presumably stayed behind to discuss.

But I knew she was still annoyed at me because she deliberately took a seat as far away from me as she could find.

Now Rizzo's grandparents put in an appearance too, Caterina shepherding them out of the house. Rizzo's grandfather caught sight of me at the far end of the table and a broad smile of recognition came over his face. He waved away Caterina's direction to a seat nearer the door and came down the length of the terrace to sit at the head of the table, his wife following. Old habits died hard, I supposed.

Looking at Rizzo's grandmother I could see where Caterina got her looks from. No heavy-boned peasantry in their family line. Her grandmother's features were still fine and regular under the aged skin. I could well imagine why fifty years ago the former stormtrooper might have gone to the lengths he did. Sitting together, I noticed they both wore the same steel-coloured wedding band, with an inscription in either Italian or Latin around its circumference, which I thought was quite touching.

As if he'd read my mind, he repeated his line about taking the girls you wanted, just as Caterina returned to the table with their plates. At least, that's what I guessed it was from the way she blushed again. Maybe his saying meant something cruder in Italian, or there was some sly double-entendre she hadn't translated for me.

Sophie was regretting her standoffishness now, because the party was all at our end of the terrace. I could tell this because of the sharp looks she was darting our way, especially at Caterina who'd sat opposite me and kept tucking in loose hair behind her ear as we ate. Sophie could have shown her how to do a braid.

We all looked up as the others finally joined us. Rizzo and his father came down to our end to exchange kisses with his grandparents. I watched as Rizzo walked back up the terrace to take a seat next to Sophie. There was no air-kissing though. As he sat eating, he steadfastly avoided looking my way, as if still disturbed at hearing my revelation in the study.

I wasn't the only one observing all this. The Mafia princess, as Sophie had described her, was also watching shrewdly as she sipped her mineral water.

The men who'd come out seemed to be in a good mood, but it was more akin to the atmosphere of relief after there'd been tension in the room. Not my problem, I hoped. Collect the weapons, drive to the ferry, hide them in the secret cave, steal a couple of rockets as samples and somehow get everyone back to Berlin. Then a handshake from Johannes and General Fiedler as they signed the release papers for Karin.

Lunch ended and the guests began to disperse. Borghese and Rizzo's father went back inside, as did Sophie and Rizzo, before I could fix a time with him to visit the factory and inspect the weapons. De Mauro wandered off down the garden.

The caterers for the party arrived and Caterina and her mother began to clear the table. I made to pick up a few plates myself, because growing up with a single parent you did. My gesture seemed to confuse Rizzo's mother and I saw embarrassment on her face. I let Caterina take the plates off me, our fingers touching as she did so. She frowned as she looked down at my hands, taking a closer look for a few seconds as we both stood there holding the china.

I wandered off back towards the pines, intending to smoke a rare cigarette on the stone bench looking out towards Bari and kill some time. I'd decided to give Rizzo half an hour after lunch before I went to find him for our reconnaissance trip.

At the edge of the lawn, under the shade of the trees, I saw De Mauro sitting on another bench, a notebook laid alongside him, gazing into the middle distance.

I gave him a wave of acknowledgement which was a mistake, for he got to his feet and called me over.

I went to him unwillingly, reluctant to expose myself to these guys any more than I needed to in case I inadvertently said the wrong thing and they changed their minds about using me.

'So, you're the German. What's your interest in this affair, apart from your payment?'

I thought for a moment.

'I was called in to do the job as a favour to Signor

Rizzo's family. What's yours?'

A smile played around his lips, the smile of someone who knew many secrets and enjoyed slowly doling them out for his pleasure.

'How well do you know them? Do you know who Signor Rizzo really is? And Borghese?'

'Not him. Why, should I?'

'Do you know what he and Rizzo got up to during the war?'

'No. Sorry.' I said, trying to hide my impatience. 'Are you going to tell me?'

There was another slight smile, as I asked the question he was obviously waiting for and joined in his game.

'Borghese was the commander of the Decima Mas, the special underwater attack unit of the Italian Navy.'

I frowned. 'You mean frogmen, limpet mines, that kind of thing?'

The rumour in Hamburg was that it was French commandos who'd attached a mine to the underside of a ship in the harbour in the late fifties. The French had believed the owners to be running guns to the Algerian nationalists.

'The attack on Alexandria,' he said, still carefully rationing out his facts.

I replied with my own question. 'What did the Egyptians do to upset Mussolini?'

'Borghese's men penetrated the British naval base there and sank two battleships.'

I raised my eyebrows. 'Good for them. But I thought Signor Rizzo was in the Italian Army, not the Navy? I was told he served in Africa before 'forty-three.'

'After the partition of the country the Decima Mas took on all kinds of special duties for the Germans in the North.'

'Hunting down partisans? That's what Rizzo's son told me his father was made to do after escaping from Tunisia.'

De Mauro smiled faintly.

'So he says. We had to gather intelligence and search out their bases. It wasn't all action with guns and grenades.'

I frowned again. Otto Skorzeny had said something similar to me about his wartime unit when we'd met.

'And you were part of that too, the intelligence side? Torturing people for information?' I asked, none too kindly.

'We did what had to be done.'

'So what are the old comrades of the Decima Mas up to these days? With this shipment?'

He'd provoked me into asking the big question, as no doubt he'd wanted me to do from the start.

Now he fully turned off the tap, the next part of his game.

'That's for you to discover. That's my daytime job,' he said cryptically.

So, riddles now.

'What do you work as? Are you a cop? A newspaperman?'

At this his face fell, for I'd guessed too quickly. I tried to be solicitous, but I wasn't sure why he deserved it.

'Don't worry. I come from West Germany. Our tabloid journalists are like wolves when it comes to hunting out information. Axel Springer would have eaten some of the charmers in our former regime in a couple of mouthfuls.'

He shrugged. 'I write for L'Ora in Palermo. That's public knowledge.'

'Sicily, then? As far south as you could get from the northern state?'

'We knew it informally as the Salò Republic.'

'Tell me. On the way down here, I met a Sicilian family. The wife was very sensitive when I brought up the Mafia in conversation. She was impatient with me, saying it's all that people ask about the island.'

He shrugged again. 'What can I say? They're part of life there and have been for centuries. Not even Mussolini could suppress them, and he tried.'

'Signor Rizzo's son describes the other half of their family as property developers with menaces.'

'It's Italy's curse. We've never got government right. On the surface it appears to be highly centralised, but underneath people always find ways of getting around Rome's instructions. Mussolini could tell people to shut down the Mafia and the Freemasons, but it didn't mean that it happened.'

A nation of people thinking for themselves wasn't entirely without merit. Germans recognised that now.

'So people shouldn't be surprised by the existence of the Mafia, especially that far from Rome. When governments don't function, other people step into the vacuum.'

His eyes narrowed but the rest of his face was all innocence.

He was being too clever for his own good. It was time to play my game now.

'I spoke with a friend before I came here,' I said tentatively. 'He took part in the student protests in Belgium in 'sixty-eight. What happened in Italy that year? Were people as equally dissatisfied with the government here as they were in Brussels?'

'Sixty-eight? It's still going on. We have a rare burst of economic growth to catch up with the rest of Europe and then the students and the other protestors undermine it all again.'

'Which "other protestors"? The communists?' I prompted.

'You had the right idea in West Germany when you banned your Communist Party. But we have even crazier people here on the left than the PCI. People who are just waiting for an opportunity to pour gasoline on the flames.'

I was beginning to suspect Borghese and his buccaneer crew might be thinking of themselves in some way as Italy's firemen. For the time being I moved onto slightly safer ground.

'Speaking of flames. Do you have a light?' I asked, proffering my pack of cigarettes at the same time. He waved it away and clicked a gold lighter for me.

'So what are the Mafia today, really?'

He couldn't resist a prideful grin. 'You're asking the right person. Eight years ago, I drew up the definitive chart of the current generation's organisation. I won the Premiolino prize two years before that for my other exposés.'

'Sounds risky,' I ventured, drawing on my cigarette.

'I did it from stitching together the police reports of the shootings and bombings which took place during the Mafia war,' he replied, drawing out his answer. 'They suddenly started killing each other off in 'sixty-two after a big shipment of heroin went missing. Almost seventy people died over two years. We saw revenge killings, car bombs, the lot.'

'What brought it to an end?'

'Eventually the state took an interest and aggressively cracked down on the Mafia for a while. Over a thousand arrests with serious disruption to their activities. That's when their hierarchy was revealed.'

'So where does Di Luca stand? Is he a bishop or a cardinal?'

'If he's anything, he'll be a *soldato* - the first rung. Then come the *caporegimes* and finally the *capo* himself.'

'What does a *soldato* get up to?'

'They don't just take orders. They make money themselves from running their own scams and protection rackets. They pass a cut from the proceeds up the hierarchy of course, like in any business organised along franchise lines.'

'Don't successful *soldati* sometimes get impatient? Want a bigger territory or want to create openings above them? Isn't that how wars start?'

De Mauro gave me a sly, knowing smile.

'They had something back then called the Regional Commission, sometimes known as the "Cupola". A kind of Mafia council, if you like. They were meant to adjudicate disputes, keep the peace, and stop disruption to the families' businesses. But after their failure to prevent the Mafia war it was dissolved. It's recently been reconstituted though, according to my informants.'

'I thought *omertà* meant there were no informers?'

'Someone, somewhere always knows something. And with the right persuasion they'll talk. That's what I learned during the war.'

He frowned. 'Don't look so cynical, it's not always what you think. Borghese himself used to say it was easier to get an Italian to lay down his life than to make the sacrifice of holding his tongue.'

'No wonder the Sicilians take *omertà* so seriously.'

'Indeed. But when I drew my map of the Mafia all sorts of hidden connections came to light. Not least between the families and the DC.'

'I guess when you've been continuously in power since nineteen forty-eight that kind of thing might happen.'

His smile was replaced with a harder look.

'They pay off the DC for things like rezoning, building permits, and other construction-related fraud. You should see what they've done to Palermo. They've ripped out its old heart to squeeze in as many flats as they can get away with. Probably too many, when it comes to the earthquake building regulations.'

'So is that why you're here, to provide advice on dealing with the Mafia?' I asked neutrally. I wondered if he was more than that, but it would be strange if an anti-Mafia journalist was the one negotiating the arms deal with them for Borghese.

'Signor Rizzo doesn't really know them. You know the history there? About his parents' elopement?'

I nodded.

'The other half, the Di Luca family is a low-to-middle-ranking clan, originally based in Ragusa province. The southern corner of the island, about as far away from Palermo as you can get. They're the real go-betweens.'

I stubbed out my cigarette and made to get away.

'What do you think of Italy?' he suddenly asked.

'I hadn't realised how much progress had been made here over the past twenty years or so,' I replied diplomatically. 'Or how successful Italian businesses have been in the rest of Europe. The growth of Olivetti, Candy, Signor Rizzo's own firm, I guess.'

I was being generous. West Germany were the world champions at economic recovery from a standing start.

His chest swelled with pride a little. 'Our real success of recent years was ENI, the oil and gas company. We discovered natural gas in the Po valley in 'forty-nine and by the sixties, ENI's founder, Enrico Mattei, had grown the company so much that it was seriously upsetting the Americans. He made Italy into a serious geopolitical player again.'

'How come?' I asked, suppressing my scepticism.

'We only found gas in the Po valley. So, in the late 'fifties, Mattei started importing cheap Soviet crude oil for refining.'

'I thought Italy was on the side of the US?'

'In addition to securing crude supplies from the Soviets he also signed exploration agreements in countries like Iran, which the Americans regarded as their natural domain. Egypt too, just before the French and British attacked Suez. And Algeria, where he signed a deal with the nationalists before the French had even left.'

'That's living dangerously.'

He gave a grim smile.

'Then he died in a plane crash on final approach to Milan. An unexplained one. Virtually on the last day of the Cuban Missile Crisis, as the world was looking the other way.'

I flicked my wrist to glance at my watch and dropped

my stub onto the grass, grinding it out with my foot. I was out of time to ask him more about Borghese's political angle, but De Mauro wanted to unburden himself further about Mattei.

'I have a theory about Mattei. An obvious one, really. ENI's imports helped fund the Soviet regime. So Kennedy asked the Mafia to get rid of him, just as he did with Castro. But later, the Kennedy brothers learnt the hard way that you don't double cross the Mob - I wonder if Mattei somehow ended up that way too.'

It was one way to sell newspapers.

'Can you prove it?'

'Next Monday I'm speaking with someone high up, connected to both ENI and to the Mafia. We'll see after that.'

'Isn't that a bit risky, running a story on the Mafia, when you're meant to be shipping them arms? Or is it part of the plan?'

'Read the papers next month and you'll find out.'

'Excuse me,' I said. 'I need to find Signor Rizzo's son.'

Mafia organisation charts, Soviet oil, dead American presidents. De Mauro was a man with too many secrets in his head for his own good.

I knocked on Rizzo and Sophie's door, but there was no answer this time. As I wandered around the ground floor of the house trying to find them, Rizzo's father caught sight of me through the open doorway to his study. Borghese was sitting off to one side, out of line of sight from the hallway. He looked round in impatience as Rizzo's father waved me into the room.

'What's the problem?'

'I'm looking for Giovanni, so he can show me the factory.'

'Isn't he in his room by the terrace?'

I shrugged.

'*Cazzo*. He's probably fucking a blonde German girl

somewhere in private instead.' He looked back and forth between Borghese and me for a moment, as if weighing something up. He said something in Italian, and I caught the word '*tedesco.*'

Borghese shrugged but didn't look that happy. Rizzo's father picked up the phone and dialled someone, speaking in a low, urgent voice that brooked no refusal.

Down went the receiver again and he snatched up a set of keys from the desk.

'My wife and daughter will come and keep the Comandante company until the other guests arrive. Let's go.'

With a nod to Borghese, he left the room and marched ahead of me down another arm of the hall and out of the house through a side door. An Alfa Romeo was sitting there, of a type which I hadn't seen before, with grilles for air vents all the way up the cabin pillar to the roof.

I got in and we accelerated away in a spurt of gravel.

'"The Comandante"?' I asked.

'It's the title he's always used. He gets annoyed when people call him "Prince."'

'"Prince"?'

'You've heard of his family, right? They're noblemen. In English they're called the Borgias.'

'I didn't even know he was a frogman in the war.'

Rizzo's father laughed.

'He was a submarine captain, got the frogmen in close to the target to drop them off. But he never got wet himself.'

So, different from Skorzeny then. At least the old Austrian SS man had gone with his men into harm's way. And no one would have mistaken him for a prince.

We reached the end of the drive. Rizzo's father looked at me askance as he pulled out onto the main road.

'So, you like her too?'

I guessed he didn't mean Caterina.

'She has lots of friends in Brussels. Giovanni is the only

one who's like a real boyfriend.'

'What job exactly do you do at the EEC?'

'I said last night. It's a kind of special assignments office. We fix problems that no one else wants to touch. But coming out here is personal, not business.'

'Is it true what you said back there, to Di Luca? About shooting that guy?'

'Yes. That time it was both personal and business.'

'Di Luca is a hothead. He went to America and lost all sense of restraint or honour. They sent him back here because he's an animal, capable of anything. I wasn't joking about you keeping him away from my daughter tonight.'

Rizzo's father took a hand from the wheel to rummage in the driver's door side bin. He found a pack of Marlboros and shook one out into his mouth. Then he swapped hands to unplug the lighter coil from the dashboard and puffed the cigarette into life, all in one smooth motion.

'What do you think of Giovanni's work at the EEC?' I asked. 'Do you believe that once Europe has a common government, Italy's problems will go away?'

'What problems?' he asked sharply.

I blundered on. 'I spoke with De Mauro just before I found you. He was talking about the industrial unrest and the student protests, saying that Italy wasn't well governed.'

'He likes to talk.' He let this hang for a second before adding, 'But yes, some people in Italy place their faith for the future in the EEC.'

'Do they understand that the EEC makes common laws that all the member states have to follow?'

'Yes. That's the attraction. They think it will stop our national politicians making bad decisions.'

'They might be waiting a long time for their federal utopia to arrive. There's various political factions inside the EEC, each with different ideas on how fast the Project should develop.'

The scrubby hills had fallen behind us as we descended to the plain. Now we hit a straight stretch of road and his right foot hit the floor.

'Ever heard of Altiero Spinelli?' I asked speculatively.

'No. Why should I? Who is he?'

'Italian politician at the EEC. On the opposite side to you during the war.'

'That was a long time ago. Even if people like the Comandante don't always realise it.'

'Did your wartime record affect your business afterwards?'

He waved his hand over the dashboard of the Alfa with its stubby gear stick, push button controls and split dials. Compared to the console of my Type Three, it looked like a jet fighter.

'What do you think?' he said. 'We're one of the West's principal suppliers of miniaturised sensors for missile guidance systems.'

I got the point and shut up for a bit. But the thought occurred to me that Johannes might find more intelligence value in samples of Rizzo's father's gyroscopes than whatever was buried under his factory.

We turned into an industrial estate. He pulled up at the double gates into his factory to undo the padlock, then walked over to the building itself to open up a roller door with a loud rattle.

'Let's see what we have in here,' he said, as he got back into the Alfa and drove us inside, the throaty roar of the engine echoing off the walls. The factory floor was completely bare, a faint smell of fresh paint and damp concrete still lingering.

He parked up by an office built against the end wall and asked me to roll down the exterior door. I rejoined him as he finally found the right key to the office.

Once we were inside, I helped him move a couple of

filing cabinets away from the wall. Underneath was the outline of an access hatch set into the concrete. He handed me a lifting tool and together we hauled the heavy cover up and off to one side, revealing a set of steps going down into the gloom.

He straightened up again. 'When you come back for real, smash the glass of the office door, make it look like an attempted burglary. You can cut through the padlocks outside with bolt cutters.'

'Don't you want it to be discreet?'

'I want a report to go on file with the police that there was a break-in. To provide me with cover in case the Defence Ministry suddenly wants to inspect the store. Not that they're likely to.'

'Won't they do so when they hear that there was a forced entry at this address?'

'This is Italy.'

He descended a few steps into the darkness until he found a switch which he flicked to illuminate the space below.

'*Buon Natale,*' he said.

I followed him down into a small storeroom stacked to the ceiling with olive green-painted metal cases and wooden crates. A real mixture of all shapes and sizes.

'This is a lot. It'll take a couple of hours to load at least,' I said speculatively.

'When you come back next time, wear gloves. And don't take them off if you get sweaty. No fingerprints.'

'Let's look inside one,' I suggested.

Rizzo's father grinned. 'Okay.'

He went along the stacks until he found the one he wanted. Together, we lowered the topmost case down onto the floor and flipped the catches. Inside were a row of assault rifles packed alternately muzzle to butt. We each pulled one out.

'Spare magazines and rounds are in another case somewhere,' he said, as he extended the folding stock and put the rifle to his shoulder, pointing it at me.

'Bang, bang. You're dead.'

I turned my rifle over and saw how the stock folded up under the barrel, hinged from the rear with the shoulder piece independently hinged too. With the stock fully extended and the rifle up in the crook of my shoulder, the stance was solid as I squinted along the sights. I hadn't had an assault rifle in my hands since the day I returned my G3 to the armoury for the last time in 'sixty-four.

'These are AK-47s,' I said. 'Why?'

'If the Soviets invade, we won't be making spare parts for Berettas anymore.'

'Same for missiles? Are they storing Soviet RPGs here?'

'Not sure. The store record book is over there.'

He went back to the foot of the stairs and picked up a ring binder lying on an empty shelf. 'Here, take a look,' he said, passing it over.

I scanned as many of the pages as I could before it started looking like more than idle curiosity. I wasn't sure of the NATO acronym for 'anti-tank guided rocket' but I recognised 'SAM' for an anti-aircraft missile. Johannes would have known.

'There's enough here to start a war,' I said, still mesmerised.

Rizzo's father brushed off my assertion. 'No there's not. There's enough buried elsewhere in the South for a strategy of keeping the Soviets pinned inside the towns while we wait for the Americans to land in Sicily or Sardinia and rescue us.'

'Will it ever come to that?' I asked.

'Why take the chance? Let's go back, if you've seen enough.'

I sorrowfully folded forward the stock of the AK-47 and returned it to its case. If I did get to come back here, I'd take one home for myself.

On the return journey to the house he asked me again

about Sophie.

'How serious are they?'

'Like I said, she makes male friends easily. She treats men as her equals which means she's open with them in a way that most other women aren't. But because she gives the impression of bringing them into her confidence, all men think that they're something special to her.'

It was a more refined version of what Rizzo had said to me over a year ago at that first dinner party, but then he'd been tipsy at the time.

'She didn't seem very friendly towards you last night.'

'We have some history.'

'Did she ever like you the same way she goes after Giovanni?'

'No,' I said, a little curtly. I didn't think Sophie ever had to go after anyone. Men fought each other to prostrate themselves at her feet, metaphorically of course.

'He's given up on all his other girlfriends. It's always "Sophie this" and "Sophie that."'

Rizzo had been hit hard - anyone who knew him even a little could see it.

'I kind of understand,' I said laconically.

'Anyway, as I said earlier, dinner is at eight. The family are having drinks on the terrace beforehand. Come and join us, because you're on sentry duty in case Di Luca decides to put in an appearance.'

I read my Italian-English primer for a while then got changed. Through the open door of my balcony I could hear the clink of bottles as the drinks things were set out on the terrace below and began to get thirsty.

Caterina and her mother were already down there but weren't serving this time. A waiter offered me a glass of prosecco as I walked onto the terrace to join them. The evening was still warm and the cool wine slipped down easily.

The three of us were the first to arrive. I imagined

Rizzo's father was still closeted with Borghese - the Comandante looked like someone who needed a lot of attention.

When it came to looks, Caterina appeared at least five years older than this morning in her closely fitted black knee-length dress and heels. The single string of pearls around the high neckline helped too.

She introduced me to her mother now, as we hadn't met properly at lunch. I got a nod, a fleeting smile, and a few words in Italian that I tried to respond to as best I could, putting my time spent with the primer to some use. I guessed she didn't speak any English, but she seemed pleasant enough.

Caterina looked round as her grandparents joined us on the terrace. Just as at lunch, her grandfather went to the head of the table with his wine. But instead of going to sit with him, the grandmother stayed by the door with Caterina, her mother and me. To my surprise, she nudged Caterina aside and installed herself opposite me for a closer inspection.

With lively, darting glances she surveyed my hands and cheek. Then she gently took my hands in hers, turning them over and over to look at the scars, tracing the tops of the fingers on my left hand. Suddenly, without warning, she lifted both my hands to her mouth and kissed them. My eyes widened in shock. Then she said something in Italian, and I looked at Caterina for assistance.

'My grandmother says that evil men did this thing to you.'

To my horror and utter mortification tears welled up in the corners of my eyes. No one else had shown compassion of that nature to me over the events in Ireland. Even my mother didn't know what had happened yet. And no one else so far had acknowledged the agony the wounds had inflicted. It was as if a dam had broken inside.

In the way that these things sometimes did, the wetness

in the corners of my eyes set them all off too - just as Sophie arrived with a swish of silk on Rizzo's arm. I looked up at her over the bowed heads of the Rizzo women, hoping she wouldn't notice anything amiss in my face.

Compared to Caterina's minimalist elegance, Sophie couldn't help but appear overdressed. But however pure and wholesome as Caterina might be, this evening Sophie was beyond beautiful - to my eyes at least.

She had performed some kind of sorcery on her face with green eyeshadow delicately blended into her natural skin tone. The structure of her cheeks was subtly highlighted with a touch of bronze. I now understood why she thought it might have been possible for Karin to escape East Germany, armed with nothing more than a make-up set sent through the mail with instructions on how to make herself look twenty-five years older.

But her grand entrance had been for nothing, for I was surrounded by a gaggle of Italian females from various generations, all quietly weeping for my pain.

As I stood there gaping, my eyes quickly dried. I was instantly suspicious. She'd made a special effort, gone way beyond her usual level of care over her appearance. She didn't need to have been at the men-only conference earlier. Whatever had been discussed after I'd left, she was going to screw out of Rizzo later tonight I thought bitterly to myself. Or whomever else she needed to.

She flicked me a glance as she took a glass of wine, but her make-up wasn't the only mask she was wearing tonight.

The women collected themselves and I went to sit down next to my fellow hazelnut gatherer. We grinned and silently toasted one other for a little while, until some new family members arrived. I got up and took myself off to one side to make space. From the way the middle-aged women greeted Rizzo's grandfather, while the men with them were reserved, I guessed I was looking at Rizzo's aunts, and assumed that his father didn't have brothers.

As I stood looking out over the grounds, I kept one eye on the door in case Di Luca tried to show. Once, I glanced back to the gathering to see Rizzo standing by the drinks table. His hand was inside the pocket of his jacket and he was fiddling with something there which looked hard and square as he twisted it around and around.

Dinner was served on long tables set up on the lawn under canopies, anti-mosquito candles burning in the corners. I sat opposite Di Luca, with a view of the family table and of Caterina, who was facing in our direction. Di Luca couldn't see her, he'd been placed with his back to the house.

I wasn't really sure why Rizzo's father was concerned. From the little I'd seen of her, the *cattolica* Caterina wasn't anything like the girls that Di Luca said he'd known from his time in New York. And she certainly wouldn't have taken part in the things he claimed women had let him do to them there. I didn't react to his descriptions with as much surprise as he hoped. As I'd told Caterina at breakfast time, little shocked me. I'd been in the police in Hamburg after all.

Other members of Borghese's wartime gang had also been invited to the party and were seated near the family at their own private table. They'd kept their distance from the other guests, right from when they began to turn up at the house, Rizzo's father excusing himself to leave the terrace early to host separate pre-dinner drinks for them in his study.

I watched De Mauro as he sat there with them, on the edge of the group. He was looking somewhat pensive. More pensive than nervous, I thought.

Di Luca, on the other hand, didn't know the meaning of either word.

'So why did you leave New York?' I asked, at the conclusion of his latest story.

'It got too hot for me,' he said, casting a sly, appraising look at a girl on one of the other tables.

'That one's giving me the eye,' he informed me, without breaking stride.

'I upset some people. Went too far on a job once. I'm not ice-cold like you Germans.'

He pointed with two fingers at his mouth and thumbed an imaginary hammer. '"Ze disrespected my mudder." Bang.' He winked at the girl over my shoulder again.

'So, what's business like in Brussels? What scams can I get into through the EEC? Or have the German Mob got there before us?' he asked, still seemingly confused as to my exact status.

The guy was irrepressible. But under the charisma I sensed an instability too, as Rizzo's father had hinted at it in his study. Di Luca would pull a knife on you as soon as tell you a joke.

Still, if he was bored of his stories of blackmailing girls into bed and wanted to know what opportunities Brussels provided for the criminal community, he'd chosen the right people to ask. Sophie and I had effectively written the manual on CAP fraud before my trip to Ireland.

'The EEC is the only one running the scams in Brussels,' I replied.

'So what scams are those then?'

'The EEC collects a mountain of cash from the members. Then they decide who gets it in the form of agricultural subsidies, allocated through a combination of rules on farm sizes and products. No one explicitly says "so-and-so percentage of the budget goes to France". It's done indirectly, by fixing the regulations. You guys must know about that in the area of construction.'

He looked at me with a new admiration. 'So that's why Giovanni is at the EEC. Those Rizzos are slick bastards.'

I'd never thought about it that way before.

'I always assumed he was there because he was a true believer in a Greater Europe,' I said lightly.

'Then they're still fascists if he believes in that.'

I regretted my jibe.

'Giovanni's father is smarter than he seems, you know,' Di Luca continued. 'He's always looking out for new ways to play the system. He never misses the chance either, to show off that he's making more money than us. He's always looked down on the Sicilian side of the family.'

'I thought the Rizzos don't own land in Apulia anymore? I don't see how they would benefit from an agriculture scam.'

'Fuck the Rizzos. They'll have had it all worked out somehow; the EEC thing. Just like with the other thing that's going on right now - the thing you're involved with.'

He paused. 'You've heard of our tradition, so don't ask.'

I had heard and I didn't ask, but I couldn't see how the friction between the families boded well for whatever Borghese had planned.

At the end of the dinner, Rizzo's father got to his feet for a short speech in Italian. He dropped in a couple of jokes which made me feel even more out of place as the other guests at the tables reacted. The jokes must have been good ones, because he even managed to raise a wry smile on Di Luca's face. We stood to toast Rizzo's grandparents and then people drifted away from the tables. A bar had been set up by the pool where Sophie had gone swimming this morning and chairs had been laid out under the hazelnut trees.

Di Luca turned to me. 'Work's done for today and now it's time for fun. With my reputation and your scars, we should do very well for ourselves tonight. I'm going to find that girl who was giving me the eye earlier.'

He opened his jacket slightly to show me the top of a cellophane packet tucked into his inside pocket.

'I brought help, just in case. I always try to bang them first though, before I give them any. It doesn't count if they're out of their minds.'

I didn't comment that maybe it was the other way around, that some girls went with him just to get a free snort.

He drifted through the clusters of people in conversation, hunting for his target. We stopped in front of a group of three girls sitting in cane armchairs around a low table. Several glasses of wine were standing on its top, all drunk down to different levels.

He went up behind one of the girls who was wearing a golden sheath dress, the one he'd been winking at earlier. He placed his hands on her bare shoulders and bent down to her ear to murmur something in Italian. She turned around sharply, then softened into a smile when she saw who it was. He gave a mock bow, then went around to pull her up out of the chair so he could sit down there himself. He drew her back down to perch on his knee, draping one of her arms around his neck.

He clicked his fingers and pointed at me to pull up a chair for myself while the four of them started talking languorously to one another.

I sat opposite a hennaed redhead, the first girl's particular friend guessing by the way they spoke to each other. Before long they'd moved on to the next stage of pretending to ignore Di Luca by talking past him while presumably talking about him at the same time too. The last of the girls was mainly watching, stretched out with her feet up on the table, the points of her shoes peeping out from under a long ultramarine blue dress.

After half a minute of their impudence, Di Luca said something rude and slapped the first girl's behind. She turned around and wagged her finger, the Italian flowing now like a babbling brook. Her redhead friend nodded over to me and asked Di Luca a question which he answered in a sly tone.

'What's she saying?' I asked.

'She's asking who you are and where did you get your

scars from. What do you want me to tell her?' he asked, one eyebrow raised.

Blue dress girl was also listening to hear what I'd say, her dark brown eyes almost black as she watched me from behind a wave of tawny hair highlighted with light caramel streaks.

I turned back to face the redhead, tempted to say something clever, not that I would know how Di Luca would translate it for me.

'Tell her I met a drunk Irishman in a bar but that he came off worse.'

Di Luca replied to the girl. Whatever it was he told her, it took a lot longer to say than my words in English and was delivered with a lot more expression and intonation. I heard my name mentioned a couple of times too, which hadn't been in the original script. He finished with a flourish addressed to the first girl, who had turned round to face him properly now, putting both her arms around his neck. She slapped him lightly on the cheek, then leaned in and whispered earnestly in his ear.

Di Luca unlinked her arms and pushed her slightly away from him. He started speaking instead to her redhead friend and to the blue dress girl who answered him coolly. The latter had paid no attention to me so far but the redhead was eyeing me up more and more frequently as the conversation carried on.

This was all very interesting to Di Luca, but I was getting bored waiting to see what would happen next. I looked over across the lawn and caught a glimpse of Sophie's side profile as she stood talking in a group which included Rizzo's father and Borghese.

I was brought back by the sound of a louder slap on Di Luca's face, swiftly followed by him pushing the first girl off him, then getting up and leading her by the hand into the bushes behind the blue dress girl's chair.

The other two women seemed to think nothing of this and carried on chatting. They didn't even appear to hear the occasional grunt, which after a couple of minutes was just audible over the noise of the party and the cicadas.

I was suddenly desperate for a drink. I stood up to signal a passing waiter carrying a tray with more glasses of prosecco. As I did so, the redhead looked over in alarm, accompanied by obvious relief when I sat back down again with a fresh glass and took a slug. Blue dress girl now started speaking with the redhead, distracting her until the first girl and Di Luca reappeared, sitting back down again on top of each other and looking pleased with themselves.

Now the redhead looked a little sour. She said something to Di Luca who turned to me with an unpleasant smile.

'She wants you to bang her like I just banged her friend. But it doesn't count unless you make her moan.'

'Then you'll need to do your one again,' I said coldly.

Just so I got the message, the redhead got up and came around outside the circle of chairs to stand behind mine. She leant down over me, sliding her fingers between the buttons of my shirt, stroking my chest and nibbling my ear.

'What did you tell her earlier?' I asked him, trying to ignore what was going on.

'I said it's been so long since you've had a woman that your balls have shrivelled to the size of chickpeas and that screwing you is a medical emergency.'

He repeated something else too, but in Italian. She leant down even further and pinched my crotch.

'*Non vero!*' she announced shrilly, causing heads to turn in the groups around us, just before I half-shrugged her away.

'Well? Are you going to do her or not?' Di Luca demanded impatiently. 'I've done all the work for you. And now you've upset her.'

Blue dress girl was looking at me appraisingly, waiting on my response. But watching in a way that reminded me of Sophie when she was judging me for being working class, unable to hide her low expectations of me.

'You've done the work. You have her. It's no fun when it's given to you on a plate.'

'Suit yourself, fag,' he said, as he got up to comfort the redhead, intending to take her away.

As I looked up, I saw Sophie and Rizzo head past, arm-in-arm like an old married couple. Going back inside the house I guessed. She half-turned toward me as they went by, taking in a tableau of the redhead undraping herself from around me as Di Luca stood behind her, his hands slipping up over her breasts as the two other good time girls looked on. At least Caterina hadn't seen it.

After Di Luca was gone, dragging the still complaining redhead by the hand behind him, I finished my drink and got up too, unsure of how to leave the other pair. In the end I opted for a kind of half-bow and a '*Scusi*,' again watched with interest, but no intent, by the blue dress girl.

I set down my empty glass on another passing waiter's tray and walked off to find the start of the path through the pines. I followed it to the stone bench at the end, brushed away the fallen needles, and sat gazing down the long wooded slope of the hill. The stars were out again, and a gentle breeze soughed over the treetops. The hurried cigarette with De Mauro earlier didn't count. I lit up properly for what felt like the first time in a couple of weeks and took a long drag, exhaling slowly.

There had been a lot to take in today. As I sat and smoked and thought, the nervous newspaperman troubled me. If his day job was writing investigative stories on the Mafia at the same time as his wartime buddies were trying to work with them somehow, maybe he was right to be jumpy.

Rizzo's father troubled me too. He had a lot to lose if he was caught stealing arms, much more than Borghese I guessed. He didn't come across as a man who'd been coerced into it either, as Sophie had suggested in Wismar. What was he getting out of all of this to make it worth his while?

And what was Rizzo doing with a box for a ring, if that's what had been in his pocket earlier? And what should I do about it? Sophie and he hadn't reached the stage of using each other's language in conversation and in normal circumstances he'd struggled to get her to meet his family. Nothing serious relationship-wise had happened between them so far. Maybe I should just let him fall into a trap of his own making.

A rumble in the sky made me look up. After a few seconds, I spotted them by their flashing anti-collision lights. A couple of fighter jets in formation, occluding the stars as they made their way north and out of sight.

I lit another cigarette and sat for a while longer, the occasional shout coming through the trees from the party. The minutes ticked by and Mars rose over the far horizon of the sea beyond Bari, glowing pinkly. My very own warning light, set in the sky just for me.

-

There was a knock on my door at six the following morning. When I arrived in the hall with my bag, Sophie was already there, waiting.

'Giovanni's gone to bring the hire car round from the garage,' she announced. 'The rest aren't up yet.'

I waited, knowing what was going to come next after a few short seconds.

'So, did you have fun last night?' she asked with a hint of jealousy.

'Did you?' I replied in a perfectly flat tone.

'Di Luca did, that was obvious. I got Giovanni to organise enough girls to take care of you too, as well as his cousin.'

'You shameless bitch,' I said quietly. 'No. When it comes my cousin, you shameless, evil bitch.' She'd been asking for it for the past three days.

She did a double-take, shocked, as if not really believing what she'd just heard from me. Her mouth opened and then closed again. I'd successfully shut her up for once.

Rizzo came back in, somewhat stony-faced himself, to usher us out to the drive. He picked up Sophie's cases, seemingly either ignorant or careless of the dumbfounded look on her face. I thought that if he had been paying attention, the lack of comments from her and instructions on where to stow her bags should have given him a clue as to her mood.

I didn't offer to help along the conversation on the way to the airport either. Whatever had happened or not happened between Rizzo and her last night, that and the early start had made him as uncommunicative as she was. If I was in luck, she wouldn't find her tongue until we were on the plane.

But that was a fanciful idea, of course.

'Before we get back to Brussels,' she announced from the back seat to Rizzo and me, 'we need to agree how often Lenkeit is going to report to us on his progress.'

'Can't you bring yourself to use my first name?' I asked, half-turning towards her.

'Sophie,' said Rizzo remonstratively, looking over the steering wheel at her in the rear-view mirror. 'He's part of this, whether you like it or not. If you didn't want to use Oskar, you shouldn't have suggested it.'

I was surprised at his boldness but maybe he was tiring of her vicious streak too.

I massaged my temple, which I tended not to do these days, not liking to hold my hands up to view. Today was Wednesday. I had to consult with Johannes about the next steps, in person if I could manage it.

'I should have something to tell you this time next week.' I said. I thought that would give me enough time for the other conversations that I had in mind too.

I was glad neither of them could see my face, for I was

planning to share all my suspicions about them with the Major. I wondered if there was a way to put the strange looks and half hints from De Mauro to a sterner test.

'Don't you also want to take some senior advice on this affair from within the EEC?' I asked.

'What about?' she replied suspiciously.

'Giovanni, you say it. We all work for Commission. What if this shipment gets into the wrong hands and destabilises Italy further, given everything else that's already going on? What if political turmoil here interferes with plans at the EEC which we know nothing about?'

'That's none of your concern, Oskar' she said, not giving him time to reply. 'You have a very specific job to do.'

She wasn't taking me seriously, so I upped the ante.

'I think we should find an Italian high up in the Commission to meet with. Someone whom we can trust to be discreet,' I suggested.

I twisted round in my seat to look her full in the face. She was frowning and biting her lip, but I couldn't tell if it was from anxiety or annoyance. Whatever she was feeling, it seemed to be another new experience for her, because it kept her quiet until the departure lounge this time.

We all perched at the bar. Rizzo clicked his fingers for espresso.

'How long are the flights today?' he asked.

'Lenkeit is the transport expert,' Sophie said acidly, recovered from whatever had troubled her on the way here.

I looked at my watch out of habit. 'We get into Brussels at ten past two.'

The drinks arrived and Rizzo took a sip.

'Well?' I asked again. 'Who are we seeing tomorrow at the Commission?'

Sophie suddenly got down from her stool and stood glowering.

'Excuse me, Giovanni,' she smiled falsely, 'I need to have a word with Oskar on his own.'

With a jerk of her head she beckoned me over to the far side of the lounge and switched into German.

'What do you mean calling me what you did back at Giovanni's house? And why didn't you go with those girls we'd laid on for you?'

'You know exactly why not. I wasn't going to disgrace myself in front of you.'

She reddened at this, but only momentarily. 'You could have taken one back to your room.'

I shook my head. 'The way you say it, it sounds almost like you wish I had. As some kind of punishment to you.'

She looked away with pursed lips for a couple of seconds, but her face was more troubled than angry.

'You already know too much of what Giovanni's family are up to. I don't want you involved any deeper than necessary,' she said cryptically, changing topic. 'But you have to make this shipment happen, for all of our sakes.'

She paused, before continuing quietly. 'I can't manage this on my own. I need you.'

That sense that she was sometimes more vulnerable than she showed on the surface came back to me, and I had a sudden, mad desire to wrap her in my arms there and then. She looked me shrewdly in the eye, saying nothing as I shuffled half a step forward. She didn't shrink back either, though.

'Yes, I understand,' I replied, calming down. 'We both know why I have to get this thing done.'

'As long as we're certain of where we stand,' she said, her head slightly tilted to one side as if to better see the scar on my cheek.

But that was something I never really knew with Sophie, at almost any time. It gave me something to think about for the rest of the day, though, all the way back to arrivals at Brussels and then home.

Chapter Six

Thursday was the regular day for my weekly report to Kramer, my sponsor at the EEC. He was my true boss there, not Masson, the department head to whom I officially reported.

As far as the rest of the EEC were concerned, Masson ran an odd little sub-department of Internal Affairs, unlisted in the internal phone directory. To Kramer and the other senior political sponsors, we were 'External Investigations' a pet project to give the Commission an embryonic intelligence gathering capability. But even that was a deception. For known only to Kramer and me, we were his future secret police force – intended to one day spy on, and if necessary, smear his rival power brokers at the Berlaymont. That day would come after Masson had moved on to his next job – so it wouldn't be for another couple of years at least. I assumed at that point, Kramer would manoeuvre me into the vacancy, but he'd never said so explicitly.

Regardless of what might happen in the future, in the meantime, Kramer had agreed to protect me from the fallout if I was ever caught informing for the Stasi in Brussels. The plan was that he'd claim I'd been working for the French SDECE all along - and he had enough connections back in Paris to be convincing and to bring any investigation to a halt. It would probably be the end of my career here, but I wouldn't go to jail.

In exchange, the French heard what the Stasi wanted me to get up to at the EEC. I was sure that the Ministry had other informers at the organisation, but Johannes was too professional to ever let anything slip. It wasn't quite a double agent arrangement, because I wasn't actively spying on the Stasi for the SDECE. But it was close enough. And close enough to keep me on my toes as regards what I said to whom.

But even a counter-espionage play against the Warsaw Pact was a sideshow compared to Kramer's real mission at the EEC. The existential struggle to ensure that France kept a stronger hold on the levers of power in Brussels than any other nation, and that the organisation itself didn't become more powerful than France one day.

I knocked on the door to his inner office on the top floor of the Berlaymont, and he beckoned me in.

He was smoking, shirt sleeves rolled up as he annotated a document spread out on his desk. A pair of gold spectacles were pushed up over his thinning hair and a narrow black tie that had been in style ten years ago completed the picture.

Almost. For in my mind, if you added a roof fan, the sound of car horns and motorbikes outside, and drew the blinds to imagine he was keeping out the heat of a Saigon summer, he could have been a French colonial official in Indochina. For all I knew, he might well have spent time out there, alongside everything else he'd got up to during the course of his career.

There was a gap in my knowledge of what he'd done between the Liberation, which seemed to have included hunting down former collaborators in dawn raids, and an actual quasi-colonial administrator job in France's post-war Saarland Protectorate within West Germany. Saarland was his last posting, just before he joined the EEC in 'fifty-eight. Sometimes the collaborators were shot whilst trying to escape, for his mild-mannered looks belied the man inside. I didn't know how he'd treated the Saarlanders, but they'd voted to become part of West Germany in 'fifty-seven.

'So, what's Masson been up to so far this week?' he asked.

Thursday was a good day for a weekly report. I had something to say from the first four days of the week, and any follow-up questions he gave me could be answered by Friday lunchtime, meaning work would still finish early for the weekend. The etiquette at the Berlaymont was only to conduct the most essential meetings on Fridays.

'This week's news isn't about Masson. It's about Sophie von Barten's boyfriend, Giovanni Rizzo.'

'Go on.'

'Prepare yourself, because it's the strangest story you'll have heard for a while - here in Brussels at least. She and he are involved in helping his family broker an arms deal between the Sicilian Mafia and a wartime gang of anti-partisan fighters from the former Salò Republic.'

He raised his eyebrows. 'Mussolini diehards, eh?'

He reassembled the document he'd been working on and dropped it into one of his desk drawers. Then he turned his notebook over to a new page, clicking out some lead from his propelling pencil as he did so.

'Who's selling to whom?'

'The Mafia are buying. Kind of.'

'Who in the Mafia?'

I wondered at the question. Who did he know there?

'The only name mentioned was Gianni Di Luca, from the Sicilian branch of Rizzo's family. I don't get the impression that the Di Lucas are big shots within the overall organisation in Sicily.'

De Mauro had told me explicitly that they weren't, but I always like to keep something back from Kramer. He sat quite still, listening intently as I said all this.

'When did you find all this out?'

'I was invited to a meeting held at the Rizzo family place in Apulia on Tuesday.'

'The Mafia and the far-right? Rizzo's people are getting themselves into some murky waters there. There's money to be made in trafficking arms, I suppose. More in drugs, of course.'

'I came away with the impression it was more political than criminal.'

'Why were you down there in the first place?' Now he started to scribble some lines in his notebook.

'Rizzo and Sophie von Barten wanted me to hear what was going on. They think that because I was in the police in Hamburg, I have some experience of the type of organised criminals they're dealing with.'

'That's weak. You were in the police for hardly a year.'

'I know, but they know even less.'

Normally my lies to Kramer were smoother than that. Sometimes, when I held things back, a half explanation didn't really work.

'It's only an impression about it being political,' I said, quickly moving on. 'From some of the things said in conversation about Italy being difficult to govern. The threat from the local communists and so forth.'

'So why has Rizzo's family got themselves mixed up in all this? I thought his father was a successful military contractor. And why is Sophie von Barten involved too? She and him aren't that close, are they? Next you'll be telling me that they're engaged or something.'

'Not as far as I know. Rizzo's father has some history with the wartime anti-partisan band, the Decima Mas. These days, he seems to be involved, as a collaborator at least, in an anti-communist stay behind resistance network run by the Italian military.'

The light, chatty tone Kramer habitually used in conversation with me was long gone. He leaned further forward over his desk, laying his pencil down.

'That's a lot of information. Who else was at this meeting?'

'Someone who occasionally goes by the name of Prince Borghese and a Sicilian newspaper journalist. They both arrived together in the morning. I collected them from the airport. Then some old comrades came later for a formal dinner in the evening who I didn't get to meet.'

Kramer cradled his head in his hands, rubbing his brow.

I carried on. 'Should the EEC be worried if they're somehow trying to destabilise Italy?'

Kramer looked up. 'That's a big leap of imagination you're making there, Oskar.'

'But what if they are? You've seen the reports of bombings and riots.'

'Why would we at the Commission worry? For the supranational wing who work here, there's no such thing as a bad crisis. If the six EEC member states end up in disagreement over something, it only reinforces the Commission's claim to be an honest broker. And, of course, its claim for the transfer of further powers from the national capitals.'

I wondered if that was Sophie's interest in the affair. It made as much sense as any other reason I could think of right now.

'But don't we need to find out how far these guys are prepared to go? What if they go too far?'

'What do you think is "too far"?'

'I'm not sure. Maybe provoke further civil unrest, as is happening in Calabria right now. Maybe take up arms against the leftist militants because the government won't? All to change the shape of the political landscape, lead Italy back down a more right-wing, more nationalistic path?'

'And what form do you imagine that might take these days?' he asked.

'Break links with NATO, as France did? Maybe even take it out of the EEC?' I hazarded.

He shook his head dismissively. 'That will never happen. Of all the European nations, Italy is the most fanatical for federation, left and right, even on the fringes of each. The only party who might have reservations about Italy becoming fully part of a bigger European entity are the communists, but only because they want it to be the sixteenth republic of the USSR.'

'It's in the Italian constitution,' I said thoughtfully, remembering Jan's lecture.

'How do you know that?' he asked, puzzled.

I tried to steer the conversation back to the immediate question of the arms deal.

'Shouldn't we at least alert someone responsible in Italy to what's going on?'

'Why are you suddenly so concerned about Italy? Or is it someone involved in this affair whom you're worried about? Are you *secrètement amoureux* for Sophie von Barten?'

'You must know something of her temper? If she is up to something and I go behind the scenes to try to stop it, life won't be worth living if she finds out.'

And in the case of my cousin Karin, it wasn't a turn of phrase.

'There's your answer,' I concluded uncertainly.

But it wasn't. I was being torn between doing what I'd been asked by Johannes for Karin's sake and my concern that Sophie really was getting herself into deeper waters than she knew. More fool me, for she didn't feel the same way. She'd dragged me in after her when she'd manipulated my cousin.

'You want to break her and Rizzo up, don't you?'

The possible last hurrah of Italian fascism was clearly of less interest to Kramer than Berlaymont office gossip just now.

'You're being too French about it,' I said.

'If I was being French about it, I'd suggest inviting her over for dinner, cooking her a special meal served with expensive wine, and then making love to her afterwards. You're being too German about it. Anyway, what's she done to you that you want to stop her making a little money on the side? Everyone does it. Haven't you hurt her family enough already?'

Until last week, Kramer was the only person in Brussels

who'd known what I'd done to her uncle. That was the other hold he had over me, apart from his knowledge of my work for the Stasi. I had some influence over him too, arising from the same events, for his hands weren't entirely clean there either. Not that I was going to use it, not while I had hopes of becoming the next boss of External Investigations when the directorship of the department rotated between the two countries who actually ran the EEC.

'Aren't you concerned about the potential for further destabilisation of Italy - even to a degree? Doesn't the Quai d'Orsay have its favoured allies within the factions of the DC? Italian politicians whom they've bought, who are friendly to France? Wouldn't this be useful information to your Minister of Foreign Affairs?'

Kramer gave a slight smile as I trotted out my theories.

'I don't know enough about what we're doing out there, not in detail. I would need to consult Paris first,' he said, humouring me.

'Can't we do something in the meantime? Confront Rizzo and Sophie von Barten, shock them into some further disclosures? Shouldn't we at least find out why they're really involved?'

'How would you propose we do that?' he asked, humouring me some more.

'Let's start off by telling Altiero Spinelli what I've learned so far and see what he thinks is going on.'

'How did he come into the picture? He's only just arrived at the Commission. Who put his name into your head?'

He shook his own head in either amazement or frustration that I wasn't letting go.

'He was mentioned to me by the person who told me about the constitution. My friend from the Free University. The one who unknowingly helped us with von Barten last year. In any case, we ought to speak with Spinelli – my friend thinks he's up to some political intrigue in Brussels.'

'Oh, that old canard of the European Parliament running the EEC instead of the Commission? I know something of Spinelli from a while back, from the early days.' Kramer pondered for a moment.

'My friend is planning a left-wing takeover of society by stealthily taking control of the commanding heights of cultural and political life in the West, starting with academia. He thinks Spinelli is on board. A "Long March Through the Institutions" he calls it, because it's going to take decades.'

Kramer tutted to himself.

'That doesn't sound like Spinelli. Are you sure that's what your friend meant? A decades-long plan won't work for Spinelli because he's already sixty or thereabouts. His political career is almost over, not that he ever made much impact in Italian politics from what I've heard.'

But if he'd failed to build a big enough patronage network for success in his early days, that could work to our advantage now.

'Even so,' I insisted, 'given his long experience he must have an intimate knowledge of Italian politics. Won't he be as good as anyone to give us a hint as to what might be going on with Borghese? And if he's on the fringes, not well connected to the DC, then no one will take him seriously if he talks.'

Kramer was still musing.

'The time of all the old pre-war and wartime federalists is almost past. Spinelli's ready for retirement and Monnet's even older - over eighty and hasn't held any office for fifteen years. Did you know that he and Spinelli clashed after the war during the early years of the European federal movement? In the end, the EEC and its predecessors were only big enough for one ego. Monnet won the battle to lead the movement because he had the better connections to America and the CIA.'

'But right now Spinelli's a Commissioner,' I said,

bringing him back to the present. 'If we can persuade him to take an interest, I can go to Rizzo and Sophie von Barten and tell them, or threaten them, that a Commissioner knows what they're up to.'

'Spinelli doesn't like Germans. His wife is a German Jew.'

'What's new? Does Monnet like Italians?'

'I don't care what traitors think.'

My eyes widened. I knew Kramer was an unashamed Gaullist and hated Monnet's supranationalism, which if carried to its logical conclusion would eventually mean France's demotion to the status of a European region. But Kramer was also a senior official at the EEC and even in private with me, whose fate he held in his hands, he was normally oh-so-careful in choosing his words.

'But did you know,' he continued, 'completely coincidentally, Monnet's wife is actually Italian? And that he's in debt to the Soviets for allowing his wife to acquire Soviet citizenship so she could divorce her first husband and marry Monnet in Moscow?'

'What?'

'No, for real.'

'When was this, in the early idealistic years of the Revolution?'

'No, under Stalin. In the mid-thirties.'

'No surprise he kept that quiet then,' I said, wondering if the Soviets had ever called in Monnet's obligation to them. But I had a problem to solve here and now.

'Regardless of what you think of Spinelli, shall we use him or not?'

Kramer looked at me askance.

'You just don't let go, do you Oskar? You're not meant to have your own political opinions. You're meant to do whatever I decide is in the national interests of France.'

I nodded silently.

'Okay. I'll give my blessing to bring in Spinelli because if I don't, you'll do it anyway. I suppose it's also an excuse for me to meet him politically in private, early on in the life of the Malfatti Commission. I don't believe your friend's claim about Spinelli and a socialist Long March, but I also don't trust him not to be up to mischief over the Parliament. Happy?'

'Yes. And you'll talk to Paris too and see if they have anything going on in Italy right now?'

'I'll think about it. But I will ask if the SDECE knows something about Rizzo's wider family in Sicily.'

'Why would the SDECE hold information on a minor Mafia clan?'

'We keep files on all kinds of people.'

I looked at him questioningly.

'Come on, don't be naïve. We both have trusted international networks of operatives. We both move money, people and weapons around the world on a regular basis, covertly and outside of the law. Of course it makes sense for us to cooperate from time to time.'

'So exactly how close are the SDECE to the global drugs trade?'

'There's some things it's better for you not to know. I'll have Rizzo's family checked out because I don't want you stepping on people's toes in Sicily and getting hurt. But Frau von Barten can take her chances.'

'Serves her right.'

'I suspect you're too caught up with her for your own good. What do your Eastern friends know of all this so far?'

'They know nothing of the Borghese connection,' I said, choosing my words carefully.

'Well, this is our affair. Whatever Paris chooses to share with me concerning France's links to the various players on the Italian political scene, I don't want it repeated as gossip to Berlin. And if it does turn out that there are rogue actors at the EEC, involved in something more serious than a corrupt arms deal, then we in Brussels need to put our own affairs into order.'

I left Kramer and spent some time in the central EEC library, spooling through microfiches. I had my own research to do on the things I hadn't shared with Kramer. For although I trusted the French more than the Ministry, I still didn't trust them.

I was constantly being surprised at the lengths the SDECE were prepared to go in supporting France's political objectives. Even when all the evidence to date, such as sunken ships in West Germany's principal port should have told me not to be. Maybe he was right, and ignorance was my protection.

I searched for the 'Premiolino' that De Mauro had mentioned. There were a couple of articles, but from different decades, 'fifty-four and 'sixty-seven. Six journalists each year were awarded the prize, but the 'sixty-seven story didn't mention De Mauro's name. I found the story about Mattei's plane crash though. The oil magnate's plane had taken off from Sicily before it went down a few kilometres from its destination, and there were any number of theories as to why.

There was a lot more material on the Decima Mas. Borghese seemed to have been a Skorzeny-type figure with high profile commando operations to his name - like the sabotage attack on the naval base at Alexandria in the earlier part of the war. But he was also tainted by the murky, ill-defined policing operations carried out by the Decima Mas during the time of the Salò Republic. He'd been tried and convicted for collaboration with Germany after the war but was given a much-curtailed sentence. After release, he'd been involved in Italian right-wing politics for a while during the fifties, but more as a figurehead. Latterly, he'd dropped out of view. At least up to 'sixty-seven when the microfiche record ended.

My last port of call for the day was Am Karlshof, a German pub in the Stalingrad district of Brussels where my contact from the East German foreign trade office sometimes drank. He made it a habit to go there a couple of times a week, so as to lull any regular shadowers into complacency. Not that the Sûreté could follow everyone all the time anyway. As part of his dissimulation, he also struck up genuine bar conversations with random strangers too. If nothing else, it gave him a sense of the current mood of ordinary people in the West. Sampling the Trappist beers of Belgium was a compensation for the inevitable risk of pub bores, but it definitely beat steaming open letters in some backwater regional office of the Stasi.

He was there now at the counter and I stood next to him to order, nodding in his direction. For want of any better general topic of conversation, I asked him what he thought of Jochen Rindt's crash on Saturday. My beer arrived and he joined me at a table at the back.

'Well, "Thomas", I never had you down as a Formula One fan.'

'I'm not. People only watch it for the crashes. Otherwise it's boring.'

'Suit yourself. It's like anything else, you need patience to understand what's going on.'

'I'm working a job with Johannes but I need to discuss some developments with him in person.'

'You need to go over again?'

'I need to see him here.'

I'd had a think about it on the way back from Bari. I could have passed a message to Johannes about the number of crates to be transported and let him work out a date by when we could move them. But my meeting with Kramer had only sharpened my suspicions that Borghese's wider plans might be more serious than the far-right simply stirring trouble for trouble's sake. Mainly because he'd been trying to avoid the topic.

'That's a big ask.' He looked at me narrowly. 'That's a card you only get to play very occasionally. For his sake too.'

I guessed the Stasi vetted their foreign intelligence officers extremely carefully and got suspicious of Berlin-based staff travelling abroad for anything other than the most essential reasons.

'You'd better be certain this is the time you use it.'

'I'm not certain. But it's the potentially biggest piece of news I've had yet.'

'That's why I'm here.'

'It's that big.'

It might be, but I didn't really know yet. All I knew for sure was that Borghese was no ordinary retired naval officer or even a middle-aged Italian businessman. To put it a different way, if someone had told me that Skorzeny was supplying arms to the Hamburg underworld, all my alarm bells would have been ringing right now. I was calling Johannes over on the assumption that when I met with Spinelli, he would have some special insight to explain how the pieces of the jigsaw might fit together into a bigger, more sinister puzzle.

He took a drink from his glass while he thought about it.

'We have a trade official coming into Luxembourg at the weekend. I'll ask if Johannes can come along too. I'll call you tomorrow in the evening at your flat. Will you have company?'

I frowned at him and he backed off.

I did get a call that evening though, but not from my drinking companion at Am Karlshof. It was Kramer. He'd moved faster than I'd bargained for and we were on for Spinelli tomorrow afternoon, meeting at Kramer's apartment.

I thought that was a good excuse to pour some whiskey and finally get around to reading Spinelli's manifesto, written whilst in confinement on the island of Ventotene and smuggled over to the mainland. I wondered if the original was in a vault at the Commission somewhere, a holy relic of the federalist religion. Maybe not. Maybe Monnet had had all the originals destroyed as being heretical.

My overriding impression on reading it was that Spinelli hated the nation-state with a deep and burning intensity as the source of all evil. There was plenty of socialist rhetoric for sure: the confiscation of private property from selected individuals by government decree, nationalisation of large corporations, handing estates to farm workers and the elimination of the parasitic landowning class, free secondary school education, and a state-guaranteed minimum income. But despite what Jan thought about Spinelli's politics, the socialism seemed merely to have been used as a skeleton on which to construct the arguments for his real ambition - the erasure of the individual European nations through their absorption into a single federal state, which itself would merely be a stepping stone to world government.

I wondered if his views had mellowed over the past thirty-odd years. After all, the belligerent countries had been restored to self-government when the Allied occupation had ended. West Germany had even been allowed to have an army, navy and air force and we hadn't managed to start a war with anyone yet.

When it came to the trappings and marks of nationhood, Spinelli was obsessed by armies, or at least his co-author, Ernesto Rossi, was. He was the one who'd written the preface to the manifesto. In Rossi's list of European federalist principles, a unified army was the very first item.

'These principles can be summarised as follows: one single federal army, monetary union, the abolition of trade barriers and emigration restrictions between states belonging to the Federation, direct representation of citizens within federal assemblies, one common foreign policy.'

Some of the others, like the abolition of tariff barriers, had already happened - if by that he meant the customs union. A single European currency was targeted for nineteen eighty under the Werner Plan. But the rest seemed quixotic right now. Maybe once enough of the other principles had become reality, the remainder would inevitably happen too. Just like the progressive stages of the 'Long March' which Jan had referred to.

As I swirled the amber liquid in the glass, I wondered what a semi-professional womaniser like Jan would think of Sophie's antics. He'd probably assume that her displays on the Apulia trip to make me jealous were just that, and if it was him, he'd move straight in for the kill. But that didn't make sense to me. Almost the entire three days had been provocation, belittlement and attempts at revenge. Continuous little jabs and twists of the knife which I tolerated almost to the end, given what she knew about me and her uncle now. I just didn't believe that love and hate could exist together in that way.

Unless she was trying to provoke me into making a physical move on her so she could accuse me of an impropriety. But in my heart, I felt that wasn't her nature, her hates were transparent and uncomplicated. It was that clarity of purpose which attracted me to her, even as I hated her in turn for destroying my cousin's life, humble as Karin's prospects had been. And I decided after the third whiskey, that on balance I really did hate her, if that was still the right word for what I felt.

A half-remembered story from a sermon I'd heard at my mother's church in Hamburg came back to me. King David, possessor of a harem, rebuked by a prophet for having had the soldier husband of one of his new acquisitions killed. The husband sent into battle by the king to effectively be murdered by him when a deliberate, treacherous retreat left the man alone on the front line. Karin had nothing, Sophie had everything, but the little Karin had, Sophie had taken away.

But in the final analysis, there was only one thing to be said about the situation. I might hate the Prussian landowner's daughter, it might even be justified humanly speaking, but like it or not, I had to forgive her. Just as I too had been forgiven, one afternoon in Dublin.

Chapter Seven

Kramer and I were sitting around the low table down in the sunken conversation pit in the lounge of his apartment when the doorbell rang. He went to answer it himself. The Kramers had a part-time maid, but presumably she was sent off duty during the private political meetings he held here away from the Berlaymont. I knew his wife was.

Altiero Spinelli was of middling height with a strong, square face. He was bald on top, the somewhat straggly hair at the side already white. If I didn't already know he'd been in prison in his youth, I'd have assumed he was an unkempt academic rather than someone who'd seen hardship but whom jail hadn't broken.

Kramer made the introductions whilst casting a loving eye at the drinks cabinet. It was late on Friday afternoon and any official business had long finished in the rest of Brussels.

'Signor Spinelli, this is my associate Herr Lenkeit.'

I got a cold nod. I guessed Spinelli really didn't like Germans after all, just as Kramer had said yesterday.

'Earlier this week, while he was on assignment for me in Italy, Herr Lenkeit came across a group of former fascists whom he wasn't expecting to meet. He heard some troubling things which we'd like to get your opinion on, as a veteran of the struggle.'

Kramer could turn on the lies and the charm more smoothly than anyone else I knew at the Berlaymont. Since the day I'd shot von Barten, that was.

Spinelli gravely inclined his head, just as an elder

statesman was meant to do.

'*Dimmi. Dites-moi.*'

I cleared my throat. 'I was invited to a private family gathering outside Bari - a birthday party. There the host introduced me to Prince Borghese and some of his wartime comrades.'

At the mention of Borghese's name, Spinelli's face clouded over.

'He's not a real prince.'

That was attention to detail which smacked of petty-bourgeois envy, if nothing else.

I ploughed on. 'There was some discussion of the current political discontent in Italy, suggestions of possible actions that should be taken to steer the country back into calmer waters.'

The hints had mostly been ones imagined in my head, but I had to give him something to react to.

'And you called me here on a Friday to tell me this? To ask me about Borghese whom everyone in Italy knows has been at the centre of every extreme right-wing and monarchist plot for the past twenty-five years?'

Kramer smoothly interjected. 'Of course not, Commissioner. We need to protect our sources. But this time, based on what Lenkeit tells me, I believe there may be a harder edge to their discussions.'

When Kramer put it as neutrally as that, I began to worry I'd let my imagination run away with me and had called in Johannes over some amateur dramatics by the extended Rizzo clan. But I'd seen the storeroom of weapons, I'd held the AK-47 in my hand.

'Where do you want me to start with the Borghese stories?' Spinelli asked the room. 'How in the 'fifties he had ambitions to be named as king if there was ever any restoration of the monarchy? How he started a new far-right movement two years ago, the Fronte Nazionale? Within the organisation he calls himself "Comandante," by the way. Not a mimic of "Duce" at all.'

Then he directed his attention to me. 'How much do you know about Italy in the first place? You probably weren't even born when the war ended,' he said brutally, if accurately - although only by a few months.

'A little,' I replied. 'I know that the DC are politically well-entrenched and that nothing seems to disturb them, even the unrest of the past two years. I know that despite the PCI being the biggest communist party in Western Europe, they haven't made an electoral breakthrough since 'forty-eight.'

'You're missing the point. The DC isn't a monolith but rather a collection of parties within a party. Depending on the national mood, over the years different factions end up on top, which gives the electorate the illusion of a change in government. Not that Italians believe much in government anyway. We became a unified state only relatively recently. The centenary is in nine days' time.'

Now Spinelli steepled his hands and looked over the top of his fingers at me.

'But because the DC has been able to act like a chameleon, reflecting the concerns of society in the moment, they've taken the oxygen away from the far-right. And although the neo-fascists and the monarchists still have representation in the Italian parliament, today they're very much a shrinking minority movement. They posture and parade but have no meaningful popular support. We know this because it was tested in nineteen sixty.'

'What happened then?' I asked, as I was doubtless expected to.

'The neo-fascist party, the MSI, announced they were going to hold their annual congress in Genoa, a centre of the Resistance during the time of Salò Republic. That alone was enough to trigger riots in the city and elsewhere across Italy. People were shot by the police in Sicily. The trade union federation announced a national general strike. And don't forget, this was all long before the protests of 'sixty-eight.'

'So whatever these murmurings were that I heard in Apulia, it can't be a mass uprising led by former Salò Republic fighters?' I suggested. 'If different flavours of the DC have been running the country since 'forty-eight anyway, what would the Italian right have to gain by orchestrating a popular revolt now?'

Spinelli shrugged. Kramer was watching him with interest, though.

What's the most extreme action that Borghese might realistically be planning today?' I asked. 'Would he go so far as to use arms?'

Spinelli raised an eyebrow. 'Lots of people are using arms right now. The Piazza Fontana bombing wasn't carried out using firecrackers, you know? But if Borghese is trying to relive his glory days from the war, then there's an outside chance he might be taking part in something like a replay of the De Lorenzo affair in 'sixty-four, when the Socialists were manipulated into coalition with the DC.'

'How did that work?'

'After the election that year, President Segni, a DC appointee, tried to broker a deal between the two parties to form a new government. A few weeks beforehand there had been a leak to the press of the Defence Ministry's counterinsurgency "Plan Solo," just to give people's imaginations time to wander. *"Tintinnio di sciabole"* - "the clink of sabres", as someone later called it. Then, at a critical point in the coalition negotiations, the president extended an official invitation to the head of the Carabinieri, General De Lorenzo, to a meeting at the presidential palace the day after the latest talks had broken down.'

'And then what happened?' I asked. Maybe Kramer knew all this stuff already.

'No, that was it. That's all that was needed. The invitation to De Lorenzo was a signal by the president to the Socialists and right-leaning factions of the DC to settle their differences. Otherwise, he was prepared to go over their heads and take special measures to form a technocratic government of civil servants. The Socialists realised that "technocratic" was code for the industrialist and land-owning clique and fell into line accordingly.'

Kramer nodded approvingly. Gaullists appreciated the proper exercise of presidential power.

'What were the special measures exactly? "Plan Solo"?' I asked.

'*In extremis*, yes. Segni was hinting at how far he might go to ensure the Socialists played their part in keeping the door firmly shut on the PCI.'

'But Plan Solo was just a plan,' I countered. 'When people heard the so-called clink of sabres, what did Segni want them to think was going to happen?'

'It would have been the classic play; call out the soldiers under a prearranged contingency plan to supposedly suppress a coup, all the while they're unknowingly carrying out an actual coup. Just like your lot tried in nineteen forty-four in the hours after the attempted assassination of Hitler.'

'And they bought this?'

Spinelli had his hands down by his sides now, softly clicking his fingers in frustration at my stream of questions. He still answered them, though. Showing off to us must have been more entertaining than anything else he had planned for a slow Friday afternoon in Brussels.

'The full story broke in the press three years later, in 'sixty-seven and last year there was a parliamentary inquiry. There were arrest lists apparently. For both the PCI and the MSI, communists and neo-fascists. Did you know that Borghese was the honorary President of the MSI for a couple of years in the 'fifties?'

'I still don't understand. How can Borghese be taking part in a rerun of the De Lorenzo affair now?'

'Don't you get it? For a counter-insurgency plan to be activated, there has to be an insurgency, or at least a credible report of one. Look at the German generals who took part in the Stauffenberg plot in July 'forty-four. What excuse did they give to their subordinates who weren't in the know, to explain why the troops were being moved out of barracks?'

'That there had been a coup against Hitler.'

'There you go.'

When I replayed Spinelli's theory to myself it seemed utterly fantastical on so many levels. Not least because it implied that the inoffensive Rizzo and the darling of the Berlaymont were in on the plans. Although Sophie's involvement was somehow the least surprising of the two. To me anyway.

If Spinelli was even half-right, then if I'd thought she might be clinically mad when she revealed her plans to steal weapons from NATO, I now knew it for sure. And even if he was only a quarter-right, and there was only the possibility of an anti-democratic plot, then trying to stop her was still a crystal-clear moral decision, for her sake too. But if she suffered or, what was worse for Sophie, if her career suffered in the fallout from having taken part in this craziness, then so be it.

'But that bluff won't work on the Italian left wing a second time?' I countered, trying to stay grounded in reality and avoid getting carried away by the talk of conspiracies.

'And it surely won't work on the right wing, either, given the reports of arrest lists for the MSI in 'sixty-four?' I asked. 'Borghese must know not to trust the DC and the Italian security apparatus this time? If there is a "this time."'

'He survived the war, so he knows how to take care of himself,' said Spinelli, another survivor.

Maybe Borghese was buying himself some kind of insurance from the Mafia with the secret arms shipment.

'Who exactly was behind the De Lorenzo plot six years ago?' I asked.

He shrugged. 'Everyone was suspected. The Carabinieri, other domestic intelligence services, the CIA, other foreigners. It's what makes it difficult to work out who might be involved today.'

Kramer recrossed his feet under the table.

'But now someone might be paying off Borghese to simulate a coup, in order to justify a military takeover of the country?' I asked, trying to prompt him into giving a definitive answer.

'You're going too far there, Lenkeit,' said Kramer.

Spinelli clicked his fingers. 'I don't really much care what they're getting up to. Anything which weakens and undermines the Italian nation-state is good for the Project.'

'That seems a little harsh on Italy, Commissioner, if also somewhat selfless?' said Kramer unctuously. 'But you can be frank with us. We're friends. Lenkeit and I are the very model of Franco-German cooperation, blind to borders.'

Yes, I thought. Napoleon's model, where the puppet states he'd created along the eastern bank of the Rhine jumped and danced to his tune. Marched into Russia for him and froze to death on the way back out.

Spinelli shook his head contemptuously. 'The more that Italians become disillusioned with Rome, the more easily their leaders can be persuaded to transfer further powers to Brussels. If nothing else, so they can blame the West Germans for the inevitable unpopular economic decisions coming their way over the next few years.'

It was cynical, but I supposed that was the way politics worked.

'Even better,' he continued, 'if we can get the Italians themselves to lead the call, rather than the Commission, then the larger member states will be under pressure to agree for fear of appearing to be nationalist reactionaries.'

I was fascinated by the way he referred to 'Italy' and 'the Italians' in the third person. I guessed when you hated nation-states, you started with your own.

'My ambition before the decade is out, is that there should be a real European Parliament, where the deputies are directly elected by the people, not appointed by the member states.'

'It read it in your manifesto,' I said. 'In Rossi's preface to it.'

I'd have thought he'd have appreciated that. But he didn't look pleased that I'd mentioned his co-writer.

'He only joined our canteen because he was kicked out by the *giellisti*,' Spinelli muttered to himself.

He left internal exile on Ventotene for now and came back to the present. 'We need to capture the hearts and minds of those Italians who still think in the old nationalistic ways by inspiring them with dreams of a New Rome. Not Mussolini's fascist dream, but that of the Treaty of Rome.'

All well and good, I thought to myself. But whether fascist or not, a European federalist's empire was still an empire. Which was another reason to keep an eye on Sophie's own ambitions at the Berlaymont, given her allegiance to Monnet's cause.

'Don't look so cynical, Herr Lenkeit,' said Spinelli. 'You've read my manifesto. A democratic, unified European state is a real prize for us all. Think of Spain and Greece. A powerful, confident people's Parliament in Brussels could be a beacon to those nations still languishing under military government.'

'Won't a strong Parliament with teeth upset the Commission, sir? Don't they love being able to manipulate the Council from behind the scenes?' I asked.

'Right now I am the Commission. Well, one of the Commissioners. But don't you agree that the Commission should wither away over time and that a democratic parliament should take its place? Don't you think that's worth striving for?'

Kramer nudged me with his foot under the table. He was listening with what I recognised was a higher-than-usual level of intensity. I wasn't sure if he wanted me to shut down Spinelli's subversive talk or keep digging into his plans.

I steered a middle course. 'Indeed, sir. If I can ever be of any assistance to you in that regard, just let Monsieur Kramer know.'

Kramer withdrew his foot and I brought Spinelli back to the topic of Borghese, hoping to force him into a firm conclusion as to the Comandante's intent.

'But what's in it for Borghese right now?' I asked. 'Is he a mercenary? Is he doing it because he's short of funds?'

'I've no idea. He's always had rich allies and supporters, seeking to bathe in the glory of his wartime commando operations.'

It was the same reason why Skorzeny had been hired by unrepentant West German industrialists as a sales agent to various right-leaning regimes around the world.

But for all the useful background that Spinelli had shared, apart from the coup idea, he'd offered nothing else. There had to be a plausible reason for Borghese's arms dealing which was less extreme than an overthrow of the Italian Republic.

'Would you be prepared to meet some of the other people who were at the party in Apulia? They also happen to work here at the EEC. Maybe I missed hearing or understanding something which they didn't.'

I had no real idea why I'd said that. I'd only suggested to Kramer yesterday that we canvass Spinelli's opinion on the situation, to get some ideas with which we could challenge Rizzo and Sophie. Not that Spinelli would be the one to directly confront the pair. But if Spinelli, as a Commissioner, presented them with a theory based on the De Lorenzo affair, the *fonctionnaires* would be forced to respond with a real explanation.

'I'll consider it, if Monsieur Kramer thinks it really necessary.'

'Indeed Commissioner. Perhaps we can meet anyway

early next week, to discuss further any little service you might wish Lenkeit to perform for you.'

'Is that it? Are you done with me? My driver is waiting down below.' He got to his feet and we did likewise.

For the first time he eyed up the scar on my cheek and I was reminded once again he'd spent time in a fascist prison. And that the Italian communist leader Gramsci had died in one.

On impulse, I asked him one final thing.

'A last question if I may, Commissioner. The Decima Mas, what was their reputation as anti-partisan fighters?'

'They had a certain cachet because of their earlier underwater sabotage exploits. But as anti-partisan fighters, in practice they would have been little different to the myriad of other ad-hoc units created by the fascists in the last year of the war.'

'At the end there was no glory for anyone,' I suggested blandly.

'In their desperation to delay the final reckoning, the puppet regime encouraged any enterprising commander to set himself up as a warband leader. Like the *condottieri* during the Renaissance times. But they were really little better than criminal gangs, outside anyone's control and a law unto themselves.'

'And the Decima Mas were just as bad?'

'I don't know exactly. Think summary executions of wounded partisans, torture of prisoners, and if they captured female Resistance fighters, rape too. The full range of war crimes,' he said, looking at my face again.

'But Borghese was lucky in that regard,' he continued. 'He chose to work directly for the German military rather than the Italians of the Salò Republic. That's what saved his men from being shot outright by the Resistance at the end of the war. German command gave them the status of enemy combatants.'

'It was described to me by someone as a civil war up there,' I said.

'It was complex for sure. As well as fighting for the Germans, Borghese also allied himself with anti-fascist partisans in the east in Istria, who were trying to defend it from annexation by their fellow anti-fascists, the Yugoslavs. But despite Borghese's efforts, after the war only Trieste remained Italian, the rest of the peninsula was lost to Tito.'

He looked inquiringly at Kramer. 'I have to go,' he said. '*Arrivederci.*'

Kramer motioned me to sit while he escorted Spinelli to the door. When the Commissioner was gone, he finally went over to the drinks cabinet to pour himself a brandy and offered me one too.

'Can you stay for ten minutes or so, Lenkeit?'

'*Je suis à votre disposition.*'

'Do you really think it's worth monitoring Spinelli's democracy project? For the Parliament to displace the Commission?' he asked. I was surprised that my opinion was being sought after what he'd said yesterday about me merely taking orders.

'Don't we have a bigger problem to discuss? About a possible coup plot in a former fascist country?'

Kramer waved his hands dismissively. 'The Italians will take care of it. Never get involved in someone else's civil war. You heard how nasty they can get. We can only deal with the problems on our own doorstep. Which right now is a failed Italian politician potentially giving some hotheads in the Parliament ideas above their station. Maybe even upsetting the delicate balance of power between the Council and the Commission. The one that no one talks about in public.'

'Is that what you were indicating to me under the table, then? Stay close to see who he's recruiting as allies? Or you think he really is washed up and it will all come to nothing in the end?'

'It never hurts to watch and see what people do, as

long as you're spending time watching the right people,' he replied delphically.

'I have a question for you,' I said.

'Okay, we have a few minutes. I still need to ask you about something else, not related to Italy.'

'But I do. Was there a SDECE link with De Lorenzo? And how deep are the SDECE's connections to the Mafia, really.'

He drummed his fingers on the table, wondering how much to tell me.

'The threads joining the players in the global drugs trade are highly intertwined. It's public knowledge that we arrested two Frenchmen a couple of years ago who were wanted by the Americans for heroin trafficking into the States, the "French Connection" it's called. The trade between Marseille, where the Corsican underworld has its mainland base, and New York, where the American Mafia distribute the product.'

'Are you suggesting that the men who were arrested moonlighted for the SDECE?'

'It started in Indochina in the 'late forties. France had no money to fund the war, not to the extent that the army wanted to prosecute it. So the French intelligence agencies had to be resourceful and make use of whichever business opportunities lay to hand.'

'Vietnam is a long way from Europe.'

'The Corsicans were out in Saigon too, along with the SDECE. So there's one link in the chain.' He gave a secret smile. 'But we're gone from there now. Someone else has taken over in Vietnam.'

I was a believer in the strategy of saying nothing in these situations and letting the other person fill the silence.

'But to answer your question on the interplay between France and the Sicilian Mafia, you have to understand that the French Connection will eventually be shut down. So the heroin refining that takes place in Marseille today will have to move somewhere else in the Mediterranean.'

'And how do you know about this development?'

Kramer sipped his drink and looked at me carefully.

'Because we did a deal with Nixon at the start of this year. He stood for election on a policy of cracking down on drug use. Some say it's a proxy campaign to disrupt the anti-war left. The Americans are also concerned because their troops in Vietnam are becoming increasingly addicted to heroin.'

'This week Nixon announced no more offensive operations in the South.'

'The climate's changing. Pompidou is much less anti-American than de Gaulle. He's open to cooperation on shutting down the French Connection and he wants to clean up the SDECE at the same time too. The Algerian war left a poisonous legacy at the agency - especially the divided loyalties over the OAS, as you can well imagine.'

'What does France get in return for cutting off the Corsicans?'

'We got it already. At the start of this year Nixon blessed our sale of Mirage fighters to Saudi Arabia, America's other client state in the Middle East.'

Fighter jets made my truckload of rifles seem pathetic by comparison. And I wasn't even getting paid for them.

If we were discussing geopolitics, then there was something else which took place in Sicily that the SDECE might have also been involved in.

'What did you think of the Italian ENI group stepping in to help the Algerians exploit their oil after independence?'

His face clouded over. 'Where did that come from?'

'The Sicilian newspaper journalist that I met in Apulia mentioned it. De Mauro he's called. He's investigating the plane crash of ENI's chief executive, Enrico Mattei, in nineteen sixty-two. He's meeting someone who claims to know something about it next week. The plane took off from Sicily, apparently.'

'What do you think?'

'If I was in the SDECE's shoes, I'd have asked myself, what was the point of the sacrifices in Algeria if France didn't even get to keep the hydrocarbon exploration rights?'

'That's your supposition, Oskar. At some point you have to stop trying to make connections to everything. Otherwise you'll go mad.'

'Okay.'

He got up and went to the drinks cabinet again. This time he rummaged around in the back for a minute, bottles clinking as he moved them to get to the one he wanted.

He returned to the table with a dusty bottle, a thirty-year-old cognac by the label.

'What's the occasion?' I asked.

'A toast to the success of your next mission.'

I stiffened, instantly suspicious.

He motioned me to finish my glass and refilled it with the new stuff.

'Okay. Now listen carefully. I have something else I need to say to you. Something may need to be done about England's accession to the EEC.'

'Why is it in danger?'

'No. Not yet.'

He placed his glass down on the table and leaned forward confidentially.

'We may need you to go there and kill some people.'

The floor fell out from under my feet.

'Jesus, Kramer. Couldn't you have dressed it up, even a little bit?'

'No. Because I need to know. There's some people there who really don't deserve to live. Ones who'll never be tried in a court of law because no one will ever give evidence against them. Not credible witnesses anyway.'

'Why the moral crusade?'

'These people who need to be rubbed out could taint our British friend by association, undermine the political will for accession.'

'Our friend? Oh, him. The guy in charge over there?'

He nodded knowingly at me.

'We don't use his name when we speak of him. I'm working on an insurance plan to protect him - you already know why this is so important to the EEC.'

'You told me.'

And he had, earlier this summer. The cost of the CAP kept growing year on year, faster than the EEC's income and the Commission was accordingly becoming ever more desperate for Great Britain's future financial contributions. Paris also wanted to use accession to force the British to stop importing cheap food from outside the EEC and instead switch to French produce.

'But what could these people possibly have done that would harm him by association?' I asked, before realisation dawned. 'Oh. It's because he's a "bachelor," isn't it? It's some kind of sex crime?'

'This is beyond sensitive. We have to find someone way outside the usual sources to take care of it.'

'If you're asking me and not the drug dealers at the SDECE, then yes, you could say that,' I said, trying to buy time.

Of course, if I got caught by the British, it was the Germans, West or East, who would most likely get the blame.

'But why go to such extremes? I'm telling you now, I won't go that far.'

'You may not have a choice,' he said.

'It's not easy, you know. A part of you dies inside when you pull the trigger. And I have a conscience too.'

'I thought it got easier, the more that you did it?'

'You think or you know?'

Kramer leaned back, disappointed.

'No, I never got to find out. There were always other people for that.'

'Think about it some more. There has to be another way to discredit his enemies and protect him.'

Kramer opened and closed his mouth. I wondered if he was going to suggest a payment to me of some kind. A bounty they would have called it in the Wild West. A hundred dollars for each body.

Instead he said, 'I'm waiting for some decisions to be made in Paris. We might ask you to go to London early next year.'

'I know I'm obliged to you. But I won't do that thing.'

'Maybe once you get to know the people in question and realise the level of protection they enjoy, you'll see the difficulty of taking a softer approach. It will be a professional challenge. It will stretch you.'

I shook my head in mounting despair.

'You also haven't heard yet what it is that they get up to. Someone needs to serve them justice.'

He looked grim now. Maybe he really did have a conscience when it came to concern for the victims of Heath's associates. When it came to asking a subordinate to commit murder though, not so much.

Or he was simply depressed for having uncorked the XO prematurely.

Chapter Eight

Luxembourg - Sunday, 13th September 1970

It was another Sunday, another day I supposed I should have been in church rather than driving down to Luxembourg to get myself even more deeply implicated into an illegal arms deal.

The address given to me by my contact at the East German foreign trade office was on a leafy street of prosperous bankers' houses in the Limpertsberg district of the city. Each one nestled behind low fences or neatly trimmed hedges, just as you might expect to see elsewhere, but the matching steel gates told a different story of subtle exclusivity.

I checked the numbers on the buildings and drove on around the corner to park. Then I trotted back to the East German house and buzzed the intercom fixed to a post by the gate. A man dressed in what looked like a kind of domestic servant's uniform came out and spoke to me in French.

I suddenly realised, absurdly, that I didn't know how I was going to introduce myself.

'I'm here to see a colleague from Berlin.'

'Who are you?'

'Thomas Hofmann.'

He looked blankly at me. I peered past him through the gate. In one of the downstairs rooms the net curtains hanging in the window had been pulled back slightly on one side. As I looked again, Johannes suddenly appeared in the gap, standing there, large as life, impatiently beckoning me forward.

'I'm here to see that guy,' I said, pointing.

The butler looked round, but Johannes had stepped away into the room again and let the curtain fall back into place.

'Oh, why didn't you say? Come on in, then.'

Johannes wasn't in any better mood when I saw him up close inside the house. He gave me a curt greeting and took me into an office just off the entrance hall, a different room from where I'd seen him standing before.

We stood facing one another across a desk. The office had a weekend look about it - the filing cabinets and roll-top units shut up tight and the desk things: calendar, stapler, legal pad all neatly tidied away to one side.

'What is this place?' I asked.

'An office for the Ministry's commercial activities in the West. Also, the place where we make payments to various friendly organisations around Europe.'

'Oh,' I said.

'The building is very secure. All the records are carefully protected, so don't even think of letting anyone on this side know about it. Your remaining family not yet in prison want it to stay that way. Especially as they haven't had any news about their daughter for almost a month now.'

'Have they had any message from her at all since her arrest?'

He looked at me coldly. 'Sit down. This had better be good.'

I'd had a while to think on the drive down this morning, about how I could tell my news for maximum effect. But now he was provoking me, and I was letting him.

'You'd better warn your comrades in the PCI,' I said frostily. 'A right-wing coup, or something like a coup, is coming in Italy.'

He stared at me sceptically.

'Well, that escalated quickly. One day you're stealing arms for your girlfriend, the next she's planning to assault the presidential palace.'

I slammed the flat of my right hand on the table. He watched me with cynical amusement while I gave myself a few seconds. He didn't stop there though.

'You really think Fräulein von Barten is involved in a coup? You should know her better than that. You're the one she's meant to be sweet on.'

Needling me might be amusing for him, but I'd just suggested he might have hit the biggest intelligence jackpot of his career. And my career, too, I supposed. In the depths of his eyes I saw a spark of greed as part of him hoped I was right.

'The arms are real. I've seen them.'

I watched his avarice grow stronger. The acquisition and hoarding of secrets made misers of everyone who played the game.

'There's a lot. Cases and cases of assault rifles, ammunition, and plastic explosives. Surface to air missiles too, I'm fairly certain. I read the manifest of what's to be transported. It's enough to create serious mischief.'

'Go on. Where's this idea of a coup coming from then?'

'Because when I went to Italy with Frau von Barten at the start of last week, I met some of the other players in the affair. One of them is a former fascist commando, a Prince Borghese. According to the senior Italian politician I spoke with at the Commission, Borghese is notorious as an agent of reaction.'

'Who did you speak to in Brussels?'

'Someone called Altiero Spinelli, a Commissioner. I believe he's a socialist fellow traveller too.'

I looked closely at Johannes for a sign that he recognised the name, but he was giving nothing away.

'Spinelli thinks that certain factions in the DC may possibly be attempting to stage a fake coup, like in 'sixty-four, as a pretext for a military crack-down on the left. If that's what it is, then Borghese may be the man of action they've chosen to trigger Italy's counter-insurgency plans, sweeping the leaders of the PCI into jail.'

Johannes scribbled the names on a piece of paper he'd detached from the legal pad on the desk. No imprints of this spy's writing on the sheet underneath.

'Who else did he say was behind this? Anyone from outside Italy?'

'He said there were too many possible players last time to be able to say with any confidence who might be stirring the pot today. He mentioned the CIA and other foreign agencies, but only in passing. He suggested the Italian agencies too, of course.'

Johannes leant forward on his elbows for a few seconds, hands up over his face, covering his eyes. Whatever he was thinking about wasn't straightforward, because then he got up to go and stand by the window for a minute contemplating the shrubbery.

'Can you prove the involvement of any intelligence agency, Italian or foreign?' he asked, turning round to face me again.

I shook my head. 'It's only Spinelli's supposition so far.'

He looked at me shrewdly.

'I see,' I said. 'It's a bigger game than a domestic coup d'état. This is about exposing CIA interference in their politics and kicking America out of Italy, isn't it?'

It wouldn't just be the biggest jackpot of Johannes' career. It would be one of General Fiedler's career highlights too. It would shift the balance of power in Europe. A repeat of nineteen sixty-six when France left NATO.

'So your man Spinelli supposes these things? That there may be a simulated coup. That Borghese may be the tool of the plotters?'

'It's the only theory I have right now. I'm not an Italian

expert.'

'Nor am I. But if I go with this and it turns into an intelligence disaster because you've been spinning yourself a yarn, or have been deliberately misled by the other side, then it's not your cousin you'll need to worry about. There'll be an internal Stasi investigation, and if you get Mielke on a bad day, the dispatch of an assassination squad to hunt you down.'

No pressure then. He came back from the window to the desk but didn't sit down.

'Let's hope the football season starts well for Dynamo Berlin in that case,' I said, looking up at him. 'What else can we do for now, but to go along with Borghese's shipment of arms to the Mafia? It's our only way to stay close to what's happening.'

'It's not as simple as that. If you really have stumbled across a neo-fascist coup, especially if elements of the CIA are involved, then this is a matter for Moscow.'

'Isn't it a PCI matter too? They're the ones in the firing line if there's a military crackdown and the president declares martial law.'

Johannes finally sat back down at the desk. He started tapping it with his forefinger.

'It depends. When's this shipment to take place? Your involvement might be over in a couple of weeks, before we have time to mobilise properly on our side.'

'They didn't give me a deadline to move the weapons, they just asked me to tell them when I'd be ready.'

'And who within the Mafia is getting the shipment?'

'That's not clear. Rizzo, the boyfriend, has a second cousin who's a member. We're delivering the arms to him in Sicily. I guess he's the liaison. Apparently, they have a coordinating body called the Regional Commission which has recently been reconstituted after several years of dormancy.'

'Who are you close to in this affair from Rizzo's side? Who might know the planned date?'

'His father might. He had a secret chamber built under the floor of his new factory where the weapons are currently being stored. I assume he's somehow connected to the Italian Defence Ministry's stay-behind resistance network.'

'It's called "Gladio". That's the NATO codename for their terrorist organisation.'

'What other codenames do you know? I skim-read the manifest, but I didn't recognise all of the abbreviations.'

He tapped the desk some more. 'I wonder if Rizzo or Fräulein von Barten know the date.' He looked at me with narrowed eyes.

'You should do something there,' he said appraisingly.

'What do you mean?'

'Prise her away from Rizzo, seduce her. Get her to tell you everything.'

'Why do you think she'd be open to that?'

'Or is she special and you're both saving yourselves before you do the deed, waiting for the right occasion?'

I threw up my hands. 'Again, Johannes, where is this idea coming from?'

'I told you a few weeks ago. I read her letters to your cousin,' he smirked.

'The ones that were lies. The ones which you'd said you'd let me read, but then in the end you didn't.'

'Because you smashed up an office at Hohenschönhausen prison.'

I frowned as I remembered Johannes' assistant laying his hand over his pistol holster as he watched a chair disintegrate against a wall.

'So what did the letters say,' I asked, intensely curious now.

'I can't remember every word exactly. Something about you being different to anyone she'd ever met. About you having hidden depths to your character that only she could see.'

I frowned, shaking my head. 'Sounds like teenage girls'

talk to me. Don't forget that's who she was writing to.'

'So what is your relationship to her, really?'

'You've met her, you've seen her magnetism. She drives men crazy. I'm no exception, I suppose.'

'But do you have any special claim on her, apart from shooting her uncle? Don't worry, the question was rhetorical.'

'She wrote those letters before she knew about her uncle.'

'You should still try to get her to tell you what she knows. Maybe she feels guilty about leading your cousin astray.'

'Perhaps. She didn't show many signs of remorse on the trip to Italy. But in the end, it's none of your business.'

'Every part of your life is my business.'

Johannes stood up again and went back to the window to inspect the shrubbery, just in case it had changed since the last time he'd looked. After half a minute he turned back to me, newly resolved and deadly serious.

'I'm going straight back to the Normannenstrasse this afternoon to write this up.'

'It's Sunday.'

'I want to hit the relevant people early on Monday morning, before anything else leaks out of Italy. I want to be first with this news and you want me to be too, for obvious reasons.'

'Will you warn the PCI?' I asked.

'We'll see. They got worried again a couple of years ago after the Greek military coup about their lack of preparedness to go underground if the same thing happened in Italy.'

He gave me a wry smile.

'You see? It's not so crazy an idea after all,' I insisted.

'The PCI used to have a paramilitary group which came out of their wartime partisan movement, but they let it wither away. So in 'sixty-seven they asked the Soviets for help to rebuild their capabilities. In turn, Moscow asked us to provide the Italians with training in counter-surveillance techniques.'

'Where, in Germany?'

'Yes, back home in the Republic.'

He looked up at the ceiling.

'I think we need to send some people with you to Italy who are better suited than the ones I was originally thinking of.'

'Better suited for what?'

'To stop interference from the Mafia, the fascists, whomever. People who can provide us with harder options than the HVA people we were going to send.'

'What do you mean, "harder options"? People with guns?'

'People able to do more than just take photographs and drive a lorry. If we come to believe a coup is a real prospect, we might want to throw a spanner in the works.'

I frowned. 'Sabotage?'

He shrugged, but his eyes were glinting.

I pressed him again. 'Will these be the Ministry's people? I thought NATO weaponry would have been more the domain of Volksarmee military intelligence?'

'Anyone we bring in will be at our invitation only. I'm not going to give up control of this prize. If there really is a coup plot, you need to find out who's behind it and then everything else about it too. If we can somehow disrupt their plans, maybe even show we stopped a coup from happening, then there's a good chance I'll make lieutenant-colonel. If we can get credible proof of outside interference in Italy and expose the CIA, then I'll definitely get a promotion. Maybe a head of a Department.'

He thought for a while. 'I'll make some calls when I get back to Berlin. The specialists I'm thinking of might need to be pulled back from overseas. You'll need to meet us again to get properly briefed before you go to Italy. It's a tricky country for us and dealing with the PCI is tricky too. Both with the old guard and the new.'

'Why?' I asked.

He tutted disgustedly.

'Oh, I see. The usual reason.'

This really had escalated far faster than either of us had anticipated. Sophie and Rizzo's plan to hire a truck and driver, cash paid and no questions asked, was turning into a full-blown Stasi operation. And I was worried that career-wise, Johannes was betting everything on red, or rather, black, the party colour of the fascists.

'Have you ever been there? To Italy?' I asked him.

'No. But I do both enjoy and dread hearing your holiday stories. Something seems to go wrong every time you leave Brussels. Not this time it won't.'

So I was going to Italy under supervision.

'Are you ever tempted to stay over in the West?'

'Why? My wife and children are in the East. Are you trying to tempt me with a 'seventy-one model Volkswagen? But seriously, never, ever put that question to me again. You don't know the damage that even asking it can do.'

'When can I tell Rizzo's people that I'm ready to go?'

Johannes thought some more. He picked up a desk calendar, tracing it with his finger.

'The week after next, in seven days' time,' he announced. 'I'll send someone to Hamburg to meet you next weekend. The comrades at the foreign trade office in Brussels will tell you where to go.'

'I don't think I should take more than two people with me to Italy. I'm meant to be charging the Italians for the service,' I said, somewhat guardedly. I supposed I could use what I'd paid Pavel as a basis for working out an amount.

'Planning to keep the proceeds, were you?'

'You tell me,' I said more neutrally now.

'Don't look so guilty.' He glanced at his watch. 'Anyway, I've had an idea. Five more minutes and I'll introduce you to the person I travelled here with.

'Did you meet the PCI when they came to East Germany for training?'

'No, not me.' He pursed his lips as if he'd been about to say more.

I wondered if his daughter had. Based on the two wild, drink-fuelled nights I'd spent with her at the Stasi training college this summer, I'd bet she'd have enjoyed all the socialist fraternisation that went on there after dark.

'What's your next step as regards the various players you work for at the Berlaymont?' he asked, while we waited on the hour hand of the wall clock reaching twelve.

'I'm going to use the old anti-fascist agitator I told you about, Altiero Spinelli, to confront Rizzo and Frau von Barten and put some pressure on them. See if I can get them to tell me what's really going on.'

'When you meet the person I'm sending across next weekend, pass me a message with what they said. Let's go,' he said, standing up.

We crossed the hallway and Johannes knocked a set of heavy double doors. Judging by the ornate plasterwork on the ceiling, the salon we entered must have been one of the principal reception rooms when the house was a private residence.

'Herr Doktor Schalck-Golodkowski, may I introduce Herr Lenkeit, a friend of ours who works at the EEC.'

Schalck-Golodkowski was a bluff, stocky man, a little younger than Johannes I thought. He was dressed like a Western businessman with cuff links and tie pin, which somehow made him look more out of place than not. He was sitting at a polished walnut conference table, a pile of papers stacked in front of him and a gold fountain pen lying on top.

'Lenkeit's cover story for his family in the East is that he works as an export consultant to the Republic, advising on trade with the EEC. I have a notion of turning it into a real story at some point and wanted to take the opportunity to introduce him to you.'

I looked across in surprise at Johannes. I'd thought his colleague was going to let me know whether I could keep the payment for moving the arms.

'Do you want to earn some money on the side? What experience do you have of business?' Schalck-Golodkowski asked.

'None directly. I was in the police before I joined the EEC.'

'But you must know about EEC commercial matters like export subsidies and other payments?'

'Again, indirectly. I did some work in that area earlier this year.'

'So why should we make use of you?'

'He has a specialist job at the EEC,' Johannes interjected. 'Special assignments. He does unusual things for them.'

'What sort of special assignments?'

'Killing people who get in his way,' Johannes said flatly.

I shook my head slightly in disagreement. He was over-selling, but maybe I didn't do enough of that myself.

'So how did you end up working with us?' Schalck-Golodkowski asked.

'I grew up in the West, most of my family live in the East.'

'His father is Russian,' said Johannes slyly.

I turned towards him, ready to land a punch.

Schalck-Golodkowski didn't notice. 'Well then, we Russians should stick together. My father was Russian too. But I was adopted by a German family.'

I listened in silence, not knowing how to respond to the idea that I might somehow be more Russian than German.

'He was a Tsarist émigré who ended up in Berlin. He served in the Wehrmacht during the war. But he didn't come back from captivity in the Soviet Union after it ended.'

He said this sombrely. I still didn't know whether I was meant to comment.

'How can I help you?' I asked instead.

Schalck-Golodkowski collected himself. 'Oh, much the same as you do for Major Johannes. Let us know of any opportunity you come across where you think we might be able to make some money. Companies trying to break trade embargoes, blackmail, even actual business opportunities where we can supply something and turn a profit. Think creatively. Here's my card with the direct number for my office in Berlin,' he said, sliding it across the desk, face down.

'I'm sure if you tell the Comrade Major first, we can have a conversation next time you're there.'

'Do we sell arms?' I asked.

'Of course. But only to the politically reliable. We don't want them falling into the wrong hands. Sometimes we can't help it, of course. Business is business.'

'Who do you work for in Berlin?' I probed again, even though I was sceptical I would get him to admit to any juicy details at a first encounter.

'The Comrade Herr Doktor is the Deputy Minister for External Trade,' Johannes said.

My jaw dropped a little.

'Oh, don't worry Herr Lenkeit, we're very egalitarian in Berlin. Anyone can speak freely with anyone else,' the Comrade Minister said smoothly.

That I doubted. In Brussels I worked for an organisation of supposed idealists too. Human nature didn't change that quickly when you passed through the Iron Curtain. And Schalck-Golodkowski oozed with the arrogance that came with success, or at least, success as measured by the East German regime.

On the drive back, my thoughts began to turn to how Johannes and I might wreck Borghese's plans, if he really was taking part in a conspiracy inspired by the De Lorenzo affair. After we'd stolen the samples, of course. But I also wondered if it was Johannes' call. The Ministry had ten times the employees of the EEC. What was the betting there was a dedicated Italian department with other ambitious majors also seeking colonelcies out of a successful intervention in Italy?

Maybe that was why he was so keen for me to worm something out of Sophie. There was no point in putting in most of the effort, only for the Italian specialists in Berlin to complete the last piece of the puzzle and get all the credit.

I didn't think his proposed technique would work though. Despite the number of men who hung around her, my impression was that she was actually quite abstemious. After all, if she wasn't unobtainable, they wouldn't be so crazy about her. She knew how to play men to her advantage only too well. Sigrid Johannes, on the other hand, would have gone through them all and not thought twice about it.

The idea from Johannes and Kramer that I could press all the usual buttons to get into bed with her was preposterous. She'd wasn't some lonely secretary posted to NATO headquarters in Brussels looking for love, the intelligence weak link which the Stasi liked to target. There was only one language she respected. But any power or influence I did possess at the Berlaymont was hidden away, known only to Kramer. And both he and I wanted it kept that way.

Chapter Nine

Today was going to be the moment of crisis for Sophie and Rizzo, but they didn't know it yet. I'd spoken with Kramer when I'd got back to Brussels on Sunday. Spinelli was attending a conference today in the Agriculture Directorate's building, finishing with drinks at five. We would all have a reason to be in the same place.

I'd asked Sophie and Rizzo to meet me there in her second-floor office, on the pretext of discussing my search for a truck and driver. Sophie already knew who was supplying the labour but Rizzo didn't. Not unless she'd told him, which I thought was unlikely.

Sophie didn't qualify for an office of her own at her current grade. But somehow, she'd managed to have the three other people she notionally shared with moved out. Earlier in the summer, she'd pushed a couple of the empty desks together to form a makeshift meeting table. Now she'd gone a step further and replaced it with a proper table and even added a sofa off to one side with a coffee table next to that. She must have raided a storeroom somewhere in the basement, because the tables had chips and the sofa was slightly worn, but I presumed she'd wanted nothing fancy so as not signal her ambitions too obviously and too soon.

When I entered the room, she and Rizzo were already sitting down, looking at one another across a corner of the meeting table.

They didn't look very happy together. I supposed it was one thing pairing off now and then for a quick hookup to relax, but quite a different thing when you were working together to subvert one of Europe's democracies, imperfect as it might be. I wondered if she'd drifted into this affair without fully realising it, getting into deeper and deeper water as the weeks went by. Maybe the trip to Apulia had brought home just how far from shore she was.

I stood by the table to open the discussion, leaning forward on my fingertips. Some of them anyway.

'So, what night is the coup planned for?'

'Shut up, Lenkeit,' said Rizzo irritably. 'You have to help us whether you like it or not. Sophie made sure you had no option.'

'Oh, I have lots of options. More than you want to know.'

Two of my harder options, as Johannes might have called them, were sitting under the base of my wardrobe in my flat, well-oiled and neatly wrapped in cloth.

Sophie looked more worried than I'd ever seen her before, even when on the way back to Bari airport the morning after the party. She'd won against me in Wismar in front of Johannes, but now she wasn't so sure of herself.

'But you're right Rizzo. Like it or not, you've sucked me into this,' I said sharply. 'Yourselves too, of course.'

I gave both of them a cold stare.

'You think it's my neck that's on the line if we're caught, because you're not the ones actually carrying out the theft from the Italian Defence Ministry's cache. But if our truck does get stopped, maybe they'd like to know who hired me and what else those people are up to?'

Rizzo sneered. 'Don't be so sure of yourself. You're not Italian. You don't know what's going on. And you certainly don't know how to navigate in our waters.'

'Neither do you,' I said abruptly. 'Why else are you having to use Di Luca? Not the highest ranking *mafioso* you could have picked. By the way, he's my new best friend. We shared drugs and girls at your party.'

'Again, Lenkeit, you underestimate your own incompetence. What are you trying to say?' Rizzo said in a low voice.

'So it's "Lenkeit" now, Rizzo?' I growled back at him.

'Stop this,' snapped Sophie. 'Giovanni's right. What is it that you want, Oskar?'

'Just what I said. I want to know if I'm going to be moving arms at the same time as a coup is about to commence. What if I'm the decoy used to distract the Carabiniere while you take over the Quirinale?'

'So much for showing you some hospitality in Rome,' grunted Rizzo.

'You know we can't give you complete certainty, Oskar,' Sophie replied, attempting to mollify. 'Even if we told you the coast is clear to move the goods, you'd have no way of knowing if we're lying. But in any case, you've created a fantasy for yourself, if you think that it's a coup which is taking place.'

'I can make one of you come along with me, to test your assurance on that.'

'Why the cold feet, Lenkeit?' Rizzo asked. 'Are you getting scared?'

'No, he's not,' said Sophie slowly, before continuing. 'I asked you in departures at Bari not to probe the political side of things. If I tell it to you now, you'll no longer be able to claim ignorance if things go wrong,' she warned.

I sat down and waited.

'Giovanni's father was threatened by Borghese that unless he made the arms deal happen, he'd expose him to the press for having taken part in a war crime atrocity in late 'forty-four. They have photographs and enough former members of the Decima Mas are prepared to testify against a former comrade on behalf of their old commander to make it stick. Giovanni's father has a lot to lose.'

'Okay,' I said. 'But why does Borghese need to make money from selling arms? Why not just extort it from the

Rizzos instead?'

She paused for half a heartbeat. 'His far-right faction is withering away with the passage of time. The Fronte Nazionale was set up to try to rejuvenate their movement. But they need a long-term source of funds to sponsor candidates at elections. This weapons sale is just the first deal planned with the Mafia,' she said in a confidential voice.

I glanced at Rizzo. He wasn't giving any indication that he supported her story.

'Now do you understand?' she asked.

'So there's no coup, is that what you're saying?' I replied innocently.

'It's just an obligation that's being discharged. As you're doing for me,' Sophie added, her eyes narrowing.

Rizzo didn't look happy at all. But I was unhappy too, that she really did think I was so stupid as to fall for her fairytale. She didn't know that I'd met with De Mauro alone in the garden in Apulia let alone with Spinelli here in Brussels. And with every new convoluted explanation, it was becoming abundantly clear that whatever it was, this was no straightforward underworld deal.

I got up again and pointed at each of them in turn with a false half-grin.

'Don't go anywhere. I'll be right back.'

The reception was being hosted on the mezzanine floor. Kramer and Spinelli stood a little way apart from each other in the crowd, each with their own cluster of hangers-on. Sophie knew that I'd worked with Kramer on the investigation which had ended in her uncle's death. But she didn't know the details of just how closely we'd collaborated back then. And I didn't want her to know I was still working for Kramer now, if I could help it.

'Signor Spinelli, Monsieur Commissaire. If I may ask for your indulgence for five minutes.'

He didn't look very pleased. He mumbled something to

his other guests about having to take care of a 'national matter' and made to follow me down the corridor. The group he was holding forth to looked suitably impressed, though. Maybe the scar on my face reinforced the air of mystery.

As we walked, he straightened his tie and buttoned his jacket.

'These are the Brussels people you mentioned the other day? The ones who attended the same party in Italy? Or are they more deeply involved?' he asked shrewdly.

'Both,' I said. 'We need to shock them, sir. Kramer will take care of any fallout. Let's remind them where their loyalties lie.'

I opened the door without knocking. The pair of them were glowering at each other as I entered, but had rearranged their expressions into ones of careful neutrality by the time Spinelli appeared in the doorway behind me.

Rizzo recognised Spinelli first. He mumbled something in Italian under his breath which sounded like '*por catrolia*'. I didn't know the phrase, but I got the sense of the words.

'I invited Commissioner Spinelli here to give his opinion on the Borghese affair. He wasn't very impressed, no, not at all the other day, when I told him what the two of you were up to.'

Spinelli didn't bother waiting for a response. He immediately rattled off something in Italian to Rizzo in machine-gun staccato. I could tell it wasn't going well for the younger man by the increasing gesticulations on each side.

I flicked a glance at Sophie. She was sitting there ashen-faced. Caught in a political scandal, she might now be looking at the end of her EEC career. From her very first day here she would have been manoeuvring for a top job in ten or fifteen years' time. She was making progress too; the office she'd arranged for herself indicated that. She was even due to accompany the Agriculture Commissioner, Sicco Mansholt, to Ireland next month to help present his plan to restructure the EEC's farming sector.

Now the colour returned to her cheeks and I sensed her rising anger as she prepared to step into the conversation and take control of her destiny once more.

'In French please, Giovanni.' But she wasn't asking nicely.

The two Italians paused for breath.

Spinelli noticed her for the first time and gave her the evil eye. As for me, I was enjoying the whole performance immensely. Perhaps too much for my own good.

'Who are you?' Spinelli asked coldly.

'Augusta von und zu Wehlau. I'm working with Signor Rizzo to come up with a political recommendation for the EEC in this matter.'

Well, I occasionally went by my nephew's name 'Thomas Hofmann', so maybe she was playing the same trick. And being as vague about her involvement as I would have been, before I knew how the land lay.

Rizzo glanced at her suspiciously as the realisation dawned that she might be intending to abandon a sinking ship. It was the first time I'd seen his face without the faint, dreamy look of the addict that it took on whenever she spoke.

'Who are you working for at the Commission, Frau Wehlau? Who authorised you to get entangled in Borghese's latest escapade?'

'It's the Industrial Commissioner,' Rizzo said to her unnecessarily, out of the corner of his mouth.

'With respect, Monsieur Commissaire,' she replied. 'You've only been here since July. All I've been asked to do is look at different ways we might restructure the CAP to transfer more money to Italy after the accession of the new applicant countries.'

'Why would France agree to that?' he asked sceptically.

'The idea is to promise the powers in Italian politics some fresh benefits from EEC membership.'

She was light on her feet when it came to making up

stories on the spur of the moment. But then, who knew? She might actually have been working on such a scheme anyway as part of her regular job. Everyone wanted a slice of the new, bigger pie which the British were going to provide, along with the Norwegians, Danes and Irish of course.

'Benefits in exchange for what? I spent sixteen years imprisoned by the fascists. Now you're advising factions of the DC on how far Italy can twist the arms of the other five EEC countries using the illusion of a fascist threat to Italian democracy?'

She opened and closed her mouth. Spinelli was quick at hypothesising, too.

Rizzo spoke. 'It's not what you imagine Dottore Spinelli.'

'I never went to university. I was in jail during the years I should have been there,' he said in an icy voice. But he wasn't done.

'And how were you going to ensure the EEC project benefited from Italian blackmail? Eh? How were you going to advance the course of European federal democracy?'

I could have told him that Sophie wasn't. At least, she had no interest in the democracy part.

'Why did you imagine you could entertain even an indirect connection through the DC to the far right and remain untainted? Don't you know enough to get as far away from the crazies as possible? Who here in the organisation has been so naïve? Tell me and I'll shut them down.'

They were getting into deeper and deeper trouble. I'd only wanted to shock them into confirming whether there was an extra-parliamentary plot to crackdown on the left, not have my friend Bernd from Internal Affairs march them off the premises.

I cleared my throat. 'I think, Signor Spinelli, that Frau von Barten's approaches to the right wing of the DC, or whomever, may still be of benefit to us.'

I was rewarded with a look of hate from her and momentary confusion from the Commissioner. But only momentary, because he didn't seem to be that bothered about who she actually was. Rizzo was the one who I guessed was really in trouble.

'The complaint of the far-right agitators like Borghese is that Italy's government isn't working. I agree that Frau von Barten and Signor Rizzo have been foolish to let themselves get involved with these people but if something is going on in Italy, we at the EEC still need to know what to expect and when.'

Sophie shot me a look of even more intense hate at this.

I carried on while Spinelli let me. He knew Kramer was just down the corridor if I took things in a direction he disagreed with.

'Tell us what you know and Signor Spinelli will make sure it goes no further,' I instructed them.

'Herr Lenkeit is correct. We can turn this to our advantage if you cooperate,' Spinelli said.

'Well?' I asked. 'What's really happening?'

Rizzo threw his hands up into the air. 'My father knows Borghese from some years ago. And yes, he suspects certain elements of the Italian intelligence agencies are indirectly supporting him, in order to keep tensions high between left and right in Italy. They want to ensure that the communists continue to be seen as the enemy of Catholic Italy and that their share of the popular vote doesn't grow any bigger than it is today.'

'And that's it? That's as far as they're going to go in order to create tension?' I demanded.

But now Spinelli interjected before anyone else had a chance to speak.

'Has no one given any thought to how the Americans will see this?' he asked, almost shouting. 'If a faction of the DC says it's time to repress the PCI with coercive means, the CIA won't complain. In fact, if they know in advance they might even help Borghese if he's the one who's been tasked to do it. They helped him out once before to get his jail sentence shortened after the war. He's probably still their man.'

I looked solemnly at Rizzo and Sophie, then picked up the baton from Spinelli. I wanted to test Rizzo to destruction to see if he stuck to his story.

'You fools. Did you stop to think that you might be giving Nixon an excuse to interfere in our affairs?'

I got a nod from Spinelli. But this was the point at which a boundary was finally crossed with the others. I could see the rage on Sophie's face, the needle wavering on the red line which signalled an explosion. As for Rizzo, he'd gone past it. His Italian male pride could take no more.

With another muttered swear word he got up and threw his pencil down hard on the table, breaking the tip. He swung his jacket onto his shoulders and stormed out without a backwards glance at any of us.

'*Cazzo*,' said Spinelli after him, as he disappeared down the corridor.

He turned to Sophie and pointed directly in her face.

'You,' he said, fixing her with a stare. 'Work with him.' Now he pointed at me.

There was an intake of breath from her.

'Finish your plan to rebalance the agricultural subsidies. Do it quickly and we'll send it to all the factions in the DC, so that no one of them has an advantage over the others. At least that way we'll be able to start extracting the Commission from your and Signor Rizzo's nonsense.'

I noticed he wasn't offering to fix things back home himself. But Sophie didn't seem to recognise this. She stared at him, her eyes ice-cold again.

'I want it by this time next week. No, give Herr Lenkeit a copy of the plan. I don't want to be seen with you or that southerner again.'

'He's from Milan,' she said angrily. 'It's only his former

family estate which is in the South.'

'He still thinks and talks like one,' said Spinelli callously. He turned on his heel and left.

We were left staring at each other across the table. After the fact, I realised I was sorry for her humiliation.

'Well, that went well.' I said, trying to make light of it.

She was furious.

'I told you to stay away from the political side. Why couldn't you have been a coward like Rizzo just now and run away? Why did you think you had the right to interfere?'

'Why did you drag my cousin into this? She was innocent, you bitch.'

She gave a shout of anger and hammered both fists on the table. 'Fuck you, Oskar.'

She stormed over to the door, kicking it shut instead of leaving. Getting ready for a tirade at the top of her lungs, I guessed. By nature she could never let things go.

I'd had enough. I wasn't going to take her arrogance any longer and went after her. She was still facing the door as I came up behind her. I grabbed an elbow, pulling her back and turning her around at the same time. In the heat of the moment I slammed my hands down onto her shoulders and forced her up against the door.

'Cool it, will you? You don't know what you've got yourself into. I'm trying to help you.'

'Get your hands off me,' she said, giving a half shrug. 'I thought you were doing this for your cousin's sake to get her out of the jail I put her in?'

Now I approached the red danger line myself. I leant in and pressed my forehead hard against hers, grinding my teeth. It wasn't great behaviour but it was way better than slapping her repeatedly across the face, which I really wanted to do just then.

She stopped wriggling and stared back angrily for a couple of seconds. Then something broke inside. She linked her hands behind my head and pulled me in even harder. The fury was still rising in her eyes, but there was just the hint of something else there too - the briefest flash of calculation, right in their very depths.

Without warning she punched a fist up between my legs, still gripping the back of my head with the other hand. With a hoarse gasp, she opened her mouth wide and began to chew at my lips and cheek, and not gently either.

Everything was happening so fast I didn't have time to think. I had the sense of us being roped together as we slid down a mountainside. Hurtling towards a precipice with no handholds and no way to stop. Not that I wanted to.

We carried on like this for a minute or so. Then, with another growl, she pushed me away while tugging the belt of my trousers at the same time. As she waited impatiently for me to sort myself out, she quickly locked the door then reached around behind with both hands to unzip her skirt, letting it fall to the floor before kicking it away to the side. She clawed at my buttocks as she pulled me in close to rub against her crotch, merely kissing me fiercely this time, rather than trying to draw blood.

'The sofa,' she said in short breaths. I lay back while she slipped off her knickers and settled down astride me.

'Oh fuck,' she whimpered as she started rocking back and forth. 'Oh God.'

But it was too late for us to have second thoughts now.

She began to unbutton her shirt, getting halfway down before she had to stop and put her hands out to each side to steady herself. For a minute I was treated to a view of black lace-clad breasts moving rhythmically in and out of the open front of her blouse. Then she leant forward, placing a hand on either side of my head and dropping down low so she could grind in harder and faster. She gasped with each movement, her cries becoming progressively louder and harsher with each thrust.

With a final, shuddering groan she came, her forehead knotted in strain, eyes screwed tight shut. She carried on moaning through clenched teeth as she came down off her high, gyrating to hold onto the last of the sensations as they subsided away for her.

'Oh Jesus,' she announced faintly when she was done.

She pushed herself upright again, hands pressing down on my chest.

'Fuck you Oskar, you bastard. Look at what you made me do.'

But there was a note of uncertainty in her voice I'd never heard before.

She avoided my eyes as she got off me to go and find her knickers, showing me all her curves from the rear as she bent down to slip them on.

I wasn't going to let her get away as easily as that. I got up off the sofa before she had any more ideas of leaving and went over to stand behind her, circling her hips with my hands, nuzzling away the long blonde tresses to gently kiss the back of her neck.

She stood quite still as I did so, not resisting but not encouraging me either. Then I heard her breathing slow and she gave a deep sigh which was repeated a couple of times. She turned around to face me, her eyes closed, head bowed to my chest. A hand was placed on each of my shoulders and she pulled me in again to press against the silk material of her briefs. Then after a few seconds she raised her head and started kissing me delicately on the mouth, the tip of her tongue darting in and out.

I unbuttoned the rest of her shirt and slipped my hands up behind her back to unclip her brassière. But she took hold of my wrists before I could do so, shaking her head even as we kissed and gently guided my hands to cup her breasts instead.

After a couple of minutes of this, she pulled away with a jerk. 'Fuck, Oskar. I'm going to come again,' she whispered huskily.

Now, if possible, she was even more frantic than before. Down came the knickers once more, and this time, every remaining stitch of clothing came off too.

She laid back along the sofa, one foot resting on the floor, the other leg up on the cushions. She flexed it slowly back and forth as she watched me get ready, then she reached out and took me by the hand, drawing me down on top of her.

This time as we moved together, she looked on gravely with penetrating blue eyes. But as the seconds and minutes went by, they gradually softened as the last signs of some inner turmoil faded away. And unlike last time, she was silent as we pressed against each other, apart from calling out right at the very end, after which she burst into tears.

Well, I hadn't expected that today.

I rolled off to lie on my back beside her and tentatively took her hand in mine, desperate not to break the spell. Her body relaxed for the second time this afternoon and she turned towards me to pillow her head on my chest. I stroked her hair to help the remaining tension flow out of her.

After a short while she unburrowed her head from under my arm and propped herself up on one elbow. I saw her take a breath, about to say something. But before the words came out, I laid my finger on her lips.

'Shhh.'

The early evening sun slanting in through the window reflected off the slickness on her skin and I traced a trickle of sweat down between her breasts. If ever there was a moment, this was it. I knew what Jan would have said, but I didn't care.

'I love you. I've always loved you, right from the moment I first saw you.'

And I meant it, foolish as it was.

'I know,' she replied. But that was all.

Suddenly she reached down between her legs. '*Scheiße*,' she said with a faint giggle and began to search for her clothes again.

She found my boxers first and gave herself a quick

wipe down before slipping on her knickers. Before she got to put anything else on, I went to stand before her once more, my arms around her waist. Hope rose in my heart as she reciprocated, putting her arms around mine, gazing softly back at me as I held her eyes.

She puckered her cheek briefly. 'I need to get dressed,' she said lightly, releasing me. 'I need to compose myself to go back out there.'

'You're the one they're waiting on. You go first, I'll follow after five minutes.'

We got dressed in silence and she left quickly, unlocking the door to take a quick glance up and down the corridor first.

I locked the door again. I was sky high. There was literally nothing she could have asked me to do just then that I wouldn't have done - beaten Kramer with an iron bar to drive him out of the EEC, walked into the nearest *poste de gendarmerie* to confess to her uncle's murder, or gone to the BND and offered to spy on Johannes.

I floated over to the window in a daze, still not really believing that the thing I had longed for with a burning intensity for so many months had just happened. I peered out between the blinds and looked up into the sky. The way I was feeling, I could have opened the window, stepped off the sill and tripped from sunlit cloud to sunlit cloud.

I knew that what had happened here might vanish like the mist in the morning, but it had been worth it. Even if it was just for this one fleeting moment in time.

Still floating for the present, I drifted back down the corridor to the reception. Everyone was still there, even Rizzo. Maybe after Spinelli's tongue-lashing in Italian, which neither Sophie nor I had understood, he needed to redouble his networking efforts.

Sophie was studiously concentrating on her

conversation with an overweight, slightly-sweating older man – a Belgian politician, going by the odd word that I caught over the hubbub. She was giving no indication in public of what she'd just got up to with me in her office earlier. I drew closer and some sixth sense made her tuck a loose strand of hair behind her ear, a moment before she turned to look coolly past me. A few metres away from her, Rizzo was looking on too. I wondered how sensitive his antennae were. Probably more than I would have liked.

I took a flute of champagne and made my own earnest conversations with anyone and everyone but Sophie. We didn't speak to one another again that evening. I didn't know how she felt, but I knew I didn't trust myself to speak with her.

When it was time to leave, Rizzo collected her coat from the cloakroom attendant and stood behind her as he put it around her shoulders. She shot me a hungry look as he did so, and I knew that this thing wasn't over yet.

Chapter Ten

I was still high when I got home on Tuesday night. Sitting in the dark in the ancient chair in my lounge I replayed those last few minutes in her office over and over again, trying to guess what she might have been about to say before I stopped her. I spent too long analysing the tone of her 'I know' to my declaration and trying to remember the shape of her lips as she made the words.

I was determined not to blow my one chance with Sophie. Having unexpected spur-of-the-moment sex was one thing, but now I had to get her to actually want to spend time with me.

But eventually I'd done it to death. Somehow, I was going to make this real, whatever it took. Anything apart from abandoning my cousin to her fate in East Germany, and I even began to think I might do that.

All throughout Wednesday I mulled over the possible next developments, distracted from my day job in the Charlemagne building. This was more problematic than sounded, because hiding in the tiny sub-department of Internal Affairs which we called home wasn't easy.

Apart from myself, the so-called External Investigations unit consisted only of Willem, with whom I shared an outer office, and our boss, Masson, who had his own inner sanctum.

After arriving back from Ireland earlier in the summer with a cut up face, Masson had eased off me a bit. Instead, it was Willem who was lumbered with most of the pointless, make-work tasks which Masson had dreamt up during the course of his new department's first year of operations.

When the department was originally set up, Bernd had wanted my job here. But little did he know how boring it was. When we weren't compiling background profiles of foreign trade delegates attending treaty negotiations with the EEC, we spent most of the rest of the time transcribing Interpol reports into internal memos. Masson called them 'security briefings', but I doubted anyone was fooled, and I doubted even less that anyone actually read them.

But although Willem wasn't a natural complainer, by the afternoon he'd become tired of my pacing up and down the office to stare out the window, the sighs, and the fiddling with my pen.

'Go to the park and smoke a cigarette. You're driving me crazy here.'

The Dutch didn't hold back when speaking, the Italians didn't like to hide their emotions - they were probably long-lost cousins of a kind.

Up the Rue de la Loi past the Berlaymont was the Schuman roundabout. I crossed over and walked into the Parc du Cinquantenaire to find a bench.

I had something else to think about as I sat there. Early this morning, before leaving for work, I'd received another call from the East German foreign trade office, giving me a rendezvous in Hamburg on Friday morning. I'd have to take yet more leave and travel down tomorrow.

I was curious as to who Johannes had in mind within the East German security apparatus when he'd talked about 'harder options.' I knew the Ministry had their own private army so to speak - the Felix Dzerzhinsky Guard Regiment. But I assumed they were there to keep an eye on the Volksarmee, to defend the Stasi against an insurrection by the military, unlikely as that sounded these days. Then again, only seventeen years ago, there had been a workers' uprising across the Republic, so maybe they knew what they were doing.

But if the Felix Dzerzhinsky were getting bored at the lack of opportunities for internal repression, I'd happily take a couple of their soldiers to Italy. Johannes' proposal left open the further question of who would be in charge on the ground. I guessed it would be made clear in Hamburg, although I had my own ideas on the topic.

Whatever was agreed, if the Felix Dzerzhinsky did turn up, it would be a small additional bonus. I assumed that NATO had a good idea of the capabilities of the Volksarmee - they'd been watching each other across the inner-German border for long enough by now. But my guess was that the Stasi's guard regiment was more of an unknown quantity. I might learn something new, intelligence nuggets I could offer to Kramer for use in Paris to keep up his credit there. I supposed that in about fifteen years' time he would be retiring, and I'd need my own relationship with the SDECE. But that was a long way away for someone not yet twenty-five to be thinking about.

As for the other thing, after my second cigarette and a day's introspection, I'd made a temporary truce with myself. If I'd learnt anything about her at all in the past eighteen months, it was what I'd been reminded of on the plane to Bari, when I heard how Rizzo had previously tried to get her to meet his family with limited success. No man possessed her. If we were to carry on it would be her decision, and little I could say would persuade her one way or the other.

I got back to the office at three and worked some more, Sophie out of my head now for a while.

Then my desk phone rang, an internal call.

'Oskar?' she said.

'Yes?' I replied, my mouth dry.

Whatever happened next, I was never going to reveal this episode to anyone at work. Even though the dishonourable part of me very much wanted to tell people I'd done Sophie von Barten in her office yesterday, while a quarter of the Agriculture Directorate were gossiping just down the corridor.

'Do you want to come to my place for dinner tonight? To discuss the assignment Spinelli gave us?'

'Sure. What time?'

'Eight.'

'Okay.'

'Who was that?' Willem asked, as I laid down the receiver.

'Some new piece of work that's been given me.'

I sighed for effect, so he understood what a chore it was going to be.

I already knew the apartment where she lived. I'd scoped it out when I was planning her abduction. But I'd rejected it because it was on a busy street, overlooked by too many other flats for my liking.

On the way back from the Charlemagne to my own place I bought a couple of bottles of wine, wishing I'd paid more attention to the labels served at the various dinners and functions I'd been to in Brussels so far.

Just to be sure, I bought the most expensive bottle of each flavour and put the white one in the fridge. My patriotic West German AEG rather than a Candy.

A shower, a shave, and a dash of sandalwood. Then it was time for action.

She buzzed me into the building, and I made my way up the stairs to her landing. The door to her flat was slightly open but there was no reply to my knock. Something tasty-smelling was cooking so I pushed my way inside and followed my nose.

'There you are,' she said laconically as I appeared in the

kitchen doorway. She'd changed out of her work clothes too and was looking down at a pot she was stirring on the stove. She gave the contents a final, suspicious prod before turning to face me.

I held out each bottle by its neck. 'I wasn't sure what you were making, so I brought both.'

'You only needed to bring one, either would have done.'

For an instant, the memory of a parsimonious von Barten arguing the toss with Kramer about whose national budget should be hit for setting up a fifteen-thousand-franc slush fund came back to haunt me.

'It's my Russian-German nature,' I said. 'The German half plans for success, while the Russian part knows that whatever happens it's going to turn out badly.'

My attempt to bury the hatchet brought a passing smile to her lips.

I didn't imagine she normally bothered too much in the kitchen, being out in the evenings as often as she was. She gave me plates and cutlery to take through to the dining area in the lounge and followed along after, carrying a saucepan of pasta mixed with what I had my own suspicion were heated-through cans of sauce.

'*Bon appétit,*' she said, still not meeting my eyes for more than a second or two at a time.

I was relieved she wasn't intending to dissect the events of twenty-four hours ago, not immediately anyway. Then again, she would have known not to, for she instinctively sensed what men were thinking. It was why we all fell for her.

'*Bon appétit,*' I replied.

If we weren't going to talk about that topic for now, we had to fill the time with something else.

'So, Spinelli's question about rebalancing. How much money is available in the agriculture budget? What can realistically be redirected to Italy?' I asked.

For a moment she looked disappointed that we really

were spending part of this evening talking business. Then again, work and career were her favourite topics for discussion, as far as I'd worked out.

'Not much. The CAP is already underwater. It's not clear that the British contributions will be enough to make a difference right away,' she said bemusedly.

'When are they expected to start paying into the budget?'

'The accession discussions only got underway properly this month. It will be a year at least, then the four countries have to ratify the accession treaty. Mid 'seventy-two at the earliest.'

'Do they all have to join at the same time?'

She raised an eyebrow.

'We're making all of our calculations at the Directorate on the basis that they are. It will upset a lot of delicate trade-offs between the Six if they don't.'

Maybe Kramer was more desperate to keep the British on track than I fully realised.

She poured herself some of the red, looking down at her glass as she did so.

Now that I'd started this thread of conversation, I had to carry on, for a while at least, so as not to appear too eager for the next stage. I had other questions for her to answer at some point, too. Like what was really going on in Italy and why she was helping Borghese. But maybe not tonight.

For all Johannes's talk of me pumping her for information, it was a lot harder than it sounded. Especially when it wasn't a casual fling where you could tell any lie you liked to get the woman to confide in you.

We ate some more and to make conversation I asked about her work colleagues. I knew a couple of their names and hoped she wasn't going to tell me they were the ones she'd moved out of her office. I wouldn't be able to hear about that room again for a while without feeling embarrassed. She warmed up as she described how they worked the budget trade-offs she'd mentioned earlier, chattering on about the various tricks she'd played to manoeuvre people into them.

For all the boring office talk it was still a surreal situation. As she gossiped, a stack of olive-green weapons cases was waiting for me under a factory floor in Apulia. But it was what animated her, so I let her carry on.

'Are you still going to Ireland with the Agricultural Commissioner next month?' I asked during a brief pause.

'Yes. Now that you're involved, I've no need to go back to Italy.'

'What's your interest there, really?' I asked carefully.

'I had an idea of coming up with a political solution on my own and claiming it for myself. Something to make my mark with. But it's been taken out of my hands now,' she said quietly.

I thought for a moment. 'There is one thing you can make your own,' I said. 'In your report to Spinelli on fairer agricultural subsidies for Italy, point him in the direction of a sector controlled by the Mafia.'

'Why?' she asked, genuinely curious.

'Wean them off the mischief they normally get up to. Make honest lemon growers out of them, or whatever. Or at least give the law-abiding inhabitants of Sicily something legal to make money out of. How about hazelnuts, *nocciole*?'

She gave me a wry smile. 'I admire the sentiment Oskar, but I think the Mafia are tougher to deal with than that.'

I thought some more as I topped up her glass and mine with the last of the bottle.

'I want to ask you something, about one of the people we met in Apulia.'

'Go on,' she said warily.

'The journalist who came with Borghese. The one they called De Mauro. Why would a northern Decima Mas man end up as an anti-Mafia journalist in Sicily?'

She pondered for a moment.

'I imagine the far-right hate the Mafia and the threat to the Italian state they represent. Mussolini tried to repress them. But I think Borghese is so desperate for funds, he'll sell arms to anyone.'

I was troubled though, and not just because I was annoyed she'd trotted out her far-right fundraising story again.

We finished our wine and I collected the plates and cutlery to carry back to the kitchen. She tried half-heartedly to tell me 'no', but I sensed she was faintly relieved to have the lounge tidied away. Yet again the ghost of von Barten hovered behind her with his compulsive need to align his pencil in the centre of his notebook when not using it.

She put water on to boil in her mocha and leaned back against the island unit, legs crossed as she watched me stack the used dinner things in the sink. That was all I was planning to do for her, she could wash her own dishes. Either her or her cleaner.

We went back to the lounge carrying our cups. I sat on one of the two sofas while she lit a couple of candles and switched off the main light. She came to sit down on the other one, placed at right angles to mine. We looked at each other for a moment across the corner made by the two.

'What really happened in Ireland?' she asked. 'What did you tell those weeping Italian women on the terrace at the party?'

'Nothing. His grandmother said something in Italian, Caterina translated it. "Bad men did this thing to you." She was right, the guys in the pub were nasty pieces of work.'

But even right here, right now, I felt compelled to hold something back, if only not to repeat the exact words which Rizzo's sister had used.

'But why were they all crying?' Sophie asked, more softly now.

I shrugged Italian-style.

'They felt sorry for me.'

Suddenly, despite myself, I was worried I was about to let go and tell her everyone I worked for and everything I did for them: Kramer, Masson, Johannes - the whole lot. I gave a sigh and rubbed my head with my knuckles to clear the thought.

'I have to go to Hamburg first thing tomorrow. I have to meet the people Johannes said he'd recommend. The fixers in the shadows whom they trust.'

'Are you going to stay the night?'

I stood up to see what would happen.

She stood up too.

'I still have to pack for my trip and besides, I brought no nightwear.'

She came up very close to me and flicked my cheek with her finger, just under my scar.

'Don't be obtuse,' she said.

Chapter Eleven

I hadn't needed to leave as early for Hamburg as I'd allowed Sophie to believe. We'd made love again as the dawn spread over the sky and she'd asked me if I would stay until she left for the office.

I still couldn't believe that eighteen months after first meeting her, it had actually happened. And had happened properly. Not the mad rage-filled loss of control in her office, but an actual coming together.

As we lay next to each other in the warmth, I willed the minutes to stretch out forever. But of course, they didn't.

I found shaving soap and a razor in her bathroom, Rizzo's things I presumed, and got to work. When she came in after me to make sure I was still really there she looked askance at the razor in my hand.

She slipped her arms around me from behind and rested her cheek lightly on my shoulder, watching me in the mirror until I gently shrugged her off so I could shave on that side too.

She followed me back to the bedroom and we got dressed. I offered to find her some breakfast in the kitchen, but she shook her head and said she didn't feel like eating.

As we walked down the stairs of her apartment block together and out to the street, reality seeped back in. We parted on the pavement with a half wave but no kiss.

'When are you back in Brussels?'

'Tomorrow night sometime.'

'I need to hear what they say to you. Come straight

over. Don't waste time going home first.'

Her rationalisation amused me. It wasn't like I needed much encouragement to come back to her bed.

On the drive to Hamburg, along the same route that Pavel and I had taken her towards the border, I had plenty more time to think about the past thirty-six hours.

Before too long, the German side of my character kicked in and I began to go one by one through the possibilities for what came next.

Had she permanently ditched Rizzo? She was forceful by nature and I guessed that once she'd made a choice that was it. Skorzeny would have approved. He'd told me in Madrid earlier in the summer that in combat any decision was better than no decision.

But was it really permanent, or had she simply tired of Rizzo for the time being? I certainly had little to offer her compared to him - no contacts, no national influence, no network of university alumni. True, she imagined I had some special skills in confidential work, which I was using in Italy, but that was for Rizzo's benefit, not hers.

And if she'd merely got bored of Rizzo and wanted a change in bed, wouldn't she eventually get bored of me too?

Johannes thought there was something between us, but he was going on the basis of letters written for the express purpose of deception; letters I'd never seen.

When it came to her intentions, there wasn't enough to go on yet. I knew I wanted us to have something real, something permanent, but for the time being I'd take the other arrangement. I was only human after all, just as she'd said to me about herself on our last journey north.

It was the first time I'd seen my mother since Ireland and the first time she'd seen, or even heard about my scars. She was dubious about my story of how I'd come by them, especially after she'd inspected the wounds more closely with her nurse's eye. But although she wasn't particularly happy, she didn't bring it up again. Over dinner, she asked about my trip to East Germany instead.

'What did you find out over there? Who did you meet?'

I wouldn't lie to her as such, but I might not tell her everything.

'I eventually got hold of a policeman in Wismar who knows something about Karin's case. The story I was given was that she was being considered for release. I assumed I was being humoured to stop bothering them and to get me to leave quietly, but he appeared genuine in believing it to be true. There was no indication of when it might happen, though.'

'What happened to change their mind?'

'You said the church was praying. I can't explain it. There's so many other ways it could have turned out.'

'I'll tell people at church this Sunday. Can't you stay for the weekend?'

'I have somewhere I need to be on Saturday.'

Somewhere on Saturday which would be much more fun than church on Sunday.

'Did you pray for her at all?' she asked, not really expecting a positive answer.

'A little, yes.'

She raised her eyebrows in surprise.

Something much more real and permanent had happened in Ireland than hooking up with Sophie. I couldn't not tell my mother, even though right now it seemed more difficult than telling Sophie I'd shot her uncle.

I also had to start admitting it properly to myself and that was a big problem. For not only was I a semi-professional liar working for the enemies of the state, whatever had happened in Sophie's office on Tuesday evening wasn't in any sermon about marriage I'd ever heard - not that I'd paid them much attention in the past. Apart from the story of King David and Uriah, I supposed. The problem with being forgiven was that it had to mean a change in your behaviour. That much I couldn't pretend ignorance of.

And like it or not, I had to begin sometime. Behind me lay the black guilt of murder. Guilt that had crushed my innermost soul for a year and more until Dublin. At the very least I had to be grateful for that and try to prove by my actions henceforth that my gratitude wasn't empty. Faith without evidence was no faith at all.

'When I was attacked in Ireland, it made me think.'

My mother had stopped breathing, I sensed her willing me to say what came next.

'I realised I was on a wrong path.'

Now a tear pricked the corner of each of her eyes.

'I… I repented of my life so far and for what I've done wrong.' My pride wouldn't let me use the word 'sin'.

'That's the best news I've ever had,' she said simply, dabbing her cheeks.

I was embarrassed at the idea that this was the highlight of her forty-five years on earth. But I supposed she was right. Forever was a long time, after all.

At least my news had distracted her from any further discussion about Karin for the time being, and about what exactly had prompted my cousin to try to leave the country illegally.

I wondered if my aunt knew who in the West had been sending Karin letters this year. Would the first couple have read as if they were simply innocuous chitchat between pen pals to put her parents off the scent when they demanded to see them? To put Karin herself off the scent of where Sophie was intending to lead her? Because for all Sophie's cleverness, my bet was that the innuendo had been too subtle for a sheltered seventeen-year-old to pick up on. Not too subtle for the Stasi, though.

How much had my uncle and aunt been told by them when they'd searched the house, as I assumed they had? Or did Karin have all the letters on her when she was arrested? If I was lucky, no one in my family, apart from Karin, realised Sophie's involvement yet.

My mother knew who Sophie was in general terms. She knew we'd posed as an engaged couple on the assignment to East Germany for von Barten in 'sixty-nine, when we'd gone on the pretext of a family visit. Using a family visa meant I actually had to meet my aunt and cousins, which was bad luck for Karin because Sophie had met her too. But I'd never mentioned her name since. I had no reason to and no desire either - then or now.

But my news from Ireland wasn't the only headline in the Lenkeit household today.

'You remember Stefan Benke?' she asked a little nervously.

I'd first met him in Hamburg just as the von Barten affair had started, and I'd seen him the odd time since. He was the only male friend I'd ever known my mother to have.

'We're getting married at Christmas. After I came to the West, I never thought I'd say those words one day.'

I smiled encouragingly, making a big effort for her. 'Congratulations. I'm pleased for you, I truly am. How do his family feel about it?'

'Okay, I suppose. Maybe not his son in West Berlin. They didn't really get on, even before the divorce.'

Thankfully, she'd hardly ever asked me about myself in the romance department. Not really at any point in my life that I could remember. Either the war had desensitised her, or it had pushed her the other way and made the whole topic too painful to discuss.

At least her lack of interest had spared her from hearing about the full craziness of Brigitte two years ago, that walking bundle of neuroses introduced to me by Jan. If things carried on with Sophie, in time I would of course tell my mother. But given that Sophie and I had lied for three days to my aunt about us being engaged, I didn't imagine that either sister would be overjoyed if she really was the next girl.

-

In the morning, I gave my mother a lift to the Wilhelmsburg hospital where she did her nursing. Then I parked up by a dock in Speicherstadt, on a cleared bombsite where you could park for free. I kicked around the centre of town by the canals for a while and even thought of trying to meet up with Jörg, the sergeant in the Hamburg police who'd taken me under his wing when I was a probationer cadet. I found a phone and called his flat on the off-chance, but no one was home.

In the afternoon, I made my way down to Saint Pauli and the former Communist Party drinking den I'd been given as a rendezvous. It was still a drinking den, but the KPD had passed on, banned in West Germany in nineteen fifty-six, much to De Mauro's approval as he'd told me in the garden in Apulia.

I was there in plenty of time - I had plenty of time to kill. Just like being back in the army. Two of them came in and up to where I was sitting at the back with an Astra, just as a good FC St. Pauli supporter should.

'Are you Thomas?' asked the older of the pair. Probably the Ministry's local man in Hamburg.

'Yes. Who sent you?'

'A friend of ours from Room 1701,' he replied.

It was the number of Johannes' office at the Normannenstrasse.

'So who's coming with me to Italy?' I asked.

'Not so fast,' the Ministry man said. The second man watched me silently. He was lean and lightly tanned, with worry lines around his eyes as if he'd spent time squinting at the sun. An operative at a guess.

'I was given two messages to pass on to you,' the Ministry man said. 'Firstly, if this goes wrong, your relative stays in jail.'

The operative looked slightly troubled at this, as if it was the first time he'd heard it.

'Secondly, any contact with the local comrades you'll be staying with is to be kept to minimum. It goes without saying that you share nothing with them about what it is that we're doing down there.'

'Okay,' I said.

Now the operative spoke up.

'You're the local liaison for Italy?' he asked doubtfully, taking in my age and possibly my scars.

I looked at him in turn, wondering which part of the security apparatus he was from.

'Yes,' I replied. 'Who are you sending?' We need to agree how we're going to work together on the ground,' I said, aiming to regain the initiative.

He flicked his wrist to look at his watch.

'There's some specialists airborne as we speak. Flying in from somewhere in Africa.'

'I'm not ready to use them yet. I don't know exactly when we're to carry out the move.'

'They won't mind a few days off. They've been away for almost nine months already. When do you get told?'

'I'm to let the people in Italy know as soon as I've got a crew together. I expect they'll ask us to get moving right away. They don't want the goods hanging around in case their owner does an unexpected stores audit.'

'We were told you saw a manifest. What was in it?'

The Ministry's man had said his piece and sat silently now.

'Assault rifles, grenades, explosives, detonators. What I think was a SAM. We opened one case - AK-47s with folding stocks.'

'AKMS rifles, if they're the modernised AK-47. The "S" stands for "*Skladnoy*" - Russian for "folding."'

'What are you really looking for? What if the specialist items aren't there?'

'We'll learn something from whatever's brought back.

Even the inventory tells its own story: the type of partisan activity they're planning for in the event of an invasion and the length of time they expect to hold out until a counterattack.'

'How much do you already know about their organisation?'

'We know the arrangements in some countries better than others.'

'They all have a hidden resistance network? Even West Germany? Who within the government controls that one?'

I wondered if local interests across Europe were being tempted to misuse Gladio for internal political ends.

He didn't reply to my question. The Ministry man frowned and shook his head slightly.

'How are my crew getting to Italy?' I asked the operative.

'On the ferry from Yugoslavia. They'll drive down in a truck with West German plates, posing as engineers working for a machine tool manufacturer. They'll supposedly be making a round of visits to their clients' factories in the south of Europe to service equipment.'

'And getting back out again?'

'The same way they came.'

'How many are you sending?'

'Two. Both sergeants. One is senior, he'll be in charge,' the operative said in a very definite voice.

The Ministry man was either getting bored or he was scanning the bar automatically out of habit for people from the other side.

'We need to be on the first ferry from the mainland to Sicily the morning after we collect the goods,' I told the operative. 'We'll need to load and leave the previous evening and drive through the night, regardless of what time your people arrive in Italy.'

'You haven't already arranged somewhere for them to stay, have you?' he asked.

'No.'

'Fine.' He nodded across to the Ministry man. 'My colleague here will pass you the names of some East German sympathisers down that way who'll put you and the guys up for a couple of nights.'

'The ones you're going to tell nothing to,' the Ministry man reminded me.

The operative carried on. 'I want my men in position well before the move takes place. I don't want them being rushed off the Dubrovnik ferry into the arms of an arrest party.'

'I need to be in charge in Italy. I need to make the call if we're ready to go ahead. I know the players we're supposedly working for.'

He weighed this up for a few seconds.

'Once we lay hands on the goods my senior sergeant runs the show. I don't want any confusion in the chain of command. Understood?'

'Do they speak English or Italian?'

'Neither. Perhaps a few words of English and French which they picked up in Africa.'

'Then that's not going to work. The people I'm working with speak English. And they'll expect me to be in charge.'

He frowned. 'What's your experience of covert operations?' he asked sceptically.

'None.'

'If my guys decide they need to use their weapons, from that point you're taking a back seat.'

He didn't say how they would make me, but I guessed with guns in their hands, they always had a last resort if I got in the way.

'As soon as my guys have collected the arms, from that point on you ask them first before you go off making any decisions with your local contacts. And no tricks, because they've been told to use force if they find themselves in an awkward situation.'

'If we're in Sicily and something goes wrong, they're a

long way from home, or even Yugoslavia.'

'That's not your concern,' interjected the Ministry man. 'Just make sure things never get that far, or your relative stays in prison.'

It was good of Johannes to get him to remind me - twice. But he hadn't passed on any hints that, so far, this operation was anything more than a simple theft of arms. As opposed to setting a devious trap for the CIA.

'How many items do they plan on taking back with them?'

'Depends what they find of interest.'

'It can't be excessive.' I'd thought about this on the way up to Hamburg too, along with everything else.

'I'm going to have to say it's part-payment in lieu of insufficient cash up front, or a last-minute extra bonus that we've demanded,' I said.

'How many will there be of them on the receiving side?' the operative asked.

'I've been told to expect only one person in Sicily, but I don't trust the reliability of Italians and their messages.'

'Have they let you down before?'

'Just a little disorganised so far, nothing serious.' I thought back to the non-appearance of the driver when the three of us landed at Bari.

'Our guys are used to uneven odds.'

'Who are they again?'

'Training team. Like the American military advisers at the start of the Vietnam War.'

'They didn't just advise the South Vietnamese.'

'I said it was the start of the war.'

I had a suspicion that Johannes' bright idea might not turn out to be so clever once we were on the ground.

'Cheer up,' the said Ministry man. 'It's just like a propaganda movie. Where you're playing the partisan behind enemy lines, but with the NKVD agents arriving by car ferry this time instead of by parachute.'

'Until Bari then.'

We left separately. I did a few twists and turns as I walked back to my car to put off any shadowers, just as I'd been taught at the Stasi college this summer.

But when I got onto the autobahn, I left prudence behind and put my foot down so as to get back to Brussels at a reasonable hour of the night. It was a little stupid, especially when I crossed the Belgian border and speed limits applied in the outside lane once again. That said, in my limited experience, the Belgian traffic police were erratic in their application of the law. I didn't think they were keen on working after seven in the evening, either.

It was all crazy. The notion that I was going to spend the weekend in the bed of the girl I'd brought coming out the other way hardly two weeks ago, chained to the floor of a truck.

Chapter Twelve

Her bedside phone rang in the morning, just before ten. She propped herself up on one elbow to answer, half-pulling the sheets over her chest in a semblance of modesty.

'*Allo?*'

It was Rizzo. I listened to her side of the conversation with interest.

She slumped back down onto the pillow, receiver in hand, looking up at the ceiling with a look of impatience as she listened. I suspected, to the point of certainty, that she hadn't told him anything about us so far.

I heard times being discussed and a rendezvous being agreed. But that was it. A practical conversation, containing no clues for Rizzo of where she'd been since Tuesday. And no clues for me either, that she'd seen him on Thursday night when I'd been in Hamburg.

My ears pricked up as the conversation neared its end.

'I'll pick up Lenkeit and bring him to the cafe.' As she said it, she hooked her right leg over my left under the covers and began moving her foot up and down my calf.

I supposed she thought she was being cheeky, but more than ever at that point I hoped I wouldn't find myself in Rizzo's position one day. Even though right now I was the next man, it wasn't amusing or anything else for that matter. I unlaced myself from her and went to get in the shower.

We arrived at the cafe together, to find him waiting at a

table in the courtyard to the rear.

Despite her warning to Rizzo on the phone that she'd be bringing me along, I could see the suspicion on his face, even as he tried to master it. Four days and a lifetime ago when I'd brought down the wrath of Spinelli upon them in Sophie's office, he'd paused for thought when she'd given a false name, wondering if she was going to shift the blame for their games onto him. Now I might be her ally, helping to shore up her position in the aftermath of the Commissioner's reprimand.

I gave him some news as reassurance that we were all friends again and to distract him from thinking too deeply about why Sophie was showing me the way to a café I could easily have found myself. Not that after the bad temper of the meeting last Tuesday he could have imagined the real reason, not in a thousand years. I could still hardly believe it myself.

'I met with my people,' I told him cheerfully as the drinks arrived. 'They're ready to move when you are.'

Now Sophie looked at me suspiciously and I regretted the comradely tone in which I'd referred to Johannes' specialists.

In response, Rizzo pushed across a day-old Italian paper.

'I'll tell you what it says,' he said.

'On September the sixteenth, Mauro De Mauro, journalist at L'Ora in Palermo, was abducted outside his house on the Viale delle Magnolie, two days before his daughter's wedding. It says the Carabinieri have used *elicotteri* to search for him and set up roadblocks. Hopes of finding him alive have receded in the absence of any ransom demand.'

'That doesn't sound good. Will he talk?' I asked.

'How do you mean?'

'If he was abducted instead of being assassinated outright, someone must have had some questions for him.'

'Whatever De Mauro's fate was, his disappearance

means we have to go right away, in case Rome starts a full crackdown on the usual suspects in Sicily. You say your guys are ready?'

He meant I'd have to go, of course. It didn't seem like the smartest timing to me, but then again I was the one taking the risk on this job, so he was the smart one really.

But it also wouldn't give Johannes much time to get guidance from Moscow, or to do his own checks on what the CIA might be up to in Italy right now.

'They have to drive down from Germany with their truck. They'll need three days to get to Bari. Today's Saturday and I'll need the rest of the weekend to alert them, so expect them in Apulia sometime on Wednesday. I'll fly out on Tuesday and find somewhere low-key for them to stay.'

I'd refuse any suggestion for accommodation Rizzo might make. We needed as much operational independence from him as possible, in case this really was all some elaborate sting by the Italian espionage agency, the SID.

'Same plan of timings for the move?' I asked.

'Yes,' he replied.

'Then I'm guessing we pick up the cargo on Thursday evening at the earliest and deliver it on Friday. Are you still coming out to Sicily to meet me the day after?'

'Yes.'

'Then we'd better hurry,' I said glancing at my watch. 'I need half the payment now. The banks are closing in an hour's time.'

Rizzo shrugged. I guessed he'd have preferred to have spent more time together with the two of us to work out what was really going on.

As he and I walked to the bank we negotiated the fee. I'd paid Pavel six hundred Deutschmarks for a fourteen hundred kilometre round trip, Hamburg to Brussels and back again via a diversion to the border. I reckoned that

Hamburg to Bari was three times the distance and I'd be taking twice the number of people. Then there was the leg to Sicily to consider too, and stopovers on top of that.

I hit up Rizzo for two and a half thousand Deutschmarks which he grimaced at and then looked even more pained when I said I wouldn't take it in lire. But he didn't negotiate either, so I reckoned they were more desperate than I was to do the job at that moment.

As we stood in the queue of last-minute Saturday customers, he decided to do some probing around the thing that was really on his mind.

'I'm going to see Sophie after we're done here. I haven't heard from her since Tuesday when I saw her home,' he said to me confidingly.

I was unsure if his tone was part of a trick to get me to say more than I should, or if he really didn't suspect me as being the reason for her silence. It could as easily have been down to someone else. There were enough of them, the group of broken, hopelessly lovesick *fonctionnaires* who drifted in and occasionally out of her orbit.

I was in a quandary. Rizzo had stormed out of her office last Tuesday, but I was beginning to understand that Italian moods were generally a passing thing. The gesticulations and swearing were simply how they expressed themselves, getting whatever was troubling them off their chests and allowing them to move on. But surely the discovery that he was yesterday's man would trigger a whole new level of passion.

I didn't trust him not to lose his temper again and get physical with her when she eventually told him. I wouldn't trust myself if I was in his place, which I might be one day of course.

I could tell him myself where he stood right now, but I didn't want to be presumptuous – it was her right to be the one to break it off. After all, they'd been together for long enough, probably much longer than I realised. But if his only real connection with her was to be entertainment in bed, did he have any connection at all?

What did I have? We'd just moved from hate to something quite different, but what it was exactly wasn't clear yet. I had no choice. Not if I was genuinely concerned about what he might do to her when she told him.

I introduced Rizzo to a world of hurt.

'I'll come with you when you go to see her. My overnight bag is at her place.'

His face drained of colour, just as it had done in his father's study in Apulia when I told him that I'd killed someone.

'What are you saying?' he said slowly, as if he didn't believe the words coming out of his own mouth. 'She hates you. She kept telling me over and over again how much she hates you.'

I didn't feel that much sympathy for him now. His alarm bells should have been ringing loud enough to wake the dead, if that was her level of obsession with me. Maybe Johannes was right after all. Maybe she'd revealed more in her letters to Karin than she even realised herself.

'Sometimes these things happen.'

His lip trembled and for a moment I thought he was going to break down, but he pulled himself together.

'I'm not stopping you going to see her,' I said. But I was and he knew it.

A sour look stole over his face.

'How can I trust you to help my family now?' he rasped. 'Who are you going to betray next?'

He didn't know that by helping his family I was saving mine. I'd made a promise to Johannes about it as we yelled at each other in a side office in Hohenschönhausen prison, Lieutenant Petzold watching us, checking his Makarov was within easy reach.

I looked at Rizzo more coldly now. 'But if you go over there and pressurise her - either today or at another time - or if you make even a hint of a threat to her over this, I will destroy you.' I'd let him work out for himself whether that meant a bullet in the head.

He wasn't sour now. Instead he looked indignant, as if he couldn't believe what he'd done to justify this kind of treatment. And he hadn't done anything, to be fair. I was the one who'd been only too happy to take advantage of her infidelity.

We reached the head of the queue and the teller called him forward. There was a long, awkward delay as she went to fetch the Deutschmarks he'd requested.

Back outside the bank he unwillingly handed over the fat envelope, holding on to it for a couple of seconds too long before we parted ways.

'Goodbye Rizzo,' I said in a lighter tone. 'I'll expect to see you sometime next Saturday in Sicily with the rest of the cash. It'll be good to see the sun again too, after all the rain we've been having here recently. If Di Luca doesn't put me up on Friday night, I guess I can stay in your house in the valley outside Ragusa?'

'Do as you please. I no longer care. I'm going to get drunk.'

I went to my own apartment to hide the cash and get ready for the trip.

I wondered if Rizzo's desperation would get the better of him and if he'd ignore my warning to let her make her own mind up. Would he mount a full-scale counterattack, pointing out to her how irrational it was to invest her time into me, compared to him who had so much more to give?

But I knew Sophie. She was determined and headstrong and was pretty much only ever swayed by her own arguments. I was under no illusion that if she was ever done with me, I'd be dropped as fast as Rizzo had been, and there'd be nothing I'd be able to do about it. This was the problem with the way in which things had occurred. There'd been no reconnaissance, no build up, no preparation of the ground for an assault, so to speak.

I left it. The past three days up to this morning had been a whirlwind, but now it was time for a pause with her. I remembered Brigitte only too well and how I'd got sucked into something without realising what had really been happening.

I opened up the space under my wardrobe and took out both my pistols. I weighed them up, one in each hand, then checked that their actions were still smooth.

The Makarov was smaller, more compact and better suited for concealment. But the trade-off was a magazine that only held eight rounds. The Browning was more of a cannon. The NATO standard 9mm round it used was slightly longer than the Makarov's and it carried thirteen of them in the magazine.

The Browning's other advantage for my purposes was that it was more readily available in the West. As I was planning to take a folding-stock AK for myself back to Brussels, I'd have enough explaining to do as it was if I was stopped along the way, without being equipped entirely with weaponry from the Warsaw Pact.

The time ticked by. As I did my domestic chores, my mind wandered. Scrubbing away, I did fix on one thing for certain. After Sophie, I didn't ever want to do it again with anyone else. I wondered if that counted for something, morally speaking. Then again, I supposed Rizzo had thought the same, so maybe not.

That made up my mind for me. I wasn't going to follow Jan's playbook of being cool and distant any more today. Either Sophie and I had something that had a chance of lasting, or we didn't.

I picked up the phone and she answered after a couple of rings.

'Rizzo wants to come over and see you at some point. Do you want me to be there?' I asked her.

'He called already. We're meeting for lunch tomorrow. To talk things over.'

There was a pause and then down the line I thought I

heard her clearing her throat. 'Are you… are you coming over tonight?'

This thing with me was real - for now. Tough luck Rizzo.

Chapter Thirteen

To my disappointment, when I got to the airport on Tuesday morning Rizzo was waiting at departures. The very last person in the world whom I wanted to see just then. I'd really hoped the next and last time would be in Sicily when he came with the second payment.

On Sunday evening I'd asked her how things had gone with Rizzo that lunchtime, but she was tight-lipped. The only thing I'd got out of her was that he wasn't taking things well. Then she'd flicked off the light and we'd lain in darkness together for a while. That was all we did. Not even a week had gone by and already we were half-domesticated.

At one point last weekend it seemed like Sophie was going to expect me at her flat every night from now on. But yesterday was the first evening since last Thursday that we hadn't spent together. The excuse we gave ourselves was that she had an EEC dinner to attend and that I didn't want to miss my flight, but maybe we both knew it was time for a few days' break.

However, if I was disappointed to see Rizzo, he wasn't. Not on the surface anyway. He even gave me a wave to come and join him at the bar next to the gate.

'*Ciao.* You're wearing your Italian sunglasses again?'

'*Si.*' I waved the Percols at him warily.

'You want a drink?'

I accepted the peace offering.

'I didn't realise you were coming out on this flight too,' I said.

'I have to leave you at Rome. I need to make some last-minute arrangements for Sicily. There's been a slight change of timings. I'll see you when you arrive on Friday, not Saturday like I said before. So after you drop off the goods where Di Luca is going to show you, stay at the house until I get there that day.'

There was an awkward minute or two as we tried to find topics to keep the conversation on professional lines.

'Do you know the guys coming to join you?' he finally asked.

'Not really. But they were recommended by people I trust. I know some of the senior people in their gang.'

'You brought protection?'

'In my hold luggage.'

Our flight was called. We weren't sitting near one another on the plane and there were no winks and smiles to the stewardesses to request a seat swap.

At Rome we caught up with one another in the passport queue but stood together in silence. I got a wave and a forced half smile as we parted company to go to our separate gates. I didn't see which flight he was taking next, but assumed he was going on to Palermo or Catania.

At Bari I hired a car, paying with the cash I'd exchanged yesterday in Brussels, putting Rizzo's family's money to work.

I'd been given the name of a small hotel owned by a PCI member in the outskirts of the city, hard by the outer ring road. I wondered if he was one of those who'd been sent to East Germany for espionage training but didn't ask him. Johannes had told me via the Ministry people in Hamburg to keep a low profile while I was here.

The establishment was mean and shabby, and the corridors smelt strongly of floor cleaning fluid. But it had a yard at the back big enough for the truck and no questions asked.

The hotel was run by the owner, his wife and daughter. A son had gone to work in the North now it was the end of the tourist season. Not that they'd see many tourists here I'd bet.

Once in the room I turned up the knob on the weak air conditioning, lay back on the bed and thought some more about Rizzo, whiling away the time.

How had his conversation with her gone? What had she said to him? 'It was fun while it lasted but...' But what? That was what I really wanted to know. What did I offer her that he didn't?

And what did 'taking it badly,' as she'd described it mean? Would he throw himself into this political plot, possibly a coup? In his rage at the unfairness of the world would he try to drive his father and Borghese to go further than they were already planning?

As the day cooled towards evening, I drove down to the ferry port to see the lie of the land. My crew were to park up once they were off the boat and wait in the port until I identified myself to them.

There were docks all around the bay and a parking lot next to the ferry terminal, just as I'd been told in my instructions. But it wasn't a large one, so I couldn't hang around there too long tomorrow. After I'd driven past a couple of times, I made my way back to the hotel, picking up some pizza on the way to eat in my room.

The evening was still pleasantly warm. I sat out on the tiny balcony with a cheap bottle of wine and a view of the main road south - eventually taking you to Taranto, I supposed. A partial view, past a faintly humming electricity pylon holding up a rats' nest of cables running to the buildings along the street. I wondered what the workers streaming home in their underpowered Fiats and Innocentis accompanied by the occasional hooting would say if they knew that right now, shadowy actors in the North were plotting a different political future for the country, but without their say-so.

I also wondered what they'd say, if they knew that, in the east, other people were possibly counter-plotting to turn those same plans on their head. Hoping to expose American interference in Italian affairs and take the country out of NATO's orbit.

The stars came out, but the city lights were too bright for Mars to be seen. He was keeping his own counsel tonight. As the night wore on, the traffic noises faded and were replaced by the rasp of the cicadas, coming from somewhere out there in the scrubby wasteland between the road to Taranto and the ring road. Reminding me of how far south I was and how far away from home.

Far away from Brussels and all alone. Apart from the two East German soldiers setting off from Dubrovnik right now, two hundred kilometres and a world away to the north east. And the family of communist comrades downstairs, who'd been sensible and stayed well away from me and from trouble all day.

-

The noonday ferry pulled in. Several heavy-duty trucks drove down the ramp, but only a couple pulled over to the lorry park by the side of the terminal.

I walked over to find my customers. As I neared the first truck, a grey-haired driver jumped down. He ignored me as he walked to the rear of his vehicle, checking the tautness of the tensioning straps along its tarpaulin side as he went.

Through the cab windshield of the next truck along I saw a couple of men who looked much more likely candidates for being members of the Felix Dzerzhinsky regiment, as I assumed in my head they were. Hard faces with the golden-brown tans of people who'd spent time outdoors in a hot country. One of them pointed at me as I approached.

I rapped on the door and the window was rolled down. 'Show me your left hand.'

I held it up. I was getting too used to my scars, forgetting how well they marked me out. I hoped Johannes wouldn't suggest some kind of plastic surgery one day in a fit of enthusiasm for his craft. Sophie had tried to get me to use some of her beauty oil on the one on my cheek, claiming it would soften its lines over time. Maybe that was why she was so keen for me to come over each night, to make sure I followed her regime.

'I'm driving the green Fiat 128. Follow me out of here. We're going to the hotel first.'

The driver didn't look happy. 'We haven't eaten since last night.'

'I'll get the Italians to serve you something,' I replied, unimpressed.

At the hotel I mumbled something in a horrendous mixture of pidgin Italian and French about '*camarades*' which seemed to do the trick. It transpired that the daughter, Paola, knew some English, which helped too. I learnt that 'comrades' in Italian were '*compagni.*'

The two East Germans were beckoned through to the kitchen and sat down with bread, salami and a bowl of olives. I was ready for lunch as well, but something held me back. Paola went in and out, looking at us curiously as she brought the food and cleared away the plates for the other two.

It had only been a few minutes, but I was already getting suspicious of the driver's attitude. I sensed I was going to have to lay down the law at some point and I began to understand for the first time why our officers in the Bundeswehr kept their distance and ate separately from the conscripts.

I quizzed the pair of them as they ate.

'None of the hotel people speak German,' I announced. 'First of all, what are your names?'

The driver's mate looked at his colleague, who'd just taken a mouthful of bread.

'I'm Roth, he's Müller.'

'I'm Thomas.'

When I'd checked in, I'd used the fake East German passport Johannes had given me in Wismar.

'Who's the most senior?'

'I am,' said Müller, his mouth clear now. Worse luck for me and the mission then.

'Where have you just come from? Not Yugoslavia. Before that.'

Müller eyed me up, the first test of will. Then he broke and looked over his shoulder to make sure we were alone.

'Sudan. Training the police and then hunting for some westerners who were doing some training of their own, of the Anyanya rebels in the south.'

'How long for?'

'Almost a year.'

'You been home since then?'

A sour look came over Müller's face. Roth answered instead.

'Once, back in the spring.' Then he paused. 'It's hard on the families.'

Something about his tone told me not to enquire further.

'We're moving the goods tomorrow night, at eight,' I said instead. 'I've already been to see where they're stored.'

'I want to drive past tonight around that time. See what the area is like after dark,' Müller said.

I was in charge until the operation actually started and wanted to keep it that way. But it wasn't a bad idea, I supposed.

I glanced at Roth to see what he thought, but he was letting me make this call on my own. In the end I judged there was no point in being a bastard until I had to be.

'I'll drive us over at seven to take a look. It should be even more deserted tomorrow night when we go there an hour later.'

I thought some more. 'We can eat in town afterwards. We'll go somewhere expensive.'

They deserved a change from whatever they got served in the bush. Probably goat stew on a good day.

They went upstairs to wash and change out of their work clothes. Paola hovered at the door to the kitchen. After the others had gone, she approached and asked me about them.

'How long are they staying for?'

'We're leaving tomorrow night. Do you have somewhere private where they can wait tomorrow if they get bored in their room?'

'They can come in here, into the kitchen.'

Her English didn't seem too bad now. Maybe her confidence was growing, or it had just been my poor first impression earlier.

'Are you all from East Germany?' she asked.

I eyed her up.

'Are you a Party member?' I asked her back, attempting to deflect.

'Yes, all of us are. Including my brother who works in Turin.'

'What do you do for the Party?' I asked.

'Not a lot. Not enough.'

I wondered if there was a young guard in the PCI, impatient at the lack of action in the years since 'sixty-eight and before that too. People who might have ended up in the PCI's paramilitary organisation if they hadn't let it wither away, as Johannes said they had.

'What do you want to do?'

'Fight. Like my father, the partisan.'

I raised my eyebrows. The proprietor didn't look like a man handy with gelignite.

'He fought the fascists,' she said proudly. 'Right here in the South, helping the British after they landed at Taranto.'

'Those times are past.'

'They will come again. There will be no victory for communism without bloodshed. If we rise up, the Soviet Union will answer our call as it did in Czechoslovakia.'

So, some people in the West really did believe the propaganda about how the paratroopers had only dropped in at the request of the Czech government.

I looked at her more closely. In her simple working pinafore she had a touching earnestness. The copy of L'Unità neatly folded on the kitchen table added to the overall impression too. A simplicity of faith, like that of Caterina who left her Catholic magazines around the house for her father and brother to read, hoping against reason for a change in their characters.

'Why are you so angry?' I asked.

'My brother was to have gone to university. Our cousin went to the one here in Bari, but he was cheated. Apart from lectures there was no other teaching, and the university didn't even bother to set written exams. Unless you could afford to pay for extra tuition, you had little hope of graduating. So my brother gave up that idea and went to work in a factory instead.'

'I never went. The Party has given me all the education I need,' I said, making the counter-surveillance course this summer stretch a long way.

But I admired her passion. It was what you needed if you were to change society. I wondered if she'd ever get the chance to harness it and make the difference she hoped for.

The industrial estate was almost deserted at seven. It was still twilight, but Rizzo's father's factory was already shrouded in deep gloom, which wasn't so good I thought. Any lights we used inside would be bound to leak out somewhere and risk attracting attention, through the skylights if nowhere else.

The two soldiers seemed happy enough for now. In the privacy of the car, I'd asked them which organisation they were with. They'd rattled off the number of a Volksarmee training regiment, without hesitation and so openly that I assumed it must be a cover for a secret unit somewhere else in the regime's hierarchy. So no real surprise there.

We drove into town and parked in the centre. On the way in, they'd both kept looking out of the car windows as if they were unused to being back in civilisation. Close to where we parked was the entrance to a nightclub and Müller nudged the other sergeant as we walked past. I ignored it for now, but I was wary of them forgetting themselves and going on all-night soldiers' bender. Even if we weren't moving out for another twenty-four hours, I didn't want to have to deal with them waking up tomorrow morning in the backstreet room of some floozy with strangely empty wallets.

I chose what I judged to be the smartest-looking restaurant on the Piazza Mercantile and tried to keep them there for as long as possible. I used Rizzo's cash to make sure there was always a bottle of wine on the table, in the hope they'd have their bender in plain sight.

As they became more uninhibited, they started to ask me personal questions. There were the inevitable ones about my scars, to which they got the same answers as everyone else. They were sceptical, but didn't say so out loud. I guessed they knew not to ask about the details of the Stasi's operational work and I paid them the same courtesy when it came to their activities in Africa.

I did want to ask them something though - the usual treatment for people attempting to flee the Republic - but Johannes had warned me in Luxembourg about how such questions might be misinterpreted.

At midnight they announced they wanted to go to a club to sample the cocktails available in the West.

'I want to be back at the hotel for two,' I said. Despite my unease, I didn't really have much choice but to let them go.

We only queued for a little while to get into the club, which was called 'Piovra'. The letters on the sign outside were made up from the octopus tentacles of its namesake. Given it was Bari on a Wednesday night the owners couldn't be too picky about who the bouncers allowed in. Tonight, this had evidently included a handful of sailors off an American warship in the harbour, going by their accents and the odd tattoo.

Inside, the music was loud and the newfangled disco strobe lights hyperactive. They had to make up for the lack of movement on the dancefloor somehow. We even got served in a reasonable time too. The prices were sheer robbery, but I wasn't paying with my own money, just as I never did back in Brussels for anything to do with work. Forget subsidies for French famers, the expense accounts of junior *fonctionnaires* needed topping up with British pounds and shillings.

Müller drifted off towards the source of the music, while Roth shouted drunkenly in my ear. I kept one eye on the senior sergeant for a while as he moved in and out between the dancers but had to keep turning back towards Roth to shout my answers.

The cunning devils had planned this, for when I next looked around properly, Müller was nowhere to be seen.

With a curse and a punch into Roth's shoulder to get him to stay where he was at the bar, I went off to find Müller. He wasn't anywhere on the dancefloor that I could see as I pushed my way past groups of girls swaying together in inward-facing circles - either for protection from the sailors or to provide them with a bigger target.

My mind jumped to the obvious conclusion. If he'd already found a woman and was still on or near the premises, then he'd most likely be in a cubicle in the toilets or in the alleyway at the rear. All nightclubs had an alleyway at the rear, it was virtually a rule.

I ran into the men's lavatory and went down the row of stalls, thumping them one by one. Most were empty and hardly any had working locks. Not that I needed the curses from the occupants to tell me that. Through the half-open door of one stall I caught a glimpse of a pair of buttocks as I hurried past. It wasn't Müller pumping the woman from behind as she bent over, leaning with outstretched arms against the cistern, but something seemed vaguely familiar about the scene.

I left and hunted for the rear door. There was a single bouncer slouching just inside. I brushed past him, holding my cigarette pack out in front of me as if going for a peaceful smoke away from the noise.

I didn't have far to look. Halfway down the alley I found Müller with one arm wrapped around the silver-sequinned back of a girl with long brown hair, his other hand up her skirt, clamped to the side of a tanned hip.

I tapped her on the shoulder and pulled her away with a baleful look that brooked no refusal. Sometimes the scar on my face was useful.

Müller looked at me insolently as he zipped up his fly with a yank. 'What are you looking at, *Bundi*? Never seen a real man at work before?'

'You idiot.' I jabbed his forehead with my finger. 'Start thinking with this.'

The thought crossed my mind that maybe I should be taking my own advice back in Brussels.

I could tell he wasn't taking kindly to being reprimanded by someone ten or fifteen years his junior by the way he took a step back and balled his fists, an arm to each side.

But I didn't have time for this. I was fed up with sorting out everyone else's problems. The cynical thought came into my head that there was no point in working for a police state if you didn't get the chance to put the frighteners on people occasionally.

I looked up and down the alley. The girl was tottering away on her platform heels and Roth was arriving. He might as well hear what I had to say.

I leant in a little closer to the wine fumes and spoke in a low voice.

'I am personally known to General Wolf, head of the foreign intelligence service. That doesn't happen very often for Western colleagues of the Ministry. We're a very select circle, those of us who know him. And you're not in it.' I was guessing all of this, but he didn't know that.

He spat on the ground. I felt a tug at my sleeve as Roth tried to get me to step back.

'Please, sir. Not here,' he hissed.

We all walked back inside. As we approached the bar on our way out, a girl standing there looked up and waved at me.

'*Ciao Oskar.*'

I did a double-take. It was Blue Dress Girl from the party, or rather not tonight because she was wearing a short green number which only reached halfway down her thighs. But I recognised the tawny hair with lighter streaks - I'd just seen it five minutes ago in the men's toilets.

So Rizzo had hired escorts of some kind that night after all, the bastard. He didn't deserve to be with Sophie. So much too, for Blue Dress Girl being demure and reserved at the party in comparison to her friends.

And I really didn't like coincidences, either. She came a couple of steps closer, then backed away again as I strode past with a grim look, followed by my two lost sheep.

We went back to the car in silence and got in. I was tempted to say something but thought better of it and pulled away from the kerb instead.

There was hardly any traffic at this time of night - apart from the red Renault which had been parked a few cars back when we left and was now following us out of town. I knew the pension was on a main road, so it wasn't that surprising that someone else was going the same way, but again, I wasn't happy.

I drove on past the hotel. Roth was sitting beside me and looked across in a silent question. I jerked my head to the rear, and he turned round to see for himself.

'Let's drive on some more.'

I joined the ring road, anti-clockwise, and the red car followed us on too.

'I'm going to get off this road and see what happens next.'

I heard a click from the back and glanced round to see Müller working the slide of his Makarov, holding the gun in front of him, still glowering at me as he did so.

'Idiot,' I said again for the second time tonight, maybe somewhat unwisely.

I let one junction go by, then put on speed to try to lose the Renault before I pulled off at the next one.

We slowed down for the off ramp and I swung the car onto the overbridge to cross to the other carriageway. Roth twisted in his seat and I glanced down too. We saw the headlights of the Renault go past, keeping to a steady ninety.

'What a waste of time,' I said.

'Better to be sure,' said Müller. I acknowledged him in the mirror with a nod.

'Okay. *Auf gehts!*' I replied, a truce restored for the present.

Chapter Fourteen

We watched the Messina Straits ferry cross over in the dawn, tracking it by its running lights from when it left the Sicilian side. We'd driven all night having loaded the truck the previous evening. My shoulders still ached even now.

The three of us were dressed in navy blue overalls with the logo of a fictional West German engineering company stitched onto the left breast pocket. We had matching baseball caps too, but the soldiers didn't bother with theirs.

After the performance at the nightclub, they'd stayed in the hotel yesterday until it was time to drop off the car back at the airport. Nothing needed to be said in the end. I guessed they wanted to get some sleep before our drive across Calabria in the small hours. I did anyway.

The ramp came down with a clang. Müller started the engine and we drove onto the ferry, the mainland behind us now, Sicily within touching distance.

The crossing was short, less than thirty minutes, and before we knew it we'd arrived. A lot quicker than the thirty days it took the Allies to force the last German soldiers here to travel in the opposite direction.

The drive down to Ragusa in the south-east corner of Sicily, was another three and a half hours. I couldn't believe we were on the last straight and that Karin might soon be let out from wherever she'd been held since August. My patience with East Germany was wearing thin, and not just because of the nonsense at the nightclub on Wednesday night.

The following morning Roth had come to me on his own and sheepishly told me that Müller's wife had left him for a factory supervisor while they'd been in Africa. He hinted that Müller really didn't want to be here either, but back home salvaging his marriage. That was as far as he would go in front of a personal friend of General Wolf. I was only a possible personal friend, of course, but people tended to give the Stasi the benefit of the doubt.

I wasn't sure how the girl in the alleyway in the silver top fitted into Müller's plan, but Rizzo wasn't the only one on this trip with woman trouble it seemed.

We followed the coast until we reached Catania. Frustratingly, along the way we could see construction work for a new autostrada which would have got us there even faster. As we turned inland and then slowly climbed, the countryside gradually acquired a dusting of green. On up the massif we went, the truck straining as we growled over the undulating folds of the mountains between us and our destination, the Rizzos' hidden valley in the hills above Ragusa.

We pulled off the main route onto a minor road and then off that one too. Roth jumped down to undo the chain strung across the private track which led to the Rizzo family bolthole from communism.

The track quickly lost its tarmac surface and began to narrow, forcing Müller to carefully inch along. Then it took a sharp turn to the left and zig-zagged viciously down the side of a steep valley, almost a gorge. At each hairpin, the heavily-laden truck swayed alarmingly from side to side, but I guessed the soldiers had negotiated more difficult roads in Africa. There was a final hairpin at the bottom as the track turned to cross a river by a shallow ford, before it followed the course upstream, the river's channel becoming increasingly choked with boulders as we drove alongside it.

I didn't know if there was a paradise on earth, but after

the last few kilometres driving on the parched plateau, this came pretty close. The sky above the valley was a slash of deep blue against the light grey, almost white-coloured rock of the gorge wall. Hardy trees with dark green foliage lining its sides provided a cool contrast and along the river was a carpet of wild mint. When the truck veered onto the verges, the smell from the crushed plants lingered in the air, mixing with the scent of the pink-flowering bushes interspersed among the trees.

'All this is one family's property?' Müller asked incredulously. 'How much further are we going?'

'That's capitalism for you,' I replied. Never in a thousand years would I make enough money to come anywhere close to the Rizzos' level of wealth. No wonder Di Luca was envious.

'My guess is we're taking the weapons in there,' I said, pointing to a place where the track widened out for a stretch before meandering further up the valley. The open area ran right up to the gorge wall where there was a large head-height opening in the rock which looked like it had been shaped by human hands.

'Let's get to the house first. The Italians are meant to be waiting for us there.'

'This might be the last place we can turn the truck before then. We should check the house out on foot before we drive further into the valley,' said Müller.

'Makes sense. We'll park and you'll scout on ahead?' I asked.

'Okay.'

The suggestions weren't quite orders, but Müller seemed happy enough. The end was in sight for him too.

'Stop by the cave.' I told Roth.

I jumped down with Müller and asked him to help me lift out the case with the AKs which Rizzo's father and I had opened back in Bari and the one with the spare magazines and ammunition which I'd found next to it there. I'd marked them both with chalk after we'd brought them up from the underground store, making sure they were loaded at the back of the truck.

'Got your eye on one of those?' he asked.

'You can never have too much firepower.'

We carried them a few metres inside the cave, down a roughly-hewn tunnel or perhaps a natural fissure, right up to a locked gate set in heavy ancient iron bars extending from the floor to the roof. Between the bars I could see the passageway running deeper into the darkness of the hill. We flipped the catches of the cases and Müller picked through the rifles, giving each one a shake until he found a couple that rattled less than the others. While he made his selection, I tore open cardboard boxes of ammunition and charged the banana-shaped magazines as fast as I could manage in the half-light.

When I'd finished, Müller took a magazine from me, rammed it home under the body of the rifle and walked up the track toward the house without a backwards look.

I charged more magazines. I heard Roth slam the door and jump down. For want of anything better to do, he came into the cave to watch, unhooking his walkie-talkie and placing it on top of a stone just outside the entrance.

The radio crackled and Müller came on the air.

'I'm by the house. There's no one here that I can see. We should wait up here with the truck, there's better cover.'

The house was substantial, built in the same pale grey stone as the rocks of the gorge. With two storeys it was more like a proper farmhouse than the goatherder's cottage I'd somehow imagined it to be. There was a gravel-covered area in front of the building, but Müller directed us to park up on a scrubby patch of grass screened by trees at the rear of the house. He joined us there as we jumped down.

'Typical Italian punctuality,' I said.

The others looked unimpressed.

Whilst we waited, I had a play with the AK in the shade, the soldiers showing me how to break it down and then reassemble it. I repeated the drills for myself, getting faster and faster until even Müller grunted in approval.

Unlike the G3 rifle I'd used in the Bundeswehr, you could only select either single shot fire or continuous burst. The G3 had an additional setting for a controlled burst of three rounds. But the AK was almost a kilo lighter and shorter too, even with the stock fully extended. And when the stock was folded up under the barrel, the weapon was only around sixty or seventy centimetres in length, making it much more practical for use in a confined space.

Eventually, a red sports car arrived, sweeping up in a hurry to the front door of the house. I watched from the corner of the house as Di Luca jumped out, swore when he couldn't see anyone, and then cursed when I trotted round the side, surprising him.

'*Ciao*,' he said, forgetting his English for the moment.

'*Ciao. Come stai.*' I replied.

'Where are my weapons?'

Not the usual reply to that greeting, I supposed, but then it wasn't a normal situation. I jerked my thumb backwards over my shoulder.

'Where are we taking them?' I asked, already knowing the answer.

'Back down the track to the cave. There's a gate there. The keys are inside the house. Want to take a look?'

He hurried to unlock the front door which gave straight into a large stone-flagged room. An opening framed in the rear wall showed a stairway descending into gloom.

'They've stocked the cellar ready for Armageddon,' he said, nodding towards the steps. He lifted a key from a hook behind the door and a torch from a shelf by the side which he flicked on and off again. We left as quickly as we came.

We drove back to the cave in both vehicles. He opened the gate and flashed the torch down the passageway beyond it. As far along its length as I could see were the black outlines of entrances to side chambers.

'Who uses this place?' I asked.

'Who hasn't? The Garibaldini last century, the Resistance during the war and Sicilian freedom fighters afterwards.'

I frowned in puzzlement, but he didn't explain.

'And from time to time our own people of course. This is Di Luca family territory after all.'

I guessed the Di Luca clan's protection extended to the Rizzos' property too. They were still family, when all was said and done.

Although there were no stairs to climb this time, it took almost as long to unload as to load. The ground was uneven, and we had to keep going further and further into the cave to find space to dump the crates and cases. It took longer too, because once the soldiers had carried them inside, they did an approximate check of the contents of each container against the store record book we'd taken with us from the underground chamber in Bari.

Just as we got started with the unloading, I asked Di Luca if he knew about the new arrangement whereby Rizzo was to join us at the house today rather than tomorrow.

'No. When did he say that?' he asked sharply.

'He told me at the airport on Tuesday, but he didn't explain why there'd been a change of plan. I thought you knew?'

'No. This is something he's decided on his own.' Di Luca furrowed his brow.

'It makes no sense, either. I don't like it. Did he say if your guys were also to wait here with you?'

'He didn't mention them. He probed a bit more as to what sort of people they were and asked if I was armed.'

Now my antennae were twitching too.

Di Luca eyed up the pile of cases still to be unloaded in the back of the truck and glanced at his watch. 'How much longer will you need?'

'Another couple of hours before we're done. Well past one o'clock.

'Okay. I'm going into Ragusa to ask around in the meantime. Keep an eye out for me, or for anyone else who comes down that hill.'

'Okay.' It was fine by me because it gave the soldiers time to find the SAMs and pick out the most interesting of the other equipment whilst he was gone.

He got into his car and bumped down the track along the river. But when he crossed the ford and got to the zig-zag, he raced up it in a cloud of dust, taking the hairpins faster than I would have done.

The soldiers looked up at the car disappearing over the ridge as they came out of the cave together, having just finished manhandling a heavy wooden crate inside. Rocket Propelled Grenades, we'd thought, by the airbrushed stencils on the lid.

'What's happening?' Müller demanded.

'He's gone to check out something in town. This is our chance to take what we want for the Ministry and get it hidden in the back of the truck. *Los!*'

Di Luca was gone for almost the full two hours. The soldiers made the most of the time and finished packing their selection of items into a couple of cases, which they then secured behind a false wall in the cargo area of the truck. Just as soon as Di Luca returned, they would be ready to leave.

'Did find what you were looking for?' I asked Müller.

'We got a couple of things. Some infra-red night sights. No anti-aircraft missiles though. We checked every crate against the manifest that we picked up at the factory. It's not the same list as the items we brought from Bari.'

'So what did we transport here?'

'A mixture of Western and Soviet small arms. Some anti-tank mines, plastic explosives, detonators. Radios and other electronic equipment. Things you would expect to arm a partisan force with. But it was a mixture of old and new, like the cargo had been made up from several caches hidden at different points in time.'

I supposed I could have let them go there and then, but I didn't want to be stranded in the middle of nowhere without a vehicle. Let alone having to single-handedly guard an unsecured cave full of enough weapons to start a second Mafia war.

My suspicions about Rizzo's message crystallized when I saw Di Luca's car zig-zagging down the side of the valley again before bouncing over the potholes back up to the cave. He was driving even faster than when he'd left, if that were possible.

'It's a double-cross,' he shouted at me as he jumped out, slamming the door.

The soldiers didn't speak English, but they got the sense well enough from his tone.

'What's up?' Müller growled at me.

'What do you mean?' I asked Di Luca in turn.

'Rizzo's coming here sure enough,' he said grimly, 'But he's bringing ten men from the Saraceno clan with him.'

'Who are they?' I asked.

'Our family's rivals. We have unfinished vendettas.'

'Why the hell has Rizzo done that?' I demanded, pretending as if I didn't already know the answer.

Before Di Luca started speculating, I asked him a different question. 'What do they want? The weapons?'

'Of course they want the weapons. They're coming to kill us and take them for themselves. With a truckload of guns, they'll be able to come after the rest of my family and our businesses too, if the Cupola will let them.'

It was the slang name for the Regional Commission which De Mauro had described to me in Apulia. Not that I would be revealing to Di Luca that I knew it.

'When will they be here?'

'Twenty minutes at most.'

'What's going on?' Müller asked, even more insistently now.

'Wait a minute,' I said to him.

'Well fuck Rizzo,' I said to Di Luca, feigning indignation. 'We haven't come all this way to return empty handed. He owes us the second half of our fee. We'll have to take it in the form of rifles instead.'

'You'll not get off Sicily in one piece,' Di Luca said contemptuously.

'If we leave now, we might.'

He shook his head. 'They know you'll be in a West German truck and there's only one road out of here. They'll be watching both directions. We might make it in my car if we leave now.'

'Enough! What's happening?' shouted Müller, planting himself between Di Luca and me.

'Some other criminals will be here in a few minutes to take the weapons off his criminal gang,' I pointed at Di Luca. 'Which right now is us.'

I let my news sink in for a second.

'We're trapped down here. If we want to get away with the sample weapons, we'll have to fight our way out.' I told him, although they had probably already worked that out for themselves.

'That wasn't part of the plan,' said Müller.

I ignored him for now and turned back to Di Luca and back into English. 'Rizzo has betrayed us all. You want to stop the Saracenos from arming themselves for a war? Then we need to fight it out here.' I said, looking at the narrow width of the gorge.

'Can your guys do that? Are they prepared to? I thought they were the German Mob.'

'We've all been in the Bundeswehr. You'll need to stay too.' I had no idea what he might be able to do, but I wasn't going to let him run.

I turned back to Müller and to Roth who'd come up close to listen too. I only had their boss's word in Hamburg that neither of them could speak much English.

'What are we in the middle of?' asked Roth.

I felt I owed them a more meaningful reason to stand and fight, than simply to make sure my sample weapons got back to Germany. Right now, there was nothing stopping them hijacking Di Luca's car if they wanted to, although I judged it unlikely.

'The criminal gangs are two rival factions within Italian neo-fascism. There's a coup against the state planned for later this year, which I've been investigating,' I said, painting them a crude picture. 'The factions have fallen out over this shipment and if we can get them to fight each other now, we might stop the coup from happening completely.'

Müller looked sceptical. I appealed to Roth.

'What's the point in struggling against imperialism and fascism in Africa if we don't fight it when it reappears in Europe?'

Müller cursed and spat in the dust.

'There's ten men coming down that track in,' I glanced at my watch. 'Fifteen minutes. How do we stop them?' I asked, turning it back into a practical problem.

'You did conscription, right?' Müller said sourly. 'Tell me you didn't train as a cook.'

'I was infantry.'

Roth spoke up now. 'We have RPGs and what looks like an Italian copy of a MG 42. How many vehicles are they coming in?'

'How many cars?' I asked Di Luca.

'I don't know, probably two or three for that many people. They might leave some men up top for a roadblock, but I'm not sure they're that thorough. They're the Saracenos after all.'

'He says three down the track, maybe one at the top to

block the exit onto the main road,' I told Müller.

'Okay,' he squatted down to draw in the dust with a stick.

'Look. Here's the track down the side of the valley. It's going to be the simplest ambush plan there is. Hit the first vehicle when it slows down for the last hairpin bend, just as the track reaches the valley floor. Hit the last vehicle with another RPG when the column stops after the first strike. The MG 42 will be the main killing weapon.'

'How do we stop them escaping up the track?'

'You and him go up top.' He got to his feet to point with the stick at a clump of scrub by another hairpin, almost halfway up the side of the gorge.

'Wait in those bushes, below the parapet of the road, until they've gone past and we've sprung the ambush at the bottom. Take assault rifles and shoot anyone that tries to escape uphill. Make sure that no one comes down the hill either, if they do have a roadblock at the top.

'Okay. He needs a rifle then.' I said pointing at Di Luca.

Müller beckoned us to follow him into the cave and then into one of the side chambers carved out of the living rock. He flashed his torch at the row of boxes stacked neatly against the wall and flipped the catches on the cases I'd chalk-marked to identify the AKs.

'Make sure he knows how to use it,' he said to me as he handed Di Luca a rifle, a couple of magazines, and cardboard boxes of ammunition. 'And make sure he doesn't open fire before our command.'

Di Luca fumbled, trying to keep a hold on everything as he walked back outside into the sunshine. Müller cursed as he watched the performance.

'Help him charge the magazines here, then when you're done, run like hell. You have a radio?'

I nodded in acknowledgement and he went back inside the cave to find his other toys.

'Here,' I said to Di Luca, as I ripped open the cartons

and showed him how to press the rounds into the magazine. 'Bet you wish you hadn't dodged conscription now.'

'I had five fun years in America instead, so I got the better deal.'

'Right. Let's go.'

I set off at a trot up the track, Di Luca puffing and panting behind me. As the road climbed, I could sense him falling further and further behind, but I was focussed solely on the scrubby bushes growing inside the bend of the turn half-way up the road.

I carried on up around the hairpin, then jumped down off the roadway and leant against the retaining wall below. We could see a good portion of the track as it zig-zagged its way down to the valley floor, but tucked in close to the hairpin we would be out of sight of anyone above us.

Di Luca didn't bother with the long way round. Cursing, he fought his way through the scrub instead, before slumping down beside me against the wall.

'I'm going to kill Rizzo when this is over.' he said simply. I knew he meant it.

'Your boys had better know what they're doing,' he added.

'Or what?'

'Or else we're all going to die.'

I quickly finished my instruction to Di Luca on the use of the rifle, showing him the safety lever and how to push it all the way down to fire. I didn't tell him that the bottom setting would only let him fire single shots because I didn't trust him with continuous fire on fully automatic.

As we waited, the initial burst of adrenaline wore off and anger set in. That preening peacock Rizzo with his hurt feelings had completely compromised Borghese and his father's operation. And more importantly, the task that I had to complete to get my cousin out of jail and from whatever went on in there behind locked doors.

But even worse than that, a detachment of the East German Volksarmee was looking down the barrels of several guns, a long way on the wrong side of the Berlin Wall. What happened to détente if we were discovered shooting back? Forget the irony of communist soldiers defending the Rizzo family refuge from communism, this mission was going wrong in so many ways right now, none of which I'd bet Johannes had even dreamed of.

Rizzo's pride was going to end up in people getting killed today. And just as I'd finally got into bed with Sophie too, worse luck. I suppressed the thought that it was my whoring after her which had caused his treachery.

And then after anger came depression. What was the point of turning over a new leaf in Dublin, or protesting to Kramer that for my conscience's sake we had to find a different method in London to assassination? I was sitting here with an AK-47 lying on my lap, knowing I was going to use it, and worse, fearing that I would get a taste for killing again, too.

The radio clipped to my breast pocket crackled into life and Müller's disjointed voice came through the set.

'Ready?'

'*Jawohl.*'

'There's movement on the ridgeline to the east. Three vehicles.'

Di Luca and I looked at one another as the noise of car and truck engines in low gear floated down the mountainside, gradually becoming louder.

'Don't fire until I do,' I told Di Luca, as I saw him finger the trigger. 'I mean it, or I'll shoot you myself.'

He twisted round to hear the sound better. We both felt the vibrations as the vehicles drew near.

'And sit still, damn you, until they've gone by.'

I didn't put it past him to loose off a few rounds when they slowed for the bend. He was too unreliable to be a real soldier.

Müller came on again, his voice calm and steady,

experienced killer that he was.

'*Achtung! Achtung!*'

A few seconds passed and suddenly they were there. A grey Lancia followed by a flatbed truck and then a panel van. I peered through the scrub to try to catch sight of the men inside, but they were past and accelerating away from the turn in a flash.

'Quick, let's go,' I said. We scrambled through the bushes to the road. The van at the rear of the convoy was just making the next turn below ours, while the leading car had almost reached the last hairpin at the bottom.

There was a momentary burst of static from the radio, followed by a second's hissing silence.

'*Feuer Frei!*'

A heartbeat after we heard a whoosh, then a bang as the first RPG hit. There was a flash, and the car was jerked to one side, followed by a cloud of dust. No one was getting out of that. Just for good measure the MG 42 opened up. I could see rock splinters being kicked up as rounds struck the boulders on the far side of the track from the car.

Di Luca crossed the road to look over the edge, trying to get a better view of what was going on below and making himself a target for anyone who happened to be looking up. Not that the Saracenos had much time for that right now.

There was a second RPG strike, on the cab of the panel van, but the grenade must have glanced off it and exploded outside the vehicle because five or six *mafiosi* tumbled out the back.

We heard the buzzsaw sound of the MG 42 again as it spat out a thousand rounds per minute and bodies began to fall. It was going to be over almost before it started. The thought was a foolish one, because just then the gun jammed.

Now we began to hear the crackle of return fire from behind the cover of the truck and van, not that they would have been given much to aim at by the professionals on the other side of the river. Some of the men who'd escaped the initial contact had left the road to crash the last few metres down the slope, closing with their tormentors at the bottom. The two soldiers had given up trying to unjam the machine gun, because we began to hear short, controlled bursts of automatic rifle fire.

'Move,' I shouted at Di Luca.

I spoke into the radio. 'We're coming down to hit them in the rear.'

We ran down to the next turn and I pushed Di Luca behind the large rock on the corner itself. Amidst the sound of shouts and firing the random thought came into my head that the hairpin had probably been built around it.

Peering cautiously to one side, I saw some of the men who'd survived the rocket and machine-gun fire trying to take cover behind the wrecked vehicles. They should have stopped hiding and moved like the others who'd reached the bottom of the slope and were working their way across the river using the boulders upstream of the ford as cover.

I brought the AK up onto the rock, flipped the lever to fully automatic and fired down the gap behind the vehicles. As if from afar, I watched the Saraceno clan members turn unthinkingly towards the source of the new sound, and the strikes of my bullets as they were punched back and fell to the ground.

Di Luca's blood was up. I hadn't waited on him before firing and now he didn't wait on me. Suddenly, he left the cover of the boulder and scrambled down the slope after the surviving *mafiosi*. The fool. He was going to get shot by the soldiers, if not deliberately, then by a stray bullet.

I peered round the rock again. There was still movement behind the truck. I couldn't chase after Di Luca until the coast was clear up here. I gave it another couple of bursts, then ran down the road weaving from side to side, keeping the smoking panel van between me and the figures lying prone on the ground.

The firing from the valley floor was becoming more intermittent as I peered round the corner of the van. One of the *mafiosi* was propped up against the rear wheel of the truck, groaning softly. When he caught sight of me, he tried to raise his pistol so I shot him again. I walked towards the others. Another couple were also still alive. One tried to drag himself away as I came up to them, but otherwise they were both well out of it. There was a lot of blood. I picked up pistols and a couple of small Uzi-type sub machine guns and tossed them up onto the empty flatbed of the truck. No wonder Di Luca's rivals had wanted the weapons we'd brought from Apulia.

The firing down below had stopped altogether now. The whole engagement couldn't have been longer than about five or six minutes at most. From the height of steps up to the cab I looked down into the valley. Müller and Roth were going from body to body and Di Luca was bending down to one too. Now we had to clear up this mess and decide what to do next.

I slung the AK behind my back and jumped off the parapet, scrambling down the slope to see what Di Luca was doing on the far side of the ford.

He was crouching with his back to me, so I couldn't tell what was going on at first as I splashed across the river. The Mafia guy lying on the ground had received a gaping chest wound but was still alive and arching his back in agony as Di Luca sawed at his genitals with a knife which had appeared from somewhere about his person.

'What the fuck do you think you're doing?' I asked him as I reached down and roughly pulled him away. Di Luca looked up at me angrily, eyes filled with blood lust.

'Sweet Jesus,' I said, when I saw how far he'd got. I pulled the Browning from the side pocket of my overalls, chambered a round, and gave the dying man a mercy shot.

'You're an animal,' I told Di Luca as Roth arrived. I presumed he'd seen worse in Africa.

He ignored me and began searching around for another

victim, the veins in his temples still bulging.

Unnoticed, Müller had come up behind Di Luca as I remonstrated with him. I saw the sergeant look down at the red knife in the Italian's hand, some slimy stuff mixed with blood dripping from the point.

Müller checked his AK's safety was off and brought it up to point at Di Luca's back. Everyone was pumped with adrenalin. The soldier and I exchanged glances. If ever there was the chance to rid the world of this mad torturer, it was now. He'd just be another body in the pile to be disposed of - the next problem to solve if we were to get away from here cleanly.

Müller was looking at me more pointedly now, hefting his AK as he waited on a decision. My mouth went dry as I tried to think. Deciding to fight back against the Saracenos had been an easy choice - it was kill or be killed. But now I realised that Rizzo was right about what he'd said to me in Brussels, about me not understanding Italy or being able to navigate its waters. I needed Di Luca alive to make peace with the locals and minimise any long-term repercussions from today for Sophie and I.

There were other people caught up in this too. Caterina and her mother didn't deserve to have a bomb planted under their car one day. And above all else, as far as possible, I had to make sure that none of the events in the valley today could be traced to Berlin.

'We need to be gone,' Müller said, bringing me back to the present.

I looked at Di Luca. The craziness in his eyes was fading away and with it my initial gut instinct to get rid of him.

'All this mess needs clearing up first,' he said. 'If you want to get your truck past the wreckage on the road, that is.'

'How long do we have?' I asked him. My mind was racing on while I said it, as another idea came into my head.

'No one lives within two kilometres of this place. Not for a decade or more. They've all sold up to Rizzo's father and gone to Palermo or the north of Italy.'

'Carabinieri?'

He snorted contemptuously.

'Let's put the bodies in the cave,' I said to him, having come to a decision. 'Then we'll blow the entrance.'

'The weapons are in there.'

'The word on them is out. How else are you going to stop the family from the next town along coming to take them? Better that no clan gets them now. Isn't that the best outcome?' I suggested.

But it was really Johannes who'd put the idea into my head, with his talk back in Luxembourg about throwing a spanner into the works. This play was almost over, though. I doubted that I'd be getting any clues on a CIA connection now. Sabotage was the best I could do for him and his promotion prospects.

Di Luca chewed his lip as he tried to work out what the people he was answerable to would say to that.

'It's an exceptional situation,' I insisted. 'You need to stop this escalating into another full-blown Mafia war. It's bad for everyone's business, your bosses will understand that. Take what you want for yourself and we'll seal the rest in the cave.'

Di Luca grunted. I took it as a grunt of assent. He could always claim that we'd outnumbered him.

'Why do you care, anyway?' he asked suspiciously.

'I don't especially care. I only got paid to move them, and only part-paid at that. But I don't want to be accused of having started a Mafia war and end up bringing Italian trouble north to my people in Germany. You mentioned unfinished vendettas between the Di Lucas and the Saracenos. I want this settled now.'

I didn't tell him which Germany I was referring to, or which people either.

I turned to Müller. 'Do you have enough plastic

explosives to blow the entrance to the cave?' I asked in German. 'We need to stick the bodies in there and make sure no one gets the weapons. Because of the fascist coup.'

'You're asking a lot.'

'If we don't hide how bad things got here today, then my cover will be blown and the Ministry's work will be put back by months,' I said. 'He says the police never come this way and that no one lives nearby, not for three kilometres at least. You saw for yourselves how sparsely populated the area is on the way here. I reckon we have a couple of hours.'

Müller weighed something up and looked at Roth.

'Okay, we'll take the slow way home.'

He didn't explain what he meant.

We walked back up the zig-zag together. The driver and passenger of the car were still in their seats, badly burnt and looking pretty unpleasant. I hoped we could leave them to last.

I walked over to the two *mafiosi* who I'd shot and wounded as they hid behind the truck. In the heat of battle I'd disarmed them rather than finish them off there and then, but now their luck had run out. Looking in their eyes, they knew it too. One of them tried to say something but just dribbled blood.

I sensed the soldiers watching me and I also sensed their expectations. Since the end of the battle, I'd taken on the leadership of the operation and now I bore its burden.

All the *mafiosi* had to go into the cave. I glanced at Di Luca and saw the gleam in his eye as he felt the edge of the knife which had reappeared in his hand. So I got my Browning out again and shot them where they lay. At least, that was how I justified it in the instant before I seared my conscience and gave myself over to the thing I couldn't name.

We kept walking towards the rear of the convoy. The truck seemed relatively undamaged, the keys were even still hanging from the ignition. But the driver of the van was as equally deformed as the occupants of the car. All his passengers had escaped the worst of the RPG, only to be killed later elsewhere.

'Use their truck to push the car and the van off the road down into the river,' I growled at Roth, hating him.

I stared at Müller next.

'Get the bodies lying in the riverbed ready for loading onto the truck. The three of us will bring down the ones from up here.'

I glowered at Di Luca. 'Now it's your turn to help us, if you like blood and gore so much.'

It was nine minutes I tried really hard to blot out from my memory afterwards. The worst part was picking up limbs which had fallen off the corpses inside the vehicles. Everything went onto the back of the truck.

The bodies of the two men I'd just shot weren't anywhere near as bad by comparison. We dragged them round to the back of the truck and Roth and Di Luca climbed onto the flatbed to haul them up over the tail. I watched with morbid fascination as they appeared to exhale after death when their torsos flopped down onto the floorboards.

When we were done, I slapped the cab door for Roth to get moving and sent Di Luca down to help Müller collect the other bodies. For their sakes, I hoped none of them were still alive.

Roth revved the truck back and forth, carefully nudging the other vehicles down the slope without going over himself. I kept a watchful eye on the manoeuvre, thumping the cab door a couple of times when his wheels got close to the edge.

The van had further to travel than the car and rolled straight into the river. If the floodwater from the winter rains got high enough, over time it would eventually rust away, the engine block the last to go. The car only slid slowly down to rest half in, half out of the water. I picked up the radio and told Müller to get back to the cave and start rigging for demolition.

Roth drove me down to the bottom of the track. I let him and Di Luca get on with loading the remaining bodies which had been collected together in a heap of splayed-out arms and legs, while I took a closer look at the wrecked vehicles.

The car was already fully burnt out but there was still a smell of petrol from the van. Ducking down there was an even stronger smell and rainbow eddies in the water. I thought of setting fire to it there and then, but my guess was that if the tyres caught, the black smoke might be more likely to attract investigation than the gunshots that had filled the valley for those five minutes earlier. If we chose, we could always burn it when we finally left here.

But even if the police didn't come, at some point someone from the Saraceno clan would arrive to see what had happened. And my bet was that they'd bring Rizzo, the Judas.

All three of us were smeared in blood as we rode in the Mafia truck back to the cave. Then we had to go through the whole gruesome business again.

'Worse than that village down by the Congolese border,' said Roth after we'd carried the last corpse inside. 'The hyenas took care of the bodies there.'

'Take what you want,' I said to Di Luca, as I stuffed more cartons of ammunition into my side and breast pockets and grabbed another couple of magazines for good measure too. 'We're done here. My guys are about to blow the cave.'

He and I waited outside while Roth helped Müller finish setting the charges.

We stared at each other warily. A lot of big decisions had been made so far today, and all at high speed.

'Are you leaving now too?' he asked. 'If you really want the loose ends tied up then I need help to catch Rizzo. I want to put him in front of the Cupola to make sure he takes the blame for what happened here, not us.'

I forced myself to care. I couldn't hide away for the rest of my life because of what I'd done back at the ambush site.

'So you're not going to kill him, like you said you were when we were waiting up the hill?' I asked cynically.

'It's in my family's interests,' he said. 'He needs to persuade the big bosses to stop this getting any worse than it already is. You said it yourself half an hour ago.'

'What's the odds someone will send Rizzo to the house to see what happened?

Di Luca thought about it for a moment.

'They might. I know a hidden spot where we can watch from the side of the gorge. There's a goat track which leads right on up to the top if we need to get away.'

'How do you know this place so well?' I asked.

'Rizzo and I used to play here as boys. Just after the time Caterina was born, I think. Before his family got seriously rich and bought the rest of the valley. Before they became too good for us.'

'Okay, we're ready,' said Müller as he emerged with Roth from the cave.

'Do it.'

He ran back inside, appearing again in under a minute. Di Luca and I stepped well back.

He sneered. 'It's on a three-minute timer.'

We waited some more and then came a dull boom and a rumble of falling rock from inside the cave. A cloud of dust rolled out of its mouth and across to the other side of the river. I tried not to dwell on the eleven entombed *mafiosi* inside – Di Luca's estimate had been out by one.

I made a final decision and announced it to the soldiers. I didn't much like it, but I didn't really have a choice.

'I'm staying in Italy to finish this business and to make sure you get away from here cleanly,' I said, adding the second part for Johannes' benefit.

'One of you drive their truck back to the start of the zig-zag. We'll get rid of all of the vehicles later. Leave your overalls with the truck and I'll get rid of them too.'

Müller bridled at the last-minute instructions and yet more time used up from his safety margin.

'A fascist coup? You're sure of that? Here in Italy?' he asked.

'I'm the local liaison. That's what it is.'

Roth looked at me in a silent appeal to hurry up and finish so they could go. I nodded and the three of us shook hands.

'I'll make sure the people back in Germany know what you did,' I added as an afterthought. I got a grudging half nod of acknowledgement from Müller, then they turned and left.

Di Luca and I drove back to the house in his car. He parked and we went round to the rear to find where the goat track started under the trees. We climbed up the steeply winding path, AKs slung over our backs. I'd charged all four of the magazines I now owned and the three spare ones in my side pockets clanked with each step that I took.

Once we were high enough, we paused to look down the valley along the twists and turns of its course. Almost a kilometre away, Roth was just getting back into his own truck. Like good Germans they'd parked the Mafia's flatbed neatly on the verge, exactly parallel to the track.

I'd much preferred to have been driving home over the hill with them. It was early afternoon and I had a raging thirst, not helped by all the dust and gunpowder fumes I'd breathed in today.

We turned a corner and carried on a little way up the track until it flattened out where an ancient fault-line formed a kind of shelf on the side of the mountain. The feature was a few metres wide, a couple of bushes clinging to the crevices. From up here we could watch the valley floor, hidden from sight of anyone down below.

'This will do,' I said. Peering over the edge of the cliff, the whole of the house and the gravel area in front of it was visible, Di Luca's car parked off to one side. He and I each found a rock to sit on, the AKs resting across our laps.

'What did you hear in town? What made Rizzo betray his own family?' I asked innocently.

Di Luca shrugged. 'All I know is that he turns up in Ragusa on Tuesday night, says he knows when a big arms shipment is due to take place and starts asking around for certain kinds of people to help him intercept it, offering them a cut.'

'Did he know he'd end up with your family's rivals?'

'We'll need to ask him.

'How did you come to hear of this?'

'The Saraceno clan put the word out for their associates. Some of them work for more than one of the clans. I went to our family's bar in town, they told me the story and that a crew had set off for here a short while previously.'

'What part did the weapons play in the coup plot? What happens now?'

'So you worked that out for yourself, did you? We don't talk about our business.'

I knew it. How had I guessed, that out of all the possible permutations for a sinister political intrigue in Italy, it would be the craziest one which Sophie would be involved with? It still needed corroboration, though.

I eyed up Di Luca, trying to hide my sense of vindication. And I was suddenly feeling a lot better too, at just having been given a new justification for what I'd done at the ambush site. A coup was way worse than mere terrorism. A deadly serious, anti-democratic act, I told myself. I also told myself that the *mafiosi* probably wouldn't have made it anyway.

'Why did the Mafia kick you out of America?' I asked.

'You don't stop asking questions, do you, wise guy?'

I offered him a cigarette. He leant over to take it from me, cupping his hands as I lit it for him.

'We probably shouldn't,' I said. 'The smell might carry or something.'

'This is Rizzo we're talking about, not Tarzan. If no one turns up in the next half hour, I'm going back into town. I need to warn my people.'

'There can't be any Saracenos left to come after them? Not after today?'

He shrugged. He knew better than to take chances, I presumed. By the lack of gunfire after the soldiers' truck crested the rise, I guessed there had been no roadblock at the top after all, despite his earlier caution.

'Did you recognise any of the bodies?' I asked. 'What did you have against the guy whose...' I didn't know the slang word in English.

'The guy with half a pecker? Him? I just felt like it.'

He exhaled a long stream of smoke, daring me to challenge him.

'I knew a couple of the stiffs,' he conceded. 'One was a lieutenant.'

'A *caporegime*?'

Di Luca frowned. 'Who's been talking to you? The journalist?'

I didn't talk about my business either.

'How well did you know Rizzo as a kid?' I asked instead.

Di Luca shook his head in half despair and decided that answering my questions was the path of least resistance.

'We spent some of our summer vacations together, before my grandmother died. After that, the occasional family celebration.'

'How well do you know Caterina?'

He looked at me darkly. 'They're just rumours. But she's too trusting for her own good. Always thinks the best of people. She's only a kid, she's just turned twenty.'

I looked at him sceptically. Twenty was my mother's age when I was born.

'You know me well enough by now. If anything had happened, don't you think I'd have told you? I got kicked out of America for banging the wife of one of the other soldiers. It was that or be killed.'

I raised an eyebrow. 'Won't the husband still come after you over here? For his honour?'

'I killed him just before I left. Problem solved.'

'And how about her?' I asked, fascinated despite myself.

'She moved to Las Vegas.'

We carried on sitting in silence, finishing our smoke.

'Listen,' I said, dropping my stub to grind it into the dust. We could hear the sound of a car descending the zig-zag, the engine note changing as it rounded the hairpins. We scrambled back to the path, then down it a little way to the corner again where we could look along the valley's length.

A black car had stopped just before the ford and two people were walking around the wrecked vehicles lying there. I wondered if they'd caught sight of the bloodstains on the surface of the truck's flatbed. One of the pair might have been Rizzo, but I couldn't tell for sure at that distance.

They got back in and came on up the gorge. If it was Rizzo, he was either incredibly brave or incredibly foolish to keep going, or else someone was forcing him at the point of a gun.

The car slowed down at the collapsed mouth of the cave, just before we lost sight of it behind some trees around another bend.

'Might be Rizzo,' I said.

'Let's go down and take a look.'

'I'll go up to him when we get down there,' I said. 'I was the one he told to wait and meet him here. The blood looks like oil stains on my overalls. You can cover me.'

I reckoned two versus two would be easy after what we'd dealt with so far today.

We arrived at the bottom of the track and waited, watching from the shadows of the trees as the black car pulled up next to Di Luca's coupé. Just before the car stopped I handed over my AK to Di Luca. I really wished the overalls had been designed with an external belt so I could have stuffed the Browning into it to hide behind my back. All I could do was make sure that the studs of my side pocket were undone.

Rizzo and his companion got out, slamming the doors and started looking around them.

The walk across the gravel up to the car was only a few metres but seemed to take forever. Rizzo turned toward the sound of the crunch of my boots, bitter disappointment flooding his face when he saw who it was.

His companion came around the car to join him by the driver's door, a pistol held by his side. Rizzo walked up and kissed past each of my cheeks, like the Judas he was.

'What happened here?' he asked brazenly, even managing to drop a hint of manufactured concern into his voice.

'Tell him to drop the pistol,' I said. 'No one will get hurt.'

To encourage Rizzo's friend, Di Luca emerged from the shadows where the trees ended and fired three times with his AK into the gravel near the *mafioso's* feet.

Rizzo said something in Italian to his companion, maybe an imprecation to lower his weapon. Instead, the other guy jumped back in the car, started the engine, and drove off in a cloud of dust. Di Luca didn't fire again. He walked slowly over to us, his rifle held at the hip, mine slung over his back.

He stood in front of Rizzo for a couple of seconds, looking him calmly in the eye.

'*Ciao cugino.*'

Then he hit his cousin on the side of the head with the butt of his rifle. Rizzo went down immediately, blood flowing profusely from his scalp.

Di Luca swung his foot back ready to follow up with a kick.

'No,' I said. 'Not yet. Not here.'

He brought his foot down short, scuffing the gravel to strike Rizzo where he lay moaning, curled up with his hands clasped over his head.

'Up you get,' I said, hauling him to his feet. I opened the passenger door of Di Luca's GTA, released the catch to pull forward the seat and forced Rizzo into the back.

'What now?' I asked Di Luca, once I'd slammed the door shut on Rizzo.

'I'll take him to the house of a lieutenant in a neutral family I know. Hold him there while the bigger bosses decide what to do.'

'How long will this all take?'

'Some days. Why do you care? You've helped me catch him. You're done now, if you want to go. Take their truck and get out of here. I'll tie him up and put him in the trunk of my car.'

Di Luca might think this was over for me, but it wasn't. Not for the next twenty-four hours at least, which was how long it would be before I could be confident the soldiers had reached a friendly country.

I had no real idea how me staying was going to help them, but my instinct said to see it through. And I had to make sure that Rizzo didn't somehow shift the blame onto Sophie. Her name needed to be kept out of this calamity.

If I hung around for a couple of days, there was also the chance that I might learn something in passing of what Borghese was planning with the Sicilians. If anyone in the Mafia knew, it ought to be the Regional Commission. Not that I was going to start actively snooping on them, of course. I hadn't abandoned all of my survival instincts.

I put it in terms I thought Di Luca would understand.

'I told you already. I don't want any unfinished vendettas. No new Mafia War spilling over into Germany. If you need me to, I'll back up whatever you say to your people about Rizzo. I can help you bring this thing to an end.'

'You really mustn't like him to want to stay. The Cupola isn't a New York community council, you know. You say the wrong thing, give the wrong impression to them, and you're done,' he said dubiously. I wondered why he was so confident about his own situation.

He handed me back my AK, though, so I'd established some level of trust with that lunatic today.

I stripped off my overalls and rolled them into a bundle before getting into the back of the car with Rizzo. I sat with the rifle on my lap, pointed in his direction, its folding stock now proving its worth in the tight confines of the Alfa.

Not that I really needed to go to all that effort, because Rizzo just sat there quietly stunned. The bleeding from his head seemed to have stopped and his face was drained of colour, but probably more from the dawning realisation of the enormity of what he'd done. He was a long way from the Berlaymont now, that was for sure.

We bumped back down the track and past the pile of rubble at the choked entrance to the cave. I got Di Luca to stop at the bottom of the hill.

'We should try to burn their van. How about the truck? I also need to get rid of these,' I said, holding up the overalls.

'Throw them in the river. Leave the truck.'

'I need to burn them, and my guys' overalls too. And I need to get that.' I nodded to my holdall which the soldiers had left by the side of the track.

I jumped out and stepped up onto the flatbed of the truck to retrieve the other overalls. The wood was stained with dried brown streaks where the bodies had been dragged over it.

I rapped the truck's fuel tank and fired a round just below the level of the diesel with the Browning. I held the bundle of garments to the puncture until enough fuel had glugged out to soak them thoroughly, then walked down the riverbed to the van, tossing the sodden mass inside the cab up onto the remains of the seats. I took a step back and struck a match.

Di Luca got going again, crunching over the broken window glass and spent casings as we drove past the ambush site and on up to the ridgeline.

Once we were back on the main road, Di Luca put his foot down. As we wound our way across the island's dusty interior, now climbing, now descending, the canyon was soon left far behind us. Not far enough behind, for my liking. After a good three or four hours he turned off the *strade statali* and drove on up onto a windswept plateau. Rizzo sat in deathly silence for the whole journey. When I looked across at him from time to time, he was staring out of the window with hollow eyes.

What I thought of as the Mafia safe house was actually a dilapidated farm, a kilometre away from where the broken pasture ground began to rise again to a thin forest of scraggy trees. A couple of mouldering broken-down cars from the time before the war rested on their rims in a courtyard. Incongruously, in its centre stood the stone basin of a dry fountain, choked by tendrils of ivy. Off to one side under a rickety lean-to, a broken-down cart rested on its shafts. We seemed to have stepped back thirty years in time.

We got out and I slung the AK over my back. Rizzo definitely wasn't running away from here. Someone who was either the farmer or the landowner came out to kiss Di Luca on the cheeks. A proprietor surely. A farmer would be working outdoors, unless it was a mealtime.

We all trooped in. Rizzo and I were shown to the

kitchen for some refreshment. Di Luca disappeared elsewhere inside the house to confer with the owner and explain why we were here.

The kitchen was the domain of the women. A matriarch type dressed in black, of similar age to the man, ruled this part of the house. She directed a younger, middle-aged woman wearing the same style of black dress, who despite being treated like a servant had a look of quiet determination underneath.

They didn't resemble mother and daughter, and the matriarch sounded none too pleasant in the way she spoke to the younger woman - although that in itself didn't prove they weren't related. She snapped at the other to place bread, cheese and wine on the table and invited us to sit.

No one reacted to the sight of the AK lying within easy reach on the chair beside me, so I guessed they were used to hosting men on the run with guns.

I ate and drank properly for the first time in almost a day, but Rizzo sitting opposite me had no appetite. He sat silently, taking the occasional sip of the rough red wine. I wondered if he was trying to work out his next move. He should have jumped in the car and escaped with his companion at the house, but he'd missed his chance.

Di Luca bounced back into the room and gave the serving woman a look I didn't like.

'Time to take him upstairs and lock him up,' he said, staring grimly at his cousin.

At this, Rizzo looked even more sorry for himself and gave a kind of groan. He opened his mouth to say something but then thought better of it.

We prodded Rizzo into motion and took him to a room on the first floor with a view over the rear of the property. It wasn't a typical guest room though, because it had bars on the window and a bolt on the outside of the door.

'You're still alive, unlike the other schmucks you sent to do your dirty work today,' Di Luca said to Rizzo, as he pushed him down to sit on one of the two single beds.

Rizzo slumped forward, elbows on his knees, head down and refusing eye contact. We left him, glad to be gone from that picture of misery.

'We're sharing in here,' said Di Luca, showing me to the neighbouring room which was a mirror-image of Rizzo's, also with two single beds, one against each of the long interior walls.

'I'm going to bang Federica tonight,' he said matter-of-factly. 'I need to, after I've killed someone. You can have her afterwards.'

He saw the look of disgust on my face.

'Oh, I forgot. Back at the Rizzos' party with those girls. You're a fag. You can always pretend and take her...' I held up my forefinger.

'Shut up.'

He did.

Dinner was the strangest I'd ever had. Even stranger than the solitary meals I'd taken in the East German prison cell last year, over those three days when I was waiting on my interrogation to commence.

Each time the unfortunate Federica came in to serve or clear away, Di Luca watched her with hooded eyes. She ignored it, wearing the same stony look that she'd used in front of the matriarch earlier. At the table, the proprietor, his wife, and Di Luca spoke to each other in Italian and I tuned out.

I went to the kitchen and found Federica eating her own meal. One hand chapped from washing was laid on her lap as she ate with the other. Grey was threaded throughout hair that once had been raven.

I mimed serving out an extra portion with the intention of taking it upstairs to Rizzo. She gave me a plate and I spooned out some of the rich meat sauce from a large pot simmering on the stove, taking a piece of bread from the bowl in the middle of the table.

Just as I was climbing the stairs to his room, a car pulled up outside and some new people arrived in through the front door. At least there was plenty of food on the go.

I slid the bolt on Rizzo's door. He was lying on the bed, staring at the ceiling.

'I brought some food,' I announced unnecessarily, laying the plate down on the bed.

'Up you get.'

There was no table in his room, but by the low window was an old bentwood chair. I picked up the plate and carried it across to place on the sill. Then I sat back on the spare bed and watched him heave himself up to go and eat. Somewhat late in the day, I took a swift look around the room for places he could hang himself from.

The food seemed to revive him. That, and us being alone. When he was done eating, he turned in the chair to look at me.

'What have they said?'

'Nothing. Di Luca understands the need to avoid a war. He's going to take it to the Mafia's Regional Commission. They'll decide all our fates. There's a meeting about it downstairs as we speak.'

At least, I guessed that's why the newcomers had arrived.

'Why did you stay? Your people weren't in the valley when I arrived. You could have cleared out with them.'

'Believe it or not, I didn't want Di Luca to kill you there and then.'

'Why? Don't you hate me? I suppose not. You have no reason to be unhappy, none at all,' he added sourly.

I wasn't going to get into a discussion about Sophie in the middle of all of this.

'I stayed out of respect for your family and my concern for what happens to them next because of this vendetta that you've started. The world won't miss eleven *mafiosi*, even if their mothers might,' I added reflectively.

'Help me escape. We'll pay you well.'

'You know that's not the right answer. You know you have to go to this peace meeting and say whatever's necessary to prevent the Saraceno clan from declaring a new war.'

'You're not Italian. You've no idea what's going to happen next. What if I blame it on you, say you were going to betray Di Luca to the Carabinieri, or that you and your guys were going to take the weapons for yourselves and that we only came to stop you?'

I looked at him sceptically. His shoulders slumped and he shrank in on himself. He looked in a state, to be honest. The blood on his scalp had crusted to the same black colour as his hair. His chin was blue with stubble and his clothes were crumpled and stained with sweat.

'Tidy yourself up before tomorrow,' I said, getting up off the bed to take away his plate and fork. After I left, I threw the bolt across hard.

Downstairs, I heard the rise and fall of voices behind the closed door of the main room. The new men who'd arrived earlier were still in conclave. I looked briefly in the other rooms, even though I knew Di Luca would be with the others.

I went outside to the courtyard and sat on the lip of the disused fountain. Above me, as far as the eye could see and beyond, the stars were out in force and the fireflies too. I fingered my pack of cigarettes but left them for now because I had the sense that Sophie didn't like me smoking too much and I thought I should try to cut down.

Sophie. There had been another woman with a Greek name once, a woman for whose honour men had launched a thousand ships and started a war. I wondered what the Mafia would think when they found out about this one. She was my real reason to stay and try to limit the blowback.

Chapter Fifteen

Sicily - Saturday, 26th September 1970

When I woke on Saturday morning, I found that Di Luca hadn't slept in his bed. Yesterday evening we'd agreed a basic schedule for guarding our prisoner, so it was my turn to take him to the bathroom. According to what Di Luca had told me yesterday evening, the Regional Commission was to meet tomorrow afternoon in Palermo.

I slid back the bolt on Rizzo's door and kicked it open, in case he'd had any ideas overnight of jumping us in the morning. But I'd overestimated him because he was still under the covers. To get him moving I gave the leg of his bed a kick too.

'Out of bed Rizzo. Time to make yourself presentable.'

'Is it today?' he asked.

'Can't say. *Omertà.*'

'So they're not telling you anything then, either?' His voice had a faint echo of hope.

I made him pick up his chamber pot and marched him to the bathroom.

'It's got bars in the windows too,' I said. There's soap, but no razor, obviously.'

When he was done, I marched him back. As I was about to leave, he looked up at me from where he was sitting on the bed.

'You'll have no career in Brussels after this. Not if I get away from Sicily.'

'You tried to have me killed, Rizzo. Use your free time today to work out what you're going to say to the Regional

Commission and how much money your father should offer the Saracenos to stop them coming after the rest of your family.'

I bolted his door and wandered downstairs to see what there was for breakfast. Federica was there, scrubbing pans and keeping her head down while she worked, meaning I didn't have to avoid her eye.

Her everyday tormentor bustled in and gabbled something in Italian.

After Federica had been given her instructions for the day, I guessed, the older woman turned to me.

'*Caffe?*'

'*Si, signora. Grazie.*'

She gave a faint smile at my pronunciation although I didn't see how I could have gone very far wrong. Then she clicked her fingers for Federica to do the work.

I didn't know why the younger woman hadn't gone north to Turin or Milan with the rest of them. Maybe she was a widowed daughter-in-law or something. In which case, where were the matriarch's own daughters?

Now Di Luca turned up and bold as brass asked Federica to pour for him. She did so with what was by now her usual reserved sullenness and Di Luca winked at me out of the corner of his eye. I really hoped it was for show and he'd actually gone into Palermo or the nearest big town last night and found himself a willing woman of some description. The guy was still an animal, for all his smooth fast talking.

After breakfast Di Luca went upstairs, saying he was going to speak with Rizzo.

Yesterday, I'd spotted shotguns hanging above the fireplace in the main room, so I went to ask for a cloth and oil to start cleaning my AK and the Browning.

After several fruitless attempts to explain what I wanted, the matriarch fetched her husband. He understood, and I got to work scrubbing off the powder residue as best I could. Not that being in a case for several months or years had stopped the AK from firing yesterday at the first pull of the trigger, but then Soviet weapons were designed to take abuse.

Di Luca arrived back downstairs and watched me with interest.

'Aren't you going to clean yours?' I asked.

'Why don't you do it for me?' he suggested instead.

I gave a shrug. 'There's nothing else to do. What did Rizzo say?'

'He still won't explain why he did it. And we can't ask the people who were with him because they're all dead.'

'I don't know why his family were doing this thing for Borghese in the first place. But I can guess,' I said, trying to divert the conversation away from Rizzo's possible personal motivations for yesterday.

I put the bolt carrier assembly back together, giving myself a few more seconds to think.

'We touched on it yesterday, when we were up on the goat track, waiting for Rizzo to arrive. There's a coup, but it's one which Borghese might only be intending to stage. Not to actually carry out.'

I glanced at him for confirmation. He wasn't giving anything away, but he wasn't stopping me from speaking, either. I carried on.

'Someone in Brussels told me about the De Lorenzo affair from six years ago. It could be like that, the intent being to give the mainstream right-wing politicians a pretext to crack down on the left, under the cover of a threat to the state. Borghese is their tool of choice. But he might simply be doing it for the money, of course - like a mercenary.'

I stopped again to look for a reaction.

'We're having a political discussion,' I said. 'Nothing I've suggested so far is to do with your family's business. Tell me what you think as an Italian,' I prompted.

'I'm Sicilian. No one is Italian.'

'Okay. Tell me then, what do you think as a Sicilian under Italian occupation,' I asked, skating over the assertion that Garibaldi's work to unify the country was incomplete.

'It could be that.'

We had all day, and I'd never get a better chance to probe him.

'Rizzo's father is connected through his manufacturing company to the defence ministry,' I continued. 'Which is where the weapons secretly stored under his factory came from. Unless he acquired the weapons illegally, of course.'

'Not in that quantity he didn't.'

'But no one trusts anyone else. Not really. Even if, or perhaps, because the Italian security services are in on the plot, the old Decima Mas men have decided to buy some extra insurance from elsewhere. This arms transaction is a side deal so secret that they went outside the country to make it happen.'

'Maybe.'

I reassembled the rest of my rifle and checked its action three or four times to make sure it was smooth. I laid Di Luca's weapon in front of me, about to start breaking it down.

'Did you fire this during the actual battle?'

'A few times. But then I got closer and used my knife and pistol. More personal that way.'

I drew back the bolt and looked at the AK suspiciously.

'There's a case stuck in the chamber. What if it was a misfire and the round is still live?'

He shrugged. I shook my head and removed the entire bolt assembly before extracting what turned out to be an empty cartridge.

I carried on with my hypothesis, now on less sure ground.

'Part of the plot is to stage atrocities which will be blamed on the left, or even perhaps the extreme right. The DC establishment doesn't care, they just want an excuse to…' I wasn't sure what came next, so I made something up. 'I don't know. To imprison the leaders of the PCI. To pass emergency legislation, maybe rewrite the constitution so that Italy gets stable governments,' I hazarded.

Di Luca looked sceptical. 'The communists have one and a half million members, the police can't arrest all of them. And the DC have ended up running every government since 'forty-eight,' he said. 'Why would they change a system that works for them?'

Then he added slyly, 'People in Sicily are asking the same questions.'

'But if someone offers your people military-grade weapons, why would they ask any questions at all?' I countered. 'There must be several potential buyers around the world these days.'

Open any newspaper and you could almost guarantee to find a report of yet another terrorist attack. Everyone was at it. The Palestinians had hijacked no less than four airliners all on one day at the start of September.

'Worth a lot to the right buyer,' Di Luca agreed. 'Especially if they're imported from another country and are unknown to local law enforcement.'

Like into America from Italy, I'd bet. I was also professionally curious as to the hard currency value that someone like Schalck-Golodkowski would place on the inventory which the soldiers were bringing back to Berlin.

'That's what I think so far,' I concluded.

'Rizzo said before, and again just now, that you'd only ever worked for the EEC. He says that if you do any private work on the side, it's not with the German Mob. He also says that you've been to East Germany and have family there.'

'He's clutching at straws to divert people from his own guilt. I grew up in Hamburg, that's where my home is. And that's where I know my crew from.'

But now I was getting worried.

'Which organisation in Hamburg do they come under

the protection of, then?'

'Do I ask about the details of your guys' business? I hadn't even heard of the Saracenos until yesterday.'

'I'm not sure I like that answer. There'll be some questions for you tomorrow too.'

'From the Cupola?'

'Don't be stupid. You're not getting sight of them around a table. Someone else will question you.'

'Am I being questioned or am I there to argue the case for a truce between the parties?'

'You helped me out yesterday in the valley when the chips were down, even though you could have run away. You had the right ideas too, about respecting the bigger picture here. That's why you're on this side of Rizzo's door and not the other. But you need to curb your curiosity to stay on the one without the locks.'

I recognised sound advice when I heard it. It was probably excessive curiosity about the workings of the world which had got De Mauro into trouble. Anyway, *omertà* or not, maybe I'd already learned enough in Sicily from Di Luca to give Johannes something extra for his report, on top of the samples. No hints that the CIA were behind whatever Borghese was planning, though, which was what Johannes really wanted to know.

The rest of the day dragged on. Di Luca paced around like a caged tiger when he wasn't cheating at cards. He was giving Federica the eye again when our paths crossed and she wasn't liking it, looking back at him with a hard set to her mouth.

As for myself, by the end of the day I just wanted to get through tomorrow and get back to Sophie. I really hoped it had all been worth it. If Johannes hadn't got enough useful intelligence material to at least come good on his assurances over Karin, then I was all out of ideas for what to do next.

We ate as five at dinner, with Federica joining the elderly couple, Di Luca and me, as I guessed she normally did when no one else was there. She frowned at Di Luca's sly glances during the meal, but her resistance was only encouraging him. I wondered if he relished the hunt just as much if not more than the final entrapment.

Then it was my turn again to take Rizzo's food up to him. And possibly my last chance too, for me to quiz him on the details of Borghese's plans, and how he and his father fitted into them. I didn't plan to confront him over his half-hints that I had more than a personal family connection to East Germany. I would just brazen it out tomorrow in front of the Regional Commission's representatives.

I hadn't seen Rizzo since this morning and he'd taken a definite turn for the worse, shrinking back as I entered the room.

'Have you come to do it?' he asked nervously. 'Di Luca said it wouldn't be him.'

I shook my head in contempt.

'I've come to bring you dinner, not a bullet. What has he been telling you all day?'

I now suspected that when Di Luca had been going upstairs from time to time today, it had been principally to drip poison in his cousin's ear. Out of boredom probably.

'He said the Saraceno clan wants revenge. He said that the Commission had De Mauro tortured for several hours before he died. With the same techniques that the Decima Mas used on their own prisoners during the war.'

That didn't sound like much fun.

'I don't know if Di Luca was being serious,' I said neutrally. If Rizzo didn't want to be in fear of his life right now, then he shouldn't have tried to have had me killed along with Di Luca and my men.

'You need to get a grip on yourself. How are you going to keep your mother and sister out of this tomorrow if you don't? Eat up.'

Rizzo shook his head and shuddered. But I made him sit and eat by the windowsill again. Maybe that was why there was no table, so the prisoners had to look out at freedom as they ate. He picked at his food, chewing slowly, but I was happy to wait.

'If things go badly for you tomorrow, how can I help the rest of your family?' I asked.

'Why would you do that?'

'Because I have a mother too. And your father asked me to watch out for your sister at the party, to keep Di Luca away from her.'

He looked embarrassed. I guessed he was remembering how else they'd planned to distract Di Luca that evening.

'How can you help them?' he asked sceptically.

'You tell me. How deeply has Borghese got your father into this thing? This political plot?'

He chewed his lip and ran his fingers through his hair. Then he mumbled something I couldn't make out.

'What?' I asked.

'I don't fully know myself. It started in the early summer. He had some meetings in Milan and Rome. There was talk of a political demonstration to shake Italy out of its stupor, make them realise how seriously we should be taking the threat from the left. A spectacular event.'

'What, like the train derailment or the Piazza Fontana bombing?'

'Bigger than that.'

'Involving foreigners? American foreigners?'

'Don't believe all the stories you hear,' he said.

'Who else in Brussels knew?'

His eyes narrowed and a faint smile played on his lips. No loose tongue there when it came to Sophie and her involvement.

'And you agreed to go along with this? That's not your nature, Giovanni. I know you, I heard you in Rome talking about how we at the EEC had to set an example.'

His mouth dropped open for a second. Maybe he wasn't expecting even a modicum of sympathy right now, after a day of speaking with Di Luca.

'I knew it was on the fringes.'

'And the Mafia? Didn't that give you a clue as to just how illegal this was?'

'They came later. It was too late to back out at that stage.'

It didn't stop him making a pact with the Devil and the Saracenos yesterday though.

'So what can I do for your family? What are we going to tell the Regional Commission?'

'It's not them you're trying to protect.'

I looked coldly at him.

'Everyone's caught up in this now,' I said. 'Me too.'

'No. I'm not going to help you, or anyone else,' he said with more than a hint of malevolence.

'Anyway, you don't deserve help. Who was it that you killed? The man that you told us about in my father's study the day of the party?'

I looked back at him, my face set in stone. So much for my showing off to Di Luca. That was the last time I'd tell anyone anything about what I did.

'Was it Ernst von Barten?'

Gott rette mich vor den Folgen meiner Sünden.

I looked around the mean room with the bars in the windows and the gaps in the floorboards, the cracks in the plaster and the greasy marks on the wall behind the bed where several people must have leaned back over the years. What a way to spend your last couple of days on earth. Maybe. To outsiders, Italians could seem erratic. Who knew what arrangement they'd actually come to tomorrow?

I got up to go, collecting his plate and fork.

He looked up at me, his last card played, anticipation now turning to hollow disappointment. His position was so hopeless, he wasn't even worth a reply to an accusation of murder.

'Does she ever speak of me?' he asked faintly.

I slowly shook my head. 'No, not at all. Which, to be fair, still shocks me somewhat. You didn't deserve that from her.'

As I opened the door to leave, he was sitting slumped forward onto his elbows. If ever there was a picture of utter despair and brokenness, he was portraying it now.

I took Rizzo's dinner things back down to the kitchen.

Federica was standing at the sink washing up. She took Rizzo's dirty plate from me to put by the side with the others. I really wished I knew enough Italian to tell her to say 'no' if Di Luca tried to inveigle her into bed tonight. But maybe she didn't care either way and I would just be interfering.

Speaking of the Devil, just then the man himself wandered in and stood by the table in the middle of the room.

'What took you so long upstairs?' he asked suspiciously. 'Are you cooking up something with Rizzo? Some kind of story for you both?'

'What have you been saying to him all day?' I retorted. 'He's completely despondent, he's in no fit state to be coherent tomorrow.'

'It's none of your business how he performs.'

'After all this, they'll still be family, you know. I thought that was important in your tradition?'

'Do you remember what he laid on for us yesterday? What's the point in family ties if that's what your relations do to you?'

Maybe he had a point, and it was me who had the fixation with the idea. After all, I was the one running around Europe trying to undo the consequences of decisions which Karin had taken for herself. Ones for which she knew the risks full well.

'I don't know. I don't have much family.'

'You're not family, but as I said to you earlier today, you got me out of a tight spot yesterday. But, again, don't push me, otherwise you'll find out what happens once mutual interest ends.'

All through this exchange Federica continued to wash up, stacking the soapy dishes on the rack. I glanced across to her. From the back view, all the domestic chores clearly kept her in trim. Not that Di Luca needed much incentive.

I shook my head to clear the thought. 'I'm done for tonight. I'm going up.'

Di Luca didn't appear in the room again that night and I began to wonder if I was the one going crazy and not Rizzo. Maybe I'd misunderstood what was said when we arrived and Di Luca actually had his own room elsewhere.

The night was still warm and I couldn't sleep. Neither could Rizzo. Through the wall I could hear him pacing up and down his room and rattling the shutters of the barred window. Later, he started kicking the door, the racket interspersed with occasional thumps of his fist on the plaster.

I endured the performance for a while, but it was the sound of weeping which finally made me get up and go to his room. I took the Browning along because I was dealing with a desperate man. However, when I drew back the bolt and opened the door, the only thing trying to overpower me was the smell emanating from his chamber pot in the corner.

Rizzo looked up at me from where he was lying curled on the bed like a beaten dog, tear streaks on his face. I couldn't believe this was the guy whom Sophie had exclusively paired off with for over a year. He looked to be almost beyond help. But then, by the end of my trip to Ireland, so was I. Just not with the histrionics.

'Talk to me,' I said gruffly.

He uncurled and cautiously sat up, back against the wall, knees tucked up under his chin.

I nodded to reassure him. He stared back, the wariness fading a little.

'Tell me what you need to say,' I said again.

He sighed, then took another deep breath before finally forming the words.

'After she and I spoke at lunch on Sunday, I thought some more. I went to find her on Monday night at the drinks reception after the ministerial accession meeting that day. I took her to one side and told her you were no good for her. Even though I knew how she would react.'

We both understood. No one could gainsay her once she had set her mind on something. Her stubbornness was a strength and a weakness. An image came to me of him in a corner of one of the upper-floor meeting rooms at the Berlaymont, stammering out his piece while she impatiently glanced at her watch. Her hangers-on giving both of them sly, knowing looks from across the room as they silently celebrated his downfall.

'True love is prepared to sacrifice itself for the other person. By telling her what I did, I knew I was killing any hope that what we had together up to that point would survive. But I was prepared to do it for her sake, to save her from you.'

In vague terms it was almost Christian. Unconditional love which was just that, given selflessly, without expectation of a reward. Love which cost everything.

I was taken aback, and a little ashamed now of my own brusqueness towards him since his capture.

The feeling got worse as he continued to speak.

'But if you truly love someone, you have to be willing to sacrifice yourself for them. Otherwise, how can you ever say that you loved them?'

I frowned, wondering now if I'd fully understood the implications of what I'd said to Sophie as we lay together afterwards on the sofa in her office. Would I have been prepared to go as far as Rizzo had done? But how could it be love if she didn't love him back? Or if she didn't love me back.

I sat down on the bed opposite him, my back against the wall too.

'You're worried about tomorrow, but it's not a foregone conclusion. If it was, Di Luca would have shot you there and then in the canyon. I know, because I saw him kill other people in cold blood.'

Strictly speaking it was a lie, for Di Luca had only started to torture his rivals to death. Only one person had shot the wounded in the valley yesterday, as far as I knew.

'You don't know them. I keep telling you that. Nothing can save me now.'

'You're being melodramatic. There's always hope.'

'Not for me. I don't have anything to live for anyway,' he concluded mournfully.

I pursed my lips. Being a Good Samaritan was harder work than it looked.

'You're Catholic, right? Don't you take any comfort in that?'

'I go to Mass from time to time, but only to keep my sister quiet.' A new sadness crept into his voice.

'Well then, you know that God can save you, even if you die,' I said, trying a more robust approach.

He frowned. 'How do you mean, save us if we die?' he asked slowly, more interested now, or at least more distracted, which was already better than the state I'd found him in.

I ploughed on with the catechism.

'You know - the body dies, but the soul carries on. Either in heaven or in hell. But true repentance from your sins can save you. The belief that Jesus Christ has paid the punishment for those sins can save you.'

There was a sharp intake of breath and a bitter look from him at the mention of the name.

'Who do you think you are to preach at me? Sitting here, as today turns into tomorrow.'

There was new loathing for me in his eyes. Some fear

and some guilt, too - a cocktail of the human condition. But maybe the words had woken something else inside him at that moment. Just underneath, I sensed it trying to break through the anger. That most precious of emotions - hope.

Hope. Sometimes foolish and forlorn, but so necessary to sustain life. And right now, the broken man before me, his fear and shame stinking out the room, needed it badly.

He licked his lips, weighing something up.

'I asked them, if possible, not to kill you right away. I asked them to bring you back to me so I could watch them cut off your balls and stuff them in your mouth, just like the Algerians did to the French soldiers. I promised them a bonus if they did.'

No wonder the SDECE might have decided to take revenge on Enrico Mattei, and no wonder the war had left a poisonous legacy at the agency, as Kramer had said.

'I wanted to make sure that if Sophie refused to have me, she couldn't have you either. What does God say to that?'

Time slowed. Above all I felt pity for him, at how much he'd hopelessly invested into one person. And for all her strength of self-belief, one who was still a frail, selfish human being.

'Ask Him yourself. But I forgive you. I've done worse. I've no right to hate you.'

'How can you say that?' he said angrily. It was like he needed my hate to feed off, but I was denying it to him.

I shrugged. 'I've been forgiven, how can I not do the same?'

I wasn't completely certain about the theology, but then there was a lot I was falling short on these days in that area. Rizzo frowned, trying to work it out for himself.

'But ultimately, it's not me or Di Luca or the Saraceno clan you need forgiveness from,' I said.

'There's no priest here in this room to hear my confession and give absolution.'

'Then you have no option but to get on your knees and ask for it.'

He shook his head. 'This is heavy stuff, the night before my execution. I won't grovel to anyone or anything.'

'Then you will die.' I felt like adding 'you arrogant bastard,' but refrained.

I got to my feet. 'You have the rest of the night to think about it and to pray if you wish. No one is stopping you. Only your pride.'

He looked at me with deep, dark eyes, calm for the moment as he chewed this over.

Some impulse, maybe a desire to show him the opposite of pride, prompted me to go to the corner to pick up his chamber pot, even though I had to avert my eyes from the foul-smelling contents as I did so. He watched me, puzzled, as I left the room. I locked the door behind me, went to the bathroom, and wondered what to do next.

Leaving it for Federica in the morning was the obvious option, so I trotted back to my own room, remembering that I'd seen one there. As I opened the door, I wondered who I'd find inside, but it was as empty as it had been the night before. I found a clean pot under the bed and returned to Rizzo.

He was lying face-down on his bed again, weeping inconsolably. I pushed the pot under the other bed with my foot and left him, for there was nothing more I could do for him.

In my own room I stared at the ceiling as the sobs in the next room faded away. His question troubled me, whether I loved Sophie enough to abandon her, if that was what it would take one day to save her.

My mind went back to an East German interrogation room in 'sixty-nine, a typed confession lying before me, ready for my signature. I had been faced with a choice back then: to sacrifice my future in order to save her from what Johannes had hinted might be happening to my cousin in jail right now. Sophie would never know the decision I'd been faced with. I hadn't told her then and nor would I now. My pride wouldn't let me.

Nor would I stoop to proving to the mournful Rizzo my worthiness for her, as he wallowed in what sounded like self-pity but what I hoped for his sake was the occasional sob of true repentance next door.

Rizzo was the moth who had fluttered before Sophie's flame. In Brussels, he'd taken on the self-appointed task of trying to warn off the others. But he himself had spent too long there, drunk too deep of that draught, and had destroyed himself, as well as the eleven men who'd died in the canyon yesterday.

I wondered if Sophie would ever understand that either.

The thought occurred as I drifted off, that I should really have tried harder to probe him as to why she'd got herself involved in what seemed like a profitless venture for her. I doubted she'd done it out of loyalty to a friend, based on what I'd seen of the man underneath tonight.

Chapter Sixteen

At ten o'clock a car arrived for Rizzo to take him away.

I thought, when the moment came, he would be despairing or in fear. But as he got into the back, he seemed to have accepted whatever was to be in store for him today in Palermo.

I'd taken it upon myself to make sure he shaved and washed properly before he faced the outside world again. When I'd gone upstairs with his breakfast, neither of us brought up the night just past. He was calm, but I still watched him carefully while he scraped at his face with a spare razor.

Di Luca told me we were to ride together, so I put my holdall in the boot of his car, the guns hidden under my spare clothes.

'The Commission will speak with me first,' he said, forgetting to use its slang name, 'while someone else, one of their advisers, speaks with Rizzo. Then that same person will speak with you.'

Di Luca didn't seem that bothered about the loss of the weapons, so I guessed the Mafia weren't immediately out of pocket on this shipment. If I was them, keeping it quiet would be my main concern. We had the same mutual interest there.

Keeping quiet was easy this morning anyway. One of the men who'd arrived with the car for Rizzo joined us in the back of Di Luca's GTA which put a dampener on conversation for the rest of the trip. Bodyguards tended to do that.

We'd been staying further from Palermo than I realised, for it was almost lunchtime before we arrived at the premises of a law firm on the outskirts. I knew it was run by lawyers by the brass plate listing the names of '*Avvocato*' this and that on the outside and by the quality of the furnishings on the inside.

We split up. I was shown into someone's office to wait, while the main meeting got underway. I waited, then waited some more, my apprehension rising as the hours passed. I got out my Italian primer again and started memorising the vocabulary at the back as a distraction. I skimmed the grammar section as well, and the excessive number of tenses which Italians seemed to use. I guess they needed them for all the talking they did.

I also tried to think of some lines to take in front of the Regional Commission's representative, to explain my involvement with Rizzo. I didn't know what story he'd be telling them, and I suspected I'd be improvising before the day was done.

A receptionist earned her Sunday overtime pay by bringing in coffee - the good stuff - and small biscuits too. Not so hospitable was the way she locked the door behind her when she left.

In the late afternoon I eventually heard muttered words outside the door and Di Luca appeared to collect me. I buttoned my jacket as I walked down the corridor to meet my fate, just as I'd seen Spinelli doing on his way to confront Sophie and Rizzo.

Herr, lass mich Sizilien überleben, beschütze die, die ich liebe.

The room where I was to be questioned had a polished wooden table in the centre and low fitted cabinets down one side. It looked like an executive boardroom, reminiscent of where I'd met Schalck-Golodkowski at the Ministry's business office in Luxembourg. Not at all like the gangsters' den you might expect to see in a B-movie about Prohibition in Chicago.

Two men were already sitting there. One of them was in his sixties, at a guess, and at the far end from the door, a younger man in his late thirties, silent and unsmiling.

The older man came around the table, heavy jowled, oak tanned and wearing heavy thick-framed glasses. Somewhat disconcertingly, his mouth seemed permanently turned up in an impish smile. The smile of a shark.

'So, you're the Kraut. Di Luca has told me all about you. Rizzo has too,' he said in a rasping East Coast accent. He shook my hand the whole time he spoke and didn't let go afterwards. Instead, he carried on standing there, with both his hands firmly clasped over mine.

I inclined my head, discomforted as he no doubt intended me to be, but also somehow strangely eager to confide in him.

'My name is Oskar Lenkeit. I come from Hamburg in West Germany, but my father was Russian.'

There, that threw them, as I thought it might.

'A Russkie, eh? So that makes you a Commie?'

He finally let go of my hand and I took the chance to shuffle half a step back.

'It makes me a German. I never knew my father.'

Di Luca hadn't bothered waiting before sitting down at the opposite end of the table to the third guy. He fiddled with an unlit cigarette, turning it over and over in his fingers, tapping each end alternately on the rosewood.

'Street kid, huh? But I forget myself. Forgive my lack of manners,' the older man said, now holding his hand to his heart.

'I am Italian-American. My own father, God rest his soul, was from Sicily, but I was born and grew up in the great city of New York.'

'The Rockaways don't count,' interjected Di Luca.

The older man merely grinned.

'But in my retirement, *stronzetto*,' he said, glancing at Di Luca, 'I've returned to the old country where I now advise the men of my tradition. I'm their international political consultant. A kind of gentile Henry Kissinger, if you will.'

I inclined my head again. He might have forgotten his manners, but he hadn't remembered them to the extent of giving me his name.

He returned to his seat, clapping Di Luca on the shoulder as he walked past.

'Talkative one, isn't he?' he said, addressing the back of Di Luca's head.

Di Luca smiled unpleasantly.

'You want to stay on the good side of Johnny Di Luca, Mister Lenkeit. I retired from my business interests in New York, but Di Luca here had to leave. He upset too many people in the city for no good reason. They sent him back here to learn respect for his elders and to moderate his behaviour.'

'Who's he learning from?' I asked.

'He works for me now, off and on.'

Of course he did. So that was why the Cupola held no fears for him. Di Luca was the enforcer for the Sicilian Mob's foreign affairs adviser, just as Kramer wanted me to be for him. My own hopes began to rise.

'But I've told him. No more stabbing people in the head,' he said, wagging his finger.

'Why was that a problem, especially?'

'Because he did it through their eye sockets. Slowly. It became his trademark.'

Di Luca grinned evilly at me again.

I waited a little more and finally it seemed we were done with the small talk.

'So, Mister Lenkeit, why have you come to our country? And why are you still here?'

The most convincing lie was often the truth.

'I came here for family reasons. Some people placed a relative of mine under an obligation. I came to discharge it on their behalf. The reason I'm still here is to make sure there's no consequences for my family in Germany because this affair didn't turn out as expected. Family always comes first.'

The Adviser pulled a face.

'Di Luca tells me you killed a man who disrespected your mother. I like that, very traditional. Our mothers carry us for nine months in the womb. Not all of us are blessed in marriage, but we all have a mother.'

He got back up to his feet and came around the table again, standing before me and clasping my elbows this time.

'Respect for family and for women is important,' he said in a gravelly voice. 'I kiss you.'

And he did, thankfully only a brush of cheek against cheek. I wasn't sure of the etiquette and whether he expected me to pucker up in return, but it was over so fast I didn't have time to work it out. As he returned to his seat, this time he punched Di Luca hard in the back on the way past.

'And your boys fought off eleven men of the Saraceno clan, I hear?'

'Di Luca charged single-handedly down a mountainside.'

The older man's permanent grin widened further and the wrinkles at the corner of his eyes deepened. I'd bet he was his grandchildren's favourite *nonno* too, the indulgent one who bought them ice cream and never shouted. Not that I knew much about grandparents from personal experience.

'I told you already, Di Luca is a bloodthirsty *pazzo*. But he has a debt to you. We have a debt to you for helping to stop this thing from getting out of control.' He glanced over at the third guy.

Now the shark smile was accompanied by a flash of teeth.

'But I'm also hearing some confusing things about you, troubling things. Things that no one can explain, not even that journalist we spoke to the other day.'

I opened my mouth, ready to say De Mauro's name but Di Luca quickly shook his head at me.

'I speak to Johnny Di Luca, and he tells me you do jobs with the German Mob. I speak to Rizzo, and he tells me you work for the European Economic Community.' The Adviser pronounced it with at least three more double-ues than the name contained.

'So, which is it?'

I pushed back in my chair and crossed my arms. I'd just had several hours to think through my answers. Ones for Italy, birthplace of *braggadocio*.

'The EEC's agricultural budget is the same size as the US space programme. You work it out.'

Di Luca opened his mouth, letting it hang for a brief second.

'Okay. We get it,' said the Adviser.

'So where do you fit in?' asked Di Luca.

I shrugged. 'We're a powerful organisation and just like other such organisations, we attract our share of enemies.'

The pair of them nodded, the third guy didn't react.

'Which means from time to time we have problems which need to be taken care of,' I continued. 'Taken care of discreetly, in special ways. And when no one else can help, the bosses at the EEC call the department I work for. In turn, we make use of people in your line of business that we know of, from back home in our own countries.'

'Okay, maybe it makes more sense now,' admitted Di Luca.

He gave the third guy a nod.

'*Il bilancio agricolo della CEE ha le stesse dimensioni del programma spaziale americano.*'

The other guy whistled softly. But the Adviser wasn't so easily impressed.

'So exactly which problems does your powerful organisation have, that they need you to call on you to solve them, my Russkie-Kraut friend?' asked the Adviser.

I'd thought of a story here too, but wasn't quite so sure

of how it would go down with the crowd.

'You need to see the bigger picture. The EEC is organised to ask for contributions, moderate contributions, from each country to provide their farmers with protection. In exchange, we stop the big agricultural concerns in America, Argentina and Australia from operating in our territory.'

The Adviser rocked his head from side to side a couple of times as he mulled this over.

'But these arrangements are delicate, easily upset.' I continued. 'Our European Commission needs to keep the EEC governments in line and stop the national politicians from going behind the backs of the other countries to cut side deals. That's where our special people come in.'

It was all a nonsense of course, for the individual member states had long given up that power of independent action. But no one outside Brussels paid much attention to the details of how the EEC operated. Just how the Commission I worked for liked it.

'So is that why Rizzo recruited you?' asked Di Luca, still trying to make sense of it all. 'He knew what you did at the EEC because you worked there together? But what's this personal obligation placed on a relative that you're talking about now?' he asked in a puzzled voice.

After impressing them at the start with an imagined dollar figure followed by lots of zeroes, I sensed I was losing the room again.

'The personal affairs of my family are just that. But as I told you already, my involvement here has nothing to do with my work at the EEC.'

Di Luca looked at me with knowing eyes. But he didn't know about Karin and the Stasi. I wondered what picture they'd been painting themselves all day today to explain my involvement.

'What else do you want to know?' I asked the Adviser, playing it cool. 'What's going to happen to Rizzo, by the way?'

'It depends on you. This thing that Rizzo did. We need to know it ends here. We don't want you going back to Brussels and taking your revenge on him, whatever form that might be. We want this thing kept quiet at your end with nothing traced back to us.'

If they really wanted things kept quiet, then dead men told no tales.

'I have no vendetta against Rizzo. Or against his family. I want your assurance that no harm will come to them either,' I said peremptorily.

'No consequences for Rizzo in Brussels then, if his family is kept out of it? Either personal or professional? You can promise that?' the Adviser asked, with more than a hint of scepticism.

Like it or not, I had to give the impression of being more important at the Berlaymont than I really was. And unfortunately, only one way came to mind. I took a deeper breath.

'His future in Brussels depends on the people I work for there, and on what I tell them about the thing on the mainland that he's got himself mixed up with.'

'And what thing is that?'

The shark mouth was turned down, now almost to a straight line. I really needed a smoke.

'I heard some things when I was last in Italy. I heard that some people aren't happy with the way things are. They want to change the arrangements here. I need to tell you, out of respect for your desire for peace, that the people in Brussels will eventually hear these same things for themselves. It's the nature of such political secrets to leak out.'

Di Luca gave me the slightest of frowns, but no clear signal to desist like when the ghost of De Mauro hovered around the conversation earlier.

'What will they do about it?' the Adviser asked in a neutral voice. 'These people in Brussels.'

'If any faction in this dispute upsets their business,

they'll make a bigger pay-off to another faction to have things put back the way they were. No matter who in Italy is involved, on either side.' I was improvising for all I was worth now.

Surely the Mafia must realise that whatever threats of violence they made to individual people, they couldn't compete with the combined financial strength of France and West Germany. Especially if it was backed up by people like the SDECE, who had even less respect for the law than he did. Then again, if the CIA were involved, none of that would matter.

The Adviser didn't give any indication that America had even crossed his mind, though.

'So what you're saying is that these EEC guys can pay off an entire government? What with? The protection money they collect from all the other governments?' he asked.

'You could put it that way,' I said, as realisation fully dawned on me too, despite the nearly five years I'd spent in Brussels.

'What a sweet deal.'

He whistled in admiration at the system which Monnet had created and Ernst von Barten's faction had nurtured. I wondered if Spinelli fully understood the vested interests he was taking on in trying to democratise it.

The Adviser seemed to have forgotten all about the weapons and the battle in the canyon for the time being.

'So what do you advise us to do? We're merely men of business, practical men. We understand the limitations of our power.' He cast his eyes to the ground as he said this, but I recognised when someone was fishing too.

I gave him something to reel in.

'In the next two years, the EEC's territory will expand considerably. Four new countries will come under our protection and hand over their contributions. Which means there'll be even more money for us to pay off our friends. But this is a delicate time, the expansion isn't yet settled. For now, our Commission wants everything to stay the way it is. No military takeover in Italy. No takeover by right-wing crazies either. It's bad for our wider business.'

'If they want things to stay the way they are, what incentives can your people in Brussels offer to us? How does this new money you speak of come to Sicily?'

He was sharp - I supposed you had to be in his line of work. But for what that was worth, he hadn't contradicted my suggestions of a coup. Now I'd have to be sharper still.

'Don't be coy with me. You already work the system today, I'm sure. Bribes to officials not to check subsidy claims too closely? Or what do you guys get up to here?'

He didn't insult me with an answer. I had nothing to lose by holding back now.

'Just do the same as every other player in Brussels,' I told him. 'Place people on the inside and make payments to the right EEC officials to get the rules changed in favour of the farmers under your protection. Fix the subsidy rates on lemons, olive oil, that kind of thing. You could use Rizzo for that, if he still has a debt to you.'

There, that was my bit done to save him. He'd end up in the demi-monde of the lobbyists and other players in the CAP racket, trying to find creative ways to bribe Sophie's boss, so that no one would suffer the embarrassment of having to call it by that name. But at least he'd still be alive.

The Adviser raised his eyebrows speculatively and looked over at the third man. Maybe he'd been following after all.

'You're suggesting we act politically and use Rizzo for that? How can he guarantee an outcome favourable to our people?'

I scrambled to work out what he meant by 'politically.' Maybe he merely meant something that wasn't outright criminality. Of course, for some politicians, the labels were interchangeable.

'He can't promise you that on his own. I just said, you

have to place people, lots of people in Brussels who will be your allies. You have to invest for the long term to buy political influence, but you know that already.'

For a moment I feared they were going to suggest I started working for them. Instead, the Adviser gave me a kind of homily.

'Politics is a delicate art. It requires patience. It requires the ability not to do what your impulses tell you, but to wait on the opportune time. Do you know how to do that?' he asked.

'For Rizzo, I will be infinitely patient,' I said. I'm not a *cazzo*, like you said Di Luca was.

All three Italians smirked at this.

'I said *'pazzo'*, which is different,' the Adviser retorted. 'Listen to me. In life you need to keep hold on your instinct for revenge, satisfy it only when you know it won't affect business. And for us, everything we do is for our business, our thing.'

But the longer he spoke, the more it sounded like a lecture to the entire room and not just for my edification.

'And the opposite is also true. If someone, even a friend, makes a mistake and hurts our business, we're left with no choice but to teach them a lesson and hurt them back. Some people, a family in America, in American politics, they learnt that,' he said.

There was only one political dynasty in America that most people had heard of and I guessed he didn't mean the Roosevelts.

But he wasn't done yet.

'Back to this thing which Rizzo did. This affair was personal between you and Rizzo. Very personal, wasn't it?'

The Adviser looked at me shrewdly. 'We got Rizzo to talk in the end. He didn't want to, but Di Luca convinced him.'

'I told him I'd persuade Caterina to do what my grandmother's sister did with his grandfather,' Di Luca smirked.

I shot him a bitter look as I guessed at the degree of persuasion he might use. The Adviser glanced between us.

'So he told us. So finally we learn it was woman trouble that you pair brought to our little island. Eleven men died because you couldn't keep it in your pants.'

'And you believe Rizzo?'

'In our tradition you don't mess around with the women of your business associates.'

'Is that his story?' I said nastily. 'She did what she did willingly, it was her choice.'

He looked me up and down.

'I'm sure she did, if you say so. We're not Italian schmucks. We know more about you than you think. That warning about hurting our business was meant for everyone, including you. I've already said, we acknowledge that you've helped stop this thing from getting out of control. But we need it to stay that way.'

He took a breath.

'And now we're going to recognise the peace that was agreed earlier today between Johnny Di Luca and Enzo Parlatore here from the Saraceno family.'

I looked properly at the third man. He'd been silent the whole time, giving nothing away apart from that one whistle at all the space rockets the EEC could have been sending to the Moon instead of subsidising France's farmers. After that, even his face had followed the code of *omertà*.

'How do we do that?' I asked.

We were driven to a restaurant in the centre of Palermo and waited at the bar. After five minutes, Rizzo arrived too. He was a man transformed, a criminal on death row who'd just received news of his pardon.

The four of us looked at each other. I didn't know about peace between the Di Lucas and the Saracenos, but the expression their representative was giving Rizzo didn't look very peaceful to me. There was a strained silence as we moved from the bar to our table.

That was when I got a real sense of just who I was dealing with. Everyone knew that *maîtres d'hôtel* received special training in obsequiousness, but the Adviser was treated by this one like he was royalty. Or at least as I imagined how those class enemies were treated by their lackeys, good socialist that I sometimes pretended to be.

At dinner, the Adviser told us something of his family and more indirectly, of the things he'd done in America. He only spoke in code: "these people", "their business", which made it hard to follow. But Di Luca laughed along to his boss's jokes and I got the gist.

As the meal progressed and the wine flowed, Rizzo's evident relief turned into a growing confidence and he gradually started to take part in the conversation. But it was awkward all the same. He sat round the table with us, dipping his bread into the olive oil and spooning out the agrodolce from the same pot as his cousin and me. None of the other guests in the restaurant would have known he'd been trying to get almost half the table killed two days ago. Not that the diners were looking our way if they could help it, keen as they were to avoid being noticed by the Mafia men.

Although the Adviser had a fund of stories from a lifetime in America and enjoyed telling them, it meant he ended up doing most of the talking for Parlatore's English wasn't up to much.

I did my bit to show an interest and be sociable. With one eye on the Adviser for help with translation I asked Parlatore about life in Sicily under the fascists. I reckoned he would have been about twelve or thirteen when the war ended.

After a couple of false starts I learnt how Mussolini had been able to suppress the Mafia for a time in the twenties. Apparently, there had been a lot of switching of sides, people donning black shirts of convenience and denouncing rival clans to the authorities to get the

Carabinieri to do the Mafia's dirty work. Everyone around the table seemed to have an opinion on this, even Rizzo the northerner.

The Adviser spoke more proudly of Lucky Luciano, the American mobster released from prison in New York after the war and deported to Sicily as a reward for the support of his crime organisation on the island during the Allied invasion.

'People don't really believe us when we tell them it happened that way. But they don't know the US government the way we do.'

'Are they still playing games in Italy?' I asked, quickly adding by way of smokescreen, 'I thought they threatened to withhold Marshall Aid if the country didn't vote the right way in 'forty-eight.'

The Adviser looked at me sideways.

'Both Italy and America hate communism.'

I backed off crabwise myself.

'And Sicily? Di Luca mentioned the Sicilian separatists to me the other day.' I said, thinking back to the canyon and the list of people he said had made use of the cave in the past.

'We've never caught a break from Rome,' the Adviser explained. 'They gave Sicily its own parliament after the war to keep us quiet, but it has no real power. Italy has always been highly centralised because the Roman politicians don't trust ordinary Italians to run their own lives.'

They weren't the only ones. That had been von Barten's particular obsession too. And once you'd decoded his propaganda, Jan the socialist professor as well.

'The invasion was Sicily's opportunity,' said the Adviser. 'It gave birth an independence movement which lasted until the fifties. We even had our own Robin Hood figure, Salvatore Giuliano.'

'So if you're proud Sicilians, what do you think of Brussels?'

'What do you mean? Why's that relevant?' interjected Di Luca.

'Over time that's where your local government's powers will end up,' I said, eyeing up Rizzo as I did so. 'Any meaningful independence they've given to you in Sicily will be taken away again. The politicians in Rome will simply be there to carry out decisions already made in Brussels. How are you going to exert influence when that happens?'

'Why would the DC leaders, of all people, agree to give up their power in that way?' asked Di Luca 'They've got Italy organised to their satisfaction right now.'

'Because in the DC, just as in every European country, there's a political faction intoxicated with the dream of a New Roman Empire.'

Rizzo said nothing to this but sat there tight-lipped.

I carried on. Spinelli would have been proud of me. 'No more Italy, Germany or France. A chance to start again with a common government. For those in the DC who don't trust Italians, a chance to give the task of remaking Italy and the Italians to someone else.'

'And when will all of this happen?' the Adviser asked sceptically.

Here I faltered, for no one ever knew for sure.

'There's talk of a new EEC federal parliament in Brussels, directly elected by the people from across all of the six countries,' I said instead.

They all laughed, apart from Rizzo.

'The last guy who tried to change Italy ended up hanging upside down from the roof of a garage forecourt in Milan,' said Di Luca.

I wasn't sure why I was bothering trying to warn them. Even to me it sounded far-fetched when said out loud.

Rizzo shook his head, smiling faintly as he did so. 'The EEC is prepared to wait longer than people realise. Longer even than our lifetimes. But they'll win in the end,' he said, finally offering his opinion on the topic.

The cigars and brandy arrived, and the evening wound down. For me, anyway. I guessed how Di Luca intended to spend his, but I was going to cry off any suggestion of a sleazy nightclub. Still, if Rizzo wanted to join his cousin, he was a free agent now.

'We've put you and Rizzo up in the Grand Hotel et des Palmes. It's the best hotel in Palermo, your room has been paid for. It's only a short walk from here and a pleasant evening. Take in a bar on the way back, if you like.'

I eyed up the Adviser and glanced across at Di Luca and Parlatore too, trying to judge their sincerity. He seemed to be saying that after a bloody Friday in the canyon above Ragusa we were all just going to go home to our normal lives, or to whatever passed as normal for the Sicilians. It was fine by me.

'I thank you for your hospitality to a stranger in your city. If you come to Brussels one day, I hope to have the opportunity to pay you the same respect.' The *maître d'hôtel* wasn't the only one who could be oleaginous when needed.

The man himself brought jackets for Rizzo and me, and we stood to leave. The pair of us went round the table shaking hands, Rizzo dug deep into his pockets for a tip. Relief at being allowed to live had made him generous, judging by the amount he tossed onto the table.

As Rizzo was making the *maître d'hôtel*'s day, I glanced at the Adviser. He raised his hand, cigar between his fingers, and beckoned me back.

'I have one more question for you, Mister Lenkeit.'

'Go ahead.'

'For you alone,' he said, looking at Rizzo.

Rizzo shrugged. 'Okay. I'll see you at the hotel, Oskar.'

He was feeling confident. I'd forgiven him, but we weren't on first name terms again. Then again, stranger things had happened over time. First though, he'd have to put aside his suspicion that I'd killed Ernst von Barten.

'What is it?' I asked, sitting down again after Rizzo had

left and disappeared out of sight down the street.

'We heard something else.'

He paused to tap the ash from the end of his cigar, then drew on it slowly, taking his time.

'An East German cargo ship has engine trouble. It's in Catania port for a week. Then suddenly on Friday evening the problem is fixed and the ship sails.'

What else had Rizzo been saying about me today, I wondered?

I shrugged. 'It's like when people confuse Sicilians with Italians. To the outside world we're all Germans.'

Then I grimaced. 'But they're Commies and we love freedom. Two different nations.'

'We don't like coincidences. Not on our territory.'

But Di Luca was looking thoughtful. 'Which German Mob outfit did you say your crew were from again?'

Maybe he'd forgotten that I hadn't. I jutted my chin in the air, the Italian gestures coming more naturally the longer I spent time with them.

'I didn't ask you about your regular day-to-day business today. Out of respect for your traditions. We have traditions too. *Immer Treu*,' I said, throwing out the name of one of our own pre-war criminal gangs.

The Adviser shrugged in a slow, deliberate action.

'I think we've detained Mister Lenkeit here for long enough. Di Luca, be a good host and show him the way back to the hotel.'

As I left, I glanced back through the revolving door to the restaurant. The Adviser and Parlatore were huddled together, speaking solemnly. At least the guarded looks were being used on each other and not on me.

Chapter Seventeen

We walked out into the evening sun as it slanted down into the narrow streets, warming the yellow buildings with a golden glow. Today's work was done and now it was time to pause after the craziness of the past three days.

'How far is it?'

'Not far. No, not far now.'

We turned a corner and in the distance I saw the Grand Hotel. I started to pick up the pace, keen to get to a phone and speak with Sophie.

Then suddenly Di Luca was no longer there. I turned around to see him standing at the entrance to an alleyway a few metres back down the street. He waved to me to return and when I got there, he jabbed his finger down the opening of the narrow passage.

Rizzo was slumped behind some garbage cans, leaning up against the wall and clutching his stomach. Blood was leaking through his fingers and dripping onto the ground. He'd been stabbed elsewhere, a lot of times, but mainly in the limbs and stomach so that he wouldn't die instantly. The thought flashed through my mind that there were eleven wounds.

There was a lot of blood on the flagstones now and I sensed that the end must be near. I crouched down to see what could be done and he reached out to grip my scarred hand with his bloodied one.

But it wasn't that which pierced me to the heart, but rather the weak, broken sobs that told of a bitter injustice. The cruelty of being promised life but given death.

Hearing them was worse than seeing the tears of physical pain which welled up in his eyes and flowed down his cheeks, even as the life force ebbed out of him. Tears of regret for a life with Sophie that might have been, as he looked up at me, his nemesis.

He tried to pull me in closer and croak out something in Italian which I couldn't catch. And then, just like that, he was gone.

I felt a tug on my shoulder. 'Time to go,' said Di Luca. 'Come on, you've seen dead people before.'

Well, I had, but no one that I might have called an acquaintance. And despite what Rizzo had done, I didn't hate him. Maybe he deserved what had just happened, for the sake of the men of the Saraceno clan who'd died. But then so did Di Luca and I, if the Saracenos were being objective about it.

I wiped my fingers with my handkerchief and we made our way back to the street. Di Luca had to push and prod me almost all the way to the hotel.

'I'm easy to find here. I should check in elsewhere,' I protested to Di Luca at reception, still half in shock.

'You're under our protection. From the police and from everyone else. Otherwise you'd be back there, lying next to Rizzo.'

We walked up to my room together.

'What happened?' I asked when the door was closed.

'Work it out for yourself,' he said. 'War was averted and honour was satisfied.'

'Why did they let Rizzo think he was off the hook?'

'It's part of the punishment. We also did it to see what he'd say once he let his guard down.'

'You're sick.'

'We're practical.'

'Who's going to tell his family?' I asked.

'If you fly to Milan tomorrow morning, you can be the first. It's unlikely the police will be that quick, even once they find the body.'

'What do I tell his father? What's going to happen now with the deal he was setting up with your people.'

'You've spent half the day with our adviser. Don't you have the measure of him by now? We won't rush into any decision. I doubt the offer of arms will swing it now, though. If Borghese is still serious about this venture and if he still wants support, then the price has just gone up. You can tell them that for free.'

No wonder he got kicked out of America. Forget his temper, it was his tongue he couldn't control. Unless, of course, they'd planned all this today so as to send Borghese and his gang a message. With me being the unlucky messenger.

He left me and I sat on the edge of the bed with my head in my hands, not really knowing what I was going to say, either to Rizzo's father or to Sophie.

I picked up the phone on the bedside table and dialled internationally.

She answered after three or four rings.

'It's me.'

'Where are you? Where have you been the last few days?'

'Grand Hotel in Palermo.'

'Did it all go to plan?'

'Part of it.' Surely I'd at least salvaged something out of this disaster on the East German side of things?

I carried on. 'But only part. There was a falling out between the two parties here in Sicily. Giovanni's dead.'

There was a long silence at the other end of the line.

'When are you coming back to Brussels?'

'I have to go to Milan first. I have to tell Giovanni's father that his son is dead.'

I had to stop using that word.

'Why you?' she asked faintly.

'I watched him die. I have no choice.'

There was another silence. 'Are you caught up in this? Is anyone coming after you?'

Well, if the entire Regional Commission of the Sicilian Mafia had decided I could live, then the answer was probably no - in Palermo at least. I wasn't so sure about the Decima Mas and their controllers in Rome though.

'Expect me back tomorrow night, if the flight connections work out. Probably late. I can't say more on this line.'

'Okay. Bye then, I suppose.'

'*Auf wiederhören.*'

Better to give her some warning than none. I wondered if she suspected me of having a more direct involvement in Rizzo's death.

I guessed I wouldn't find out until tomorrow or the day after next.

-

I woke at six and took my time shaving. After having been on the go since Thursday evening, I felt a little more human again for having had a night in a hotel.

The previous evening I'd got the front desk to speak with Alitalia and the girl had earned a big tip by cajoling them to get me on the first flight today to Milan. I tipped the concierge too, to make sure she kept hers.

At the airport, I booked on to the afternoon flight from Milan to Brussels. I checked in my bag containing the AK as hold luggage, trusting that I wouldn't get delayed too long by Rizzo's father in Milan and miss my connection. The Browning went into the inside pocket of my jacket during the flight, which wasn't ideal. I should have gone to the leather goods quarter like all the other tourists and got a custom holster. A souvenir from Sicily.

We landed at nine and I made my way to the Rizzos' factory in the outskirts, on the far side of the city. After a long and frustrating attempt to make myself understood at reception, it transpired that Rizzo's father wasn't there today, but instead all the way back in the centre of Milan for a meeting. Eventually, they managed to get hold of someone who spoke German, a younger guy in a blue boiler suit who'd worked for a time in somewhere like Düsseldorf or Essen. With a grim look I managed to persuade him I was here on a matter of life and death and the woman at reception got Rizzo's father on the phone for me.

He gave an impatient 'Who is it?', his voice sounding distorted down the line, not quite human.

'It's Lenkeit. I need to see you, sir. I have some news about the shipment,' I said.

'Why isn't my son calling? Where has he got to?'

'I need to see you about that too.'

There was a long pause.

'Palazzo Rasini, by the Porta Venezia, number twenty-two. Come right away.' Then another pause for a couple of seconds. 'Ask Enrico to drive you there.'

The Palazzo wasn't a palace but rather an Art Deco apartment block. I rang and went up.

Rizzo's father opened the door. Through the hallway I could see some other men, and what I thought was the back of Borghese's head. There was a bark of conversation and just before noon, I hadn't interrupted some social gathering.

He took me through into the kitchen. There was no easy way to say this. I composed my face in what I hoped was a gravely respectful expression.

'I'm very sorry Signor Rizzo.' I took a breath to continue, but he waved me to stop.

He sank into a chair and covered his face with his hands, elbows on the table. I waited while he sat for ten long seconds in silence.

Still holding his hands up over his face he simply asked,

'What happened?'

Where to start? Forget trying to use this tragedy to worm out more details for Johannes about Borghese's plans and who was behind them, how should I tell him human to human?

'The Saraceno clan heard about the shipment. They tried to hijack it and there was a gunfight at the property.'

'A gunfight! Giovanni hardly ever held a gun, he refused to do army conscription.'

I sighed.

'The Saracenos blamed Giovanni for the action. A peace meeting was held yesterday in Palermo and it seemed there was an agreement that the dispute should go no further. But then the Saracenos broke it to pursue their personal vendetta against Giovanni.'

'Why the hell was Giovanni blamed for what they did?'

He looked up at me now, his eyes burning blackly into mine.

I clenched my teeth. 'He tipped them off about the shipment.'

Now Rizzo's father folded his arms on the table, burying his head in them. He began to sob softly. But unlike with Rizzo's midnight tears of sorrow the day before he died, I feared what would happen once his father's head was lifted.

I pulled my jacket together for the comfort of feeling the Browning. It bulged from my side without me intending it to.

Someone came and stood in the kitchen doorway behind me, then quickly left again.

Rizzo's father looked up. There were tear streaks on his face, but he quickly wiped them away with the back of his hand.

'Let's go.'

He led me out of the apartment, down the stairs to the street and round the corner of the building to a park. We walked until he found an out-of-the way spot, where the path ran under the shade of the trees.

Benches had been provided on both sides of the path at that point for promenaders to take a break and reflect on life, but we stayed standing, facing one another across the pavement.

'Why did he tip them off?' he asked coldly. The hardness was back, his eyes as bitter as I'd ever seen in anyone. Looking at him now, I could well believe that Sophie's tales of his alleged wartime atrocities might be true.

'It was his revenge. His girlfriend left him for me.'

'The blonde witch?'

It wasn't the right time. I nodded instead.

'He wanted you dead?'

I looked at him straight in the eye.

'How did he die?' he said grimly.

'After the gunfight, the Mafia held an enquiry. At its conclusion, they said they'd let us both go. But when it came to it, they separated us, made him leave the meeting on his own. Then the Saracenos stabbed him in the street like a dog. I followed and came across him as he lay dying. I held his hand right to the very end.'

His eyes were sullen now, smouldering.

He took a swing at the side of my head. I saw it coming, but thought it best to let him get it out of his system. He landed a real punch though, and I sagged over to the right. I staggered back to sit myself down on one of the benches by the side of the path, head still ringing from the blow. People stopped to stare at us.

He sat down on the opposite bench and glowered at me, watching as I shook my head to try to clear it, his hand still in fists by his side.

'Don't we need to go back up and tell the others?' I asked. 'Before they find out for themselves?'

'I knew that *puttana* didn't love him the way he felt for her. I could have told him not to bother. She's going to drop you too, one day. I know the type. The only person she loves is herself.'

There was nothing I could say to lessen his pain.

I got slowly to my feet and briefly held out my hand towards him, before indicating the way back to the apartment.

'*Signor. Per favore.*'

We went inside, back to the kitchen again, and he left me there while he went to tell his news to the others. I looked thirstily at the bottles of wine on the rack. The smell of cigarettes coming in from the lounge was giving me cravings too.

I heard raised voices and shouts from the other room, as the import of what had happened sank in.

Rizzo's father reappeared in the doorway.

'In here,' he said with a curt nod of his head. Despite the earlier scene in the kitchen and the park, now he was back to looking like someone still in denial.

Borghese was none too pleased when he saw me either. He took me aback by speaking in German.

'*Wo sind meine Waffen?*'

'Out of reach of everyone involved.'

'What do you mean?' he said, looking to his right and left at a couple of equally unsmiling henchmen.

'They're in a cave in the side of a canyon above Ragusa with eleven bodies of men from the Saraceno clan. The entrance is blown. No one's getting in, or out.'

He glowered at me.

'And you're missing a journalist,' I added, out of spite. 'The Mafia told me that they'd interviewed him.'

No one apart from Borghese reacted to this news, they mustn't have understood German.

He switched to English. 'Rizzo. You know of this? That people in Sicily spoke with De Mauro?'

Who else did he think had kidnapped De Mauro in Sicily? The KGB?

Rizzo's father replied in Italian. The conversation went back and forth, and they seemed to forget I was there, apart from the glances when I heard my name mentioned and occasionally a '*tedesco*'. This went on for a few minutes until they appeared to come to a decision.

There was an announcement from Borghese and a few of them got up and left. Rizzo's father stayed. By the sound of the jabbering they'd only got as far as the kitchen. It surely didn't take all of them to refill the percolator.

The Prince turned to me and reverted to German.

'De Mauro is the second person we've lost so far. The first one developed a conscience, went for a walk with his dog, and never came back.'

I glanced at Rizzo's father, but he wasn't giving anything away.

'Make sure you're not the third. Whatever you saw or heard the past few weeks, you forget it now. *Verstanden?*'

'Of course.'

He pursed his lips and looked at me shrewdly.

'You told me before, that your family were refugees from eastern Germany and that you want to pay back the Soviets?'

'More than you know.'

He nodded his head slightly.

'I understand something of that. At the end, it wasn't the Americans we were fighting but Tito's communist partisans in the east, in Istria.'

'You held them off in your eastern territories, we didn't. Brandt finally signed our land away to the Soviets in Moscow last month.'

But the Italians hadn't saved Istria, not really. As Spinelli had said at our first meeting, only the city of Trieste had remained Italian after the war.

'We did what we had to do,' he said. 'And in Alto Adige too, four years ago.'

I frowned in confusion at the name. Rizzo's father

spoke up, but in English.

'South Tyrol. We ran a campaign against the German-speaking locals there who were agitating for a return to Austria.'

Well, there was an irony. Earlier this summer Skorzeny had told me the story of how Hitler had personally selected him for the mission to rescue Mussolini from imprisonment by Italy's former fascist government, pending his handover to the Allies. Skorzeny the Austrian, chosen by another Austrian for the operation, because of what he'd said about the restoration of South Tyrol to its former home.

'What do you want?' I asked Borghese.

'I want your silence. But I also want you to understand the seriousness of the threat we face here in Italy today from the communists and the other socialists. The left wing of the DC can't be trusted not to come to an accommodation with the PCI, and one day bring them into government.'

'The DC's mainstream has managed to keep the PCI away from power so far,' I replied.

'The PCI's share of the vote continues to grow. Their party membership has stabilised and is no longer falling. Italy can't afford to take any chances.'

'One and a half million is a lot of people to deal with. What can I do about it?'

Borghese looked at me sharply. I wasn't sure myself why I'd made the offer. He frowned some more before replying.

'Signor Rizzo tells me you know influential people in Brussels. Tell him if you hear of anything that might help us.'

He was speaking as if I was part of what was going on. But by this point too much had happened since Friday in the canyon. Right now, I no longer really cared. The only thing I still wanted to know was whether Sophie somehow still mixed up in all this.

'I'll let him know if I do,' I said, trying not to sound begrudging. Borghese was letting me walk out of here, after all.

The others drifted back in from the kitchen, and for some reason the whole circus started up again. Once more, I faded into the background while the voices rose and fell. After a while, I looked at my watch and realised I needed to get back to the airport if I was going to make my flight to Brussels.

Rizzo's father saw me checking the time and clapped his hands to bring either the discussion or the argument to order. Given we were in Italy, it was hard to tell which. He said something while pointing at me and I hoped it was 'any last questions.'

He looked around the silent room, then got to his feet.

'Come,' he said to me. 'I have to go and tell his mother. I'll take you to the airport, if you're going. It's on my way.'

The dissonance in the words he'd used hadn't been missed by the other English-speakers in the room either.

We walked the short distance across the street to where his Montreal was parked. I'd seen it in an Alfa Romeo advertisement at arrivals in Fiumicino and finally worked out what it was. But Rizzo's father's expensive toys didn't matter anymore, not having just lost a son.

The crisis came sooner than I'd expected. Once we got in the car, his shoulders slumped, and he thumped the wood-trimmed steering wheel hard in anger. He didn't stop, but instead became frantic, violently hammering the walnut faster and faster, as if he was trying to break the wheel, or possibly, kill it. Eventually, after a final, harsh sob he stopped and hung his head down between his arms for a minute, hands still gripping the wheel.

I waited, wondering how to deal with the situation and not having the first clue. He solved my dilemma by suddenly lifting his head and turning to me, the colour in his cheeks fading away.

'You need to get out. Take a taxi.'

I risked a glance at my watch. I desperately wanted to bring my involvement in this whole sorry affair to some kind of final conclusion.

'What will Borghese do now? The Mafia won't be bought so easily next time. They told me.'

'Why didn't you tell the Comandante that back there?' he asked coldly.

'I thought you had enough bad news for him today.'

'Don't try to play games with me. We already know what the Sicilians will say, *cretino*,' he growled, the anger flaring up again.

'Get out,' he shouted now. 'And stay away from my family. You and the witch have done enough damage already.'

'I need to tell you one last thing,' I said urgently, trying to get my words in before he cut me off. 'Di Luca threatened your daughter again.'

He gave a yell of frustration and hammered the centre of the steering wheel this time.

'What did he say?'

'The same thing that you hinted to me at the party. A seduction, willing or unwilling, he didn't care which. But I warned him off. I told the people in Palermo that no harm was to come to Giovanni's family. We did a deal.'

Rizzo's father shook his head in disgust. His lip curled up.

'Who do you think you are? Get out.'

The plane journey was only an hour and a half long and I spent most of it drinking rum and coke before I dropped off for the last few minutes over Luxembourg. I normally didn't bother with mixers, but I needed to get drunk as fast as possible. I got a few strange looks from the stewardesses, but then they hadn't been picking up pieces of burnt bodies three days ago.

They also hadn't experienced the sense of power that had flooded over me when I put the Browning to the back of the heads of the wounded men and pulled the trigger, knowing in that instant that there was nothing and no one who could stop me.

Giving myself over to that thing had been like a hit from a drug, all the more intense for knowing it was wrong. But aside from the guilt, I had an even bigger problem. Because after any powerful drugs rush, at some point the addict was compelled to seek it out again.

But I didn't just shiver from withdrawal symptoms and the air conditioning as I sat uncomfortably in one of the DC-9's narrow seats. I shivered too, when I thought of what would have happened if the Saracenos had brought an extra carload of men to the valley and tipped the balance. Or if the RPGs had failed to go off after having been in storage. Or even if a passing patrol of the Carabinieri had turned up out of sheer bad luck and we had to shoot our way out.

If that had happened and we'd still managed to get away from the valley, we'd have had to run halfway across Europe to get back to safety in the East. And it was unlikely I'd ever have been able to come back to the West and to Sophie again.

As the alcohol took hold, my thoughts turned to the conversation Rizzo's father was having right now with the remainder of his family. I had enough trouble to deal with myself without getting maudlin on Caterina and her mother's behalf, but I couldn't help but feel sorry for them. And for her grandfather too. How were they going to explain this to him in a way he'd understand?

By the time we landed, I still was in no fit state to face Sophie. So I topped myself up with a couple of beers at a bar in arrivals which turned into several. But I couldn't put it off forever. Eventually, after another hour, I went to find a taxi, the magazines of the AK clanking in my bag as I walked unsteadily to the rank.

Chapter Eighteen

Brussels - Monday, 28th September 1970

I made it from the airport to Sophie's apartment by seven. I knocked on the door to give her a warning before I opened it with the key she'd given me on the morning I left.

I found her sitting in the lounge with a drink in her hand. Looking sombre and like she'd been crying at some point earlier in the evening.

She looked up at me, lips tightly drawn. I sat down and faced her across the corner made by the two sofas, just as we'd done on the first night I came here.

'What happened?' she asked flatly.

There were only so many lies I could keep track of in my head, so for this story she got the truth.

'We picked up the crates as agreed. We delivered them to the Rizzos' property in Sicily.'

'What happened then?'

'Giovanni recruited some men to go to the valley and seize the weapons from us. Another Mafia clan, rivals of Di Luca's family.'

'They attacked you? How did you get away then?' she said, speaking more and more slowly as her suspicion mounted.

I looked back at her equally grimly. 'We killed them all.'

'Jesus, Oskar,' she said coldly. 'What have you done? Did you kill Giovanni too?'

I didn't take kindly to the suggestion, either that I'd got rid of Rizzo, or that the hijack attempt was my fault. Although in a sense partly it was, for having cuckolded

Rizzo in the first place. Which meant it was as much her fault too, because I didn't cuckold him on my own.

She needed time to absorb the news in her own way. I shook my head slowly.

'He didn't die in the valley. He assumed we'd be taken by surprise and that the other gang would have killed all of us instead. He came along later to see for himself what had happened. Maybe he came to meet the Saraceno people he expected to find there, to agree what they were going to do with the weapons.'

Now she shook her head in disbelief at the mess we'd got ourselves into.

'The guys with me had left by then. Di Luca seized Rizzo when he turned up and took him to a house belonging to a neutral clan. He was held there until the Mafia's Regional Commission got together to decide what to do.'

'But you were there too, surely? You took Giovanni prisoner too?'

She was too quick for me to get away with anything less than a reasonably complete explanation. But it was easy for her. She hadn't helped load the bleeding bodies onto a truck for mass burial.

'The last Mafia war in Sicily eight years ago took seventy lives. Revenge shootings, car bombs on busy streets killing innocent people - Rizzo risked all of that starting again. The old Mafia Commission was dissolved because it failed to prevent the last war. But they've recently been reformed again to try to keep the peace.'

I didn't know why I was defending them, especially as I was mainly guessing at the next part.

'Yes, they act selfishly, for the common good of the greatest number of *mafiosi*. But it's a form of control and even though they dispense rough justice, it limits the worst of the random violence. And after what Rizzo did, there was never going to be an outcome where everyone got away free of consequences.'

'So they ran a kangaroo court, passed a death sentence on him and he was executed?'

Her eyes welled up and she began to softly weep. Why did women always take the side of the underdog?

'He sent those men to kill Di Luca, Johannes' people and me. If we weren't killed outright, they would have cut off our balls and stuffed them in our mouths while we were still alive. I'm not making that up, he told me himself. That's happy-go-lucky Giovanni for you. It wasn't a friendly act,' I said sharply.

'At least the Mafia Commission gave him a chance,' I continued, hoping to make her see things rationally. 'Di Luca knew he wasn't allowed to kill him outright there and then. Giovanni had a couple of days to think about what he'd done and…'

I wasn't ready to tell her about what he and I had discussed the night of his distress.

She dried her eyes and frowned. I saw her thinking about how to say what came next. And I saw fear there too. She sat forward slightly.

'So how exactly did he die? Did Di Luca murder him?' She paused, holding her breath. 'Or was it you?' she asked, her voice now starting to quaver. 'You have to tell me if it was.'

I shook my head.

'It was the clan he tricked into trying to seize the weapons. He was on the way back from the Mafia Commission meeting to his hotel. They dragged him into an alley and stabbed him. Once for each of their men who died.'

'It doesn't seem real. He goes off to Italy with you, but you come back and he doesn't.'

She slumped against the sofa, massaging the sides of her head.

'What happens next?' she asked.

I wasn't sure whether she was referring to the possible coup, the funeral arrangements for Rizzo, or us.

'I presume the funeral will be later this week or early next. Will you go?'

'I have their private numbers in Milan and Apulia. I'll ask Caterina.' She pursed her lips. 'I want to go. I have to.'

I wasn't in the right frame of mind to decide there and then what I was going to do myself.

'I'd rather not be alone tonight. But that's all,' she informed me.

'I understand,' I said. 'I can sleep in here. Anyway, I have the smell of death on me.'

'You have the smell of alcohol on you too.' She gave me a wan smile.

I went over to join her on her sofa and do the usual things to calm her down when she came back highly strung from work. Mainly listening with an arm around one shoulder while she held forth on whatever topic bothered her. But tonight she was out of words to say.

After a while we got up to cook together. When we were done eating, I brought my bags in from the hall to the lounge, dumping them heavily in the corner.

'What's in there,' she asked, as I unzipped the holdall to rummage for my wash things.

A scent of gun oil wafted up from the open bag.

I took out the AK and laid it on the floor to get to my shaving kit. I took the Browning out of my jacket. From habit, I worked the slide to check the action and dropped it into the bag.

She gasped at the sight of the weapons.

'So this isn't a bad dream? It all really happened?'

I nodded silently. Her mouth was still agape. She shuddered a little then got up to go into the bedroom.

The door closed and I went to the bathroom to get in the shower, part of me relieved we were done for the night. I wasn't really in the mood, despite all the alcohol I'd taken on board.

But whatever state her hormones had been in before, they

soon settled down. While I was still in the shower, the door to the bathroom opened and she appeared in the frame wearing just her robe. And that was that.

Chapter Nineteen

It seemed to me like most of Rizzo's year group had come to Apulia for his funeral, but it was probably only fifteen or twenty *fonctionnaires* who were here to pay their last respects and make a weekend of it in Italy.

It was my first real funeral in a way, at least of anyone I might have called a personal acquaintance. As a single child to a young mother who'd deliberately cut herself off from other East Prussian refugees in Hamburg, our social circle was really only people from church. My maternal grandmother had died in the fifties in Wismar of a heart condition before either of us knew the other existed.

Rizzo's friends stood outside the mausoleum in their own group as the priest intoned the words. But even now their attention wasn't really on the interment.

No one in Brussels knew yet that Sophie and I had paired off, and she appeared happy to keep it that way for now. After getting back from Sicily, the assumption seemed to be that I would be living in her flat full time from now on. There hadn't been much discussion, it had just somehow become a given.

I remembered how surprised I'd been to see Rizzo take her hand in the queue for the plane the last time we came here, because she'd never made any display of intimacy towards him on the Brussels drinks circuit that I'd observed. I knew that the worst thing I could do right now would be to lay claim to her in front of her friends. Like it or not, she would be the one to tell them when.

On the way down that decision had been easily avoided, for a gaggle of Rizzo's acquaintances clustered around her at the check-in desk and we got allocated seats in different rows.

I should have known that Sophie would be the centre of attention. I could sense the anticipation rising among them on the plane, even from three rows back, as I realised she was the one many of them had really come for. They weren't here to mourn Rizzo, but to hurry him away from her side, metaphorically speaking.

As for myself, I had to admit that I wasn't particularly happy about her spending the weekend with her old crew. Whatever it was I had to offer, I didn't trust one of the European elite not to be able to persuade her that she'd get a better deal from them.

But unlike the others on the flight, I had a genuine reason to be here. I had no choice, really. To stay away and avoid Rizzo's father would have been much easier, but also the act of a coward. And although I truly was sorry for him as a parent, ultimately it was his son's own decision to start down the path which had led to his death.

Rizzo's funeral service was in the cathedral in Altamura and we buried him in the town's old cemetery, under a sombre sky.

The family home was on the way back to Bari, and food and drink had been laid on for the mourners who'd travelled down to Apulia. We gathered in the main reception room, which had been shut up last month. All the entertainment at the party had taken place on the terrace and the lawn. And in the case of Di Luca, in the bushes too.

Rizzo's parents moved among their guests, thanking them for coming. Caterina was off to one side, standing quietly next to where her grandparents were sitting with someone who I had to assume was Rizzo's other grandmother. I didn't remember her having been at the birthday dinner.

I went over to Caterina. She saw me approaching from across the room and swallowed, holding me with solemn eyes as I drew near. Set against the black of her dress, her milky skin seemed paler than usual. I thought it might be the same outfit she'd worn to the party, hardly four weeks ago.

'*Ciao Caterina*,' I said softly. She leant in to exchange kisses.

'Thank you for coming.'

I inclined my head. Unsurprisingly, today she seemed a lot older than her years. Even her lipstick was subdued, a deep blood red.

'I've had a Mass said every night since he died,' she informed me out of the blue, trying to keep control of her voice as she did so.

'Isn't that the responsibility of your...' I trailed off. Not that I believed a Mass would do anything for someone who'd already passed outside the realm of making their own choices here on earth.

'I'm the only one in my family worried about his immortal soul,' she said quietly.

For some reason which I couldn't quite define, a sense of sadness came over me.

'I'm the only one of us who believes we'll see him again,' she said, more quietly still.

Now I felt a feeling of warmth towards her, as if for a real sister - or at least, how I imagined I'd feel if I had one. If Di Luca tried any moves on her now, I'd make him chop up his own balls first, before I fed them to him.

I attempted some words of comfort.

'I believe in the immortal soul too. Even if my actions don't always show it.'

She stood quite still, calm for the moment.

'The night before... we talked. He asked me some questions about... eternal things. I explained to him as best I could. I think it might have given him some solace.'

Now tears filled her eyes. She tried to dab them away, but they kept on coming. Always with the weeping, the Italians. And with women generally. I'd forgotten about the moistness in my own eyes the last time I was here.

She reached for my hand and pressed it to her lips. I really hoped Sophie wasn't watching.

'How has it been for your grandparents?'

'My grandmother insists that my father must do something for the family honour.'

'And…?'

A look of hurt crossed her face. 'He gets more confused these days. His seventy-fifth birthday was the last time we'll have a public celebration like we did last month.'

Caterina's parents came over. Her father looked stern and said something to her in Italian. By the way he glanced at me, some kind of warning perhaps. Maybe she was already in trouble with him for pushing the religious side of the mourning period too hard.

He looked me in the eye. 'Come with me,' he said with a jerk of his head.

I dutifully followed him out of the room, past a large group of older men and along the hall to his study. When we were inside, he shut the door tight and stood there glowering at me. It was going to be one of those conversations, the ones without small talk.

'It wasn't a gunfight,' he said. 'It was a massacre. No one in Sicily properly understood what you'd done until they went to clear up. My property there looks like a fucking warzone, or so I'm told.'

He waited on me saying something, but I didn't oblige.

'So, who did you really bring? I bet it wasn't the regular German underworld. Mercenaries from the Congo?'

'Some people who'd been in Africa, yes.'

He threw his hands into the air, palms upward.

'Some people? What people? How did you find the funds to pay for men like that?' he asked suspiciously.

He could ask, but he wasn't getting an answer.

'What did you think you were doing bringing that kind of weaponry onto the island?' I challenged him instead. 'Sooner or later the rival clans would have found out about the shipment and come after it. Di Luca and I stopped things from getting out of control.'

'Di Luca's boasting about how the four of you went around shooting wounded members of the Saraceno family, so it's no surprise they wanted my son dead.'

'It was either that or let Di Luca torture them to death,' I said grimly. 'Why do you think I warned you in Milan about his threats to Caterina?'

'You're a strange one. You seem very personally concerned for my family. Don't stick your nose in where it's not wanted.'

'I feel an obligation to look out for them.'

'Why?'

'I held your son's hand as he died,' I said thickly. 'This is personal now.'

'It's none of your business.'

'Can we sit?' I asked.

He wanted information, but so did I.

'If you must.'

He went round behind his desk, pulled out the swivel chair, and sat down very slowly and deliberately, eyeing me up the whole time as he did so.

'This is delicate,' I warned him.

'What?' he said darkly. 'You've thrown out the witch and now you want to go after Caterina yourself?'

I shook my head, trying to hide my impatience.

'No. That's not it. I tried to keep the peace in Sicily for everyone's sake, including your daughter. But I'm still with Sophie von Barten.'

He frowned. 'How long... when did she abandon my son?'

'A few days before Sicily, a couple of weeks ago.'

The furrows in his brow deepened.

'Who are you working for again?' He raised his eyebrows, and the furrows deepened some more. 'I'll ask one more time, who are you really working for, that you thought it necessary to take mercenaries to Sicily to deliver sixteen pallets of supplies in a truck?'

I wasn't getting out of this one so easily. That was the thing with fishing trips, sometimes you were the one who ended up getting snagged by a hook.

'I told you already, back in September. For EEC Internal Affairs, but for a special department.'

'So you keep saying. But special in what way?' he insisted.

I'd managed to slip past the Regional Commission - at least that's what I told myself. But the vague story I'd used with Rizzo's father so far wasn't going to work for much longer. I mentally gritted my teeth as I prepared to lay down a high card.

'Liaison with the national intelligence agencies of the EEC members.' It was the cover story which Masson allowed us to use in extreme need. 'People think we're just general problem fixers. No one really knows what we do.'

He shook his head slowly. '*Merda.* I can't believe I was so naïve. So much for Giovanni and her finding someone they could easily manipulate.'

I stared at him frostily. 'They didn't know who I worked for. That's why we're a secret department. So we stay secret, even to those around us.'

He looked up at the ceiling for a moment or two in disbelief.

'Does she know now? After only two weeks I suppose not. Will you ever tell her?'

I stayed silent.

'*Madonna.* That's cold.'

He tilted back in his chair, trying to work something out.

'Now I've told you something,' I said, 'you need to give something to me. What's Borghese going to do next?'

'Why? If you're as connected as you say you are, just ask the right people at the SID in Rome. You must know people there. Not that you'll get very far. Italy has intelligence agencies inside its intelligence agencies.'

'I'm more connected to the German side of that game. You want to sell your systems to the Bundeswehr, *vero*? Not if your company is linked to funding the far-right you won't.'

That seemed to make him pause and think for a moment.

'So who funded your African mercenaries, then? Who in West Germany is taking an interest in the Comandante?'

'I called in a favour, I had to. She told you the last time we were all together here, that I had a personal obligation to her family.'

I followed up while the door was still metaphorically ajar.

'How can you trust the multiplicity of leaky Italian agencies anyway? Don't you want to buy some insurance from people outside the country? Work with me, so that one day, if needed, you can claim you were helping West Germany all along to penetrate the international far-right networks which Borghese's Fronte Nazionale belongs to.'

'I'm going to need better credentials from you before I make any more mistakes,' he snapped back.

But then he paused, glancing up at the ceiling again for inspiration. He shook out a cigarette from a pack lying on the desk, lighting it with a match from a book lying beside the ashtray. He gave me a shrewd look as he waved the match to and fro to extinguish it. Then he made me wait while he took a couple of drags, the tip of the cigarette glowing bright red.

Eventually, the mating dance was over.

'Okay, then. You can take this back to your people as a taster. Not that it's hard to deduce, but the weapons were to have been used by the Di Luca family to buy the Mafia's participation in attacks to be carried out on Sicily and the mainland, which would have been attributed to the left.'

'If you're telling me this, does it mean you're thinking of backing away from Borghese?' I asked.

'I haven't decided yet what to do.'

Borghese had made him wait for a couple of hours in the apartment in Milan to discuss their plans, while his wife sat at home, unaware their son was dead. That had to have hurt.

'The problem with Borghese's plan is that Mafia's Regional Commission aren't that naïve. No one is. They all remember the events from six years ago involving De Lorenzo. In any case, the Mafia have enough connections in Rome to come out on top, no matter who's in government. Borghese needs them more than they need him. That's why they told me to tell you in Milan that the price of their cooperation had gone up.'

'Did they tell you that explicitly or did you make it up?' He shook his head. 'Either way, you don't know everything.'

I gave it a second, then took my cue from what Caterina had told me her grandmother had demanded of her father.

'Don't you have another reason to work against Borghese?' I prompted. 'Don't you want revenge for you and your family having been dragged into this catastrophe?'

He looked thoughtfully at me once more. 'You really don't know what kind of people you're dealing with, do you?'

I ploughed on.

'I know other people, very discreet, who can...'

'Who can do what?' he interrupted brusquely. 'Fix this? Bring back my son?'

I bowed my head in embarrassment.

'Just get out now.'

I left him and went down the hall, back towards the main

room. On the way, something made me stop at the framed family tree I'd seen on the night we arrived for the party. There at the bottom were Caterina's and Rizzo's names - his death date already written in with black ink. Rizzo had only had aunts, after all. This branch of the dynasty was at an end.

I returned to the main room. A short while later, Rizzo's father returned too. I saw Sophie look round as he came in and she cast a glance at both of us over her glass of wine. I drifted off to mingle with the other Brussels people but kept half an eye on her. Not because I was jealous of the other men as such - it was an undefined general suspicion which troubled me.

My suspicion hardened when a little later, I saw her and Rizzo's father in conversation, and then the pair of them leaving the room in the direction of his study. I wondered if I could eavesdrop from outside the room - below the windowsill, just as the black cat had done back in September. Now that I'd given my story to Rizzo's father about working with unnamed national intelligence agencies, how quickly would he pass it on to her? But why were they even talking in private in the first place? After all, he'd called her a witch in Milan and again just now.

But the decision on whether to spy on her was made for me. One of the French girls who'd come with us from Brussels latched onto me as I stood there musing and I couldn't quickly break away. She was one of Sophie's entourage in Agriculture, less arrogant than the others and easy to chat with. A friendly little thing, restraining her natural *joie de vivre* out of respect for the occasion.

But whatever Sophie and Rizzo's father had been doing, it didn't take long, for the pair of them soon reappeared. I wondered if I would find a way to get it out of her later tonight.

It seemed that most of the Brussels visitors were staying in the same hotel and a group of us assembled in the bar after dinner.

All of the younger men, and a few of the older ones too, were hovering around Sophie, now that the day's formalities were out of the way. Before, Rizzo had played the unofficial role of her watchdog, as he had done with me once. Now she would have to brush them off herself, not that that would bother her. She probably enjoyed it, at least when doing it to the *fonctionnaires* who didn't matter to her career.

The numbers in the bar dwindled as the night wore on and at midnight a group of seven or eight of us were sitting together in armchairs around a low table in the corner. Sophie's hardcore long-term admirers and girls waiting to pick them up on the rebound. The drinks kept coming, for the men were determined to break her down, one way or another.

But that wasn't why I became more uncomfortable the longer we sat there. For when I listened to their conversations it became even more apparent that I had nothing much in common with them, and I suspected with Sophie, even less than that.

They talked about university, about politicians I'd never heard of, and lower-level office politics at the big Directorates. Although these people weren't as high up the ladder as Kramer, they took every move equally seriously. Hand-to-hand fighting like Rizzo's grandfather had done in the Austro-Hungarian trenches.

And they talked about money. Trying to impress Sophie with complaints about the parsimoniousness of family trustees. For the more enterprising, boasts of the profits they'd made from share tips acquired from people on the inside of companies or from property they'd bought on the cheap.

They moved on to social comparisons. Anecdotes from holidays in places I'd only vaguely heard of. Risqué stories of weekend parties with the remnants of Europe's titled aristocracy. But eventually the comparisons were done, and as the conversation flagged, it turned to talk of going on to a nightclub. Piovra was mentioned among the possibilities.

'Are you coming Oskar?' the French girl from earlier asked, her hand gently gripping my forearm. 'There'll be drugs.'

Sophie watched her appraisingly from where she sat across the table, almost opposite us.

Dancing into the small hours was fine as far as it went, but tonight I was planning to slip along the corridor to Sophie's room later.

But before anyone made a move, the conversation took a direction I really didn't like.

'Sophie's the widow. Why make her go hunt for an Italian Romeo to cheer her up, when we're available,' said one of the men who'd been eyeing her up all evening more than the others.

'Go on, Sophie,' said another one, running his hands through his hair to show off its length.

Sophie's mouth parted in a faint smile of amusement.

'She's going to do it,' exclaimed the first one, smirking.

'Who's it going to be? Italian, French, or that German thug you brought along from Internal Affairs?' he said, looking shrewdly at me now.

She tutted and shook her head slightly as she drummed her fingers on the arm of her chair, playing along with their game.

My gorge rose, for it felt all wrong. One of their number had met a violent death not a week ago, although none of them apart from me knew just how violent it had been. But now she was encouraging them for their amusement.

I saw her lift one finger slightly off the armrest, pointing in my direction, but not so obvious as to be noticeable to anyone else yet.

I'd had enough. I'd already been feeling out of place for most of the evening. And this wasn't how I'd imagined people finding out about us. I certainly wasn't going to let it happen by acting out some sleazy tableau for them, where the lady took the peasant off into the shepherd's hut for an assignation. A kind of Turgenev's 'Spring Torrents' translated from Wiesbaden to Apulia, as far as I could remember the story.

'*Vaffanculo tutti,*' I said to the group in general, got up, and walked out of the hotel.

I carried on walking, right out of the old centre, my anger continuing to grow without really knowing why. I wanted to hit someone, beat them up until they called for mercy. I thought of going into one of the local bars to find someone to fight, but the memory of Di Luca's knife in the canyon and of the gashes in Rizzo's body put me off. Typical Italian cowards, using knives instead of fists. Then again, I was bigger than most of them.

I walked on out of town, for another three or four kilometres. I had the vague idea of staying the night at the pension owned by Paola's parents. They'd been hospitable enough the last time I was in Bari when we'd picked up the weapons.

But when I got there, the building was in darkness and I decided I wasn't going to wake my Italian comrades. If I told Paola I was on a mission for the Party, I guessed she'd be only too happy to persuade her parents to let me stay. But I wasn't going to take advantage of her enthusiasm for the cause, my problems were hardly a life-or-death situation.

And as I'd walked, I'd begun to calm down. In the end, Sophie's friends from Brussels and what they thought of me weren't worth getting provoked over. I turned around and made my way back to the hotel, getting there just after half one. I went up to her room to knock on the door.

It took her a minute or two to open up, and in that time I began to suspect that either she wasn't alone, or she'd gone with them to Piovra after all. But then the door swung wide and she stood there in the opening, hand on one hip, wearing a nightdress I hadn't seen before. She wore an ironic curl on her lip too, but let me in anyway. I really wanted to check the bathroom and closet to make sure no one was hiding but held onto my pride.

'Out of your system now?' she asked tonelessly.

For a moment I felt like pinning her to the wall there and then, just to wipe the fading smirk off her face. It was probably what she needed. Or maybe even wanted. But I also wanted to know what she and Rizzo's father had been talking about earlier, so I simply nodded silently before switching off the main light and following her back to bed.

In the morning, I left her in the room and went down to breakfast first. Some people from the group of midnight diehards were already sitting there in the restaurant and I joined them at their table.

'Don't let Sophie see you this morning,' warned the French girl. Then she added, 'Oh, you missed a good night at the club. You should have come.'

'What time did you get back?' I asked, momentarily distracted from the first thing she'd said. She was fresh-faced and starry-eyed, *joie de vivre* turned up at full volume this morning.

'About three.'

'But after you walked out on us,' said one of the men, 'Sophie was furious. I've never seen her so angry. Not shouting, just ice-cold, the way she sometimes is.'

'You should have come with us Oskar,' said the French girl again. 'We did cocaine,' she announced happily.

'Why would she get so angry at you?' the man asked, annoyingly persistent. Then he looked up at someone behind me.

'Oh,' he said sadly, as I briefly felt a hand on each shoulder, just before she went to get her own breakfast at the buffet.

The flights back to Brussels were the best of my life. I was the alley cat who'd stolen the cream and the other toms could only watch in frustration.

She asked for a row of seats on our own at check-in and got them. No one would have wanted to sit with us anyway, they were all too much in shock.

When we changed planes at Rome, we walked along side by side down the long passageways between the gates. I carried both our cabin bags and I could tell she was enjoying the sideways glances she was getting from the other men.

When we got to the plane and another row to ourselves, I decided to take advantage of her good mood and pre-empt anything which Rizzo's father might have said to her about my supposed links to intelligence agencies in West Germany.

'Now that the rest of them know,' I said with a backward jerk of my head. 'I need to tell you a couple of things about work, in case they come and speak to you first.'

She raised her eyebrows. 'It's about time we had that conversation.'

'These things are never as interesting as the rumours make out. Masson's department produces security briefings for certain of the bigger Directorates. Including for Sicco. It's nothing exciting. We recycle alerts produced by Interpol and others, picking out items we think might be of interest to the Commission. So now you know, officially.'

'I already had an idea you did that. From the questions you asked me about CAP fraud before going to Ireland in the summer,' she replied, with a hint of smugness.

'Why did you go to Ireland, by the way? It wasn't to deal arms, like you told Giovanni's father the very first evening in Apulia?'

'Of course not,' I replied, laughing it off lightly. Not that I hadn't been asked.

'Masson sent me as part of a plan to show goodwill to the accession countries by giving them the same briefings as we prepare for the Six.' I wondered if I could use the same excuse to explain away my trip to London next year.

But now it was her turn to tell me a story. Last night hadn't been the time.

'By the way, what did you discuss with Giovanni's father at the funeral?' I asked neutrally.

There was a heartbeat's hesitation before she replied.

'I wanted to say how sorry I was, to apologise to him for having introduced you to their scheme. What did he want to speak to you about?'

'We talked about the need to protect his family from any fallout from Sicily,' I replied, hoping it would stretch to cover any report he might have given her of what he and I had actually discussed.

But I did know that she'd either lied to him or to me, for in my experience she never apologised for anything. Never, that was, apart from one time. Her apology to me on the train back from Wismar.

Chapter Twenty

The nightmares started the weekend after we got back from the funeral in Apulia. I thought they might. They had done a little while after I'd shot von Barten. The Irish ones hadn't started yet, but what had happened there was so extreme maybe they never would.

I dreamt that one of the guys whose chest moved when his body was slung on the back of the truck with the other corpses wasn't dead when we buried him. I dreamt that after the cave was sealed, he woke up and tried to get out. I heard him scrabbling at the rocks blocking the cave mouth as I waited for him outside, my AK held at the alert, ready to fire. Eventually, he emerged and stumbled towards me. I emptied my entire magazine into him, but he wouldn't die. I changed magazines and fired again, but he kept coming forward.

I woke up with a shout, drenched in sweat and with a burning thirst.

Sophie didn't stir beside me, so maybe I'd imagined the shout too.

In a half-awake daze I got up to go to the kitchen for some water.

The dream annoyed me because although I couldn't see his face, it wasn't one of the burnt men from the car or from the cab of the van, or even the one who'd had his member hacked off by Di Luca while he was still alive. It almost seemed unfair that it should be one of the other ones who came after me. Maybe it was guilt, because although they hadn't been so desperately injured as the others, I'd shot them anyway, not given them a chance.

But by the time I reached the kitchen from the bedroom, the dream had gone, shockingly fast. I poured a glass and drank it down. Then the trembles started in a delayed reaction.

I went to the hall and fished out my cigarettes from the pocket of my overcoat hanging by the front door. With a shaking hand I lit up, taking a grateful drag as I went back to the kitchen.

I puffed along the length of the cigarette until the ash was about to drop. As I reached for a dirty plate from the sink, I heard a noise behind me.

I turned round and Sophie was standing there in the doorway. She'd put on the new nightdress she'd worn in Apulia, the one with the hem just below the knee.

'The smell woke me, I think,' she said softly.

She looked at me with concern. I wondered if I'd broken some domestic rule about smoking in the kitchen, but instead of a scold she turned and went up on her tiptoes, reaching to find an ashtray on the top shelf of one of the wall units. I looked at her from behind, her golden hair hanging in a braid halfway to her waist and felt a surge of affection.

'You had another bad dream?' she asked as she handed over the ashtray.

I started. I thought she hadn't woken up the past two nights.

I nodded dumbly.

'What was it this time? The cave again?'

'How did you know?' I asked stupidly.

'You talk. You tell someone to go back in there.'

Now I was worried about what else I might have said out loud in my sleep.

She took a step closer. 'You should tell me. Whatever you want to.'

I sucked on the cigarette, looking at her narrowly over the tip.

'There's some things you don't want to know.'

The softness was replaced with a glint in her eye now.

'Why?' she asked.

I took another drag through pursed lips.

'A lot of people died in Italy.'

I looked at her more solemnly now.

'I had to… I had to finish some of them off. They were still alive, but I shot them dead.' I said, my logic not at its best at four in the morning.

'Why didn't you say before? What else aren't you telling me?'

I tapped the ash into the tray. 'Do you ever smoke? I've never seen you,' I asked.

She frowned. 'Not really. They're now saying it definitely causes cancer, even with filters.'

I ground the cigarette out into the tray. She watched me as I tipped the ash and the stub into the waste bin, rinsed the ashtray under the tap and put it back on the shelf where she'd taken it from.

'What else aren't you saying?' she repeated.

'Nothing,' I said, hoping to get away with it. 'There was a lot of blood. We had to load the bodies onto a truck, drive it to the cave, unload them again…' I tailed off, hoping she'd be satisfied with a little more detail.

'How many were there? How many did you… finish off.'

'Eleven men came into the canyon,' I said in a strained voice. 'We smashed them up badly. Machine gun and rocket fire. I killed four of them.'

She came in close and put her arms around me. 'It sounds like a war.'

'You must have known what Giovanni's father wanted moving. They weren't toys.'

She held me a little tighter. But just then I had a flash of annoyance at her again for the trouble she'd got me into in Sicily, no matter how it had turned out for us so far.

There was something else on my mind now too. The

day after we'd got back from Rizzo's funeral there'd been a message for me to come to Berlin this Friday. I couldn't afford for her to hear me arguing with Johannes in my sleep.

It was a dilemma. Walking out on her that night in Bari didn't seem to have done any harm. We didn't do it every night, but that was less important than the fact that I was still spending all of them in her flat, which no one else in Brussels had done, as far as I knew.

But despite that, and despite my showing off to the other *fonctionnaires* on the flight back from Bari, I didn't have much real evidence that I was any more of a permanent fixture than Rizzo had been. We went back to bed and I eventually drifted off, but I could tell she wasn't settling down easily either.

-

In the morning I made a decision.

'I'm sorry I disturbed you last night. I think we need a break for a few days. Just until my head is clear.'

'What are you saying?' she asked uncertainly.

'I'll come and see you in the evenings, if you want. But we should sleep apart.'

She glanced at her watch. 'Why?'

'It's just being practical, nothing else. Look, you're going to be late for work.'

She wasn't happy as she left the apartment. After she was gone, I cleared out my things from the bathroom and stuffed my dirty laundry into my bag.

I wondered if she'd expect some kind of handwritten note left on the kitchen table, but decided she could do without it.

All day Tuesday I waited on her call at work to say what she was doing that evening, but none came. So she was playing it cool too. Maybe that wasn't such a bad thing, just to find out where we were.

I went home for the first time in two weeks. I'd last been in my own bed the night before flying out to Sicily. My landlady, Madame Vandenbroucke, came to complain about the post building up in my box.

The phone didn't ring all that evening either. This spelt trouble later, I was sure. But I refused to get into the whole Brigitte situation again. Not that the politics student from Ghent and Sophie had anything in common, apart from their degrees.

Maybe it was the change of scenery, or it was because I'd finally talked about my nightmares to someone, but I didn't have any dreams that night. So some good had come out of the move already.

-

As the following day, Wednesday, went by, the awkwardness of the situation became more apparent. After two days of radio silence, I couldn't casually phone her office and tell her not to worry, thanks for asking, but by the way, I'd had a better night's sleep last night.

There was no way I was actually going there in person. It would be a question of waiting to see who blinked first.

Back at my flat, there was no word from her after work on Wednesday evening either. I tried to imagine how she might be seeing things. Either the spell had been broken, whatever that spell was, or she wanted normal service to resume and was getting dangerously impatient. Or it was something else entirely.

I found out at one in the morning when the bell for the street door rang. I buzzed her in and made my way down to the bottom of the stairs to meet her in my dressing gown.

Half-way there, I met her coming up, tear stains on her face.

'Is anyone else with you?'

'How could there be, after you?'

She did bring Brigitte back to memory again just then. The midnight visits, the scenes on the staircase, the neighbours banging on doors to complain at the shouting.

But Sophie wasn't Brigitte. Not in any way. Something made me stop at the threshold of my door, though. I turned around and faced her.

'What's the password?' I asked, without knowing why.

She went on her tiptoes and put her mouth to my ear. 'I love you,' she whispered.

Well, I hadn't expected that tonight either. I really wasn't sure why she was attracted to me and hoped she'd never put me on the spot to explain it to her.

'Come on in then,' I said, flustered.

Once we were inside, I made a show of locking the door behind me and pocketing the key. Then I took her by the hand into every room in turn, to prove that they were empty. It didn't take long.

I even opened the wardrobe for her, so she could see that no one was hiding there too. Lying on the baseboard was the holdall I'd brought with me to her flat on the night I came back from Sicily, the one that had held my AK. She caught sight of it and pulled back.

'I did actually believe you, you know,' she said, sitting gingerly opposite me on the ancient threadbare armchair Madame Vandenbroucke provided for her tenants. It was probably already old the last time that the Germans ran Brussels.

'Anyway, Oskar,' she said more brightly now. 'I've decided that we shouldn't have any secrets from each other. What else keeps you awake at night, which you need to tell me about?'

I couldn't very well reply by saying that I'd been on the way to getting two nights of unbroken sleep, since I'd moved back in here. I also couldn't very well say that what

I was most worried about right now, apart from Kramer's horror assignment which he'd planned for me in London next year, was going to Berlin and hearing that the soldiers somehow hadn't made it back to East Germany and that I was suspected of betraying them. And that was on top of worrying about whether the Saracenos felt more blood was needed to avenge the deaths of their men. Or if Borghese had suddenly decided he was captain of a leaky ship with holes below the waterline which needed plugging. Or if any number of other people I'd upset wanted retribution, including her own family.

The safest course was to make her the focus of attention.

'The night before he died, Giovanni and I spoke. He said he loved you. He'd told me how he tried to warn you off me. He said he was prepared to risk a permanent rupture with you, if his warning would save you from me.'

'He was very devoted,' she said quietly.

'Why didn't you take him seriously? What do you see in me?'

She sat forward in the chair.

'No one else I know has your forcefulness. You chained me up and put me in a truck to East Germany.'

I was nonplussed. I'd done it for the sake of my cousin and would have done the same to anyone else who'd got in the way. Not to give her some kind of thrill. I wondered how she really saw me. Did she get turned on by sleeping with the son of a rapist? Maybe she was as mad as Brigitte, in her own way.

'I did it for Karin. Nothing is more important… almost nothing is more important than family.'

'I want that love for myself.'

'You have a family. You have that love already.'

She folded and refolded her hands as she sat there, her head bowed.

I judged we'd had a long enough talk and I wanted to keep up my run of better nights' sleep. I got up and pulled her to her feet. My bed isn't very big. I can sleep here on the sofa tonight.'

'Won't you come back to mine? We can call a taxi.'

It was too late at night to start playing Brigitte's old games and letting Sophie have her own way. And anyway, she'd told me she liked forcefulness.

'No, it's okay.'

I took her by the hand into the bedroom, intending to leave her there after I took a couple of spare blankets for myself.

She hadn't brought a bag to my flat and I wondered if this visit had been a spontaneous act of desperation, after my failure to call her over the past forty-one hours. Or perhaps it was an attempt to catch me unawares with another woman. But before I found my things, she'd quickly undressed down to her slip and got into bed. She lay there looking up at me sadly, her arms open wide.

I sighed inwardly and got into the bed with her. At first, she tucked herself in close. But then she began to wriggle and wouldn't settle, making me wish I'd taken the couch after all. Eventually, she did drop off, but by then I'd been squeezed to the side of the bed and didn't get much rest until morning. So much for another undisturbed night's sleep to make sure the cycle of my bad dreams stayed broken.

Even after tonight's performance, I still wasn't much surer I held any enduring attraction for her. But maybe I was thinking about things the wrong way. Maybe whatever initially attracted someone was just that, not important in itself. Maybe once you were together, other bonds developed, meaning the first attraction didn't take all the strain. It hadn't worked for Rizzo, though. It might have done for his grandfather. Maybe his advice was the best after all, take the girl and work it out afterwards.

Chapter Twenty-One

Tomorrow I was off to Berlin for whatever awaited me there. I'd explained away the trip to Sophie as a last-minute summons from Johannes for a debriefing on Sicily. Extra information he was demanding to help him put pressure on the Ministry over Karin's case. But I'd need a proper cover story for the next trip. And for the one after that. There would always be a next one. Even back when I signed the false confession in 'sixty-nine I'd realised that once they had you, they never let you go.

When I received the message about going to Berlin, I reckoned that it couldn't hurt to try to meet with Spinelli beforehand. I wanted to tell him about Di Luca's indirect confirmation in Sicily that a coup was on the cards, and the other piece of the jigsaw given to me by Rizzo's father, that the Mafia had been asked to take part in a strategy of maintaining the background political tension in Italy. Above all, I wanted to know if the bloodshed had been worth it.

After three weeks the commissioner had probably forgotten all about Augusta von und zu Wehlau, Rizzo, and I by now. At the time, he'd blustered about receiving a report quickly on manipulating the CAP to help Italy. But he hadn't chased Sophie or me for it since. I'd ask her again tonight when I moved back into her flat.

As it turned out, I couldn't even get an appointment for a meeting until I marched over to his office to plant myself there in front of his secretary. I virtually had to prise his appointment diary from her fingers to force her to find me a date.

Wednesday's news bulletins had included reports of the expiry of the Libyan deadline for the remaining twenty thousand or so Italian settlers to leave the country. People who'd moved there before the war, when it had been the Italian colony of Cyrenaica. Gaddafi had taken the opportunity to expel the remaining Libyan Jews at the same time. Having said that, both groups were still better off than the East Prussians had been during their expulsion. No one had been killed or worse this time.

'Did you see the news from yesterday?' I asked Spinelli when I arrived at his office, trying to warm him up with small talk.

'What news?' he asked, pointing for me to sit across the desk from him.

'Libya and the Italians.'

'Oh, that. It's of no real interest to me. The Libyans have done the right thing by finally erasing Italy's imperial legacy, though.'

'They were ordinary people, not criminals. Not fascists.'

'We're building a better world. A new Europe. They're welcome to move here from Africa.'

He was off on his hobby horse and away. It was my first time inside his inner office, I took a quick look around the room, always curious to see which objects people surrounded themselves with at work. In his case, it was long shelves of leather-bound legal volumes, and on the walls at eye height, large black and white photographs: Spinelli with De Gasperi, Spinelli with Adenauer, Spinelli with Schuman, and Spinelli with de Gaulle.

From the pose of the last photo, I got the impression that he thought it was Le Grand Charles who was being honoured by their meeting, rather than the other way around. This was a guy whose bubble needed bursting from time to time.

'Will the little people like the expelled Libyan settlers get a look-in in this new Europe? I read in your manifesto something along the lines of:

"The new state is formed through a dictatorship of the European revolutionary party, allowing a new, true democracy to take shape around it."'

'Yes, and?'

'But what if that second stage never occurs? What if the forward-thinking revolutionary people you approve of - the ones who are going to build a European democracy - what if they decide they need to keep the revolution going for a little while longer? With them in remaining charge of course.'

'Going to? That was written before the war ended, before Europe took on the form it has now. And anyway, you haven't quoted the sentence that came after that one:

"There is no need to fear that such a revolutionary regime will automatically lead to renewed despotism."'

'Well, that would have made it all right then,' I said. 'But how was your vision any different to that of a communist dictatorship today, claiming they're still in the construction phase of socialism? Saying they just need to stay in power a few decades longer to achieve true communism?'

'Don't be impertinent. I went to prison for my beliefs. What have you done for yours?'

Being put in prison for them didn't mean his ideas were right, though. But I wasn't going to point that out to him just now. He was already riled up enough for my purpose.

I put on my solemn face.

'After our last conversation, I went back to Italy. I met with a different set of people there, people who are also mixed up with Borghese. But the overall picture of what he and they are planning still isn't clear.'

It was becoming clearer to me, but I wanted to keep Spinelli curious.

He placed both hands flat on the desk in front of him, studying them for a moment before looking up.

'What was it exactly that I asked you to deliver when we had our last meeting?'

'A report on a possible rebalancing of the CAP in Italy's favour. The suggestion was that one wing of the DC was planning to use the threat of a Borghese coup to squeeze concessions out of the EEC.'

'Seems unlikely, now that you say it again. Especially if you're going around asking everyone about a plot. These things are meant to be a surprise when they happen.'

I ploughed on. 'That's the problem. No one is taking it seriously, not even the Mafia.'

'Are they involved now?'

'Who isn't? We just need the CIA and the KGB for a full house. But what if Borghese doesn't want it to be a secret? What if he's not as stupid as he looks, and the Fronte Nazionale are lulling their sponsors into a false sense of security because they're planning this thing for real?'

I'd been wondering for a couple of days now if that was the real purpose of the secret arms transfer. Secret from the official sponsors of the false-flag coup, was there an actual coup hidden in plain sight?

'You know that's impossible. I explained to you the time we spoke with Monsieur Kramer, there's absolutely no popular or mass support for such a thing.'

'But if it's so unexpected, that's why it might come off. Or what if it's not a coup, not even a false one. What if it's something like what Gaddafi did, something from left field? A political assassination or the bombing of an oil refinery. A declaration of independence by Sicilian nationalist politicians, accompanied by an armed uprising led by the Mafia? Something to give Rome the excuse to award itself wartime powers, like a kind of Italian Gulf of Tonkin incident?'

He shrugged, not dismissing my theory out of hand.

'If the CIA really are interfering, then there's nothing that we at the EEC can do to stop them,' he said. 'But in any case, I've thought about it, and on balance I hope that some kind of constitutional crisis does happen. Even if there's the small risk of a fascist-leaning government for a few months.'

'What?'

'This could be the perfect crisis to move things on at the EEC, to make people take my plans for the need for a federal government seriously. Make people see that we need that European army under centralised control to stop this very kind of thing from happening. A democratic federal government of course,' he added quickly, just in case I was still doubting his good intentions.

'But what if Borghese turns out to be a hard-line nationalist? What if he moves too fast for you and solves a crisis at the Berlaymont by pushing his political allies to break Italy's ties with all of its international associations: the UN, NATO, the EEC?'

'He won't do that. Most of these far-right people, from Austria to Sweden, want a United States of Europe, even if their conception is a twisted version of what it should be. Borghese's a European nationalist before anything else. His mother was Dutch, he grew up in England. He fought for Germany.'

I didn't think he was that enamoured with Germans - or perhaps Austrians - based on his campaign in South Tyrol, but I tried to humour Spinelli anyway.

'So how do we influence the outcome of any coup attempt, such that the EEC gets the maximum benefit? And how do we stop the plot in its tracks, if we find out new information and decide it really is too dangerous for the stability of Europe?'

'But I just told you, I want the Italian government to

look incompetent, so that people lose faith in it. Sad to say, we almost certainly need some people to die too.'

Thus spoke the guy who'd spent the last two years of the war in neutral Switzerland while Rizzo's father was selling his soul to the Decima Mas, fighting to save Italy's post-war borders.

'What if things go too far in that regard? What if they plan a real atrocity like the bank bombing in Milan last year when seventeen people died?'

He looked troubled. And so he should be, the old hypocrite. What was the point in boasting about being imprisoned by the fascists, if you ended up being content to see their methods being used, even if indirectly, to achieve your goals?

'I guess you'd need to find out the real leaders of the plot, not just their trained monkey.'

'How do I do that?'

'It's Italy,' he said cynically. 'Bribe someone.'

Chapter Twenty-Two

Berlin - Friday, 9th October 1970

After landing at Schönefeld, we taxied to the Interflug stand past a row of giant, high-winged Antonov cargo planes wearing the red star of the Soviet Air Force. Their rear ramps were down and military stores were being unloaded by a swarm of Volksarmee ground crew in a kind of sinister mirror image of the Berlin Airlift.

Johannes looked at me sardonically when he greeted me at arrivals.

'Well, what have you done now? Blown up half a mountain in Sicily, or so the Volksarmee tells me. It only took them ten days to get back to Germany on that freighter. I heard they got pretty seasick in the Bay of Biscay.'

'What's happening out there?' I jerked my thumb back towards the runway.

He looked at me appraisingly for a moment.

'Exercise "Comrades-in-Arms". Joint war games involving the Volksarmee, Group of Soviet Forces in Germany, and the Polish People's Army. Paratroop drops and an amphibious assault up by Rugen Island. Practising for an assault on Denmark, I believe.'

I was tempted to ask more. It was the sort of nugget of useless information which would have sent the field intelligence people in the Bundeswehr into transports of delight. But it would have been unseemly. Plus, of course, it might have been a trap too, speculatively laid by Johannes on the spur of the moment to see if I leaked the details to the West.

'When's my cousin being released?'

'You're not taking the Cold War very seriously, are you, Oskar?'

'People are still people the world over. We all want peace.'

'Whatever that means,' he said contemptuously.

Then he looked me in the eye. 'But I am allowed to tell you that some of the various pieces your own comrade-in-arms brought back were interesting.'

He held up his hand to stop me speaking. 'Some of them. Don't get excited. They weren't the real prize here.'

I shrugged.

'We'll speak in the car on the way,' he said.

We took a long way round to the Normannenstrasse complex, almost up to Hohenschönhausen prison then down again.

'Do I get to make a visit?' I asked.

'She's not here. She's been moved to an adult women's prison outside Berlin, even though she's only seventeen. You should thank me for that.'

'*Danke sehr.*'

He grunted.

'I'm not going to play games with you. You've earned a certain amount of goodwill here because of Sicily We'll find out just how much at the meeting later. Make sure it goes well, because it will accelerate her release if you do.'

'Who are we meeting?' I asked.

'An ad-hoc Italian committee from Department III. People who've liaised with the PCI in the past plus an analyst or two from Department VII.'

'Lieutenant Petzold?'

Petzold was the one who'd briefed me before my trip to Ireland, eager to tell me that East Germany's trade with them amounted to little more than imports of butter and pedigree sheep.

'I don't think so. We'll speak more once we get to the

357

office. But listen, the reason why we're coming this way is to give us longer to talk in private. Ulbricht is on his way out. We've heard from our informants on the Politburo that there was criticism of his economic policy at the session in early September. It doesn't sound like much, but the first move has been made.'

I looked across at him in surprise. 'I didn't realise the Republic had an economic policy.'

'It was to do with over expenditure on prestige construction projects rather than investment in the production of consumer goods. That kind of thing, not really my area of knowledge. The Fourteenth Conference of the Party takes place in early December. That's most likely when the next move will take place.'

'Who's expected to take over? What does it mean for us?'

He looked at me reflectively, 'The front runner is a guy by the name of Mittag, Secretary for Economic Affairs. Don't tell anyone.'

I looked back at him suspiciously. No one needed to warn me. Being given news of this magnitude had to be a test to see if I'd leak.

His face was blank, but two could play at that game.

'So, this new guy. Does he trust the Ministry's western co-workers or not? Has he been much outside the Republic?'

'I don't know the answer to that. But if there's a new boss, people will want good news to bring him at their first meeting.'

'Haven't I already given you some? Or do you want to shore up Ulbricht?'

'No one here likes Ulbricht. No one understands how he's kept his job for so long. I guess Moscow doesn't like change. Anyway, I'm always on the lookout for good news. So keep bringing it to me.'

I was tempted to say, 'Or what?' - but they were the ones still holding onto my cousin.

'You know I can't promise you that.'
'Your call.'

We walked the long corridors of the Normannenstrasse to his office. Forty buildings containing ten thousand rooms, spread over four city blocks - but eventually we got there. I must have had the air of an outsider, because people we passed on the way avoided my eye. I hadn't noticed it the day I spent here in July for the briefing on Ireland - but I didn't have any scars back then. I felt aggrieved more than anything else, strangely resentful for not being seen as one of them.

In July, Johannes had left me alone for a few minutes in his office and whilst he'd been gone, I'd taken a closer look at the family photos on his desk. The one of Sigrid, daughter from his first marriage, was still there. She stood beside Johannes, present and correct in her second lieutenant's uniform, looking confident as she stared back at the camera - just as she'd done the night she'd walked up to me in the bar at the training college. But the snapshot of Johannes, his second wife, and son in front of the Berlin Fernsehturm was gone. Instead, there was a picture showing only his son, being awarded a prize at a gymnastics tournament, it seemed.

I really hoped his current marriage wasn't in trouble, and that the Saturday trip with his son to the football match, which Sophie and I had interrupted, hadn't been on one of his days to have custody or suchlike.

'Today, you need to be on your best behaviour,' he said as he hung up his coat. 'No questions to shock or off-hand comments. I told you, back in Luxembourg, that Italy and the PCI are tricky for us. You're here to answer our questions, not to give us advice on our Italian policy.'

'Are you on this ad-hoc committee?' I asked.

'They couldn't very well exclude me.'

He looked at me as if in challenge.

'Are you encroaching on the territory of one of your

rivals here? One of the Italian specialists?'

He came to sit down behind his desk, facing me.

'I've seen the report from the Volksarmee of what happened. I made the right call to send them with you. But being right can make you unpopular here, just as in any large organisation.'

'But it wasn't only about discovering the chemical composition of plastic explosives, was it?'

'It's a tricky time for everyone here, what with the news I told you on the way over.'

'So people are happy with a limited success? A bird in the hand?'

'Something like that,' he admitted.

'It could have been so much more,' I said.

Not that I was disappointed, truthfully speaking. If we'd proven CIA involvement with Borghese and caused a shock to the Italian political system which led to a permanent rupture with America, it would certainly have been something. But upsetting the current balance of power in Europe wasn't a responsibility I wanted any more than the next man. And I suspected, not one which the Stasi wanted either. If Johannes was stepping on his rivals' toes in Italy, then they in turn would probably have been stepping on Moscow's if they'd followed through.

'Don't remind me of what might have been,' he said sharply.

'Can you still use this to get the colonelcy you wanted? You told me in Luxembourg you needed to prove you'd stopped a coup.'

'That was before the Volksarmee destroyed the whole shipment and brought your involvement with the plotters to an immediate halt.'

I frowned at Johannes' naivety.

'What happened there?' he asked. 'Who attacked you?'

'Another Mafia gang who got word of the arms arriving and tried to hijack them.'

'That was convenient for us,' he said shrewdly.

'So you're hopeful then? Of getting a promotion out of this?'

'It depends. It depends partly on how this meeting goes. In front of them, you show absolute loyalty to me. They have to understand that access to you and to what you know comes only through me.'

'When have I ever set out to deliberately undermine you?'

He tilted back in his chair and sighed.

'The committee is well disposed to you at this point in time. You're still a prize worth fighting over for the Italian desk. Even if you're not an agent in place in Italy, you have access to Italians at the EEC.'

'So don't mention my conversations with Spinelli, then?'

'Who? Oh, him. No, let's keep that source to ourselves. In any case, they think that this intervention in Italy is finished so let's encourage them in that.'

Now he pursed his lips. 'Which means that if Fräulein von Barten and her friend have any unfinished business with Borghese and his gang, I don't want you getting persuaded by them into helping out some more.'

I gave him a nod. 'Did we do enough for your next promotion board, in the end?'

'I'll use it as part of my evidence. It's probably not enough on its own, though. But despite that, no more involvement with the Italian conspirators and their West German ally. Just like the others here, I don't want the current neat conclusion to the affair to be jeopardised in any way.'

'Yes, I get it. Do the committee know about Borghese?'

'Only in outline. I presented it as a plot by a little-known, militant group on the fringes of the right wing. There's enough of those in Italy these days. The committee don't know that Borghese's directly and personally involved.'

'You really don't trust your colleagues much, do you?'

'Don't be impertinent. Don't forget why you were sent to Italy in the first place.'

'Do they know about Karin? Can you say with any more confidence about what's going to happen to her next?'

'Later. It's almost time to go,' he said, looking up at the wall clock.

'While we still have a minute alone, the guy I met in Luxembourg, Schalck-Golodkowski - is he still open to having a meeting?' I asked.

'What do you mean? You've decided you want to work for him after all? And he's not a 'guy', he's a deputy minister.'

'No, not yet. I've enough to do at the EEC right now. But I'd like to know what my options are for the future. And in any case, the longer all this goes on for, the more robust a cover story I'll need for my visits here. No one is that fond of their aunt.'

'What do you mean? "The longer all this goes on for"? When do you think we're going to let you stop?'

I gave him a quick frown.

'I'll get the Comrade Minister to meet you again and you can negotiate percentages. But don't thank me all at once. Right, you bloodthirsty *Verrückter*, time to go.'

As we were leaving, he suddenly asked, 'By the way, speaking of Fräulein von Barten, did you do it with her yet?'

I glanced at him. The lines around the corners of his eyes were more noticeable today than they'd been in Wismar at the start of September.

'Yes.'

He clapped me on the shoulder. 'You see, I knew you would. Nothing gets past me.'

He wasn't smiling much, though.

The five Stasi men and one woman around the conference table looked a lot happier than Johannes. Maybe they were allies of Mittag and Johannes wasn't, so they were looking forward to a change of regime and a reorganisation which would put the major back in his box.

The chairman rapped the table and brought the meeting to order.

'We've received the report of the action in Sicily from the Volksarmee. You helped strike a great blow against fascism, Comrade Lenkeit.'

Immediately my hackles rose. We'd gone out to conduct some weapons espionage, not to strike a great blow against fascism as such, not unless the Ministry was given to over-exaggeration, which as the most professional intelligence agency in Europe I thought unlikely.

One of the men sitting to the right of the chairman picked up a typewritten document lying before him, tapping it a couple of times on the table to square off its sides.

'With your permission, Comrade Chairman, allow me to read some excerpts from the report. It uses Comrade Lenkeit's operational name.'

He cleared his throat.

'Comrade Hofmann showed socialist leadership in the operation of the twenty-third to twenty-fifth September, in southern Italy.

Operatives under the control of the Ministry broke into a secret weapons cache of the NATO "Gladio" terror organisation. The entire contents were removed under the guise of conducting an illegal arms sale by a fascist bandit group to criminal elements in Sicily.

Under the direction of Sergeant Müller, the following secret items were abstracted from the consignment and brought to the Democratic Republic on board the cargo vessel Freundschaft.'

Here he listed encryption equipment, low-light sensors, and anti-personnel devices - but only in general terms. Habits of secrecy died hard.

'On arrival in Sicily, a rival faction of the fascist bandit group

attempted to seize the arms. Comrade Hofmann made the decision to deny this faction the weapons and instructed Sergeant Müller to prepare an ambush which was sprung resulting in the deaths of the entire attacking force without loss to the Ministry operation.'

They all rapped the table in unison, like they'd been practising for it.

'How many fascists did you personally account for, Comrade Lenkeit?' asked the woman.

I stared at her a little too long, for I could have sworn I'd seen her lick her lips just before she asked the question.

'One during the action itself, the three remaining wounded afterwards.'

'How did you dispatch your prisoners? Did you slit their throats with a knife?' she asked. She was leaning forward on the edge of her seat, desperate for the titillating details.

I glanced around the table. They all had the same expression, their tongues virtually hanging out.

'I shot them in the head with my pistol. One bullet each.'

I wondered why the soldiers had reported it the way they did, if indeed it was the soldiers who'd written the final version of the document. Maybe Müller had still been worried I'd inform on him over his behaviour at the nightclub, so had made my role sound more important than it was.

The Stasi man who'd taken it on himself to read the excerpts coughed to get his colleagues' attention.

'Comrade Hofmann informed Sergeants Müller and Roth that this action had certainly prevented a coup by fascist elements from taking place in Italy and saved our Italian comrades from any threat of renewed police oppression.'

There was another round of rapping on the table as he triumphantly concluded his recital.

But thanks to Müller, the sly bastard, I wasn't celebrating with them. There was my answer as to why the report read the way it did. If Borghese pulled something off in Italy now, they could say I'd deceived them. And that couldn't be healthy for Johannes, not at all. It also suggested that the report had been changed since he'd last seen it.

I scanned the room, giving him the very briefest of looks as I did so.

His face was inscrutable, professional that he was. But whatever he was thinking, my Stasi boss wasn't joining in the congratulations either.

Now the meeting opened for questions, and it seemed they wanted to know all about the details that didn't actually matter, like how effective were our disguises as West German engineering technicians. No one mentioned the connection which Johannes had made in Luxembourg. That even if Borghese's coup didn't eventually come off, if he'd had support from the CIA and we'd exposed it, it could have been the other side's biggest intelligence disaster of the new decade.

Someone asked me how I knew we'd been attacked by a rival fascist faction. I sidestepped a lengthy explanation by simply saying I'd been told so by my local contact. They didn't seem surprised and I got the impression they thought the Italian far-right were merely an amateurish collection of splinter groups. Maybe in real life they were.

There were a couple of questions about Paola's father and the help her family had given, but no one seemed to be making the connection that maybe the PCI should be warned, just in case something unexpected did happen in Italy. In fact, I wasn't hearing any discussion about what came next. Johannes was right. It was as if it was in everyone's interest to claim a success, move on, and close the case. And in the case of Johannes' rivals, set him up for failure if it wasn't.

'We wish to make a gesture of appreciation,' said the chairman of the meeting.

I raised my eyebrows and looked at Johannes.

'We thought of an award of some kind,' the chairman continued.

My eyes widened in alarm. They really were doubling down on the story that the operation had been an unqualified success.

'I'm meant to be a confidential agent,' I protested. 'Besides, I'm not a member of any organisation here. It wouldn't be legal,' I said, quickly thinking of the biggest stumbling block you could put in a German's way.

I looked at Johannes, willing him to speak.

'Lenkeit still has some small obligations to us which he needs to discharge. Perhaps if there's a next time.'

Despite the refusal, it didn't seem to dampen the mood of the committee. Drinks arrived and glasses were filled with sekt for a celebratory toast. After the others had been past to shake my hand, Johannes cornered me.

'Is that how it went in Sicily? Did you say that last thing which Sergeant Müller supposedly reported?' he asked out of the side of his mouth. At the other end of the room, the chairman was still holding forth under the photograph of Ulbricht to those who hadn't yet made their excuses and left.

'No, of course not. I told them the attackers were a rival fascist faction. But that was to get them to stay and fight.'

He pursed his lips.

We left and went back to his office to discuss the booby-trap which had been planted in Müller's report. Back to sitting cramped up against his desk at the wrong height for comfort. If he made lieutenant-colonel maybe he'd get a bigger office with a proper meeting table.

'What's the chances of a full-blown coup happening now?' he asked.

'It's hard to judge. Even the Italians themselves can't make up their minds whether it's likely to actually go ahead or if it's just to be used as a threat,' I said, thinking mainly of Spinelli. 'On top of all of that, it hardly seems to be a surprise to those close to these things.'

He shook his head. 'Successful coups require planning, resources and secrecy. There's none of that here that I can see.'

'Plenty of coups before have succeeded against unlikely odds,' I said. 'And you're ignoring the personal dimension. People like Skorzeny and Borghese don't back down willingly, once they've started something.'

He leaned forward on his elbows and bowed his head in his hands for a second or two before looking up.

'You're certain you never told the soldiers the coup was definitely over, because you beat off the attack and destroyed the weapons?'

'You know I'd never make a claim of that nature.'

'Really? You weren't trying to impress them for some reason?' he asked.

'After what I'd done to the wounded?' I retorted.

'I'm almost certain I know who back in the room there manipulated the last paragraph of the report. But this is important - did you give Sergeant Müller any cause to write what he did?' Johannes insisted.

I paused for a moment, then raised my hands in an Italian-style expression of not knowing.

'You did, didn't you? What did you fall out over?'

'He was about to go off somewhere with a woman he'd picked up at a nightclub. I stopped him.'

Johannes leant back in his chair, looking at me in a way I hadn't seen before. I fully expected a reprimand for not having prevented the soldiers from getting anywhere near a nightclub in the first place, but it never came.

'Despite how the report ended,' he said instead, 'some people here would actually prefer the Italian parliament to be suspended for a while and the PCI to be put under pressure. Just to make a point.'

'What point? Something to do with Normannenstrasse internal politics or something concerning Italy?'

'The PCI isn't everything the USSR wants it to be. They have a dangerous streak of individualism.'

'You mean the attack by the PCI's moderate wing on the Soviets over the invasion of Czechoslovakia?' I asked.

'How do you know that?' he said, frowning.

'I try to have an interest in what's going on.'

'The Italian party has picked up the Western disease of indulging in criticism of their own side. Some people here see them as being ideologically suspect.'

'So the Italian committee wouldn't be sorry if the PCI experienced some light repression. Just to remind them that they're meant to be real revolutionaries?'

He glanced at his watch. 'We need to go soon, if we're to make it in time for your flight.'

'If your rivals on the committee really are hoping for something to happen in Italy which will embarrass you, then as insurance why don't we try to pre-empt Borghese's plans? Or at least try to disrupt them further? And warn the PCI too. Make it their responsibility.'

He looked at me pointedly. 'What's this? You're giving me career advice now?'

'How much do Moscow know of all this? If it really has been cooked up by the CIA and we're caught sitting on our hands, or worse, didn't warn them, what happens then?'

He didn't choose to share with me exactly what the Lubyanka knew at this point. Instead, he gazed at a point on the wall behind me.

'I don't know,' he finally said with a furrowed brow. 'I just don't know.'

I'd never seen him admit to any doubt before. Maybe he was under more pressure than I realised. I wondered what the penalty for failure was here. I knew that one punishment was expulsion from the HVA, back to the ranks of the regular Stasi, as Johannes himself had once told me before.

But I had no idea what the KGB would do to any scapegoat that General Fiedler might offer up. The thought occurred that I would most likely be the sacrifice. Better losing me than having to admit to a mistake by one of his own officers.

'What else did your contact at the Commission say?' he asked.

'Bribe someone to discover who's really behind the plot.'

'You still need to know who to bribe. Do they know?' he asked.

'If they do, they're not being forthcoming about it. How capable are the people we trust within the PCI?'

'I told you before, when it comes to covert work, their party is a long way behind where it should be. Although we gave them counter-surveillance training a couple of years ago, I highly doubt they have the ability to penetrate the Italian state security organs themselves.'

'There's another option,' I said. 'If a long enough period of time passes before Borghese tries something, then you can claim unforeseen circumstances intervened, invalidating the conclusion of the Volksarmee report.'

He shook his head. 'Maybe we could claim that, but only if he didn't make a move for at least six months. Do you have the sense they'll wait that long?'

'We might get lucky.'

'That's not a strategy.'

On the way back to the airport I asked him again about Karin.

'So, did I do enough back there for the Ministry to let her go? Did the committee even know she was in jail?'

'Of course not.'

'I thought so. All that "Comrade Lenkeit" stuff would have sounded even falser if they had.'

'You would still have been a "comrade." Socialists aren't meant to have sentimental bourgeois attachments.'

He said this with a trace of bitterness, and I wondered again about the missing family portrait.

'When are you going to confess to your latest set of murders? And who do you plan confessing them to?'

'I've told her already. Even about clearing up the bodies afterwards. Not the burnt ones though.'

'I can imagine.'

And he could, for during the war he'd been a sailor serving on destroyers. They'd been attacked from the air on more than one occasion.

But he didn't know that I'd enjoyed killing the gang members at the time. Or that I'd needed to kill someone again.

'Does she know you're over here today?'

'That's why I need that meeting with Schalck-Golodkowski. To go legitimate.'

'So how serious are you with her?'

'I don't know. We'll see how it goes.'

'Do you want it to be serious?'

'You've met her, what do you think?'

He grunted noncommittally.

'What does her Italian boyfriend think about all this? Does he know?'

I looked at him with a puzzled expression, wondering how to break the news.

'Well?' he frowned, as I still didn't answer. 'You're starting to worry me now.'

'I... I mean to say... he was killed in Italy, after the ambush. Things got complicated with the locals. I had to hang around to straighten things out.'

'Jesus Christ,' he shouted. 'Now you tell me.'

We were cruising down the Adlergestell by this point. He pulled over into the inside lane, turned off down the next side road, and parked. He got out without saying a word, slamming the door behind him. A moment later I jumped in my seat as two fists slammed down onto the roof, jolting the whole car on its suspension.

He opened the passenger door, grabbed the collar of my jacket and hauled me out.

'Let go Johannes. You're making a scene.' I said, shrugging him off as the passers-by on the pavement gave us strange looks.

He released me and growled instead.

'I need to get to my flight.'

'Did you kill him?' he demanded in a grim voice, his self-control beginning to return.

'No. I didn't. Everyone keeps asking me though.'

'I can't think why,' he said sarcastically. 'Are you responsible in any way for his death? Did you ask someone to kill him for you?'

'No, just the opposite. I was going to explain. The Mafia did it, a couple of days after the gun battle. I was the one who had to go and tell Rizzo's father his son was dead.'

'Why you?'

'I was the last to see his son alive, we came across him in the street after he'd been stabbed.'

Johannes gave a great sigh.

'It was important for us that I did,' I continued. 'It's the father who was either supplying or stealing the arms from the Italian Ministry of Defence. He's close to Borghese and he's our best option if we want to stop something from happening.'

'What does the father want to do himself?'

'He doesn't know. I think he's trapped. Maybe we can try to persuade him to take revenge on Borghese for the death of his son.'

'Get back in. And shut up until we get to the airport. I need to think.'

We pulled into the car park at Schönefeld. Out of habit, he drove to an empty row - the Ministry instinct to maintain a distance from other people was strong. After all, by definition anyone not Stasi was untrustworthy. The Mafia and their *omertà* had nothing on the East Germans by comparison.

Once we'd finally stopped and he'd jerked on the handbrake, I gave him my explanation of what had happened.

'She left Rizzo for me before Sicily. So he went out there just before the Volksarmee and I arrived, and betrayed his own father by getting a rival clan to attack us. It was pure revenge. But it didn't go as he'd hoped for, because you sent me with a more professional crew than they were expecting.'

I paused to let him catch up.

'Instead, he was captured by the Mafia gang we were supplying the arms to. They took him to kind of a Mafia court which passed judgement on him. To keep the peace between the clans, he was handed over to the gang he'd foolishly encouraged to attack us and they executed him.'

Johannes drummed his fingers on the steering wheel.

'And that's it? It's finished? You're sure of that?'

'What more can they do to him? The whole point was that they were bringing the dispute to an end.'

'You're becoming erratic. You can't not tell me things like this.'

He put his hand on my shoulder and turned me towards him, fixing me with a grim stare.

'You fall out with the senior sergeant on the operation, you indulge your twisted pleasure in killing people in cold blood, and your love rival gets a death sentence. Do you see why I might be getting concerned?'

'No. One thing led to another, it's just the way it happened.'

'I don't know what to do about you either. Again. And I don't yet know what to do about my own situation. Unless I can find a way to explain away a coup by Borghese, or by any other fascist in Italy for that matter, my rivals in the department will use it to finish me. It won't merely be about promotion any longer.'

'Then we genuinely do need to find a way to stop him.'

He removed his hand, thrusting me away.

'Don't forget your place. For now, you need to keep your head down in Brussels until I work out what to do next. And this time I really mean it. Don't interfere like you did last time when you brought your woman to Wismar. Settle down with her for a while, try to be a normal person. God knows you need to.'

'That might not be a choice I get to make.'

'And right now, I'm saying it's time to think about a pause. At least until I decide what to do.' He opened his door. 'Right, let's go. Otherwise you really will miss your flight.'

He left me at passport control and went in through the side door of the Grenztruppen post, rejoining me on the other side. I'd had a chance to think myself whilst I stood in line. Much as I wanted a break from Ministry work, as I'd said to him, I didn't think we had a choice. The plotters were still out there planning their next move, even if Johannes was hoping they weren't.

As we walked to the gate, he brought up something else, perhaps reminded by where I'd just been.

'Next time we meet, I want you to return the temporary passports we issued you in Wismar. Both of them.'

'Why? I can bring hers, but an alternative identity would be useful to me.'

I didn't tell him I'd already used it since, to check into the pension in Bari.

'I told you in the car park. It's time to put things on hold. Just for a while.'

I looked at him sceptically.

'Believe it or not, Oskar, we try to look after our own people. And you're one of us now. Give me some credit for knowing when enough's enough.'

'Putting this on hold is easier said than done. I'm still unhappy that no one seemed concerned back there about warning the comrades in Italy.'

We arrived at the waiting area by the gates. He took me by the elbow over to a corner, behind a plant.

'I appreciate your concern for them,' he said in a low voice. 'Or at least for whoever you met in Bari. But they have to take their own chances.'

He gave a short sigh.

'Despite the ambitions of the people on the Italian committee, we can only support the socialist movement in so many countries. You know where our focus lies and which country takes the majority of our investment of time and effort.'

I frowned. What was the point of international communism if the various national parties didn't work together when they could? It didn't seem very communal.

As I boarded the plane back to Brussels, I was deeply dissatisfied. I'd hoped to be leaving here confident that Karin would be released. I'd even secretly hoped I'd arrive to find it had already taken place.

My instinct was that, for me, Italy was going to drag on for months to come, whatever Johannes said. For the fact was that Karin still wasn't free - the dissatisfied, envious little girl who'd been partly responsible for getting me into this seemingly unending nightmare. And while her only advocate at the Ministry had a threat to his career hanging over him, I had to continue to do what I could to guarantee a favourable outcome in Italy. We had personal access to one of the conspirators, after all. Surely something could be made of that?

But as I turned things over in my head, the sense also came to me more strongly than ever before, that there would never be a good time to tell Sophie I was working for Berlin.

If I had to come clean, I could tell her that I'd only got

sucked into their world because of having to deal with Johannes to get my cousin's release. So that would make it her fault. Or I could claim I was spying on the Ministry for an unnamed agency in the West, which would only be slightly less untrue.

The real explanation of course, was that I'd agreed to work for them because last year Johannes had left me in no doubt of what they'd do to her if I didn't. But I doubted even that story would impress her much.

Chapter Twenty-Three

Brussels - Friday-Saturday, 9-10th October 1970

My plane landed at just after seven and by half past eight I was back at our flat, as I supposed I was calling it now. There was no suggestion that I'd be living anywhere else from now on.

She was sitting at the dining room table with a glass of wine in front of her.

I raised an eyebrow. She was free and easy with the alcohol at functions and events, but careful at home, rationing herself for when it really mattered.

'How did it go?' she asked warily.

She hadn't said anything before I left, but I sensed she'd been worried I might get stuck over there. Even to those of us on the inside of the organisation, the Stasi weren't exactly the most trustworthy of people, as I'd just heard regarding Johannes and his troubles with his rivals. I wondered at the tone of the question too, and if she was getting ready for a confrontation about my exact relationship with the major.

'It went well enough,' I said. 'They didn't make any promises, but this time I think they will let Karin go.'

'That's good,' she said, relieved. And so she should have been, for right to the last she'd shown little shame and less remorse.

'What did they say when you explained what happened in Sicily? Did you explain what Borghese might be up to?'

The East Germans had leapt on the suggestion there might be a coup and that it had been stopped. But why did she want to know what they knew?

'They'd already heard about Sicily from the people they sent with me. They were more than pleased. They spend so much time sneaking around in the shadows, playing their games, blackmailing and bribing Western politicians, that they almost wet themselves with excitement when they read a report of some real action.'

'I think I'm pregnant.'

I did a double-take, unsure if I'd heard the words properly.

Normally, half a second's pause would be enough for her to want to say something else to fill the gap, but not this time.

I started to blush, but it faded away as she let the statement hang and I caught the deadness in her eyes.

My mouth went dry for this was ten times worse than being quizzed by either the Mafia or the Stasi, worse than the series of life and death decisions I'd had to make in the canyon. The delicate discussions that I'd been putting off for some future time, so as not to disturb our cosy life of make-believe domesticity suddenly came rushing in all at once, demanding answers. A lot was riding on my response, more than I fully realised at a shrewd guess.

I didn't know what to think. I knew I'd wanted to make what we had permanent, but doing it in this way hadn't even crossed my mind.

Part of me really wanted to say something along the lines of, 'I thought you took care of that side of things', but that would have been shallow and callous.

I also judged that, 'Why do you think you might be pregnant?' would be just as bad and maybe earn me a slap in the face into the bargain.

So I turned the tables.

'How do you feel about it?' I asked.

'I don't know. I really don't know. It's not yours, Oskar. It's almost an impossibility of it being that.'

For an instant the world went dark, as if I'd just heard about the death of a relative. I was shocked at how an unlooked-for hope had crept up on me unawares, even in the few short seconds since she'd made her announcement.

She saw the sadness in my eyes and got up from the sofa to come over and stand close to me, but that was as far as the intimacy went.

'I'm sorry Oskar. I didn't expect this either.' She continued in a whisper. 'I wish it wasn't this way. I wish it was ours.'

As I folded her into my arms, I didn't press as to why all this might be, for I'd never concerned myself so far in that area. I'd assumed that if she was prepared to have uncontracepted sex with someone in her office who she'd hated a minute beforehand and very possibly afterwards too, then she must know what she was doing. I'd seen the pills in her bathroom cabinet, but not enquired as to how they worked.

'Is there a chance it's mine, however small?' I said, holding her away from me now.

'Very, very small, but I suppose so. Very small indeed.'

So Rizzo had got his revenge on us after all, from beyond the grave.

'When will you know all this for sure?' I asked, trying to buy time.

'There's laboratory tests the doctors can do. They use frogs from South Africa.'

I grimaced inadvertently. 'Sounds expensive.'

'I'll know by next weekend, even without the test.'

I let her go. 'Why do people pay to have them done then?' I probed, suspecting the answer.

'For some women, it's so they can... so they can make private arrangements. Before other people realise that they're pregnant.'

So she wasn't saying it outright. There was hope yet for Rizzo's child. Or maybe mine. It was bad enough to experience the death of a dream without having to watch her go through something like that.

'If you are sure, then when is it due?'

'June next year.'

'Who else knows?'

'You're the first.'

'What will your parents say?' I asked, probing some more.

She bit her lip some more. 'I don't think I'll like their advice.'

Here was my opening. But why was I having to clear up after Rizzo yet again? And why was it my cousin and I who'd ended up paying the price for his games? But I also knew this was going to be a critical turning point in my life.

Of course, what I really wanted to come straight out with and say, was that in the eyes of most people at the time, my mother would have been justified in having had me aborted. But that thankfully for me, she hadn't.

I swallowed and licked my lips.

'I held Rizzo as he died,' I said, exaggerating somewhat, giving the impression that I'd cradled him in my arms rather than had the tips of my fingers pinched as he tried to hold onto the unwinding thread of his life.

'He wanted so badly to live.'

There was a momentary confusion in her eyes, but I carried on anyway.

'You saw his mother and Caterina at the funeral. You saw their distress. Imagine how they would feel if they knew their grandchild, their nephew or niece was no more?'

Her eyes finally welled up and she started to gently sob. 'I know,' she said, wiping her eyes.

She didn't challenge me as to how they would ever find out unless I told them, but I guessed she wasn't thinking straight right now.

'This changes everything,' she wailed. 'Everything.'

'What has to change?' I asked gently.

'How can I have a career with a child?'

'Why can't you? Lots of women manage it in East Germany. They're proud of it.' Mainly because with their moribund economy and stagnant population they all had to pitch in and work.

'Even for professional women? You know the demands of time this job makes.'

I could have added a comment that the demands were really only on people who wanted to get to the top, as she hungered for. Otherwise the Berlaymont gave plenty of opportunity for people to happily drift along unsupervised. As I was doing right now with my frequent personal trips to Italy and Germany.

There was something else I would have liked to have added to reassure her, but couldn't. Namely, that if the real long-term purpose of External Investigations was to one day become Kramer's personal secret police force, then I could push Sophie's career along too, by spying on her rivals at the Commission at the same time.

I shrugged instead. 'Someone in Brussels has to be the first woman to make it.'

'I didn't choose this, but it's happened. It was my mistake.'

She paused before continuing. 'Only a woman knows what it's like to discover a pregnancy.'

I couldn't argue with her. Then, after another pause. 'What does your mother think of me?'

I hadn't actually told her I was with Sophie yet and I didn't immediately see the relevance of her question, either. I tried to give an answer which might cover a range of implied questions or suggestions.

'She wasn't happy that I used you to trick my aunt last year, but I don't think she'd blame you for that. And I don't think she knows about you and Karin.'

Sophie chewed her lip some more.

'She'd be supportive of any woman in your situation, for obvious reasons. If she'd wanted to, she could have done as other women did back then. No one would have held it against her. Apart from me. But then I'd either be dead or adopted.'

It was somewhat clumsy, but I had to go further if it wasn't just to be a platitude.

'If there's any chance it's mine, I will stay with you and help to raise it, whoever the father turns out to be.'

'Do you really mean that? Are you really prepared to love another man's child? Because if you're not, then there's no point in me going through with this.'

'What are you saying Sophie? That we're staying together?'

'You said that not everything had to change,' she said in a small voice.

'Do you really want me?'

'I told you that night that I loved you.'

Later in bed I asked her when she thought it had happened. By silent, mutual consent, we weren't speaking any further of the long-term implications for us.

She propped herself up on her elbow and looked at me in the light of the street lamps coming in past the curtains.

'In Rome, the day we travelled together.' I couldn't tell for sure but thought she was half-smiling.

'You did it to make me jealous?' I asked. I didn't comment that maybe misusing sex in that way had resulted in her current situation as a consequence.

She came to lie on top of me. 'Did it work?' she said, grinding her pelvis a little.

It had annoyed me, but it hadn't made me jealous for I could never have even begun to imagine that I'd end up here in her apartment at night five weeks later, worrying if sex during pregnancy led to miscarriage.

I felt her pull her nightdress up around her waist then reach back down to get a good grip.

'Are you sure this is wise?'

'Why? For a woman in my condition? In which part of a woman's anatomy do you imagine pregnancy takes place?'

'I don't want to damage...'

'Damage what Oskar? Name it. Don't be squeamish.'

So many life-changing chances tonight to make the wrong choice and say the wrong thing.

'Maybe our child,' I said uncertainly.

My reward was a smack on the lips and then she immediately rolled off me before anything else had actually happened or even properly started. Which was a disappointment, now that I'd been told it was safe. She lay back bright-eyed on her side of the bed while she stroked my hand.

Well, we were still both awake and there wasn't much point in holding off what needed to be said until the morning.

'It's not easy being a bastard. Children can be persistent with their questions when adults know to back off. They hunt out other children's vulnerabilities.'

I turned to face her as she stared hard at the ceiling.

'Do you understand what I'm saying?'

'Yes, I think I do,' she said. Now she was counting on her fingers, murmuring numbers under her breath.

'If you want to, we should.'

She turned her head to look at me.

'Really? You're proposing to me? Just like that?'

'I can't it take back now and say it again a different way.'

'Giovanni proposed to me three times. Each time he tried harder to make it a more dramatic, more romantic gesture than the previous one.'

'He did it in Apulia?' I asked, remembering the box he'd been rotating inside his jacket pocket at pre-dinner drinks. Round and around like worry beads.

She nodded.

'Giovanni warned me not to let myself be attracted to you,' I said, 'On that very first evening we met, when we sat next to each other at dinner. He said you had no one special, you were just friends with men. But he didn't listen to his own advice.'

'Nor did you.'

'No. I wanted you from that night on. Even during the months when I told myself I hated you I wanted you.'

'Why did you hate me?' she asked neutrally. 'Because we got arrested in East Germany?'

I shook my head, buying time to think.

'You're from a different class - technocrats, power brokers, those with inherited wealth. The people who run society.'

I could have said a lot more. Like how the von Barten affair of 'sixty-nine had crystallised for me for the first time that the enlightened graduates of the College of Europe wanted to steer the EEC towards a kind of Western interpretation of Yugoslavia, perhaps a new Austro-Hungarian Empire - without an actual emperor of course. An arrangement where the plebs had no say. Just as Jan the academic socialist and Spinelli the European federalist revolutionary both wanted at heart.

'But you don't mind us so much now?'

'You're different. No one tells you what to do or think. You have a lust for life which sets you apart from everyone else here in Brussels. From anyone else I've ever known.'

I was rewarded with a broader smile.

'Why is it, by the way?' I persisted. 'Why does someone with your self-confidence want to hunt down and destroy your enemies the way you do? And how do I make sure I'm never one of them?'

I'd definitely said enough of the right things because she rolled back on top of me and got to work.

-

In the morning we made breakfast together. I put on my suit, getting out one of the spare shirts I kept in a drawer in her closet.

I wasn't entirely sure if we'd agreed on something last night. I knew how Rizzo had proposed to her, but she hadn't actually replied to my suggestion. Not unless you counted moaning '*Ja, Ja, Ja*' through gritted teeth as she held onto the bedstead with whitened knuckles.

But as she got ready for work herself, she was wearing a wide grin and flashing the occasional beaming smile my way too.

'So, when do we tell people?' I asked, hoping that whatever had happened last night would be revealed by her answer.

'As soon as you buy me a ring, of course.'

Okay, so it was the good news I'd been hoping for.

'I'll get one at…'

I stopped as she raised an eyebrow.

'We'll get one?' I hazarded.

'Surprise me.'

And there was me thinking the hard part had been done. A lifetime of avoiding the wrong choices now stretched before me.

Chapter Twenty-Four

I'd gone to Antwerp in the end to buy a ring from a Jewish jeweller in the diamond quarter. At least, the name of the shop was Jewish. Whether any of the original owners had survived, I didn't ask.

I spent a third of my savings, hoping that she wouldn't mind too much what I got her. Someone with her level of self-belief had no need to show off anyway. I could imagine how other women, unsure of the constancy of affection, would want something flashy and expensive to tell themselves that what they had was real. But once Sophie had decided on something, that was it. A ring was a bauble to her. She didn't wear any jewellery normally. Apart from the evening of Rizzo's grandfather's party in Apulia, when she'd dressed like a Greek goddess.

Having said all that, I wanted her to have something she could wear to work without shame. Something suitable for the Commissioner or higher I was sure she'd be one day.

So I got her something of a decent size, but understated, with a couple of sapphires on either side to match the colour of her eyes.

Despite myself, that evening I was excited to see what she'd think of my purchase. But when I got to the flat, her face was glum.

'I spoke with both my parents today. I told them my news and then our news.'

I'd thought she said we'd wait until I'd given her the

ring currently nestling in its navy blue leather box.

'What did they say.'

'What I thought they might. They want me to end everything.'

I waited with bated breath.

'But I told them that I'd made up my mind and I wasn't going to change it.'

'Have some jewellery to cheer you up.' I handed over the box.

'Very nice Oskar, nice choice.' She tried the ring on for size, then snapped the empty box shut and put it in the drawer of her bedside table.

I knew she was determined, but she could still surprise me. A day's leave taken to go and search for the right ring in Antwerp, then thirty seconds for it to become a permanent feature on her finger.

'I'd better tell my mother then. I thought we were waiting until I got you that,' I pointed to the diamond and sapphires, looking strange on her normally empty finger.

Shallow as it might be, seeing them there made it real, the thing we'd be doing in a few weeks. For much as her parents might want it, time wasn't going to stop, nor was the baby growing inside her.

'Are you going to call her now?'

I looked at my watch. 'She does a lot of evening shifts. I'll try her tomorrow at work.'

For one, the EEC could pay for an international phone call. For two, I didn't want Sophie overhearing my end of the conversation. I reckoned that when my mother had got over the shock of an engagement, she would be shocked again by it being the fake fiancée from last year that her only child was marrying.

'Are you still going to Ireland with Sicco Mansholt the week after next?'

'Yes. Nothing will show for the next six weeks and maybe not much even then.'

'At the wedding?'

We'd decided the end of November was the earliest we could get away with it.

'Probably not. Anyway, dressmakers can do lots of tricks.'

-

The following day I waited until I knew Masson and Willem would be away for a few hours, attending a day-long seminar ahead of the fourth round of deputies' meetings which started tomorrow.

My mother answered after a couple of rings, so I knew I hadn't woken her after a night shift.

At least with her I could afford more honesty than with Sophie, for now.

'You remember the girl I went to see Aunt Hilde with last year, when we pretended to be engaged as a story for the East German border guards?'

'Yes?' she answered warily. 'You didn't tell me much about her.'

'We started seeing each other again this year. We've got engaged for real.'

She went deathly quiet. The seconds stretched out then stretched out some more. I began to worry I'd caused a serious rupture with her.

'Really? Why the secrecy? Why so fast?' she finally asked in a hurt voice.

'I haven't had the chance to meet her,' she said, more indignant now. 'I gave you plenty of time to get to know Stefan.'

I hesitated.

'Oh no, Oskar. You haven't?'

'It's not what you think.'

'It never is,' she said grimly.

'She thinks she's pregnant by her previous boyfriend.'

'Then how long have you been going out with her for?'

'Not long, not…' I was going to say 'properly', but the

word was loaded with more connotations than I cared for.

'But I've known her since last year,' I said, somewhat lamely.

'What can I say, Oskar? Is she a believer? No, I suppose not.'

I threw up my hands in the air in frustration, even though she couldn't see me down the line.

'We'll come up to Hamburg in a couple of weeks' time.'

There was another long pause.

'Oskar. I didn't have the opportunity for a normal relationship. Please don't waste yours. Please, please think carefully about this.'

I definitely wasn't going to tell her I'd just blown almost fifteen hundred Deutschmarks on a ring.

Chapter Twenty-Five

Bernd had got his promotion and Jan and I were out drinking with him to celebrate.

But it wasn't just Jan. I now got the chance to meet his obsessively tidy secretary, and as company for her, Bernd had brought his new girlfriend too. It was the first time I'd met either of them.

I had planned to tell them my news before I knew who else was going to be there, but I didn't want to upstage Bernd so decided it could wait until later in the evening.

Jan's secretary was called Fabienne. Bernd's new woman was a Belgian girl called Magda, who he'd met through work at the EEC. Like me, I supposed.

If Fabienne knew the stories about Jan I did, I wondered if she'd have been quite so bossy with him this evening. Then again, maybe she was what Jan had really been looking for all these years.

His new girlfriend also didn't seem to take his politicking too seriously either. In fact, she came across as quite petty-bourgeois. Why had he made such a big show of being a radical socialist in the years since we'd known him then? All the free love and broken hearts just to prove he was liberated from social convention. Now he was sitting here being made to give his opinion on the latest syrupy Will Tura song and whether the dry weather would hold into next week.

I was also frustrated with him, because if ever asked by Johannes to do some recruiting in Brussels, I was going to offer up Jan as a candidate. Maybe if he settled down with this woman, though, in seven years' time he'd be ready for rebellion again.

But Bernd did know where he was going. His promotion had given him one of the deputy directorships of Internal Affairs with the expectation he would have a shot at becoming its overall boss in a few years' time when the current incumbent eventually retired.

Bernd might still be a friend, but I needed to stay in his good books professionally. You never knew. Kramer wanted External Investigations to start snooping around the EEC one day, but it inevitably came with the risk of getting caught. And if that happened, it would be Bernd who'd end up investigating us - even though we were notionally in the same department.

The four of them chattered on, but eventually one of the girls asked me the question I'd been waiting for.

'Do you have a girlfriend Oskar?'

'He used to,' began Bernd. Then he realised that Fabienne might not enjoy hearing how Jan had effectively procured that nutcase Brigitte for me. And how he'd had to seduce her away from me again to break her fixation before I could dump her.

'Not exactly,' I replied. 'I'm getting married.'

'Where did that come from?' asked Bernd, spluttering into his beer.

'You kept that secret,' said Jan, suspiciously. A light began to dawn on him. 'This isn't by any chance the girl you were meant to be giving a helping hand to in Italy, earlier this summer?'

'It came out of that work.' I was turning into someone congenitally unable to give a plain answer, like a politician.

'Who is it then?' asked Bernd, hurt that I was only telling him now.

'Sophie von Barten.'

Now he choked on his beer. Really choked. His girlfriend had to slap him a few times on the back.

'Fuck me, Oskar. What can I say?'

'Who is she? Why is it so surprising?' asked Fabienne, scenting gossip and scandal. How little she knew.

Bernd looked at me in a mixture of wonderment, scepticism and a dash of admiration.

'She's the niece of someone Oskar once investigated when he was in Internal Affairs,' he explained to the others. 'It was something political. A kind of power play between France and West Germany at the EEC.'

Then he looked at me knowingly.

'And you and her uncle effectively ended up on opposite sides. Big time.'

'More or less,' I acknowledged.

'How the hell did you change her mind?' he demanded.

I coughed. 'I'm not sure really. We recently spent a bit of time together and then we began to start seeing one another.'

Now Bernd paused and put his head, first to one side and then the other, pondering.

'Didn't she have a boyfriend? Didn't he die in a mugging or something?'

I wanted to ask how he knew that. He was a devious one in his own way. Keeping tabs on people came naturally to him. All in the interests of his career, as he would have explained. I wondered if purely professionally speaking he'd be a better choice than me to run Kramer's new EEC secret police.

'Yes, they were together for a while. But he died some weeks ago in a street robbery in Sicily, after she and I started seeing each other properly.' Tomorrow would make it three weeks ago, to be precise.

'That was handy, Oskar.'

'As I said, he was already history when it happened.'

'So why the rush to get married? You haven't got her pregnant by any chance, you dirty dog?' Bernd was making all the running here. Jan was on entirely new ground with a real girlfriend in tow.

But now I had to make a decision I'd rather not have

made on my own. Telling my mother about the baby was one thing, but during the past week Sophie and I hadn't properly discussed who was to know who the real father was. What I did know for certain, was that there were only so many lies I could keep track of. If Bernd and Jan were put out by a surprise engagement, our friendship would be even more strained if they found out the child was Rizzo's later.

'I wish I had got her pregnant. We're making the best of an awkward situation.'

'How come?' asked Jan.

'She is having a baby, but by her ex.'

Fabienne looked at me with a slack jaw and wide eyes. 'You'd do that for her?' she asked.

'She's special,' I confided to her.

She looked at Jan, as if to say this was the standard of behaviour she was expecting of him now. Maybe she was wondering about getting pregnant herself, just to hurry things along and make sure Jan got off the fence.

'Hang on,' said Bernd darkly.

'The niece of the guy you investigated, who then committed suicide over the head of that affair, is now marrying you, pregnant with the child of a guy who recently wound up dead himself. You don't seem to be a very healthy person to be around these days, Oskar, what with your knife fights in Irish bars as well.'

'What can I say? *So ist das Leben*. Will you come to the wedding?'

I saw Jan jolt, as if he'd been kicked under the table. I supposed there was no way Fabienne would miss an opportunity to show Jan what he and she should be doing in due course too.

'Sure,' said Bernd, shrugging. 'If you're happy to come, Magda? Where's it taking place?'

'In Gerolstein in the Eifel, closest town to where she grew up.'

'Jesus. Well, this evening didn't go as planned, that's for

sure,' he said, clinking my glass.

Jan was brighter. 'Come on Bernd, it'll be fun,' he said, giving a quick smile to Fabienne. 'This craziness is too good to miss.'

Chapter Twenty-Six

We left Brussels mid-afternoon on Friday, as many *fonctionnaires* did. Not that he especially cared, but Sophie simply told her boss she needed the time off because she was flying to Dublin on Sunday to join Sicco Mansholt on his trip to Ireland.

It had been a week since I'd told Jan and Bernd we were getting married in Gerolstein. Now I was off there to meet her family and find out what I was letting myself in for.

Her trip to Ireland was on her mind and that was what she chattered on about, rather than her family who didn't get much of a mention at home in Brussels either. I guessed I was about to find out why.

We arrived in Gerolstein a little after six, just as the light was finally fading and the rooks were returning to their nests.

'Keep going,' she said. We drove across the river and up into the wooded hills behind the town.

'Keep going. We're driving over the top,' she told me, as the road began to narrow, and I slowed in anticipation of our arrival.

'Just round the next bend. Turn off there,' she said, pointing. 'Then drive on down to the small castle.'

It looked big enough to me in the headlights as we approached along a clearing, walled by the forest on either side, but maybe when she was growing up, she'd had school friends who'd lived in even bigger ones.

When we got there, it turned out to be a large half-timbered manor house rather than a true robber baron's fortified stronghold. Maybe at one time the original building had been. The lower storey was in stone and there was a squat stone tower of some kind attached to the north end of the house.

I pulled up on the gravel alongside a couple of large, dark-coloured Mercedes and a red Porsche 911 convertible. Suddenly, my four-year-old Type Three looked very out of place - just as I was feeling right then.

She got out and waved to someone I couldn't see inside the house. I didn't follow her gaze, instead carrying our bags to the porch over the closed front door.

We waited almost half a minute for someone to come before she yanked hard on the chain of the doorbell. We waited some more.

Just as the boar's head knocker was about to get a hammering, the door opened to reveal her brother. I'd seen photographs, but in the flesh there wasn't a strong resemblance between the siblings, unless it was a trait of impatience.

'There you are at last,' he said. She could have said the same to him and I sensed the rising temperature as I stood to one side and slightly behind her.

'Come in,' he said, looking past her to give me a cursory glance.

So that was how this weekend was going to be.

We went through to the main living room where a fire was burning in the grate. Sophie's mother and father were sitting on settees on opposite sides of the mantelpiece from each other. She went across to her mother first and briefly leant down to exchange kisses. Then she quickly turned away and went over to her father to do the same. I sensed there was more warmth there, on both sides.

So, sibling rivalry and favourite parents. Maybe I was lucky as the only child of a single mother.

Her father stood up and waited on me coming over to shake his hand. He gave me a cold look as I did so.

His wife didn't stand, and I judged it best not to go in close Italian-style as Sophie had done. Instead, I gave her a half-nod of acknowledgement, which was half a nod more than I got in return.

'Why didn't you come in the car we bought for you when you went to Brussels?' Sophie's father asked.

'Oskar drove me here.'

I had no idea she even had a car locked away in a garage somewhere in the city. I wondered what the women in the family were given to drive. Maybe Sophie had the use of another Porsche all this time.

'We haven't eaten yet,' she said.

'I think Anneliese left something in the kitchen. You can serve yourselves,' her mother offered.

'Let's go,' Sophie said to me.

I hadn't spoken a word since crossing the threshold of their small castle.

'Well,' she said, as she hunted through the pantry for bread, cheese and pickles. 'I did warn you before we came.'

'I've faced worse,' I said laconically. 'Don't let it bother you. No fuss is easier this way.'

The less her family spoke to me, the less chance that von Barten's death would somehow come up in conversation. Especially as at one time they'd suspected me of murdering her uncle. There was danger for her too, for she knew their suspicions were correct. An unexpected question could catch her out just as easily as me.

'Yes, I suppose it is,' she replied, putting on a carefully casual face.

'What do I say to them to make it easier for you?' I asked.

She looked at me with solemn eyes. 'Just don't rise to the provocations.'

'What provocations?'

'Didn't you mind them not waiting for us until they ate dinner? Just wait and see.'

We went back in and she sat next to her mother on the settee. I took an armchair facing the fire. Her brother settled himself in another leather armchair next to me and Sophie's father sat opposite his wife, just as before.

'What do you do?' I asked, turning to Dirk. No one else was offering to start the conversation. Forget provocations, I wasn't even worth that apparently.

'I'm the junior to a partner at the Swiss merchant bank which manages our family's money. I'm still learning. The idea is that in a couple of years' time, the bank will carve out a separate, dedicated partnership to manage our family foundation's various holdings. We plan to recruit other wealthy families from our network too and manage their investments as well.'

'Sounds ambitious,' I said.

His face flickered as he tried to work out whether I was complimenting him or being sarcastic.

'I'll be a senior investment manager at the new venture, but I won't run it,' he said, playing it cautious for now. 'The agreement is that no one from the family will. Avoids arguments that way.'

'Yes, Dirk is doing very well for himself,' piped up Sophie's mother from the wavering shadows cast by the firelight.

The merchant bank would hardly hold back the son of a big client who was offering to bring in even more business, so I wasn't so sure.

'What investments do you manage today?' I asked, sticking with what I guessed was the family's favourite topic.

'We have five main portfolios. But we don't ever disclose the value of the funds we have under management.'

Sophie's mother looked at me suspiciously, like she'd

caught me trying to case the joint.

'How do you find living in Switzerland?' I asked for a change.

'It suits me. Cosy place to do business, if you're on the inside. My fiancée is Swiss. We're having a big wedding by Lake Geneva next spring.'

I wondered if he was annoyed at his younger sister getting married first. What had Sophie's parents planned for her, if he felt the need to mention his was going to be a big affair. I had a nasty suspicion that Sophie was underselling the level of provocation coming our way.

Her father now did the minimum for politeness.

'What is it that you do in Brussels?'

I was so tempted to reply with 'and in Berlin'. Right now, having a rank or some other official status in the Stasi would have been worth it, just to see the expressions on their faces if I told them so - as a joke in poor taste, of course. Not as fun as having them arrested as class-traitors if the Soviets ever rolled west, though.

'I work as an internal investigator for the EEC. We look out for fraudulent expenses claims and deal with the theft of property.'

'What kind of property?' asked her mother, suddenly interested.

'Oh, handbags and scarves pilfered from offices, that kind of thing. People are always taking what doesn't belong to them,' I said innocently.

'Like my sister,' Dirk muttered clearly enough under his breath.

Her father looked at me astutely. My guess was that he knew his daughter too well to believe she'd go after a jumped-up clerk.

But that was the end of the warm-up, such as it was.

'My daughter has some big news. She's going to have a baby.'

He said this more like it was for his benefit, as if he was still getting used to the idea.

I glanced at the others. Dirk was contemptuous, Sophie's mother pursed her lips.

As for Sophie herself, she'd retreated behind a mask.

'Yes, that's right,' I replied. 'We're looking forward to its arrival next June and thought it best to get married now.'

Her mother shot me a quick look of poison. I now knew where Sophie had inherited that skill from.

'Be that as it may,' her father continued. 'You'll have to meet our lawyer to sign a prenuptial agreement first.'

This was news to me. I wasn't even exactly sure what one of those was.

Dirk saw my hesitation and was only too happy to explain.

'In the event that your marriage doesn't last, you won't have any claim on the family's money.'

'What else does it contain?' I asked, suspecting they wouldn't stop there. Maybe I'd have to pay them back for the cost of the wedding.

'The usual family law provisions,' her father replied, leaving me none the wiser.

I didn't care about getting a share of their poisonous money, but Sophie could have warned me about this little surprise.

'Tomorrow morning, before you meet the lawyer, we'll go for a walk in the woods. Just the men. We'll take something for lunch up to the lodge and make a picnic out of it. To get to know you better, you understand. I'm sure you'll appreciate this has all been sprung on us rather suddenly.'

Yes it has, I thought. By Rizzo's little *soldati*. Maybe he'd prefer if I didn't give his grandchild the fig leaf of legitimacy.

Now Sophie broke her reverie.

'I think we'll go up now, mother,' she said. She kissed her mother's proffered cheek and rose to her feet.

'Are you coming, Oskar? Or do you want to sit here for

a while longer?'

'I'll carry your bags.'

'Is this your childhood bedroom?' I asked as we entered the room.

There were pinhole marks on the walls where I presumed posters had once hung. No one had bothered to redecorate here since she left.

'What did you have on the walls?'

'Oh, the usual. Movie posters mainly.'

'Which ones?'

'Westerns with a love interest,' she said, embarrassed '"High Noon", that sort of thing.'

'Not Clint Eastwood, then?'

I put her bags by the wardrobe and she came over to hang up her dresses.

I had nothing constructive to say about her family and she didn't ask me what I thought of them. I began to wonder if her drive at work was to prove herself to her parents and brother. Or to escape them. Maybe her professional collaboration with her uncle at the EEC had been more complicated than I realised.

'I don't know where they made up a room for you, but the bed wouldn't be any bigger than mine,' she said.

'I'm used to life on the edge.'

-

Breakfast was set out in the dining room, but when we came down there were no other diners, and no dirty plates either to show that someone had got there before us. I caught a glimpse of who I assumed was Anneliese, as she went back to the kitchen down the hall where Sophie and I had served ourselves last night.

We ate together companionably enough, as the morning sun streamed through the wide window. A table stood underneath it with a coffee urn on top and I went over for my first cup of the day.

It had been dark when we arrived, so I hadn't properly appreciated the house's setting against the hill. A hundred metres to the north the clearing ended and the forest rose steeply to a ridge running east-west and then out of sight.

'Yours?' I asked pointing, as I took a sip.

'Yes,' said a voice from the doorway.

I turned to see her father already dressed for the outdoors.

'I thought we'd walk up there before lunch. I can get Gerhard to lend you a pair of boots.'

I recognised Gerhard's type when I saw him, because I'd just dealt with a pair of them in a nightclub in Apulia four weeks ago. He was about Johannes' age and I'd bet he'd been in Russia thirty-odd years ago. Then again, most men of his era had.

He had an impudent look about him and I wondered what hold he had over the family that they tolerated it. Maybe he'd been the batman to one of the von Barten clan during the war and knew things they'd rather he didn't.

He showed me a row of boots lined up along the wall of his lair on the ground floor of the tower. From the range of sizes on offer, I suspected tramping the woods was a trick Sophie's father did with all his weekend guests.

We started up the hill at a fast pace. If her father made a habit of this, it was no surprise he kept his trim figure. Dirk was soon puffing though, and gradually fell behind. With all those mountains in Switzerland he had no excuse for not staying fit.

'Who do you really work for?' her father asked, once we were out of easy earshot.

'You sound like someone who works at something they're not supposed to talk about,' he insisted. 'I know the type. We come across them in various capacities, through some of the companies we own which manufacture military systems.'

I had a shrewd idea of what he was getting at. People dealing with export controls and other intelligence types. But he would need to try harder with me.

'If my daughter wants to marry you, you must have some special qualities we're not being told about.'

He didn't like lowly employees? Well, he could have some more of that then.

'I was a police probationer before I joined EEC Internal Affairs. I've never been much more than that. We're a very small department, don't forget. The whole EEC organisation is only four thousand people.' At least, that's how big it had been last year.

'So you're still arresting pickpockets today, you say? Or are you catching bigger fish?'

'I said we're small. It means we deal with everyone. From secretaries and doormen to Commissioners who refuse to pay their parking fines to the local Belgian police.'

He looked at me curiously. Not because of my supposed job, I imagined, but more in how I was deflecting.

'So naturally we can't say everything we get up to,' I said, a little lamely.

'I bet you can't. Give me some credit for knowing my daughter.'

'What's this prenuptial agreement I need to look at this afternoon?' I said to change the topic.

'It's not directed at you personally, if that's what you're thinking. Every rich family has them. My son and future daughter-in-law will sign one too, before they get married next spring. Probably the very same document, if we can get the other side to use our contractual wording.'

I looked at him blankly, trying to hide my ignorance.

'It's nothing. Just sign it when you go over to meet Herr Sauer. Our family lawyer. He's come in especially today to open up his office for you.'

From his own deflection I was beginning to suspect I wouldn't like what I saw when I read it.

'If you're only a house detective for the EEC, then why were you involved with Sophie and her old boyfriend in Italy?'

He just wouldn't let go.

'They came to me to solve a practical problem. They thought I'd know practical people who could help them. I told you I was in the police in Hamburg, we knew all sorts of people there.'

'And then her old boyfriend died. Like my brother.'

The temperature under the trees instantly dropped by a few degrees.

'That was a coincidence. I'm sorry for both those tragedies.' And I meant it too.

'My wife hates you already.'

Oh well, at least the von Bartens had a quality of honesty about them. You could work with that.

'And she hates your mother. She thinks your mother has put you up to persuade Sophie to keep the baby, so you both can make a claim on our wealth.'

'How can you dislike someone you haven't met, or haven't even spoken with?' I demanded.

'It's ironic isn't it, because my wife didn't come from a wealthy background herself. Money is dangerous, Oskar. Being around it changes people. Even people you think you know well, like your own mother.'

'Now you're making the same claim that Frau von Barten is.'

'Hear me out. My brother became very wealthy during the war, amazingly so. But that's why my son will never run the family partnership we're setting up, there's too much at stake for my surviving brother's family and mine to fall out over. And we can't have interlopers.'

I raised my eyebrows.

'The foundation has only recently been restructured so that no one family controls it. We now all have the same class of shares with the same voting rights. But it's taken all this time since Ernst died to sort out the new ownership arrangements.'

That shot I fired in March last year had rippled out more widely than I could have imagined.

As he waved his hands for emphasis, explaining his points, I began to see where Sophie got her certainty from. Her self-belief that her solutions were the only possible ones for any given situation. And her directness, too.

I also began to realise what it meant to bring up someone else's child. Would its character be a combination of Sophie and Rizzo's, or would it copy our behaviour? And which parts of my father's character had I inherited?

We stopped to let Dirk catch up. There was a gap in the trees and down below in the valley I could see the house in its perfect setting. West bank of the Rhine too, the other side from the Group of Soviet Forces in Germany, and secluded in the surrounding woods to boot. Rizzo's father wasn't the only one with an eye to geography when it came to choosing where to live.

I couldn't help but wonder who would inherit the house. Dirk in all likelihood. The eldest child and a son to boot. I wouldn't mind a small castle for myself someday.

We walked two or three kilometres further. As we tramped along, the conversation became more desultory, even between Dirk and his father. The fun didn't stop when we got to the lodge, just as it came onto rain. I'd imagined it as a woodsman's cabin, but just like the main house, it gave the impression of being a nineteenth-century interpretation of something older. In this case, the architect had come up with a full-height, two-storey building with a confectionery of intricately carved gabling and a matching balcony.

Sophie's father unlocked the door with a large key he'd taken from his pocket and we trooped inside. There was a musty, unlived-in smell. The main room had a large-scale map of the surrounding area pasted onto a board. Pins were stuck into various parts of the green areas showing the forest.

'What are they for?' I asked, pointing.

'Kills of boar each season. A different-coloured pin for each year,' Sophie's father explained.

'You hunt?' I asked.

'We both do,' said Dirk. 'Gerhard comes too. He made the map.'

'What do you use?'

'We have .308 rifles back at the house. I'll show you this afternoon after you're back from the lawyers, if you like,' Dirk offered.

His father joined in. 'There's something spiritual about taking the life of another living thing. You can understand why the Romans had people fight to the death in the arena.'

He was talking to the right person, more than he knew.

Dirk handed out the sandwiches and coffee and we ate under the map around a dark wooden table in the main room.

'So where did you dig up Gerhard and Anneliese from?' I asked, making conversation.

'They've been with the family for years, since the war. They both grew up on our estate in East Prussia,' said Sophie's father.

I wondered how much of my own Prussian background Sophie had told them about, but I didn't fancy that particular line of enquiry.

'Did you ever meet Giovanni Rizzo or his family?' I asked instead.

'Did you?'

'Yes, in Brussels. And Italy too, at his grandfather's party.'

'You went out there with them in September?' Sophie's father asked in surprise.

'Yes. Didn't she say?

'She said she was going to consult you, but she didn't

explain what it was you did at the EEC. I hadn't realised you'd gone out there with them and that she'd end up wanting to marry you.'

'That's not quite how it went.'

But I was in a quandary, for Sophie and I hadn't properly rehearsed this conversation before coming here. How much had she kept secret from her own family, then? Did they even know she'd recruited me to carry out the theft?

'Why did Sophie get involved with Rizzo's family in the first place?' I asked him, hoping to take advantage of his surprise.

They both looked at one another quickly.

'What has she said?' asked her father.

'It was a favour to Rizzo,' I replied, not even convincing myself. 'Why, what should she have told me?'

Her father gave a faint smile, as if he was pleased at his daughter's secrecy.

'In case you didn't know,' I said, to test their reaction, 'she's still cooking something up with Rizzo's father, even now.'

'But you don't know what it is, even though you're supposedly marrying her?' said Dirk brutally.

'Do you know all of your fiancée's secrets?' I asked him back.

'You certainly don't know hers, or ours, for that matter,' he retorted.

Dirk got a warning glance from his father. It was time to try to put them on the spot again.

'In case you weren't aware,' I said, starting off diplomatically, 'as best as I can work out, the people I met at the party in Italy were dropping hints of a coup that's to take place. A coup, or something like it.'

They were glassy-eyed, impossible to read.

'I guess that might affect the value of the shares in any Italian companies you hold, if it were to take place?' I asked, probing some more. Their money was the only thing they cared about. They might open up if that was at risk.

'These things still happen elsewhere you know,' I said, pressing on. 'Look at Chile, where the right-wing tried to kidnap the head of the army and launch a coup to stop Allende being confirmed as president. Or the military coup which did take place in Bolivia a couple of weeks ago. You might need to look into that, Dirk.'

There was a slight, passing tension in Sophie's father's expression.

'None of this is any of your business,' snapped her brother. Trust him to rise to provocation.

Sophie's father tried to smooth over the awkwardness.

'You don't need to be concerned on our behalf. We invest cautiously. We make sure we're protected if there's a swing in the markets,' he said more calmly.

I wasn't quite clear what he meant by that.

'These suggestions that you picked up?' he continued. 'How serious did they sound? Was there any indication of when something like that might take place? It could be important for Dirk to know,' he said, in a slightly false, confiding tone.

But I didn't feel comfortable giving anyone stock market trading tips, let alone a future senior investment manager.

'If it happens,' I replied, 'it might be some time later this year. It's Italy's centenary year, which might count for something. But don't bet any money on it based on my say-so.'

The rain beat down against the leaded windows. Sophie's father shrugged.

'Maybe you're a useful man to know,' he admitted. He stared out of the window, ducking his head to try to see the clouds up above.

'It had better stop soon. You have an appointment in the town.'

In the end we had to get going before the rain had properly stopped. By the time we'd got back to the house, I just had time to change out of my borrowed boots in the porch where I'd left my own shoes.

I hadn't seen Sophie since breakfast and wondered what she'd got up to in the meantime. Discussing dresses and flowers with her mother, presumably.

Her father drove me the ten minutes back down into Gerolstein in his luxury SEL model Mercedes.

Their family lawyer was a dry, saturnine man, of about Sophie's father's age. He watched me from under hooded eyes as her father made the introductions.

'Herr Sauer will explain the contract and answer any of your questions.'

'Is he empowered to negotiate on your behalf?' I asked, getting down to business.

'It's a standard prenuptial contract, there's nothing to discuss,' the lawyer said, speaking for the first time.

'I have to go. Oskar, you need to be back at the house by,' he looked at his watch, 'four.'

That gave me two hours. He left without a backwards glance and after a few seconds, I heard the growl of the car's three and a half litre engine outside as he swung the heavy vehicle around in the middle of the street and drove off.

'You can sit there at the table in the corner to take a look at the contract. I'll stay in the room with you. I'm preparing for an important court case on Monday. If you finish by half past three, I can drive you back to Herr von Barten's house. Otherwise, you'll have to walk.'

He handed me a bound document with a red fake-leather cover and I sat down. Riffling through it, I guessed there to be a hundred and fifty pages, if you counted all the schedules. There was no way I could read it in ninety minutes.

I flipped the contract over onto its front, so as to work

through it from the back which was where people tended to put the nasty clauses they didn't want you to read.

'My own lawyer isn't working this weekend, so I suppose I'll have to take a look myself,' I informed him.

I was only half-joking. If I asked Kramer for advice, he'd probably give me the name of a lawyer in Brussels and tell me to charge it to the French embassy.

I started to read the text. The paragraphs at the back contained the detailed provisions for different aspects of a separation. I presumed the general principles were described up front. Although I hadn't got to those yet, from the way the sections at the back were worded, I got the gist. Namely, that any divorce wouldn't leave me with a *pfennig* that I hadn't already possessed before the marriage, and I wasn't even sure about that.

I skim-read the clause about the calculation of accrued gains. The clause about return of 'clothes, footwear and other accoutrements' struck me as particularly petty.

Then I uncovered the first real hidden landmine.

'The Second Party relinquishes their right to joint custody of any issue of the marriage. The subsequent degree of permitted access shall be the exclusive decision of the First Party.'

I flipped to the front of the contract to check the definitions and stared when I saw her full set of forenames. I flipped back to the clause.

'No access by the Second Party is assumed.'

That was me, obviously. I didn't know if Rizzo's child would come under the clause about the issue of the marriage, but even so. To bring up a kid with it thinking you were its father, and then for you both to be separated after who knew how many years seemed harsh.

Then, to add insult to injury, I found an accompanying clause which stated that if Sophie died in unexpected circumstances, the custody decision would be made by the surviving members of the von Barten family.

Given that the list of possible events 'including but not limited to' took up almost a page, I couldn't see how they might be considered unexpected. They'd even included a nuclear attack, which seemed optimistic to me as regarding the survival of either Party.

'Has the younger Frau von Barten read this contract?' I asked. I almost said 'my wife.'

A smile hovered over the lawyer's thin lips.

'Oh, I expect so. I believe she was the one who insisted on the addition of the qualifying paragraph on unexpected demise. I believe where you are involved these events aren't always so uncommon. Like with her previous companion, Signor Rizzo.'

He had to say that, I told myself. Any suggestion that she'd only seen an earlier draft, and I would be out of there in an instant. His words seemed an unnecessary provocation though, and after how the weekend had gone so far, I was ready to be provoked.

'What are the consequences if we marry without signing this?'

Now the corners of his mouth turned upwards a fraction more.

'The terms of the family's Foundation don't forbid you from that course of action.'

Cheeky devil, I thought.

'But without a prenuptial contract, a dormant right in the existing agreement between the shareholders of the Foundation is activated. That clause gives the other shareholders the right to purchase Frau von Barten's shares at their nominal value in the event of her unexpected demise, regardless of the terms of any will.'

Whether a legal basis existed to give a prenuptial contract precedence over a will, I didn't know. I suspected he might be laying down a smokescreen.

'What's the notional value of a share, a *pfennig*? So

you're saying that without a prenuptial agreement, effectively her children wouldn't inherit anything?'

'They would be unlikely to inherit much. You won't, for sure, not under any circumstances. But with this prenuptial agreement in place, such that the family gets custody of any children, the purchase right is waived and her children can inherit.'

'How do you mean, I won't inherit under any circumstances?'

He smiled at the question, as if he'd been hoping for it.

'Aside from future children, her shares can only be passed on to named people on a very short list. You're not on it.'

I flicked on through a couple of pages. It all sounded a little over complicated to me. Unless, of course, they'd only recently added these clauses especially for Sophie's and my situation.

'What happened when Ernst von Barten died unexpectedly,' I asked interestedly.

'You heard about that, did you?'

I didn't answer, but kept staring at him instead.

The lawyer looked at me appraisingly, as if wondering how to use it to his advantage.

'His estate was divided by percentages. Although the value of his other property, relative to his shares in the Foundation, wasn't large, it still took them until this summer to agree how they translated to the proportions mentioned in his will.'

He frowned at me, as if I were a slow pupil in class.

'And some people wanted their percentage made up entirely from shares. To complicate things further, they wanted the shares valued as at the time of his death. They aren't going through that kind of fight again, that's why the revised Foundation agreement and this prenuptial contract are so prescriptive. They won't negotiate any changes to it, not a single paragraph.'

If what he said was true, and I didn't have any reason

to doubt him, then I was partly responsible for the situation I now found myself in. Everyone was taking revenge on me from beyond the grave these days.

'So from what I've read so far,' I pinched the rear third of the document between my forefinger and thumb to show him, 'the trade-off is sign it and lose custody of my children so that they can inherit my wife's wealth or don't sign it and keep the children, but the rest of the family take everything?'

There, I'd finally said the word 'wife' out loud. I was getting sucked deeper and deeper into this arrangement.

'I can't agree to this, not under any circumstances.'

'That's something you'll have to take up with your future wife. I can't imagine she'll be very happy to know that if she dies in a car crash her children will be left with nothing. Unless you have some personal wealth we don't know about?'

Put that way, the wider family and greedy cousins had an incentive to encourage me not to sign and then arrange an accident for Sophie after the wedding.

'I'd better get moving then, if I'm going to speak with her.'

I put the contract under my arm and made for the door.

'Don't be a fool Herr Lenkeit. Not unless you want your engagement to be broken off when you get back up there.'

'I know her better than you,' I said, even though I didn't feel so confident inside.

'What did you expect to see in this contract? What's unreasonable about it?' he riposted.

'If you have a falling out with your future wife, lose your temper, and hit her too hard, then why should you have custody of both her children and their inheritance?'

'But this definition of unexpected death is so wide it's virtually impossible to prove natural causes. You just said so yourself, a car crash would cover it.'

'You're concerning yourself over some highly unlikely events. Just sign it and I'll drive you back now. Get married, protect your wife from harm, enjoy life on her family's wealth.'

I shook my head.

'Or walk back to the house, be late for whatever event they've laid on. "Yes *Oma*, it is very rude of Oskar not to turn up, after you made that long trip just to see him specially,"' he said in a falsetto voice.

'Shut up. Think of a solution. That's what we're paying you for after all,' I said, leaving and closing the door tight behind me.

It was actually quite a pleasant walk in the weak autumn sun back up into the hills. Four o'clock came and went and still I climbed. Not many cars passed. I had plenty of time to think.

Had she really agreed to these clauses? My sense when it came to her having custody was that she had. Especially if the child she was carrying wasn't mine. This was the real world after all. Hate had turned to love, but who was to say we mightn't end up back there again? I guessed that Johannes' first marriage hadn't worked out for him and maybe his second too, for all his boasting to us in Wismar about understanding women.

But would Sophie have agreed to such a wide, catch-all description of an unexpected or an unexplained death? Or was that paragraph in the contract a signal from her family? Sophie had said that they'd paid the police to investigate Ernst von Barten's death as murder rather than suicide. And if I kept causing them problems, these guys could afford to hire tougher nuts than the police to straighten things out.

I got back to find that I was indeed late for something. No one came to the door when I rang so I wandered round the side of the house to find them all in the south-facing conservatory at the back. The remains of cocktail things were off to one side, empty pitchers and used glasses.

'Oh there you are,' said Sophie's father. 'We had a call from Herr Sauer.'

Sophie hissed at me, not quietly enough for my liking. 'You've completely humiliated me in front of my family.'

Dirk smirked from behind his glass, clearly enjoying his sister's discomfort.

His mother looked at me coldly and turned a frosty eye on Sophie too.

'Well it's a shame. I made my special South American cocktails,' he said as he rang the bell, presumably for Anneliese to come and clear up.

'Dinner is at half six, don't be late,' said his wife as she swept past. I don't believe she'd looked me in the eye once since I'd got here.

Sophie left too and with a look from her father I went to follow her upstairs to her room.

'Where the hell have you been?'

'Not signing your prenuptial contract. Not after Herr Sauer and I had a little chat about some of its special provisions.'

'What do you mean?' she said, snatching the contract from under my arm.

I sat down in the armchair under the window as she stood and flicked through it.

'What's the problem?' she demanded.

I wondered if this was the time and the place where it all fell apart.

'Look at clause one hundred and twenty-two.'

She frowned as she scanned the lines with the help of her finger.

'This has been embellished. He's gone way beyond what I thought my father and I had agreed.'

'But in outline you were happy for it to be in there? And for us to sign such a contract in the first place?'

'In outline? I didn't have a choice. I have to keep my family happy, as far as I can. You know what they already think about you. It's called making compromises. I thought that's how you make a marriage work? Or so people say.'

'Maybe we've made too many assumptions about what each other thinks.'

'What are you saying? You want out? At this stage?' There was anger in her eyes and a touch of fear there, too.

'I'll sign the contract, but only if that clause is struck out in its entirety. If tragedy strikes, I'll make my own way in life with your child. I won't leave it fatherless as I was.'

The colour in her cheeks slowly faded but her lips remained pursed.

'I'll talk to my father. I've already had enough problems to deal with today with my mother.'

'What's been going on?'

'I'm arranging this wedding all by myself, that's what,' she said grimly. 'And it seems I'm paying for anything other than the bare essentials out of my income from the Foundation too.'

I considered what to say. I wondered how determined she was not to lose face in front of her family with a low-key affair, especially with her brother's wedding coming up next year.

'If they don't want to celebrate it in a big way, then don't make them. Let's just get married and then have some kind of reception when the baby's born next year?'

'The whole point is to make everyone think that it's ours.'

'We haven't discussed that yet. It's firstly so that the child isn't born out of wedlock. It gives us options about what to tell people later.'

She frowned again. 'There's a lot we haven't discussed yet. We need to get through this weekend first and convince my mother that this wedding is really happening. If she believes it is, her natural desire to show off in front of the crazy half of the family will take over. My other uncle's family,' she explained.

'Go get your lawyer to change the contract.'

'Let's see.'

'I have to take something back to Gerhard,' I said, looking for an excuse to finish the conversation there.

I picked up the boots from the porch and found my way back through the house to Gerhard's lair.

For all her talk, this wedding was no sure thing. Not now that I'd put my foot down over the clauses in the prenuptial contract. Like anything else in life, the theory was different to practice. I'd have done anything for her the evening we'd first made love in her office, but now reality had finally intruded into the make-believe of the last few weeks.

I wouldn't let her go willingly, that was for sure. And I had to keep remembering that it might be my child after all, despite her certainty that it wasn't. If it didn't clearly look like a Rizzo, we might never know for sure. Blood tests excluded some possibilities but didn't give a positive answer on their own.

I wasn't in the best of moods when I saw Gerhard.

'What do you do all day, hidden back here?' I demanded, dropping the boots on the floor. 'Your wife does most of the work round here that I can see.'

He smirked.

'They think it won't last, you know. Maybe they're right. The family didn't get to where they are today without being as cunning as foxes.'

'Why do they keep you hanging around then?'

'Oh, Anneliese and I go way back with them. We know all their secrets.' He smiled knowingly.

'You won't get to find out mine, so don't try.'

'You're a cocky one. You wouldn't be the first man they've driven away,' he said slyly.

I knew what he wanted, but despite myself I gave it to

him.

'Are you going to tell me?'

'Maybe. There was someone when she was eighteen, before she went away to college. They got rid of him too.'

Rationing out the details seemed to give him as much pleasure as it would have done to De Mauro.

'I'm not some eighteen-year-old they can scare off.'

'I wasn't talking about the man she was with. Only that she was eighteen when it happened.'

Well, more fool me for asking.

Dinner was even less cheerful than the cocktail party I hadn't been to.

Her father's not-so-subtle pressure on me over the contract was replaced by very unsubtle attacks by her mother. Over apéritifs we exchanged our first words, by the entrée a real row was brewing and over the main course it came to a head. Talking to Gerhard hadn't helped my frame of mind. But for someone who preferred to give people the silent treatment in awkward social situations, I shocked myself at how quickly I lost my self-control - the one time when it really mattered.

'Tell me again, Herr Lenkeit. Why didn't you go to university? It's not as if poor people in West Germany can't. Or did you lack the intelligence to take a degree?' she asked.

'Most people don't go. You can't write off nine out of ten people that way,' I snapped back.

'But people with ambition do go, those with the desire to make something of themselves in life. Or don't you care? You're happy to drift through life and be carried along by others?'

I took a breath, fighting the anger.

'I was ambitious enough to move to Brussels from Hamburg. I quit my police cadetship and the prospect of a steady job to do so.'

'Yes, but what have you actually achieved there in the

past four years?'

I knew Sophie was worth all this, but I hadn't realised how much she would cost. I tried to remember that she'd warned me yesterday evening about the provocations and tried again for her sake.

'I do jobs for all kinds of people,' I said quietly. 'I've been assigned to help one of the leading European federalists, Commissioner Spinelli. He's going to turn the EEC into a democracy.'

Sophie frowned at this.

'My daughter has already been promoted twice. You're just name dropping. She's actually accompanying the Agricultural Commissioner to Ireland next week.'

'Are you pleased that your daughter has a career? What was your profession Frau von Barten?' I asked, fraying at the edges.

There was an intake of breath from Dirk and his mother. Sophie's father was looking at me reflectively.

'There was a war on, in case you'd forgotten. My education was sacrificed for Germany,' she snapped, just as Sophie would have done.

I looked at her with narrowed eyes, estimating her age. 'Which war was that? The Spanish Civil War?'

Sophie's father slapped his hands on the table. 'That's enough,' he said sharply, glancing around the room. 'From everyone.'

He looked sternly at me now.

'We're not some bourgeois family whom you can insult as you please. Or push around either.'

Said the man who wanted me to sign away any motherless children I might one day find myself with.

'We're far more influential than you give us credit for. We're connected to all kinds of powerful people in West German politics. And in the West German security apparatus, too, as I suggested earlier today.'

The apparatus which my guys in the Normannenstrasse had thoroughly penetrated, I thought to myself.

'So don't sit at our table and play your word games with us, dropping your sarcastic comments that you think are so clever.'

I set my cutlery aside.

'However I try to describe my work or my social position to you and your wife, it won't be good enough in your eyes for Sophie. But at least give her some credit for possessing her own judgement. She's not a child. She's having a child.'

There was silence as Anneliese and Gerhard cleared away the plates and served dessert.

The silence carried on until the end of the meal. I glanced at Sophie. She was pale and withdrawn and I wondered if the pregnancy had any physical effect on her at this stage. She thought she was starting her seventh week.

We moved back to the main living room where coffee was served.

Her mother and father took up their same positions as last night when we arrived, one of either side of the fireplace on the leather settees. Dirk joined his mother on her side this time, Sophie with her father. I was on the armchair in the middle again, facing the fire.

'We're going to discuss this prenuptial contract. All of us together,' her father announced.

I burned inside for Sophie's shame. A smile played around the corners of Dirk's mouth in anticipation. His mother's lips were tightly pursed together, which did nothing to hide her frown lines.

'Firstly, it goes without saying that the only access you have to Sophie's share of the family money will be from whatever allowance she chooses to pay you.'

Sophie herself had the same set about her mouth as her mother, possibly worried about an explosion from me. But she had said before dinner we needed to get through it, so for her sake I would.

'I'm not marrying her for her money.'

'Good. Well now that that's established, you agree that it would be selfish to deny any surviving children the benefit of being looked after by the family, should an unfortunate event occur?'

'You seem very concerned about that. It took you a whole page in the contract to cover every possibility, even down to a lightning strike.'

'Then let me make it clear to you, you little fucker, just in case you're especially dense. We know you went with Sophie to East Germany just before my brother died and today we find out that you went with her to Italy, just before her old boyfriend died. A very pleasant young man, I may add. Wealthy and sophisticated. I liked him.'

'I liked him too. But you're missing the point. For any future children involved here, it would be wrong to break up the family they were born into. Their real family, not the family of their parents. That is an absolute for me.'

'I've no intention of letting go of any grandchildren. As I said, it would be utterly selfish of me to deny them the benefit of what my brothers and I have worked so hard to achieve.'

I was ready to tell him the nature of the wartime embezzlement, bribery and corruption I suspected their wealth had come from, but it was the wrong argument and the wrong time.

'That's not your responsibility, but that of the surviving parent,' I insisted.

In the end it wasn't me but Sophie's mother who exploded.

'Tch! Max, we've heard enough,' Then to me, 'Tell us what it will cost, to pay you and your mother to go away, so we can find a proper husband for our daughter.'

I saw Sophie's jaw drop from across the room. Without a word or backwards glance at anyone, including me, she got up and left. I could hear her climbing the stairs and if I knew her at all, it was most likely to pack our bags, rather than to collapse weeping on the bed.

'Are you going to go after her?' Dirk asked.

'I suspect she'll be back down soon enough.' Now that she was gone, it was time for some home truths.

I crossed my legs, took out a cigarette and lit up.

'We don't smoke in the…' Dirk began to say.

I held up my forefinger to silence him.

'If she can't get married here, with her family, we'll go to mine in East Germany. My aunt attends church in a dilapidated old building in a town on the Baltic coast. Who knows? Once Sophie experiences the real love and warmth of the socialist human community, as it's called over there, we may stay. Raise our child to think and care for others before itself, away from the fascist successor state of West Germany.'

A chill fell over the room as many questions went unanswered.

'That's preposterous,' her father finally growled.

'The problem is that you don't really know her as well as you think, not the Sophie von Barten of Brussels that is. She doesn't need you to get where she wants to go. She may have thought she needed her uncle, but I think one evening she found out she didn't.'

I tilted my head to exhale straight up to the ceiling, then turned to look pointedly at her mother, giving her a good stare. I suspected she would have told Sophie to ignore Ernst von Barten's importuning, as it had been described to me on the train back from Wismar.

'She's going to make her own way in Brussels. I've seen her at work, and I believe in her. And I'll help her too. Any obstacles or people who try to trip her up I'll deal with in my own way.'

I caught sight of Dirk looking at the scar on my hand as I raised the cigarette to take another puff.

'The EEC's empire, so to speak, is growing and her power will grow with it. Don't estrange yourselves from her, one day you might come to regret it.'

There was a long silence, broken by Sophie coming back into the room. She came up behind my chair to stand there, resting her right hand on my left shoulder, as if to transmit some of her own unbounded self-confidence to me. Not that I needed it just then.

'We're going now,' she announced to her family. 'I don't think I'll make the plane for Dublin if we leave tomorrow morning as we'd planned. We'll stay in a hotel nearer to the airport tonight.'

I got up and her hand fell away. I followed her out of the room to the hall, dropping my cigarette butt into an old brass artillery shell casing decorated with engravings which stood by the door.

She glanced at me as she picked up her bag. I shook the car keys out of my pocket, picked up my own bag and we left.

As I pulled out onto the public road, she finally spoke. 'What did you say to my parents back there?'

'I told them you're more than capable of making your own way in life without their money.'

'Do you really believe that?'

'There's no one at the Berlaymont smarter than you. And no matter how many other countries join, those of us from the original Six will always be the ones who own the place.'

She lay back in the seat. I was glad I'd got a Type Three with headrests.

We didn't speak much as the kilometres rolled by. Neither of us were really in the mood to dissect what had just gone on today. She fiddled with the radio for a bit and found American Forces Network, tapping along with her foot to The Animals for a while.

She hadn't complained to me about her family's behaviour. She'd just made her decision and got on with it. It was why I loved her.

We called it a day outside Liège and found a motel off

the A3 autoroute. I carried our bags in from the car while she negotiated at reception.

'They call it a bridal room, but I'm dubious as to how many honeymooners it's ever seen,' she told me as we climbed the stairs.

'I told your parents we might end up getting married in Wismar. I was tempted to say that Major Johannes would be a witness, but I held back.'

She snorted at this. 'I can't see that impressing Sicco much.'

'Have you told your boss yet?' I asked as I unlocked the door to the room.

'No. But I've been thinking, and no matter how liberal people say they are, if only for my career's sake I need to get married before the baby arrives.'

At this she stroked her stomach for an instant, the first time I'd seen her do so.

'My parents must understand that, at least.'

We went inside and she threw herself back on the bed, staring up at the low textured ceiling.

'What a shit day,' she said, her arms crossed behind her head on the pillow.

I lay down beside her and flicked the tip of her nose.

'Who's hosting you in Ireland?'

'The Department of Agriculture, I think. Why, do you know someone there?'

'No. I never met them. I was with other people - the Department of External Affairs. But don't ask questions about me.'

She rolled over to lean on her elbows. 'Why not?' she asked.

'They don't want me back there. Don't get tarred with the same brush.'

'Why were they so upset?'

'How do you think you'd feel if a delegation came to Brussels from Washington or Moscow, and one of them got into trouble involving the local police?'

'You get into trouble everywhere, don't you?'

'Everyone gets into trouble when they try to visit their mother-in-law.'

I got a quick kiss on the mouth for making light of it.

'Not every prospective mother-in-law tries to pay off the groom not to turn up,' she replied.

'I'm hard to bribe.'

'She's hard to impress,' Sophie conceded. 'Why couldn't you have given her a better story about what you do than investigating cloakroom thefts?'

'I said to you before, it's not possible to explain any part of what Masson's department does without revealing too much.'

As for Sophie herself, I hadn't gone much beyond what I'd told her on the plane back from the funeral, about the security briefings that we produced for the main Directorates. The monitoring of foreign negotiators and the investigation of potential leaks at the institutions she didn't know about yet. As for Kramer's future plans for a department at the EEC to carry out hatchet jobs on other *fonctionnaires*, that was staying well under wraps.

'The EEC's not the CIA,' she said. 'You're not sworn to protect the secrets of the Commission from your own family. At some point we should tell her something more.'

'Difficult, now that I've already given her one particular story.'

What I'd just said about her mother could have applied to Sophie too.

'I understand it's confidential, but you could have hinted at something. They might have accepted you more easily.'

I wanted to say that they hadn't accepted me at all, from what I'd seen today. I might begin to get their respect if I had a large bank account, but even then, there was no way I'd ever make enough money in one lifetime to come close to their level of wealth.

'Your father guessed there's more to me.'

She grunted.

'Anyway, let's not part on bad terms,' she announced, stretching above the headboard to flick off the switch to the room's single light.

Chapter Twenty-Seven

I picked Sophie up from the airport in the morning, straight off the plane from Dublin, and we set off for Hamburg there and then.

Her week had been interesting even if mine hadn't. Masson had got us compiling meaningless reports again to fill our time until the third round of ministerial meetings on accession took place in December, when we could go back to picking up gossip on the applicant countries' delegates.

'Yesterday Sicco gave a speech in a place called Tralee. We had to drive past signs saying, "Go Home Cromwell." No one really wanted to explain what they meant.'

'I guess they don't like being bossed around by outsiders. On the other hand, the people in power in Dublin just love the idea of EEC agricultural subsidies. Eventually they'll have to choose which is more important to them.'

'Well, whatever you got up to there, it can't have been that bad because no one mentioned a drunk EEC official who'd ended up in hospital after a fight in a bar.'

'Good to know,' I replied drily.

As a distraction from that topic, I gave her something else to puzzle over.

'You had a whole week with Mansholt's undivided attention. How easy would it be for someone to get a subsidy decision made in favour of a particular product?' I asked.

'You suggested something like that already, at dinner

that first night we spent together. To give something to Sicily and encourage the Mafia to go straight.'

She was sharp to have remembered. Too sharp for my liking.

'It's something I'm discussing. Could it be done?'

'Depends on how greedy people are. Often there's subsidies on some minor product that get agreed to, in combination with trade-offs being made elsewhere. If the lobbyists are clever with the wording the Commission signs up to, they can stretch the definitions later.'

'Makes sense.'

'Who are you discussing this with?' she asked.

Two or three seconds stretched out while I considered my answer, but it felt a lot longer.

'It was something that came up at the meeting in Palermo. I suggested it as something Giovanni could have done for them, to give them a reason to use him. But you know what happened next.'

'Are you still discussing it?' she asked suspiciously.

'No, it was my poor choice of words.'

Are you going back there for any reason?' she asked.

'I don't know. It depends on Giovanni's father. I told you on the way home from the funeral, that he and I talked afterwards about whether the Saracenos were still out for revenge.' Then, just for good measure I added, 'He's the grandfather. He's family now.' Not that it was likely she'd have forgotten.

She grunted.

'My own family are still extremely unhappy with you. At least my father is, and he's the one who really matters here.'

'Did you speak to them while you were in Ireland?'

'Expensively and at length from different hotels.'

I sped up a little to overtake a Ford Capri ahead of us, the Type Three valiantly giving its all to get past.

'Did you come to an agreement?'

'We'll see. It depends what the compromise is going to

427

have to be.'

'You do deals with each other in your family like that? As if you're negotiating a treaty?' I asked in wonderment.

For all my trips to Berlin to confer with the Stasi, and for all the international assignments planned for me by Kramer, sometimes I felt I knew so little about the world.

My mother kissed Sophie matter-of-factly on the cheeks and offered her a drink after the journey.

She was shown to the seat of honour in the leather armchair, my mother took the settee and I sat on a dining table chair.

They both looked at me to say something. How did you break the ice with two people from opposite ends of the social spectrum, who'd been introduced under the strangest of circumstances? We had one thing in common, though.

'Sophie's family are from East Prussia too, Mother.'

'Which part?' she asked Sophie.

'They had an estate to the north of the Gilgestrom River, a few kilometres before it emptied into the Kurisches Haff. They're both called something else now by the Russians. Very flat country I understand, a bit boring.'

'We came from Allenstein,' my mother explained. 'Much further to the West. The Poles call our town "Olsztyn" now.'

Then, to my embarrassment, she added inconsequentially, 'They've built a tyre factory there since we left.' This was followed by, 'Where were you born, then?'

'In Switzerland,' Sophie replied. 'Nineteen forty-six.'

We could have carried on with the awkward trivialities, it was the done thing in these situations. But maybe after her own mother's performance last week at their house in the Eifel, Sophie was done with respecting social norms.

'When I met your sister last year, Frau Lenkeit, I

worked some things out for myself.'

'Oh, it was you? Oskar didn't say when he told me.'

Well that had taken a turn I hadn't expected. But talking about my paternity didn't seem to bother the two women.

'Have you ever spoken with anyone about what happened back then?' Sophie asked.

'I need to go and fill up the car for the journey home, if you're okay staying with my mother for a while.'

'Take as long as you like.' she said. So I did.

When I got back, I could hear low voices in the lounge. I gave a half knock and opened the door at the same time. They both looked up. Whatever had been discussed earlier didn't seem to have caused a falling out. Sophie was stroking her stomach again.

'I told your mother something of Giovanni. I said how proud I was that you want to be a father to his child.'

I really wished I could have found another excuse to leave.

'We haven't decided when to tell his family yet,' I said. 'Not until the pregnancy is a surer thing.'

'Oskar always wanted a father. But I couldn't cope with a relationship because of the war,' my mother said.

I really didn't like this opening up game. Clearly, given that I was now moving on, there were some things my mother felt she could reveal for the first time. I just wished she wasn't revealing them to me.

'When did you and Stefan decide to get married?' I asked, out of genuine curiosity, as well as to deflect.

'Only this summer. His son in West Berlin isn't pleased about it.'

'He's an adult. What does he have to do with it?' I asked.

I wondered if Johannes' people in Berlin proper knew of him. Maybe they had an informer in the West Berlin police who could run some checks.

'Divorce is hard on people,' she said, eyeing up Sophie and I warily.

We went for a walk in the neighbourhood while my mother got dinner ready, refusing any help. There was something else on the horizon which I needed to address with Sophie.

'My mother will ask if you want to go to church tomorrow morning. I haven't been for a while. I was planning to go with her.'

'Okay. How long is the service?'

'An hour or so.'

'I'll come with you if you like. It doesn't bother me either way.'

'When was the last time you went?' I asked.

She looked at me solemnly, but with an edge.

'Oh,' I said. 'I'm sorry.'

'We're sorry too. It took eighteen months and almost a civil war in the family to work out what came next.'

Now her tone was cynical.

'How does what you do, what you did to my uncle and to all those people in Sicily, sit with going to church?'

'Where else can I go?' I asked, staring back at her.

'Does it change you in any way? Does it do any good?'

'Your uncle's death was wrong. I'm not denying that. Sicily was self-defence. At the end of my trip to Ireland I turned over a new leaf, became a new person, if you will.'

'Well that gives me a lot of comfort, I'm sure. What happened in Ireland to make that come about?'

She looked at me with piercing, gimlet eyes.

I sat down on a bench along the path under the trees.

'I repented of my sins because I came to the end of the road,' I said simply.

'Why?'

Unpleasant as this conversation was, I had to go through with it.

'Killing your uncle ate me up from the inside, like

cancer. I couldn't see any other way out. I thought of the gun in my flat back in Brussels and how easy it would be to end it all.'

'So how did you feel after Sicily? That was four more times you pulled the trigger,' she said unsympathetically.

I looked at her grimly. 'You saw what it did to me. You heard it at night. I didn't put that on.'

'But now you're going to go to church and that will make it all right?'

'No. Going to church on its own won't make a difference.'

'Then I don't understand,' she said, even more impatiently now.

I ploughed on. 'It's what I tried to explain just now. My sins are forgiven, once and for all. We go to church, I guess... I guess to be with other believers.'

'You don't sound very sure. You should speak to your aunt's pastor in Wismar. The one we met last year,' she instructed, adopting the tone she used when she was exasperated that I wasn't coming up to the mark. I hadn't heard it used since the journey back from Wismar in September.

'What do your mother and your aunt's family know about Karin's escape attempt?' she asked, less sure of herself now.

'I don't know. Major Johannes never said who knew of the background to her arrest. I guess my uncle and aunt might have been told when they were questioned. My mother hasn't mentioned you in connection with Karin.'

'If she asks, I'm going to be honest.'

My mind boggled at how honest she intended to be over how she'd tried to suborn a seventeen-year-old girl into fleeing to the West.

'Let's go back,' she said. 'We'll have to tell her sometime, you know. We can't keep these secrets forever.'

-

Sophie put on one of the business suits she'd worn to Ireland for church in the morning. Even if she hadn't been overdressed for our congregation, she'd still have turned heads as she entered the sanctuary.

She didn't seem to notice and took part in the service as if she'd always been going there, singing along to the hymns, even if she didn't know the words. I'd never heard her sing before. Her voice was as tuneful and clear as a bell, but then I was a biased listener.

The sermon was a disappointment though. I'd been hoping she'd hear something to make her stop and think, or at least understand better where I was coming from. But my mother's pastor was as weak as water.

Sophie was right, the pastor in Wismar whom I'd crossed swords with on two occasions would have been much steelier. Even if he suspected that some of his congregation might have been reporting his words back to the Ministry.

After the service, my mother introduced her to most of the people there. It wasn't a big crowd.

Although I hadn't grown up in the church - my mother had only started going more frequently when I was already a teenager - I knew most of them, even if we'd never been especially close. To their credit, they'd mostly accepted me for what I was, the child of a single mother. There had been the occasional awkward reference or clumsy word which had hurt at the time, but they hadn't been meant maliciously. No one knew of my full parental history though.

But now there was only warmth and delight at our news, as much for my mother's sake as mine, I sensed.

Sophie was also right in another area, I did have a higher standard to live up to these days. It was all very well telling Kramer I was forswearing trigger work, but I couldn't have imagined how Sicily would have blown up as it did. And despite his assurances, who knew what Kramer and France's British allies really had in store for me, once I got to London?

But that was a problem for another day.

We made our farewells and left straight from church to drive back to Brussels. As the city dropped behind us, Sophie started to chirp less and less. After a few minutes driving down the autobahn in silence, I looked over and saw her silently sobbing. She saw me looking and tried to dry her tears, but something set her off even worse. I began to get genuinely worried.

The Buddikate rest area was up ahead - the same one we'd stopped at on the way to the border the day of her abduction. I pulled off and parked up.

'What's the matter?' I asked, almost using a term of endearment for the very first time.

Now she dried her eyes properly and looked around her.

'Why did you bring me here of all places?' she complained.

'Why were you crying?'

She pouted her lip and very deliberately turned to look out of the passenger window.

'It's just a delayed reaction to the story your mother told me yesterday afternoon when you were out. Of what happened when the Red Army arrived at the field hospital.'

'Oh,' I said quietly, folding my hands on my lap.

'Yes, "Oh,"' she said sternly, turning back to look at me now.

'Come on, never mind. Let's get moving,' she snapped.

'Did she, did she say where they were from? Which part of the Soviet Union?' I asked nervously.

Now Sophie gave me the coldest of cold stares.

'There were so many. More than she could remember. Who the hell knows where you sprung from?'

I put it down to the hormones.

Chapter Twenty-Eight

It was the weekend after Hamburg. We'd come back for a peace meeting with her family and to sign the new prenuptial contract. It had been couriered to me in Brussels and I'd taken it to a lawyer recommended by Kramer. The lawyer wouldn't fully commit himself because the contract was governed by West German law, and although his eyes widened at some of the more insulting clauses, he put my mind sufficiently at rest.

I didn't know what Sophie had threatened or bribed her parents with in the two weeks since I'd walked out of Herr Sauer's office, but the clauses on children had been changed to award joint custody with either her, or with her family if she died. Percentage access for each party would be determined at arbitration. It was as good as it was going to get, the lawyer had reckoned.

Tomorrow there was to be a lunch with her surviving uncle and aunt. Her other aunt by marriage, Anne - Ernst von Barten's widow - would be there as well, which I wasn't looking forward to much. Dirk was back in Switzerland.

Whether Sophie's father had cautioned his wife or not, dinner late on Friday night was a calmer affair than last time, as we sat just the four of us around the table. Who knew? My future mother-in-law might warm to me in time. It had taken Sophie long enough, but she'd got there in the end.

'Are any cousins coming tomorrow?' I asked her mother, trying to show an interest.

'I doubt it,' Sophie's father replied. 'We weren't particularly close in that way. Dirk and Sophie didn't really see much of them. My brother's eight years older than me, he started his family earlier in life too. Sophie's surviving cousins are in their thirties and forties.'

'Margrit only turned thirty-three last year,' Sophie interjected.

'My youngest niece,' he said.

'Did one of the cousins die?'

'Hans, the eldest. He was a fighter pilot. He got shot down at the start of 'forty-four during an American bombing raid on the Ruhr. He was twenty.'

'That must have been hard.'

'He was Ernst's favourite nephew. He took it almost as badly as Hans' father.'

I knew this already and more. A few minutes before I shot him, Ernst von Barten had told me Hans was to have been his heir.

'Are they all coming to the wedding?'

Sophie's mother looked at me frostily. For what social blunder, I had no idea.

'Werner won't.'

'Ah, yes. That's tricky,' her father murmured.

I looked puzzled.

'Werner was Hans' younger brother. They were only a year apart,' he said to me.

I was still no clearer as to the problem.

Sophie cleared her throat. 'He was engaged to be married at the end of the war. She was from East Prussia too, from another estate in the next district. But they didn't escape in time when the Red Army arrived.'

I got the picture.

'Werner had a very strong sense of honour,' her father said. Sophie added, 'his own honour,' under her breath.

'He broke the engagement because of it and she later committed suicide,' he concluded.

A whole new world of hate opened up in front of me.

'So what does that side of the family know of my… situation?'

'They all know,' Sophie's father said.

I looked at Sophie. She looked back impassively. She was the first von Barten to work out who I was last year. Either she or her uncle had taken it upon themselves at some point to tell the rest of the clan.

'Do you get on with your brother's family?' I asked.

The question hung in the air for a long moment or two before he answered.

'We're a family, no different to any other. People get on, people don't get on. We're in business together, so to speak, and that can bring difficulties. It was Ernst who kept us together, he was the driving force behind the Foundation. But he didn't plan for his own demise. That's why it took so long to resolve affairs after he died.'

'Were you close to him?' I asked.

Sophie stared at me, shaking her head ever so slowly.

Her father laid down his knife and fork, steepling his hands the way I'd seen Ernst von Barten do himself on occasion.

'He was my older brother. He had a drive, a lust for winning that I've only seen in a few people.' We both glanced at Sophie at the same time.

'But he had a dark side too,' said her mother.

I wondered if she meant the Ukrainian girls - children, really - that he'd used and abused during the war. Maybe everyone knew something about everyone else.

I knew what Sophie's awkward family story was going to be. No point in avoiding it then.

'Now that we're being open with each other, I think Sophie and I should invite Giovanni's sister to the wedding,' I announced.

I hadn't discussed this with Sophie yet and she told me so.

'Don't we need to talk about that first?'

'Let's include your parents in the decision.'

I turned to them. 'You know why I'm saying this. If what we believe turns out to be true, we should allow the child to know both sets of its real grandparents.'

Her mother was wary, instinctively mistrustful of me. I tried to explain.

'I've lived a lifetime not knowing certain things. I don't want to put someone else in the same position.'

'That's very human of you, Oskar,' said her father. 'It really is.'

It might go some way to balance out what he would think of me if he ever found out about his brother.

Even Sophie's mother wasn't angry at me right now. Confused for sure, though. Maybe the sourness would come back later.

'Who inherits in that family now?' she asked, trying to make sense of the world.

'I have no idea. The daughter perhaps. Caterina,' I replied. It was the first civil exchange we'd had so far.

Upstairs after dinner Sophie had a few words of her own.

'You were damn cool out there, asking my father if he got on with the brother you…' I put a finger to her lips and frowned.

'If you can dissimulate that smoothly to my father you can do it to me.'

She let the statement hang in the air.

I waited, so as not to answer too quickly and prove her point.

'I haven't told any lies about what happened. But if someone asks me outright one day, I may have no choice but to tell the truth.'

All Cretans are liars. I had no intention of doing any such thing. Confessing to Sophie herself in the relative seclusion of an East German police station was one thing. Tapping my glass to make an announcement at the next von Barten family get together, swiftly followed by me walking into the nearest *poste de gendarmerie* in Brussels with my hands held out for the cuffs was another.

'When it comes to being honest, let me give you a warning,' she said.

'Going into this thing I have one rule only, or rather, one rule above all else. If you are ever unfaithful to me, even just the once, I will find my own Mafia guys to hold you down while I cut off your plums with a blunt spoon.'

I winced, but only inside. At least it was good to know she was taking it seriously.

-

Lunch with her uncle and aunts was a buffet, which avoided any family member being stuck next to another one for longer than they could both tolerate. Unexpectedly, one female cousin did show up after all, one of the forty-somethings. Bottle blonde and chain smoking. One divorce behind her at least, I thought uncharitably.

As soon as lunch could reasonably have said to be finished, she went off with her father and Sophie's for a private meeting. I guessed they were in conclave to talk money. She wasn't here to see Sophie or I, that was for sure.

Anne von Barten and Sophie's mother didn't get on. By now, though, I'd have been more surprised to come across someone who her mother did get on with.

Then again, Anne von Barten herself didn't strike me as being particularly pleasant in her own right. The kind of tall, aquiline woman who'd have been more at home in the uniform of a regional leader of the League of German Girls and may well have been, before she married Ernst von Barten.

The pair of them were in the middle of a long exchange, when suddenly Anne turned on her heel, cutting Sophie's mother off mid-flow and marched up to me instead.

'So you're the one she's marrying?' she said, as if

observing a new arrival at the zoo from some exotic faraway land.

Sophie was a little way off, speaking to her older cousin who'd re-emerged from her meeting looking none too happy with life. By the flush on her face, she was already on her fourth or fifth glass of wine. No surprise there, if it was money they'd been talking about. I knew how carefully the von Bartens guarded it.

The two cousins drifted closer. Sophie keen, no doubt, to hear how I was going to handle von Barten's widow.

'That's correct, Frau von Barten. I'm the one,' I replied.

Sophie and her cousin arrived just as I spoke. I got a look from Anne as if to say she was yet to be convinced.

'This is him?' her cousin asked Sophie. I'd thought that mystery had just been cleared up. Anne von Barten's expression said that she thought the same.

Without waiting for an answer, the cousin probed deeper with the logic of the inebriated.

'Can he speak proper German? And what's wrong with his eyes?'

'You mean this?' I touched the scar on my cheek where it started below the eye socket.

'No, they look funny,' she slurred slightly. 'I was told you were a mongrel.'

Well, that was one less person to cater for at the wedding. To my faint surprise, I felt nothing by her words, even though they'd just taken me straight back to Wismar in September and Sophie's insult which had triggered my confession.

She'd changed her tune now, though. 'They're perfectly normal,' she snapped back at her cousin.

'I've never even been to Russia,' I joked, trying to do the decent thing and make light of it all.

Anne von Barten gave her drunk niece a frosty look. 'And you've had too much alcohol,' she said, doing another about turn and marching off to complain to Sophie's surviving uncle. He glanced at me and came over my way. Sophie led away her cousin, still complaining, before there was another scene.

Sophie's father came over in his brother's wake too. 'Come into the conservatory, we want to ask you something,' he said.

At the back there were cane armchairs in amongst the palms. The two brothers drew three of them into a rough circle and we settled down.

Her uncle lit a cheroot and offered me one. I'd almost managed to stop as per Sophie's instructions, but refusing him now was the wrong time. Her father took one too.

All this *Gemütlichkeit* made me wary and my instincts weren't wrong.

Max tells me you have family still in East Germany,' Sophie's uncle said. 'Who do your family know in the regime?'

I frowned. 'No one of consequence. Why do you ask?'

'Do you yourself have any professional relationships over there?' asked her father.

My policy was always to try to give people something.

'Some of my connections in Brussels know people in the East. I've been toying with the idea of starting some work there on the side. Export consultancy.'

If they assumed that 'Brussels' meant the EEC rather than the East German foreign trade office, I wasn't going to make them any the wiser. I had no idea, of course, what might happen to Johannes if Borghese caught us out, so the introduction I'd had to Schalck-Golodkowski might end up being worthless.

'Hmm.'

'Why do you ask?'

The two brothers looked at one another.

'This goes no further. Not even to Sophie, yet.'

This family had more secrets than the Stasi.

'Our father, Sophie's *Opa*, died during the war. Natural causes. He was in his seventies.'

I inclined my head in respect.

'He was no fan of Hitler, didn't trust him when we invaded Russia. My apologies,' now he inclined his head in turn.

'Why has everyone got it into their heads that I'm Russian? I hate the Russians, even more than the British.'

'Okay, listen' said Sophie's father.

His brother carried on.

'He was more a man of the nineteenth century than the twentieth. To cut a long story short, he liquidated a good share of our estate in mid 'forty-three, sold it to a high official in the Nazi Party. But he got paid in gold. And he buried it near the main house.'

'Which now lies in the part of East Prussia annexed by the Soviet Union? North of the Gilgestrom River?'

'Correct.'

'How much is there? Is it worth it to try to retrieve it?'

Sophie's uncle leant over to clap me on the shoulder.

'You're getting the idea. But it's not the amount that's important, it's more the principle that the Russians shouldn't find our property one day and take it for themselves.'

I doubted the von Bartens were ever driven by principle, but I didn't say so.

'Take time to think about it,' her uncle concluded. 'It's been there for a few years. It's not going anywhere fast. Maybe we can work something out with your contacts.'

'Where have you been?' asked Sophie. 'Have you met my other aunt yet?'

Then, as I got closer, 'Have you been smoking? I thought you said you'd stopped?'

'Your uncle offered me. It was a matter of politeness.'

Einstein had said that women married men in the expectation of changing them. He was being proven right so far.

'They were telling me one of your family stories from

East Prussia,' I said to put her off the scent.

But her nose for tricks was something to be in awe of.

'They were telling you the legend of *Opa*'s gold, weren't they?' she declared, frowning. 'And they want you to help go and find it.'

I shrugged. 'They told me not to tell you.'

'Because it's suicidal, that's why. Digging up half of the military enclave of Kaliningrad in secret? That's a one-way ticket to a twenty year stretch in a Siberian gulag.'

Sometimes, for someone who had as many male friends as she did, she had no idea of how men's psychology worked.

'And don't tell me that beating the odds is the attraction,' she said, instantly proving my estimation of her wrong.

'There's nothing that can be done without the Soviets' cooperation, which is vanishingly unlikely,' I said to mollify her.

That said, they were only human. If there was enough loot to go around, there was surely a deal to be done.

-

The following morning before we left, there was another surprise for me.

After breakfast Sophie's father asked me to come with him outside. We trotted round to the courtyard at the back.

'It's yours,' he said, pointing at a black Mercedes E-model. 'An early wedding present.'

He fished out the keys, then frowned at the expression on my face.

'It's just a car, Oskar. It's not an insult. You're not obliged to me in any way for it.'

That I didn't believe for a minute. I knew his class of people better now. This family had successfully connived against Göring to siphon off more wealth from Occupied

Europe than *Opa* could ever have conceived of. They would demand payment for everything eventually.

And if I was to be bought off, to make sure I turned up to the wedding of their pregnant, unmarried daughter, or even as an inducement to recover lost gold from Kaliningrad, they could have done it with something more exciting than what a mid-level official in Brussels might drive to and from the suburbs.

'Thank-you Herr von Barten.'

'Let's go for a drive. Let's talk.' He threw me the keys. 'Let's see how fast you can get down to the town and back again.'

The car purred into life at the turn of the key and I pulled out of the courtyard. The Mercedes was reassuringly solid compared to a Type Three, and with its big straight-six engine it accelerated faster too.

As we sped along the empty forest road under the trees, her father started to relax a little, showing me a more reflective side of his character. I began to wonder if I'd misjudged him.

'I'm not really sure what sort of person her mother had in mind as a husband for Sophie,' he ventured.

'If I'm being honest,' he continued. 'I don't really think she was comfortable with the idea of her daughter going away to university at all, let alone trying to have a career in a serious profession. Maybe a fashion editor at a magazine would have been acceptable.'

I glanced over to the passenger side. A faint grin was fading away.

'She's successful at what she does,' I said. 'She's lucky to have found something she's suited for.'

'I know my daughter. I know how ambitious and determined she is. I've also sensed, for a long time, that once she'd made her choice on who she would marry, nothing or no one would put her off. Even you.'

I understood his father's pride, or perhaps nervousness,

about the gorgon he'd raised, but I didn't like the inference of me being drone to her queen bee.

'And I also realised that I would have to accept her decision, even if I felt it to be a wrong one.'

'And do you?' I asked, looking over at him again.

'I don't know yet. No one does. But you're a stranger that she's suddenly brought into our family and we have a lot of wealth to protect. That's why you signed the prenuptial agreement. It's not personal, it's just business.'

Chapter Twenty-Nine

Brussels - Tuesday, 10th November 1970

Charles de Gaulle died at eight o'clock on Monday evening, the ninth of November.

I came to see Kramer at his flat the following afternoon, as had already been agreed the weekend before. He didn't cancel the appointment, presumably the struggle to maintain France's influence at the EEC didn't stop for the death of a giant. What the man himself would have wanted, no doubt.

As it wasn't one of our regular Thursday meetings, I also presumed I'd been called in to talk about London. He hadn't brought up the topic again since the first time he'd mentioned it two months ago. The meeting where I'd refused to commit murder for him - just before I went to Sicily.

Although I'd asked for Kramer's help in recruiting Spinelli to confront Sophie and Rizzo that fateful day in her office, I'd never actually told him that I'd been asked by them to transport stolen weapons to Sicily. And I'd certainly never told him of what had happened there when I did. All that he and everyone else in Brussels, apart from Sophie, knew about Rizzo's death, was that it was a mugging which had gone wrong.

Today, I wanted to ask his opinion on Italy again, before I went any further down the path of interfering there on Johannes' behalf. Even though the major had asked me not to. The real reason for not letting go, of course, was that I wouldn't be satisfied until I knew that Sophie's involvement with Rizzo's father and indirectly with Borghese was over. Simply asking her never seriously crossed my mind. I wasn't going to trade any more of my secrets with her for the truth.

Sifting through everything I'd picked up along the way, it was Spinelli's original theory that I kept coming back to. His suggestion that right-wing elements of the DC and the Italian security establishment might be running a false flag operation to allow a crackdown on the left.

But did the DC need Borghese to create more unrest in Italy to that end? They could always point to the threat of international terror as justification for repressive measures.

Discontent was still festering in Chile over the election of Allende, where the general had died of his wounds sustained during the kidnapping attempt. A wartime state of emergency had just been declared in Canada, thanks to attacks by a Quebec separatist terror group - the one secretly sponsored by de Gaulle when he was president. The West German terror group, the Red Army Faction, had started a campaign of violent bank robberies in the country and I knew more than I cared to about the IRA.

Kramer's mood was subdued as he opened the door.

'I heard the news last night,' I told him.

'Quite something wasn't it? A few days short of his ninetieth birthday.'

'Life goes on, I guess,' I said.

'Let's sit.'

He collected two glasses and a bottle of brandy from the drinks cabinet and led me down into the conversation pit.

I poured for us both. He swirled the spirit in his glass for a second or two before starting.

'I still don't know how I'm going to use you in London. We have several options.'

'I'm telling you again. I'm not going to kill anyone. Whatever needs doing can be done without that.'

'Don't be so idealistic,' he retorted. 'Since when did you

develop a conscience?'

'You must know why, Kramer. You more than anyone. You know what happened to Sophie von Barten's uncle.'

'That's a strange way to refer to him. Why do you bring her up?'

Now I swirled my glass. 'A few things have happened since we last had one of these private chats in your apartment.'

He raised his eyebrows.

'Did you comfort her after the death of Giovanni Rizzo?'

'We're getting married.'

His eyes started from his head. I'd bet that had upset his plans to keep a tame German to do France's dirty work at the EEC. Ernst von Barten and he had been bitter rivals, and now I was marrying his niece.

'You're sick and twisted,' he said coldly. 'Does she know about her uncle?'

'Yes, of course she does.'

'That makes two of you then. Dracula and his bride,' he said angrily, almost shouting.

I threw my hands up into the air.

'You know if I'm put in a situation of necessity, I'll do what needs to be done. But I also know from experience it's extremely messy. It leaves lots of loose ends, as I'm finding out again now.'

'Don't lecture me. By your age I'd dealt with twenty times the number of awkward situations that you have.'

'Then you know we have any number of tools at our disposal in England. I can smear the dubious associates of our friend as KGB spies. The English have had enough of those for real since the end of the war. We can also smear the opponents of accession in the same way, if need be.'

Kramer poured himself more brandy.

'We can bribe the British parliamentarians to vote the way we want, either with cash or with something more subtle. I can possibly even arrange for the abduction of certain targets across the Iron Curtain. The Stasi did it to Otto John, the head of West German counterintelligence in the fifties. His career never recovered.'

'How do you know it was them?'

'I was forgetting, it could have been the SDECE, because your guys make the Stasi look like a normal, legal, constitutional police force. So don't tell me I have to kill people. There's another reason not to do it too. You might inadvertently create a martyr in England, a new Leo Schlageter. As an old Saarland hand, you must be aware of that danger.'

'You'll take a gun to London though.'

'I'm not so naïve as not to.'

I poured some more brandy for myself. A short truce reigned for a minute or so.

'So when does this assignment start? Next year I presume? We have a child due in June.'

'What?'

'I forgot to say. Part of the reason to get married now.'

'I said cook her a meal for her and make love, not start a family.'

He shook his head in amazement. 'Oskar, you need help.'

'She's the one, I love her.'

He took another minute to digest this. I wondered what my chances of the directorship of External Investigations were now.

He started speaking again, looking at me down his nose in a speculative fashion. 'I have some friends coming over in the next half hour. A kind of vigil for de Gaulle. You should stay, you'll hear some stories.'

I nodded.

'London is the big one. Do it well and do it successfully and you'll never have to work for me again. You can even do it your own way, if you can prove it's working with the first couple of targets.'

I stared at him. I'd thought I'd never be free of any of

my entanglements. I'd confessed von Barten's murder to Sophie and that was one cord snapped. Kramer had held the same murder over my head to oblige me to him and now he was suggesting he'd let that go too. I was still stuck with the Stasi, though.

And that was why I remained bound to Kramer, so the French would protect me as one of their own if I ever got investigated by West German counter-intelligence. That said, they'd abandoned their associates working the French Connection drugs run when Nixon had decided enough was enough.

'But?' I asked, knowing there were always conditions attached.

'But if you foul this up, if someone really does need to be killed to protect our friend and you don't do it, then I will confess to the Gendarmerie on your behalf over the killing of von Barten.'

Previously, my escape plan was to run to East Germany, but not now I was with Sophie and from next year, her child.

'I get it,' I said, as neutrally as I could.

'It won't be difficult,' he assured me. 'We have more supporters in England than you realise. It's the obverse of empire. The more powerful they became, the more that internal opposition to British domination in world affairs also grew - from internationalists, pacifists, artists - those kinds of people. People who were also naturally attracted to European federalism, especially after the First World War. The people in that same *milieu* are the ones setting the tone of England's debate on membership of the EEC today.'

'I thought the socialists lost power there this summer?'

Kramer smirked with delight. 'That's why our friend is perfect to sell accession. No one will suspect an ex-Army officer.'

'Of what?'

Kramer smiled to himself again.

'Do you know what the idea of France is?' he asked instead.

He didn't wait on my answer. 'For me, it's the idea that anyone can be French if they adhere to the principles of the Republic. Look at the way Napoleon emancipated the Jews, in France and in the other European territories we liberated back then.'

I frowned. 'Your name?'

'Not Jewish. German or Dutch originally. Probably a soldier from the Rhineland who joined the Grande Armée.'

'Is that why they sent you to the Saarland in the 'fifties?'

'I was the best man for the job but it didn't hurt.'

'Why are you telling me all this?'

'Success dissolves people's natural loyalties to their country. Look around you in Brussels. Look at the British elite, like their negotiator O'Neill, desperate to be part of a new European empire.'

I wondered if Kramer hoped that one day I'd seize hold of the idea of France, too.

'What's the schedule for London?' I asked.

'We have to get it right. We've only got one chance to use you. I need time to plan with our collaborators in England and then we need to wait on the right moment to bring you over there. It will be a few weeks yet before I know.'

The doorbell rang.

'The first people are arriving. Tonight is de Gaulle's night. Stay.'

Over the next hour a variety of Frenchmen of all shapes and sizes arrived. Kramer threw open his drinks cabinet and lined up row after row of bottles of brandy, cognac, anisette and other spirits on the side table.

It didn't take him long to get drunk, but in a controlled way. They toasted de Gaulle, but also other people they'd known, popular officers who'd been loyal to de Gaulle in the years of exile and Resistance martyrs too. And the names of people whose relevance wasn't explained. I wondered if they were men who'd ended up on the side of the OAS. Kramer had mentioned divided loyalties the day he and I had met Spinelli back in September.

I began to see a side of Kramer I suspected few at the EEC had ever been shown, for at the Berlaymont he acted the part of the suave diplomat, effortlessly so. Before today, in private, I'd seen that layer peeled away to reveal an unashamed, exuberant chauvinism towards the other member states. But not one which was especially malicious as such. And if he did hold malice against certain individuals in Brussels, it was because of who they were, rather than simply because of which country they came from.

But now, in his cups, with wartime comrades who'd been hidden in the woodwork of the Brussels institutions all these years, I began to see a much harder nationalism. To be fair, it was still more the nationalism of the idea, of the principles which defined France, as he'd described to me earlier. And he was consistent in making sure it wasn't directed against me, the only German present.

As I listened to the Gaullists assembling in his lounge, I began to understand the importance he attached to the fight against England. And I also began to be carried along by it too.

'This is Oskar Lenkeit, a friend of ours. He has performed great services for France in the past,' he announced to the group. I got a silent toast with most of the country's regional spirits, from absinthe to pastis.

'These are some comrades of mine. Berger and Renard here were *hommes de Londres* too.'

'You were with de Gaulle from the start, like Monsieur Kramer?' I asked. In June nineteen forty Kramer had been a junior diplomat in London.

'We escaped in a fishing boat from Bretagne,' said

Berger. 'Vidal and Le Roux joined us in Algiers. They did a very special assignment there. Changed the course of history.

'You all work at the EEC?' I asked a little incredulously.

'The French embassy, French liaison group at NATO headquarters, the Council, the Commission, French firms with offices in Brussels,' Kramer explained. He didn't say who was who.

'What was wartime London like?'

The anecdotes spilled out. French officers in unfamiliar uniforms being arrested on suspicion of being German parachutists. The rivalries between the various exiled governments and armies to get the attention of the British war leaders. And the accompanying struggle to obtain war materiel from the British, who often had insufficient to equip their own forces in those first months after their expulsion from the Continent.

As the drink flowed, more recent stories about the murkier side of the French security establishment started to be told. Not that I was any particular stranger to those. But it provided an opportunity to hear what Kramer's friends thought about Italy, and maybe even get their collective wisdom on what should be done there.

I fired a speculative shot, all the more random for my being partially inebriated.

'I met someone in Italy recently who had some political theories.'

There were blank looks all round.

Kramer coughed. 'Oskar was checking out some things for me there.'

'People who aren't happy with the way things are run politically,' I explained, slowly assembling my words.

'He wants to know your opinion about the unrest in Italy. Whether there might be another De Lorenzo affair, like in 'sixty-four,' Kramer said with more precision.

'It's a snake pit,' said Renard brutally. 'We had a fascist

government for four years, a quick civil war and a clean purge. They had twenty years of fascism and then two years with the country divided every way possible. Church against state, North versus South, worker fighting peasant. Republicans and royalists too.'

Now Vidal spoke up. 'No one trusts anyone else. They can't even agree on what it means to be Italian. Never have.'

They all seemed to have something they wanted to say. Even Le Roux joined in.

'They're secretive too. Nothing is ever as it seems. Obscure religious orders within the Vatican, freemasons, hidden factions and personal loyalties inside the established political parties.'

'Who was De Lorenzo by the way?' Berger asked as an aside to Kramer.

'Head of the Carabinieri. Suggestions in 'sixty-four he was going to mount a coup, but it came to nothing.'

Vidal snorted cynically. 'Even if a coup took place in Italy, how would anyone know?'

'What coups have you carried out then?' I demanded, trying to defend Italy's honour for some reason that only made sense in the small hours.

'None that we care to talk about.'

'Why? Because it's the CIA who are the masters at coups?'

'We've nothing to prove to them. We fought the CIA in Vietnam to stop their proxies taking over the drugs business of our allies.'

'Who, the Corsicans?' I asked. Kramer had said the Corsican underworld had made it to Saigon when the country was still a French colony.

'Operation X. We set it up after the end of the war and it was beautiful. One of the conditions the Americans imposed on de Gaulle for their wartime support was the suppression of the official opium trade in our colonies afterwards. But after the European war finished, in

Indochina we needed the colony's tax revenues from narcotics more than ever in the fight against communism. So as the colonial administration began to dismantle the official infrastructure for the distribution of drugs, we took it over. And what we had, the CIA later wanted for themselves.'

'Do the CIA want to take over the transatlantic trade? Would they mount a coup in Italy to do so?'

It was the random path these conversations took when the alcohol flowed. Occasionally they turned up a nugget, though.

'If they wanted, they could do both those things,' Berger asked. 'Doesn't mean it's the right time for them, though. They have a new coup in Chile to plan first.'

Kramer looked at me. Drunk, but not that drunk.

'What's your loyalty to France?' Renard suddenly asked.

'I believe in what Kramer believes in. And Spinelli.' They frowned at the unfamiliar name. 'That the democratic ideals of France need to be extended to the whole continent, East and West.'

Stronger than my belief in democracy was the idea that people like the von Bartens shouldn't be in charge. I supposed that at least made me an East German socialist, as much as anything else.

'Let's toast to democracy,' said Kramer.

'And governments who don't interfere with us making money,' said Berger.

Even at this time of night, the irony wasn't lost on me. That of a senior official at the Commission, an organisation, as I'd come to realise last year, specifically created by its founders to suppress democracy, about to toast the same concept.

I got back to our apartment at half past three.

'Where have you been?' she said, coming close to sniff my breath.

'With some Frenchmen - people from the Commission.

They were toasting the memory of de Gaulle.'

'What with? The entire contents of the wine cellar?'

'I didn't smoke once,' I announced proudly, maybe slurring a little.

'Oh well,' she said. 'That's all right then.' She was gradually learning to tone down the sarcasm.

'You see,' I said. 'I do listen to you.'

Her lips parted briefly, as if she was about to deliver another admonition. But then she obviously decided it would be wasted on me in my current state.

She was welcome to open them again, though, if she had any bright ideas to get me out of going to London, or to work out what to do in Rome.

Chapter Thirty

I never found out if Sophie had any clever ideas about either London or Italy, for I didn't get as far as asking her. Instead, we had a fight about who was to go and tell Rizzo's father our news ahead of extending the family an invitation to the wedding. Her news really, I supposed.

The excuse to meet him in person and push to see if he'd thought any more about abandoning Borghese was partly why I'd suggested making the invitation in the first place. I hoped the announcement of a grandchild might humour him too, when it came to asking for help for the people I supposedly worked for.

Sophie's vehemence about going herself only made me more suspicious of her own lingering intentions in Italy, and even more determined to see Rizzo's father on his own.

The original reason for the argument seemed unimportant as words went back and forth. I skated around the oldest excuse, of wanting to keep her from distress in her current state, but backed off before I got onto thin ice. It was probably wise, given that she didn't look pregnant and was planning to go skiing on our honeymoon. She told me she didn't feel it in the mornings either, as women were meant to, or so I'd heard.

In the end, I told her I'd already booked the flight and was going whether she liked it or not, but that no one was stopping her from calling him on the phone. She opened and closed her mouth, paced around the apartment and slammed a couple of doors. But I got the sense it was more in confusion than anything else, at being thwarted over something she'd set her mind on.

I did say, though, that I wouldn't invite Caterina to the wedding myself, so that she could be the one to do it. It never hurt to provide the losing party some means of saving face.

When I'd phoned Rizzo's father's office, I'd simply requested a meeting on a personal matter without giving further details. Now I was standing before the door to his town apartment, only a few blocks away from where I'd met Borghese, and squaring my shoulders for what came next.

We hadn't parted in the best of terms on the day of the funeral six weeks ago, but that was hardly surprising given the situation.

As I was shown to the living room by the maid and invited to take a seat, he was more suspicious than usual, but the reason wasn't immediately clear.

'What's this personal matter you've come to speak to me about?' he said in opening. 'I haven't heard from you in weeks.'

I nodded in agreement, just to show him that the love was still there.

'I thought that after we last spoke, you were going to go back to the people you know in West Germany and establish your credentials with them, in case I need to make use of you.'

So my fish was still nibbling the bait.

'I've made approaches to people in Germany,' I said. 'I think they can be persuaded to help out, if it comes to it.'

He leaned back in his black leather and chrome chair, crossing his legs.

'I have my own insurance plans too,' he said, drumming his fingers on the arm of the chair. 'What did the Germans say?'

'Truthfully? They're going to watch and wait.' At least,

that's what Johannes had said.

'They'll need more to go on before they take it any further, or before they'll be serious about offering you protection,' I said, trying to play it cool. 'But that's not why I came.'

He leaned forward and raised a finger.

'Before you say anything, I'm going to give you a warning.'

I frowned, puzzled.

'My daughter was grateful for your words of kindness and comfort in Apulia,' he said, not bringing himself to use the word 'funeral.'

'But that's as far as things go between you and her. I told you this already, the last time we met. I didn't ask you to protect her from Di Luca only for you to have designs on her yourself, once you and the blonde witch have got tired of each other.'

'You don't need to be concerned any more. I'm engaged to be married to her.'

He threw his hands up into the air.

'Is that what this so-called personal matter was about? You came all the way to tell me that, of all things? Given the history between her and my son?'

He shook his head in disbelief.

'You're a strange one.'

'There's more,' I said looking at him solemnly.

'What?' He gave an impatient gesture, flicking the fingers of both hands upwards.

'She's pregnant with your grandchild. Almost certainly, anyway.'

He sank back into his chair, stunned.

'That's why I'm here, to tell you this news,' I said, using lots of words to make sure it sunk in.

He gripped the arms of his chair and jumped to his feet.

'And now what?' he shouted. 'She wants money to pay off a doctor to do an abortion, or you want money so she doesn't? Or you want us to take the child for adoption? One of those. Is that it?'

'Don't be crass. You know exactly who she is and how much wealth her family possesses. It's her child. No one else will be its mother.'

His face was still dark and thunderous.

'We want to invite Caterina to the wedding. We don't imagine you or Signora Rizzo would want to come, but you are welcome if you do. That's what I came all this way to ask you.'

Now he sat back down and lit a cigarette. Then he got up again, paced impatiently to the window, looked out, and came back to face me again.

'I need time to think about all this. It will please my wife for sure. It will fucking delight Caterina. You'll be even more her Catholic hero for having your woman bring up this child. Because everyone knows you Nazis are natural-born murderers.'

He waved me to be quiet as I opened my mouth to speak.

'Even if that's not how it is, that's what she'll build it up in her mind to be. I hope for your sake the child is a boy. Daughters are only trouble for their fathers,' he finally concluded.

I couldn't even begin to imagine what trouble Caterina could possibly have caused her father, which would compare in any way to Rizzo's antics in almost setting Sicily aflame, but he was the expert in these matters. As I realised, like it or not, I was to be in a few months. But I didn't want Sophie's baby to be a boy. The only child I would be comfortable calling 'son' would be my own.

'So, you want financial help with this child, if it turns out to be half-Rizzo?'

I'd just told him it was unnecessary, but maybe it was his roundabout way of acknowledging an obligation to us. But there was another way he could pay a debt.

'We can help each other in a different way.'

His hackles rose.

'Last time we met, you told me something of what the Mafia were planning to do for Borghese. But you know the details of the main event, and you know which levers need to be pulled to stop it. Tell me and I'll go back to my people and have them pulled them for you, like I offered last time.'

'Why do you Germans keep changing your mind about this thing?'

It seemed a bit unfair. I'd only changed it once in that I'd agreed to work for them, then I'd got the soldiers to blow the cave with the weapons inside.

'You want revenge for his death. It's what Giovanni would have wanted too. He was at the Commission to help build a new Europe, a better Europe. Not in the way Borghese wanted, but with intelligence, in a way where no one got hurt.'

'You assume a lot about my son.'

I pressed on.

'A few armed men marching around Trajan's column won't do it anyway. And how do you imagine the people at the Berlaymont will look at Italians after that kind of performance? Borghese will tar Italy with the same brush as Mussolini all over again. He'll put back Italy's international standing by twenty years.'

I tried to push all the buttons I could think of. 'It could indirectly hurt your business, too, if Italy becomes a pariah.'

'Why do you care? You're German, not Italian.'

'Give us some credit for trying to learn from the past.'

He exhaled smoke from his cigarette in a long stream.

'I'm sick of the whole thing. At the start, it was just another late-night discussion, ideas that got bandied around after dinner. Then it got more serious and I got sucked in without realising it. And then my son, and then his girlfriend, and then you. Some speculative venture that was.'

'If you want me to help you, I need to know today,' I insisted. 'We're going to be family next summer.'

He jerked his head back in surprise, as if he'd just realised the connection between him and I.

'How do I know all this talk is for real?'

'Caterina can come to the wedding and place her hand on my fiancée's belly. Do you think I would lie about this to her, after what's just happened?'

'I said I'd think about it.'

'It's already the middle of November. Is something taking place this year or not? Toss me another bone that I can take back to the people I work for."

'He told you himself in Milan. The last guy who talked about Borghese's plans for the Fronte Nazionale took his dog out for a walk one day and didn't come back. Neither did the dog.'

'If I'm to do something for you,' I said, 'I need time to get ready. And I have to get their attention, so that they'll take the situation seriously.'

He got up and went to look out of the window again, standing there for a while, absent-mindedly tapping the ash from his cigarette to the floor.

He turned back to face me, lips pursed.

'Check out someone by the name of Licio Gelli.'

'Who is he?'

'He's a guy. Member of the Fronte Nazionale and some other organisations. Worked for Mussolini in Dalmatia, the part we restored to Italy from Yugoslavia in 'forty-one. Worked for the Americans after the war, as we all do now.'

'Why's he important?'

Rizzo's father shook his head.

'You wanted a bone for your people, the BND or whomever, to chew on while I decide. That's your bone.'

'Okay.'

'One last thing. Just so you know. Borghese was saved from execution at the end of the war.'

'I heard he was in trouble back then. I didn't know he

461

was under threat of execution. Wasn't he safe because he was considered an enemy combatant, having taken orders directly from the Germans?'

'It was the early Cold War. Desperate times. Borghese made friends with a young American intelligence officer called James Angleton who ran one of the Italian desks for the OSS, predecessor to the CIA. Angleton's father was an American businessman who moved to Italy after the first World War which meant James Angleton grew up in Italy under Mussolini.'

'And what's he doing now?'

'He's the global head of counterintelligence for the CIA. Think about that before you and your people do anything rash.'

Chapter Thirty-One

I was due up in Hamburg for the weekend, my last visit to my mother before the wedding. I left Brussels just after the morning rush hour, but when I neared Hamburg, instead of turning off I drove by, on up to the inner-German border. I was still in the Type Three, the Mercedes was staying at her parent's house until the honeymoon.

Earlier in the week, I'd gone over to Kramer's office and forced him to agree that he'd get the SDECE to do a search in their files for Licio Gelli.

I insisted that Spinelli was still interested in Borghese's plans. I pointed out to him that he'd never actually given me an answer on what the SDECE knew about the Di Luca clan, as he'd promised. And I played the London card again.

London was the clincher, and I began to realise just how desperate Kramer was for me to go there. I also realised it was a card I'd be able to play again and again, right up until I got on the plane for the short hop across the Channel.

But he was annoyed that I was still asking questions about Italy after all these weeks. When he'd made the introduction for me to Spinelli, he'd thought that had marked the end of my private investigation into Sophie's involvement there.

He hadn't heard of Gelli, but with a frown and a sigh he said he'd ask Paris. Now it was Johannes' turn to see what he could do.

The interview facilities at the Selmsdorf border crossing point were still as basic as before. Major Johannes kicked the duty lieutenant out of his office, so we had a little privacy at least.

'So why did you call me down here?' he asked.

'Are you sure we can talk privately? This is a Ministry matter, not for the Volksarmee,' I said, choosing my words carefully, in case we were being bugged and not wanting any listeners to think Johannes and I were plotting something.

'Yes. We can speak freely here,' he replied, eyeing me up.

I paused, weighing up which piece of news to give him first.

'I've been given a name. Someone who might be behind Borghese, one of the people pulling the strings. In fact, I've been given two names. Borghese's American sponsor, too.'

'American sponsor?' Johannes' eyes widened slightly.

'The CIA's global head of counter-intelligence.'

But he didn't look as impressed as I'd hoped. I'd been waiting all week to tell him. Even if we couldn't prove a definite CIA connection to the plot, pre-emptively sharing Angleton's name with Moscow might provide us with some kind of safety net if the Comandante's coup did come off.

'Who told you all this?' he asked.

'Rizzo's father. He's having second thoughts.'

'And why are you speaking with him? I thought I told you to stay low?'

He frowned now, but not with the quick anger that I knew from before. I began to worry that his rivals had already started to make a move at the Normannenstrasse. And then I felt something unexpected, something akin to the stirrings of loyalty – to the man who'd made me sign my life away in 'sixty-nine.

'I should have explained, I had to go and see him on a personal matter. But then we got talking, and he offered me a name, a principal in the plot.'

'Why did he do that?'

'He's broken, or at least he's considering breaking with Borghese. He's open to the idea of helping someone to undermine their plot.'

'That's handy for us,' said Johannes, but his flat tone jarred.

I carried on, less sure of myself. 'The local connection is a certain Licio Gelli, another old-time fascist, a former intelligence officer under Mussolini. If we can get to him, we might be able to significantly harm their chances.'

'What do you mean "get to"? Sniper rifle, twenty-five-centimetre hunting knife?'

'I've no idea. That's all I know. Ask the comrades in Italy to check him out, see what he's got planned in his diary for the rest of the year. Arrange a trip to Cuba on a slow cargo ship for him.'

'Let's take a walk. I need a smoke,' said Johannes by way of reply.

We left through the back of the building, keeping out of sight of the West German border guards. It had started to rain while we were inside. Through the chain link fence, the corn fields we'd seen at the start of September had already been ploughed for sowing. The north German countryside was grey, damp and depressing. Cold too, today, but that didn't seem to bother Johannes. After serving on a destroyer north of the Arctic Circle, it hardly compared.

He shook out a cigarette and offered me one, but I declined.

'I'm trying to stop. I haven't had one for almost a month.'

'What made you stop?'

I turned down my mouth.

'Who made you?' he asked again.

'She's pregnant, you know. Not mine.'

Johannes drew deeply and looked at me with narrowed eyes. The tip of the cigarette glowed red.

'Whose is it? Her other boyfriend? The dead one?'

'That's why I went to see his father, to tell him. To invite his daughter to the wedding.'

Johannes slowly shook his head. 'Wedding?' Then he shook it some more before exhaling slowly, blowing the smoke in my face.

'Are you sure you won't have a cigarette? You look like you need one.'

'Aren't you surprised? Or displeased in some way?'

He said nothing.

'You said to me in Luxembourg that every part of my life is your business.'

'When are you getting married?' he asked.

'Next weekend. In Gerolstein. It's a town in the Eifel.'

'I really called that one right, didn't I? She tries to scratch your eyes out just up the road in September and now you're getting married in December because she left you with no choice.'

I turned away from him to face the building, running my thumb over the surface of the concrete.

'Something like that,' I said. 'Why did you bring me out here, by the way? I thought the office was private?'

'Nothing's going to happen in Italy from our end, but I think you knew that already. People are preparing themselves for what happens after Ulbricht's gone. No one wants to take risks right now, even if Italy wasn't already a problem case for us. We criticised the PCI heavily over their attitude to the intervention in Czechoslovakia. I doubt they've forgotten.'

'And yourself? What if Borghese doesn't play along and your rivals use events in Italy against you? Pretending they care for the PCI, while they're happily cheering the Comandante on the whole time.'

'I've taken precautions. I've done the logical thing.'

'And what's that?'

'I've dug up some dirt. Not a lot. Nothing terminal for the people I'm up against. But serious enough to threaten them with; stop them using the Volksarmee report against me. And against you.'

I raised my eyebrows.

'There was talk a few weeks back of whether you were a special case, and if there was a mechanism in the regulations for you to one day become a Special Duties Officer, instead of a plain collaborator - an "IM", as you are now.'

'Well lucky me. Would it come with a uniform?'

'Don't be facetious. Schalck-Golodkowski is one. It's only given to high-value associates of the Ministry, to give them an official status with us. It's a mark of trust.'

'And do they? Eventually plan to make me one?'

He looked away across the fields.

'Did the boyfriend's father know about James Angleton? Or did you learn that from someone else,' he asked, turning back to me and fixing me with a grim stare.

'No, it was Rizzo's father. The plotters all know each other's secrets.'

'There are few secrets elsewhere, either. Angleton is a paranoid, and I also mean that in the clinical sense. I'd never trust him as a sponsor. In any case, your work in Italy is done.'

'I don't know why my fiancée got involved with the Rizzos, or what she might still be up to with Rizzo's father.'

'Then why not ask her, instead of spying on her?'

'She doesn't know about us. I don't want her to think I'm asking her on your behalf.'

'And I've just told you don't need to. But you can't let this thing go, can you? What is it? Some misguided sense of honour on behalf of the Italian comrades?'

'These past two months people have been obsessed by Borghese, by the Mafia, by the DC. But no one has asked the ordinary Italian people what they want. Even Spinelli, the supposed European democrat doesn't care. Like your harder-nosed colleagues at the Normannenstrasse, he wants a crisis in Italy, to further his own agenda in Brussels. He told me he needs people to die.'

'What can I say? He sounds like a caricature of a Western imperialist.'

'So you don't believe the Party's propaganda?'

Johannes declined to answer.

'Do you have any access to the PCI to ask them if they can make enquiries about Licio Gelli? Or can you search your files here for him?' I asked, without much hope.

He dropped his stub and ground it out with his foot but showed no signs of wanting to go back inside. Instead, he lit up again.

'I don't know. I can't speak with the PCI, the Ministry's formal contacts are through the other members of the Italian committee. Which has been disbanded by the way.'

His cigarette smelt good. I was sorely tempted to ask him for one.

'If the Italian operation is over as far as they're concerned, then when is my cousin being released?'

'She'll be home for Christmas.'

'*Danke.*'

He raised his eyebrows at this.

'You're getting married quickly, aren't you? Not as quick as some people had to do in the war, of course.'

Back then the regime had even authorised special distance marriages, where the service was conducted by proxy in a registry office back in Germany, a steel helmet standing in for the man serving at the front.

'And you? You were married twice. You got any advice there?' I asked,

'My first wife died of cancer. So not much.'

It sounded like his current wife was out of the picture, too.

'You said your second wife is a doctor,' I stated

blandly.

He was silent.

'Is that how you met? When your first wife was getting treatment?'

His shoulders slumped a little.

'We met under strange circumstances, as you seem to have done. If you have a child together and bring it up, that's what's going to take over your life. That's what should dominate your life. Not becoming a Special Duties Officer, or stopping a coup, or expanding the EEC, or whatever.'

'Or becoming a colonel.'

His eyes were hollow now, and as I looked at him, I saw a man approaching late middle-age, wearing a grey suit and with lines in his face. Who'd made the Ministry his life.

General Fiedler had asked me in the summer how I found working for East Germany despite having been coerced into it, although he hadn't acknowledged that directly himself. I'd sidestepped the question by saying how I'd come to realise the Ministry was staffed with real people.

Johannes had mentioned the caricatures that people in the East had of Westerners. But we had them too, and I was finding it harder to keep my distance from the real people that I'd now met on the other side of the Iron Curtain. People who weren't automatons, but living, breathing, imperfect people - just like me. And in any case, if it came to thinking in terms of national loyalties, I was half-Russian already, whether I wanted to be or not.

'I still need to get a move on with my promotion,' he said, bringing me back to the present. 'My daughter will be making captain sometime in the next couple of years.'

'How old was she when…?'

'Twelve.'

I nodded to myself.

'Your second wife was already pregnant when you got married?'

He gave a final pull on his cigarette and tossed it half-smoked into the middle of the roadway running past the back door.

'Let's go back inside.'

We sat down again in the lieutenant's stuffy office.

'Have you brought the fake passports, like I asked?' he said.

I drew them unwillingly from my inside pocket. Before I slid them across, I gave them a last quick flick through out of habit. I frowned when I came to the photograph page of Sophie's passport for the very first time.

I remembered the care that day with which the duty photographer had posed and angled Sophie's face. It may not have been her choice, but when the photograph was taken, she was looking left, towards me - although I hadn't noticed it at the time.

But the image made me pause. There was a look in her eyes, one of shrewd estimation if anything, rather than straight malice - despite what I'd just told her a few minutes previously. And while she wasn't smiling, she had a presence, a confidence as she stood there in her borrowed clothes.

'Can I keep this? The photograph?'

Johannes took the open passport from me and turned it around so he could see it properly for himself.

He looked across at me with lidded eyes, saying nothing as he reached into his jacket for a folding pocket knife. He bent back the page to insert the blade of the knife under the photo and peeled it away from where it had been stamped onto the hammer, compass and wheatsheaves symbol of the Republic printed underneath.

'Here you go,' he said sliding it over to me with one hand as he took my own fake East German passport with the other.

I opened my wallet and slipped her photo inside.

He leaned back in his chair and reached into his jacket

again, this time pulling out a plain manila envelope.

'Here, this is for you,' he said, handing it over.

I ripped it open with a finger and looked inside. It was a real East German passport, in the name of Thomas Hofmann, using the photograph that the sergeant had taken of me that day. I riffled through the visa pages. There were a couple of stamps for Brussels, several for West Germany and even one for Italy, for Rome in September. The royal blue cover of the book was slightly creased and dog-eared to reflect the number of trips Thomas Hofmann had supposedly taken.

I looked quizzically at Johannes.

'You're one of us now.'

The most surprising thing was that I almost agreed with him. How had I come from wearing a West German Bundeswehr uniform seven years ago to this point today? Before 'sixty-nine, to me East Germany had been an enemy state, just as they thought of us. But now that I knew them better, now that I had met my family who lived here, I had no desire to be part of a civil war. And if I was simply a 'German', then both halves had a claim on me, I supposed. Now I understood better too, why the Italians hadn't rushed to sack their fascist-era prefects and police chiefs. Civil wars demanded compromises in their aftermath which utterly defeated nations had the luxury of not having to make.

'Anything to say?' Johannes asked, interrupting my reverie.

'Is this a tacit blessing to carry on in Italy?'

'No, but it's not an explicit ban on going there either,' he said slowly.

'How good is the passport?'

'It's the real thing. You can use it until the expiry date, as if you were an East German citizen.'

The rain outside had stopped for the present and the sky lightened as the clouds lifted a little.

'Are you coming to my wedding next weekend?' I

asked.

'Am I invited?'

'I would, but then Sophie would start to work things out for herself.'

'We can't have that, can we?'

'Try for me. Try to see what you might know about this Gelli.'

'I'll do what I can. It will take about a week to see if we know anything. Where will you be for the wedding if I have a message for you?'

'The night before we'll be at a hotel in Prüm, the next town along from Gerolstein. Zum Goldenen Stern it's called.'

'Okay then. If you don't hear from me, then there's nothing. But whatever I send, don't let your woman see it. Ever.'

'She'll be the last to know that I have this,' I said, patting my new passport before I hid it away inside my jacket.

I drove the Volkswagen back round to the road from where I'd parked it, tucked in tight against the side of the main building and out of sight from the Western side. If the West German border guards asked me why I'd only been East for an hour I'd tell them I was picking up the parcel I'd hidden under my seat on the way over here in preparation for the question.

But that wasn't the trickiest problem I still faced today. Once I'd crossed back over to the West, I'd have to decide whether to call up Paola in Bari and ask if her family had any contacts of their own amongst the comrades in Rome, which was where I assumed we'd find Gelli.

The reason not to, of course, would be that if Johannes' Department III rivals got to hear of an unofficial approach to the PCI, it could seriously backfire for us. And what story would I give the Italians at this stage anyway? Maybe it wouldn't hurt to try Paola in any case, just to find out when was the best time to call her, if I did have to contact her in a hurry.

In one area, though, there was no uncertainty. More than Thomas Hofmann's passport, speculative phone calls to impressionable young Italian women were definitely something to be kept secret from Sophie.

Chapter Thirty-Two

My mother, Stefan Benke and I went out for lunch at a restaurant in a hotel up by the Inner Alster lake, a special meal to celebrate their upcoming wedding next month. Stefan was coming to mine next weekend, so it was a double celebration in a way.

'Where's your fiancée?' he asked, trying not to sound aggrieved at the discourtesy of her not being there.

'She's making some last-minute preparations at her parents' house.'

It was the truth - conveniently for me and my secret rendezvous with Johannes.

But everything was going to become more difficult on that score in the future. My scheme to one day do some work on the side for Schalck-Golodkowski might raise more questions than answers, especially as it wasn't like I'd need the extra money to live on after next weekend.

'Are your East German relatives coming to the wedding?' Stefan asked. 'Your aunt seemed to get over here quite a lot over the past few months.'

There was no way she'd be allowed to come now, not with Karin in jail. My mother mustn't have told him yet. People around me were too apt to keep secrets.

'We'll probably go over there sometime after the wedding. I don't want her to get into trouble on my behalf by requesting another trip so soon after the last one. Anyway, travel from the East might get easier in the next couple of years. There's talk of a treaty.'

'Brandt will never pull it off.'

'We'll see. It depends how badly the other side wants it.'

'So, are you ready for a child? I suppose it's not the way you wanted things to be?' he asked.

'There's enough trouble and heartache out there in the world already. Bringing up a child with someone you love is hardly the biggest hardship two people have ever faced together.'

I could have added that it was a lot less hardship than what my mother had faced the winter of nineteen forty-five, but I thought he got the message.

It was she who changed the topic.

'I have a friend who works at the University Clinic hospital. Guess who checked in for an operation last week? Otto Skorzeny.'

My jaw dropped. 'Why? What was he in for?'

'That's all she would tell me.'

'It must be serious if he's come back from Spain,' I said to myself thoughtfully. The others looked at me askance, doubtless wondering why I knew this and if I had a secret fascination for famous Nazis.

When I'd met him in the summer, I'd had to try hard to ignore his shambling gait when we'd gone from his office to a cafe for a drink. I wondered if that was anything to do with his visit now.

'Does your friend know how long he'll be there? When did you last speak to her?'

'Why the sudden interest?' she asked.

I shrugged. An idea had come to me, something else that I might be able to use with Borghese, if I drew a blank on finding Gelli. Despite Johannes' assurances about the insurance policy he'd taken out, I had to try everything.

'We spoke a couple of days ago. He's unlikely to have been moved over a weekend,' she said.

I cleared my plate quickly, impatient to be away but trying not to let it show. I did refuse dessert, too curtly for politeness, and I saw it in my mother's eyes.

Stefan Benke insisted on paying, so I couldn't even save face that way. Then there was a suggestion of a walk around part of the lake, but I had to decline that too. Despite my apologies, I could see the scepticism in their eyes that I really did have somewhere more important to be this afternoon.

My first port of call was a public phone booth and a frantic search through my pocketbook for Jörg's number. Bettina answered.

"Hello Oskar. What a lovely surprise. We're sorry we can't come to the wedding, but we've already accepted an invitation to another one that weekend.'

'I need to speak with Jörg, is he around?'

'He's based at the Mörkenstrasse police station in Altona these days. His shift tonight doesn't finish until eight.'

'Do you know if he's on desk duty?'

'Sorry, no idea. Just go to the station and see if he's there.'

I drove to Mörkenstrasse but they wouldn't say where he was. I said I'd wait. I watched a probationer cadet prepare to go out on patrol with a couple of older officers, just as I'd done in a different lifetime, only four years ago.

I waited on the hard back-to-back benches in the public lobby for almost an hour. By the end I was regretting my hastiness and wishing I'd simply asked Bettina if I could come round when Jörg was due home.

Just as I was about to call it a day, I felt a clap on my shoulder from behind and a guffaw.

'What trouble are you in now, Oskar? Got a parking ticket? Been caught somewhere off the Reeperbahn where you shouldn't have been?'

I got up and turned to face him. 'Can you talk?'

He glanced at the clock on the wall behind the counter. 'For ten minutes, yes.'

476

'Outside?'
'Come on then.'

We walked and talked because time was short. At least the hour's wait had given me time to come up with a story of some kind for what I was going to ask him to do.

'I've just heard from my mother that Otto Skorzeny is in town, receiving medical treatment.'

'Go on.'

'He's connected to an EEC subsidy fraud. Exporting olive oil from Spain to Italy so it can be relabelled as Italian produce. I want to ask him some questions, catch him by surprise when he's least expecting it.'

'It sounds official. Shouldn't you be going through the normal channels?'

'I need a success to impress my boss. We're not on the best of terms at present.'

If he knew which boss and which side of the Berlin Wall I meant, he'd be ramming my head onto the pavement right now. The Hamburg cops enjoyed strike breaking the left-wing unions, they did it with vim and vigour using the riot squad they'd specially created for the task.

'What can I do about it?' he asked, the jollity fading.

'Can you get me into the hospital, find out who's guarding him?'

'Are you in trouble of some kind back in Brussels?'

I weighed this up. He might be more inclined to help me if I was.

'No, not as such. But you know the sort of people he's connected with and how difficult it is to catch these slippery fish at anything. It's a chance I won't get again.'

'I'm only a sergeant, there's only so much I can do.'

'Just tell me if he has a police guard.'

'Okay. I can ask around.'

Then he seemed to relent at his lack of enthusiasm.

'You want me to come with you, when you go to see

him?'

'Let's see what kind of security he has first, official or private. I don't want to create difficulties for you,' I said, knowing a challenge would make him more likely to want to join me.

For want of anything better to do while I waited on Jörg's shift ending, I drove north to Eppendorf and parked up in one of the back streets. For what it was worth, I did a quick scout on foot around the blocks covered by the University Clinic, just to get the feel for the neighbourhood and see if there were any back ways in or out which Skorzeny's bodyguards might be using.

After I'd hung around for as long as I thought I could before risking undue attention, I made my way back down to the bar in Altona where I'd agreed to meet Jörg. I'd met him in the same bar near his and Bettina's flat in 'sixty-nine, just before the von Barten affair had started when I'd been home for another visit.

When Jörg arrived shortly after eight, he was still in uniform.

'Well, I had to ask around. In the end I went in person to the station down the street from the Clinic and asked them what they knew. He had some overweight old comrades guarding him when he first got here but that was over a week ago, so they may have got bored and drifted back to their day jobs.'

I pondered. If we got past the bodyguards and he recognised me from earlier in the summer, I shouldn't have any trouble. Presumably he wanted to keep a low profile and avoid any fuss whilst he was back in West Germany. He was the one who wanted the medical treatment, after all.

'Do you still want me to come with you?' he asked.

'Don't you want to come? To see Otto Skorzeny? It might be your last chance, if he's not well.'

He hesitated, troubled at my apparent enthusiasm, just

as Stefan Benke and my mother had been earlier. Maybe he suspected me of having an autograph book for prominent members of the former regime.

'Okay, if we're quick.' He glanced at his watch.'

'Bettina still home?'

'No, she's gone out again. She's working tonight.'

The uniform made all the difference and we breezed past the front desk and the clinical staff whom we met on the way.

When we reached the private ward, a burly older man was sitting on a chair outside the door.

'What do you want?' he barked.

'I need to see the Obersturmbannführer,' I said.

Beside me I heard a slight intake of breath from Jörg at the use of the SS rank.

'Who are you and what do you want?'

'Police business,' said Jörg. 'My colleague has some questions for your man.'

The guard eyed up Jörg, who was the tallest of everyone here, apart from Skorzeny in the next room. The broad sergeants' stripes - copied from the British when they ran the police just after the war - did their trick again too.

He rapped on the window of the door to the ward and another fifty-year-old of dubious provenance came out into the corridor. Well built like the first man, but with muscle running to middle-aged fat.

'If you're going in, then we'll need to search you,' the new man said.

'I'll wait outside,' said Jörg.

'You can go if you like,' I told him. 'I'll come by and see you tomorrow.'

'Okay, *bis Morgen.*'

I nodded and he left. The two guards didn't seem impressed with the casual pleasantries.

'Are you sure you have business with the boss?'

'He knows who I am.'

The first man patted me down and I followed the second man into the ward. Skorzeny was lying back on the pillows looking pale, a yellowish tinge to his skin. Compared to how I'd remembered him in Madrid, he seemed to have lost weight from his bulky frame, too.

He propped himself up on the pillows.

'You've changed,' he said. 'Come closer.' He waved me over with his free hand, his other one still attached to a drip.

I stood by his bed and looked down at him.

'You want a cigarette?' I asked. 'Or have they forbidden you?'

'They haven't killed me yet. But no.'

He looked at my face more closely and jabbed his chin at me.

'You got your own duelling scar now?'

'It was hardly a duel when that happened.'

'So what do you want? Who are you working for these days?'

'Everyone,' I said, dropping all semblance of pretence. At the end of July, I'd been an EEC official in the Agriculture Directorate, seeking contacts to dump powdered milk in the Middle Eastern market.

'I wanted to thank you for saving my life. For the advice you gave me earlier this summer.'

'What did I say? A lot has happened to me since then.'

'Any decision is better than no decision.'

He sank back onto the pillow.

'Maybe I will have that cigarette now.'

I handed him one and bent down to light it.

'You attract trouble. So what trouble is it now?'

'Not me. One of your allies is in difficulties. More than he realises.'

He looked up again, interested.

'Julio Borghese, sometimes known as Prince Borghese,' I explained.

'Oh, him,' he said in a strange voice. I sensed he might actually be jealous.

'You know, at Alexandria, he and his men were lucky. Someone once told me, Yeo-Thomas, I think, that the British had just opened the anti-torpedo nets to let some of their own ships back in the harbour. All Borghese's men had to do was follow them in.'

'Did you meet him, when you were in Italy in 'forty-three?' I asked.

He gazed into the middle distance, presumably thinking back to that afternoon in September when his glider had landed the top of the Gran Sasso in the successful rescue attempt on Mussolini. The mission which had made his name and transformed him into a Nazi celebrity. The aura of questionable fame still hung about him, even twenty-seven years later.

'No, we were in and out within seven weeks. Then I was busy elsewhere.'

'Well, he's in trouble now and could use your help. Wouldn't you like him to be in your debt?' I said, trying not to sound as if I was speaking to a child.

'What do you want me to do about it?'

'He may need to leave Italy in a hurry. Find somewhere else to live in the Mediterranean. Permanently. Could you ask people in Spain?'

'Why do you want to help him?'

'I'm helping some other people by giving Borghese a way out.'

'I'm getting to the stage where I'm past caring. I need to get better.'

'Would you ever have left one of your own men behind, if you could have helped it?'

'No,' he said. There was a strained look on his face, as if he'd remembered something unpleasant from his past.

'I can speak to some people, but it's not like he isn't already well connected in Spain through the various networks of our movement. I can't promise anything. I don't even know why I'm offering.'

'I understand. I'll make sure you get the credit with Borghese, if it comes to anything.'

'How did you find Ireland?'

'Confusing. They're at war with each other.'

'I know that, fool. I watch the news.'

'No. I meant in the South. You know how it goes. Different opinions within the government on what to do in Northern Ireland. That kind of thing.'

'Are you done here?'

'Yes.'

I stood for a moment in front of the bed, hands clasped before me. This was probably the last time I'd ever see him. I wanted to say something significant, but I had nothing.

He'd helped to keep alive the hopes of the regime right until the end. And afterwards he'd kept alive the hopes of its ongoing adherents too, both secret and not-so-secret. He'd shown no repentance, no remorse for his beliefs over the years and was still prideful of his actions. What did you say to such a person? My aunt's pastor in Wismar might have known.

But I felt compelled to say something.

'It was all for nothing, you know. Through the EEC, over time West Germany will get to hitch all the other nations to its cart. We could have got to the same place as Himmler, Göring and the others wanted, but without the disaster you inflicted on us.'

'Yes, but the Jews would still have been in charge. Now we get our victory, after a fashion, but without the Zionists secretly pulling the strings. We just need to make sure they don't come back.'

Some people were beyond hope of change. Humanly speaking, at least.

Chapter Thirty-Three

After another protracted fight with his secretary, I'd got a meeting with Spinelli at his office in the Berlaymont again.

I'd tried to tie him down to a conclusion over Borghese the very first time I'd met him, at Kramer's apartment. At our second private meeting, he'd told me to find a puppet master, and now I was going to run Gelli's name past him and see what that prompted.

But given that it had been seven weeks since I'd seen him last, and that I was having to chase him, he obviously had little real interest in Borghese. Or maybe he did, he'd told someone back home, and the Italians were taking care of things privately themselves.

But it seemed unlikely. At the second meeting he hadn't even been that interested in seeing the completed proposal to rebalance the CAP. The one that he'd originally made such a song and dance over, the day he yelled at Rizzo in Sophie's office.

As it turned out, she'd only just finished it, at the start of the week. I brought it along with me, all two hundred pages of it, as a conversation piece if nothing else.

When I entered, he was sitting behind his desk, thumbing through a journal. Something deadly dry and academic by the look of the dense text and line graphs which I could see interspersed throughout the page he was on. I glanced again at the black and white photos on the wall, of him and the other fathers of Europe. If he'd had any respect, he might have put a black ribbon around de Gaulle's picture for a couple of weeks.

'I took your advice,' I said, as politely as I could. 'About trying to find one of the controlling minds behind Borghese. A name did come up, a Licio Gelli. Ever heard of him?'

'No.'

'He worked for the fascist intelligence agency during the war, I was told. In Dalmatia,' I added, in case that prompted Spinelli's memory.

'He could be anybody,' he said, disinterested.

'He must be somebody,' I replied. 'If he really does have influence over Borghese.'

Spinelli shrugged. I wondered if he could ask the people he was close to in the DC. Given how widely the party's tentacles spread throughout Italian politics, everyone over there must be connected to at least one member who had a role in the shadow state.

'I was at a social function the other day. Someone said that secrecy was a feature of Italian politics,' I volunteered, trying to lead him on.

'It had to be that way, for a country under foreign occupation for so long: the Habsburgs, the Bourbons, Napoleon and his family. The unification movement last century was an illegal one for long periods.'

'The people I was with mentioned secret Church societies.'

'Garibaldi was a freemason. You can understand the attraction to the aristocratic *Risorgimento* plotters of hidden networks of like-minded people, outside the mainstream Church and royal courts.'

'I didn't realise there were freemasons in Catholic countries.'

'European aristocracy is more blind to religion than people realise. Real power and real money know no flag or creed. As I said, the Freemasons have always provided neutral ground for unlikely allies to come together. That's why Mussolini banned them.'

As did Hitler, for the same reasons, I guessed.

'What do you think of Freemasonry?' I asked, wondering if he was dropping me a hint of where I could start looking for Gelli.

'The same as Mussolini.'

'Pardon?'

'As you read in the manifesto, my hope after the war was that a revolutionary European federalist party would arise. An alliance of liberal intellectuals, backed by the power of the working class on the streets, that would force a new settlement on Europe. Purge the continent of nation-states and bring about unification. Freemasonry is at heart a vehicle of the elite, a tool of reaction. I would have had no time for them, during the revolutionary transition.'

'So you'd have had them banned too?'

'Mussolini had the right idea about how to use power. His mistake was in using it for the wrong purpose.'

'You wrote your manifesto, but in the end, there was no need for the democratic revolution you thought would be required. All the countries of Western Europe, once liberated, became democracies. So what's the point of destroying the nation-states now?'

'The principles of what I said in my manifesto still hold. Although these states today appear to be broadly democratic and sometimes even socialist, it's only a question of time before power falls back into the hands of the reactionaries.'

'So what you're saying is that the plebs can't be trusted not to return to fascism if they're given a democratic nation-state to live in? How do you achieve your goal? Your old idea, to smash these societies up and start again, initially with a federal dictatorship?'

'It's not the nineteen forties anymore. But the plan's the same in outline.'

The guy was a fanatic. He was more of a danger to Western Europe than the people I worked for at the

Normannenstrasse. At least you would see them coming to destroy Europe in their tanks and paratroop-carrying Antonovs. No wonder Jan was smitten by Spinelli. They were both equally crazy.

'Now we have to take the long way round,' he said, far too calmly for my liking. 'We won't assault the member states as such, we'll hollow them out, undermine them. We'll transfer ever more decision-making power to the EEC via the Commission, but we'll leave the national civil servants in place to enforce European federal policy in each of their own countries. The facade of the individual buildings will still stand, but only because we're constructing a new fortress home behind the scenes.'

It sounded more like a prison than a home to me.

'And the second stage?' I hoped there was some light at the end of the tunnel.

'Once we've completely neutered the nation-states and the ability of the unreconstructed, uneducated lower classes to subvert them, then we'll hand power back to the people.'

I could have commented that perhaps it wasn't his power to have in the first place, but he wouldn't have heard me, caught up as he was.

'We'll create a real European Parliament. One chosen directly by the electorate of Europe. One which will have real law-making power and which will relegate the Commission once its task of building a unified state is done, merely to the status of an administrative body. Nothing more than a European civil service.'

'And at what precise point do the nation-states disappear exactly?' I asked, half in horror, half in fascination.

'Once we have a single European army. Even Monnet knew this. That's why he went as far as he did in 'fifty-four to try to bring it about. When men fight and die under the same flag, only then will they forget their old allegiances.'

'Like Ostmark.' I said, over brightly.

He scowled. But I knew one thing for sure, it wouldn't be him and his faux-revolutionary intellectuals who would be dying for a European flag, but the working class, as always.

I had one final thought before I left him, for amusing as all this theorising was, it was still a digression from my attempt to find Gelli.

'But how about those European democracies who didn't succumb to fascism. Like Ireland, or Switzerland, or England? Or even the ones who were occupied and resisted throughout, like Norway and Poland? Why should their nation-states disappear, just because you don't trust the others?'

'It seems to me that England and Ireland are only too eager to join the EEC, even though they know full well the path we're on. Or at least, they ought to. Who are we to stop them if they don't?'

Indeed, and Kramer was determined to make the path of one of them in particular as smooth as possible.

'I still don't think people will give up their national identities as easily as you think. The elite for sure, but not the plebs. The memory of place endures for a long time.'

I was thinking of myself as I said this. I had never been to East Prussia, but when Sophie mentioned the old German names for the rivers and the lakes around her family's estate, and when my mother talked about Allenstein, now Olsztyn, something called to me.

'Once an idea gains a certain momentum it becomes unstoppable,' Spinelli said.

Yes, I wondered. But in whose head? And what if not everyone in a country was convinced that their nation should disappear? What unpleasantness did that lead to?

'Kramer said you'd be able to help me in my project to democratise the Parliament, if I needed it?' he asked.

'Yes, sir. He did.'

'Let me have a think. I'm still new to the Commission.'

And oh, how so naïve, I thought to myself. Naïve too,

because if anything, he was gradually making me look more favourably towards Borghese.

I was hunting around for ways to stop the Comandante, because I'd assumed he was no less anti-democratic than Mussolini. But what if the Fronte Nazionale really did just want to repair the democratic settlement in Italy for the health of the nation? What if they had a better grasp on the principles of democracy than the federalists? Because for all of Spinelli's protestations, I wasn't sure that he did.

I went to the Parc du Cinquantenaire to think some more, but no cigarette, even though my fingers itched for one. Sophie's sense of smell was becoming ever more acute these days and it wasn't worth the risk.

The real problem, as exemplified by Spinelli - even though he dressed it up in the virtuous talk of European federalism - was that no one really seemed to believe in Italy, or that it could stand on its own two feet.

The DC manipulated elections and ran Italy as their fiefdom, like a larger version of the Sicilian Mafia's Regional Commission. The PCI looked to the Soviet Union to save them. When the chips were down in 'forty-three, even Borghese had been in love with Germany rather than Mussolini.

And what was I to do, really? Italy wasn't my fight. There were already enough men of violence in the country for my liking. Then again, if Borghese knew the coup was a feeble one from the start, suggesting to him that he retire to a life in the sun in Spain might be more attractive than I knew.

But against all that, even if I didn't believe Borghese had a chance, it was the principle of the thing. Gavrilo Princip had started a war with a single shot. Who was to say another one couldn't prevent decades of heartache and trouble.

Surely the Ministry would help if it was put to them the

right way, despite their internal turmoil over the forthcoming departure of Ulbricht. What was the point in having the most professional espionage agency in Europe if it was never used for what it was designed for?

Gelli was an unknown quantity though. Rizzo's father could have named him for any number of reasons. As the Adviser had explained in Palermo in the 'twenties, the Mafia had used the fascists to bump off rivals whom they'd denounced, getting the Carabinieri to do their dirty work. Why mightn't Rizzo's father be doing the same with me? But Gelli was the only lead I had, so I had no choice.

And when I found him, what then? Borghese, I'd try to persuade, if I got the chance. But Gelli?

In the afternoon I met Kramer at his office in the Berlaymont for our regular Thursday meeting, before I left for Gerolstein to get married. Too many of the twists and turns of my fate seemed to have been decided in this room since spring nineteen sixty-nine.

'So, has anyone in France heard of Licio Gelli?' I asked.

'Well now I have.'

He looked at me over the top of his spectacles, the ones he hardly ever wore. Out of vanity, I supposed.

'My advice is to stay well clear of him.'

'Why?'

'He's as well connected in Italy as the Pope. He's probably connected to the Pope too, for that matter.'

'You're not helping me.'

'Vatican Bank, the Mafia, SID, UAR,… the list goes on.'

'And the freemasons?'

'Yes, those guys too. How did you guess that?'

'You mentioned everyone else.'

But it was Spinelli who'd dropped the secret society into our conversation. And Spinelli who'd claimed ignorance of one of the most connected men in Italy, apparently.

'How do I get hold of him? Do you have any personal details? An address?'

'Why do you need those things?' he said, frowning at me. 'I've indulged you more than enough already. The SDECE isn't a reference library, in case you hadn't realised.'

The thought crossed my mind that they might have better contacts with the PCI than Johannes.

'I don't know why I might need the details, not yet anyway. I just have the sense that I need to be able to find him if I end up having to go to Italy.'

'Go to Italy? What aren't you telling me?'

I wasn't going to get out of this one.

'It's a complicated situation. I didn't tell you before but the child is Giovanni Rizzo's.'

He tilted his chair back and let out a low whistle.

'Really?'

'Yes, really. It means that Rizzo's father is going to be a grandfather. I want to encourage him to disentangle himself from Borghese.'

'How are you going to do that? Did you make a penfriend in the Mafia?'

I hadn't of course, but Di Luca had given me the phone number for his flat in Palermo. You never knew when you might need a favour.

'I don't know that either. I'll work it out when the time comes.'

Chapter Thirty-Four

Yesterday afternoon, the day before the wedding, Sophie had forced her parents to put on a reception at the house for the families. Effectively this meant an extended von Barten clan gathering because there were so many of them. Not just uncle, aunts, first and even second cousins, but their hangers-on too: wives, husbands and children. Cousins at multiple removes, I supposed. Not that I'd ever had to work it out before.

Caterina had been invited too. She seemed overwhelmed by the occasion. She'd held Sophie's hand, earnestly telling her of how she would pray her rosaries and have a Mass said for the safe delivery of the baby and for our marriage. She hung around our table for a while, as if there was more she wanted to say, but eventually drifted off to speak with Sophie's mother which was brave of her.

Whatever little Sophie had expected in terms of bringing the families together, she must still have been disappointed. Sophie's father made some effort with my mother, but Sophie's mother said nothing and wouldn't even shake hands with mine. I got a limp handshake, but the distaste was obvious for all to see.

As for the other von Bartens, it was like my mother was a carrier of the plague. Which was probably how they thought of Russian war-babies.

But now the day had arrived, the actors were offstage, and the play was about to begin.

The Church of the Redeemer in Gerolstein hardly

needed decorating with flowers, given its covering of gold mosaic tiles above head height and marble everywhere else. I understood why Sophie had chosen it. Last year she'd told me that if she ever had to take religion seriously, it was the ritual and incense of the Catholics she'd go for.

But the Church of the Redeemer wasn't one of theirs. Instead, it had been paid for and dedicated by no less a personage than the last Kaiser himself. A statement of Prussian intent in the Catholic Eifel. It looked more like a Greek Orthodox church than a Lutheran one, but maybe that was deliberate.

But for all the grand setting, there were only a few flowers in the way in. The result, I guessed, of Sophie's disinterest in frippery and her mother's belief that it wasn't worth making an effort for a first wedding.

At least the scale of the service on our side of the family wouldn't put my mother's wedding to Stefan Benke next month into the shade. He'd come with us to the von Bartens' yesterday. Last night he'd stayed at the same hotel in Prüm as us, but in his own separate room. If they'd chosen a different arrangement it would have been hypocritical of me to object.

My other guests were Jan and his secretary-girlfriend, Bernd and Magda. And Caterina, I supposed, given that it had been my idea to invite her. She hadn't arrived at the church yet.

I wasn't bothered about the traditions, like having a best man. If there was someone in my recent past who might conceivably have filled the role of jolly jester, then Di Luca would have done as well as anyone.

But he was a mad murderer and a wedding attended by Sophie's emotional girlfriends would have been the last place to invite that lecher to. Plus, I'd promised Caterina's father when he'd agreed to let her come, that I'd look after her here.

So Dirk ended up being the official best man. It was no more insincere than anything else concerning the involvement of Sophie's wider family.

On Sophie's side it seemed like half the class of 'sixty-seven from the College of Europe were there in attendance. There had been no suggestion she might throttle back her guest list to more closely match mine, it was just her way. If I had mentioned something, she would probably have done so to a degree. On the other hand, if I was the sort of person who was bothered by it, we probably wouldn't be getting married in the first place.

Two rows back from the front I caught sight of a couple of the midnight diehards from the bar that evening after the funeral in Apulia. They looked more like they were attending their second funeral in two months than a wedding. Come to witness the final burial of their hopes of ever making it with Sophie, I thought smugly to myself. I wondered if they'd once been some of the more serious contenders.

They were somewhat cheered up, though, at the sight of Caterina in her Milan couture coming down the aisle to the front of the church, to sit demurely under her broad-brimmed hat next to my mother. From their sideways glances, I realised this would be the second celebration where I'd have to keep an eye out for her. *In loco parentis*, as practice for the real thing.

The service started and I stood at the front with my left hand clasped in my right to try to hide the worst of the scars as I waited on her to arrive up the aisle.

Then she was standing at the altar rail opposite me, flowers in her hand, her hair in a braided ring around the top of her head, like a crown. It was a family tradition, apparently. The photographs of her mother and grandmother on their wedding days showed their hair dressed in the same way.

I wondered if she was sending a signal to her mother, that today was a real wedding. The photographs to be glued firmly into the family album, rather than tucked in behind tissue paper.

The rest of the service passed in a blur, as it finally struck home that this was it, there was no going back - not for me, at least.

She watched me, unsmiling, as we spoke the words. I remembered her eyeing up the scar on my cheek as she repeated her names: Sophia Augusta Helena Viktoria. My single name seemed cheap by comparison.

At the reception, the von Bartens continued to avoid my mother. They tolerated me in their own fashion because today they had little choice, but they certainly didn't extend it to my guests. My guests with the exception of Caterina of course, because they always made an exception for money.

Despite the different treatment, Caterina stayed close to us and got more than her fair share of looks in reward.

Before dinner, one of Sophie's more distant female cousins, not the one who'd got drunk at the lunch the other week, came up to find out more about her, probably trying to estimate the size of her bank account.

Under the make-up, I reckoned the cousin was in her forties, maybe even the same age as my mother. The cosmetics couldn't disguise the permanent downward set to her mouth though. I did the translation, explaining that Caterina was from Italy. Somehow, the line of the cousin's questioning brought up the fact that Caterina had family connections to Sicily.

The cousin's mouth turned down further and her hand went to the wedding ring on her finger twisting it round and around. Suddenly, she blurted out in a low voice something I hadn't expected to hear today.

'*Mein Mann ist in Sizilien gefallen.*'

At least my mother had been spared that. She'd had a fatherless child, but not suffered the loss of a husband. I wondered how long the cousin had been married then, if her husband had died in the invasion of Sicily, as I presumed he had. Twenty-seven years on from nineteen forty-three and he was still her husband. What if they'd had one of the wartime distance marriages and had never actually been together?

The cousin drifted off and for the moment I was left alone with Caterina. Before I could react, she leaned in close and whispered.

'I have a message from my father. It's going to be the night of the seventh or the eighth next month.'

I looked open-mouthed at her for a second then composed myself. 'Anything else? Is that it?'

'He says he'll be at our apartment in Rome on the afternoon of the seventh if you want to meet him. That's the message.'

She gave me the address on a folded piece of paper which she slipped from her handbag. I did some quick maths. Today was the twenty-eighth of November, so I had nine full days at most. And we were meant to be going on honeymoon tomorrow to Switzerland. I couldn't do anything today, but I could try to work out who I'd need to call from the hotel.

'Okay, Caterina. Thanks.'

'Is this bad news? Is it something to do with Giovanni?'

I weighed up what to say to her, for she clearly knew nothing.

'I promised your father I would make sure his death wasn't in vain.'

Her eyes were sorrowful and doe-like, but in the depths, there was fire. She was going to play havoc with many men's hearts in the coming years. I saw Sophie, my wife, looking at us from across the room and went over to her.

Dirk gave his best man's speech. I was impressed, despite myself. He knew nothing about me yet managed to conjure up a smooth five minutes where he managed to make it sound like we'd been boyhood friends, now joined by deeper bonds. It was another reminder to me, should I need it, not to underestimate the von Bartens.

Ernst and the rest of them had got where they were, precisely because they were so plausible. I supposed in Dirk's case he'd had plenty of practice at charming Middle Eastern oil sheiks who wanted their money managed in a less volatile part of the world.

Dirk read out the good luck telegrams too. I'd passed him the one from Jörg and Bettina, but not the one which appeared to have come from a West Berlin sender. It might somehow have been amusing to Johannes, but I thought the joke was lame: *'Now you've picked a teammate for the match, make sure you don't switch sides.'*

'Why did you hide that one?' she asked as she saw me put it back into the inside pocket of my jacket.

'It wasn't suitable to be read out in public.'

'Who's sending you unsuitable ones then?'

Surely she wasn't already suspicious about other women?

'Some army buddies. If you know any barracks humour, you can probably guess the kind of things they were saying.'

But the telegram was the only message that Johannes had sent. He'd obviously drawn a blank on any information concerning Licio Gelli - if he'd even asked. I would be on my own in Italy. But that was tomorrow's problem.

We said our farewells and got in the car to drive for an hour to Bad Ems, just outside Koblenz. We were going to stay there overnight and get a head start for the long drive down to Switzerland the following day.

I closed the door to our hotel room and shut out the world of the Ministry, drug dealing French spies, Italian fascists and mobsters. There was a European federalist fanatic inside the room though, but it wasn't Spinelli.

Sophie was already in bed, watching me as I stripped

off. She was still wearing her braids, but nothing above the waist. She was probably naked below the waist too, but the sheets were wrapped around her so I couldn't tell.

I went over and unpeeled the bedclothes to check she was ready before moving her into position.

It was enjoyable, it always was with her. But it was just another time. Because over the past weeks, I'd come round to the view that as far as I was concerned, this union didn't date from today, but from when we'd fucked each other's brains out in a second-floor office in the European Quarter ten weeks ago. Taken to its logical conclusion, I supposed it meant there was no such thing as casual sex with anyone.

Chapter Thirty-Five

While Sophie went for her morning swim in the hotel, I called for help. But not from the room phone, because I didn't want an excessive amount for international calls showing on our bill.

I cajoled reception to let me call from another, unoccupied guest room on the first floor and said I'd pay cash. I had no plan yet for how I was going to explain away a trip to Rome to her in the middle of our holiday. It was force of habit which made me keep the making of the arrangements secret.

I sat at the desk with my head in my hands and tried to think.

The first place I called was Di Luca's apartment. There was no answer, which was hardly surprising given it was Sunday and the morning after the night before.

Next was Kramer. This time I did get an answer.

'*Allo?*'

'It's Oskar.'

'Aren't you meant to have got married this weekend?'

'I did. But now something important has come up.'

'More important than Madame Lenkeit? Why are you calling me on your vacation? We only spoke on Thursday.'

'The Borghese affair is coming to a conclusion. Something is taking place in as soon as eight days' time. The evening of either the seventh or the eighth.'

'Why am I dreading what comes next?'

'It's what I told you last week, I need to go down there and help Rizzo's father - the child's grandfather.'

'And I said to you weeks ago, stay out of other people's civil wars. This is not France's problem. And it's not your fight either.'

'And I'm saying I don't have a choice. Right now, I need all the help I can get.'

'And I need you in one piece for London.'

That again. Whatever he had in mind for me there, I was starting to dread it. All the favours he was doing for me would come with a price to be paid later, a price which was only going up with every request I made of him.

'Then help me out with this thing, because I'm going down there anyway. Did your people find out anything more about Gelli?'

There was a long pause and the seconds stretched out. Down the line I heard him clear his throat. I thought there might have been a ghost of a sigh before that, but the connection wasn't clear.

'They have a home address, a Villa Wanda, named after his wife. He's known to various people, but no one who stands out.'

'I'll take that. Do you have anyone you can send with me?'

'Do you know when to stop pushing the boundaries? *Mais putain*, Oskar. What are you planning to do in Rome?' he said, an urgency now starting to creep into his voice.

'I told you on Thursday, I don't exactly know. Persuade Rizzo's father to leave the country that night perhaps. Use Rizzo's father to persuade Borghese to stop.'

'And you want someone to come with you? How much influence do you think I have in Paris?' he hissed. 'I can't call up the Service Action and order them down there to assault Borghese's headquarters. You're my Service Action.'

'I left my guns in Brussels. Can you send someone to my flat and have them sent to my hotel in Switzerland?'

There was another pause and then a sigh.

'I'm not going to be able to stop you, am I? Does your

honeymoon finish before or after you march on Rome?'

'After. I'm going to tell her that you're sending me, and that it's you who's breaking our vacation. So you might as well help me all you can, to make it worth your while when I explain it to her later.'

'You've got all this thought out, haven't you? Or so you think.'

He hadn't, because under no circumstances would I tell her that I worked for him. He'd been her uncle's bitter rival. It would be almost as bad as confessing to her again that I'd shot him.

'Okay, I'm only doing this because you're going to London for me next year - and you will be doing whatever I tell you to do there. But when I say you're taking a risk by going to Italy, I don't only mean you're in danger from the Italians. Don't forget about the American agency, too.'

'I'll talk her around into forgiving you.'

I told him where to find the weapons and where to send them. They were still at my old flat, my rental agreement ran into the New Year. There was another nasty silence when I mentioned the AK and I tried to tell him that the Stasi sometimes issued their informers with assault rifles, but he got over it. That was all I could do for now. It was time to hit the road for Saint Moritz.

I left the room and went back to reception to settle up. Just as I finished, Sophie made an appearance on her way back from the pool down in the basement level.

'I had a message from work,' I said as we walked back up to the room together.

Her eyebrows shot up. 'What? Today?'

I nodded back, as if it was all completely normal.

'What's going on?' she asked suspiciously.

There was no point in delaying the inevitable.

'In a week's time I need to go to Rome for a couple of days. Spinelli's sending me.'

'I thought you worked for Masson?'

'He's taken a renewed interest in Borghese. He trumps Masson on this one.'

'Am I allowed to ask why?'

'It's the aftermath of the affair with Giovanni. Some loose ends that need tying up.'

'What's it got to do with Spinelli? Does he know what you got up to in Italy? Even Masson didn't know you were in Italy some of the times you went. Or so you told me.'

It was all starting to unravel, and it only got worse.

'You have to tell me. We're married now.'

'Spinelli's heard things through his own people. Borghese's plans aren't as secret as he thinks. Spinelli wants it taken care of, he wants me to go and persuade the ringleaders to back off whatever it is that they're up to.'

I was making it up as I went along.

'And what are Borghese's plans?' she asked.

Yes indeed, Sophia Augusta, what is it that's happening down there? As I didn't ask her out loud.

'Spinelli's obsessed with the idea that Borghese is going to stage an extra-parliamentary political demonstration, a coup of some kind.'

'So how exactly are you going to stop it, then?' she demanded. She didn't tell me that Spinelli's idea was nonsense either, though, which was a change from her attempt in her office ten weeks ago to make up a story when Spinelli had confronted her and Rizzo.

'By any means I can think of. A promise of more influence for Italy at the Commission post-accession of the Four. Your subsidy plan.'

'And?'

'It's just a conversation with the Italians. Don't worry, I'll take protection to Rome.'

She stopped and turned to me impatiently.

'Enough of the metaphors and equivocation.'

'We're almost at the room. I'll tell you more there.'

Once we were inside, she stood arms akimbo, waiting.

'Spinelli's a Commissioner and he's asked me directly. The same Commissioner who threatened to torpedo Giovanni's career, or so he told me in Sicily. Maybe yours too.'

The lies were tripping over themselves to get out of my mouth.

'Who are you going to meet with? Borghese? Giovanni's father? And why right now?'

'Spinelli's been given a date by one of the people he knows, of when something's going to happen.'

'What date?'

'The night of the sixth,' I said, intending to make sure I had an extra day to get down there and get ready.

'How long has Spinelli been talking to you about this? Is that why you mentioned a coup that day he came to see Giovanni and me in my office.'

I looked away in embarrassment, although I wasn't sure why. I wondered if her father had mentioned the suggestion of a coup that I'd made to him and Dirk in the lodge as the rain came down. If they had, she was keeping quiet about it.

'I'll only be gone for a couple of days. If it keeps Spinelli happy and means he doesn't come after you, then it's a small price to pay.'

She sat down in a chair by the window and looked out over the forecourt for a moment to the Lahn River beyond. She turned back to me, lips pursed.

'I can't say I'm very happy about it.'

'It's an exceptional situation,' I said. Any situation which threatened her career was exceptional. It was an argument I knew could count on with her.

'More than I suspect,' she replied drily.

Given her tone, I expected she was about to start building up a head of steam, ready for an explosion.

Then she shrugged. 'You're sure it was the sixth that Spinelli said? Next Sunday?'

I nodded.

'And you're just going to request one meeting with Borghese, just to prove to Spinelli you tried?'

'That's all.'

'Okay,' she said. 'Okay. Just don't test my patience and don't ever do this on holiday again.'

It was a promise I'd be unlikely to break.

'My mother would be delighted if she knew you were leaving me on our honeymoon,' she said sourly.

'I have some more calls to make once we get to Switzerland. I won't let it interfere with our plans more than it has to.'

I tried to take her hand, which was a mistake, because she withdrew it hurriedly.

'I need to get dressed. We need to go,' she said.

'I won't take any risks. You told me yourself I'm a careful person.'

'That's not why I married you yesterday.'

We made good time and arrived at Badrutt's Palace Hotel in Saint Moritz by five. After we'd checked in and she was in the bath I made another call to Di Luca from the hotel reception area.

This time I got an answer.

'*Pronto.*'

'It's Oskar.'

He took a moment to remember, it had been nine weeks exactly. 'Yes?'

'I might need your help.'

'What for?'

'I'm being sent to speak to the people in Rome. To try to persuade them not to go down a wrong path.'

'Okay.'

'It would help me if I knew what your people's final decision was.'

'You've been sent on your own?'

'Yes.'

'Then you're naïve and stupid.'

'I'm doing it for Italy.'

'You keep forgetting I'm Sicilian. I went to America to avoid the Italian draft. Let me tell you a story. Apparently, when the Saraceno clan forced Rizzo at gunpoint down that alleyway, he knew the end was coming. The last thing he said to them was "*Vi faccio vedere come muore un Italiano!*" - "I'll show you how an Italian dies!" So he did.'

'What's your point?'

'You want me to teach you how to say, "This is how a German dies?"'

'Can you tell me if they've decided to help the sailor?'

'Have you seen any reports of bombings or other atrocities in the past few weeks, leading up to today?'

'Not in Italy.'

'There's your clue.'

She didn't ask me who today's calls had been to, the ones before and after we arrived in Saint Moritz. Over dinner she did ask me to explain again why Spinelli was now giving me instructions on a national issue, and if Masson knew about it.

'You know how these senior guys talk to each other. They pick up on goings-on that they think will advance their careers or help them somehow. If Spinelli wants something done, Masson isn't going to gainsay him.'

'What exactly does Spinelli think you can do in Italy that he can't?'

'Don't you remember what he said when he met you, Giovanni and I? He's no intention of getting anywhere near people like Borghese. He's not going to jeopardise his second chance at a political career and more importantly for him, his federal democracy project.'

She pushed her vegetables around the plate with her fork for a while.

'That's why Masson's department is there. We're expendable, deniable. We fix problems no one else can.'

'Again, I wish you'd been a little more forthcoming

with my mother that night you first met her.'

'We're not playing games here. Masson's department has a serious purpose. Spinelli's concerned that we try everything to prevent the Italians playing these comic-opera games. Borghese and the Decima Mas weren't nice people. If they do something foolish, something more appropriate to Chile or Bolivia, then Italy will have the opprobrium of Europe to deal with.'

'And you're the only one he's sending to persuade them not to go through with it?'

I didn't like the speculative way she asked the question, as if she was trying to work out my odds of success.

'And when are you going exactly?' she said, stabbing a carrot.

'Saturday, around noon. I need to be there all day on Sunday and Monday. I'll be back on Tuesday.'

'Why don't I come down to Rome with you? If you're not back until Tuesday, it hardly seems worth continuing the holiday.'

My mouth went dry. I had no idea what I'd end up having to do in Rome before this thing was over.

'You told me how much you wanted to go skiing before you're unable to. When I'm gone, you can do the harder slopes. I'm only going to keep you back for most of the week.'

I'd only skied once before in my life, she'd lost count.

'But I'm not having Spinelli wreck our time away together,' I said virtuously. 'Let's delay our return to Brussels until the following Sunday.'

She took a sip of wine.

'Don't go to Rome,' she said quietly. 'Let's not go back to Brussels at all.'

I looked at her quizzically.

'I've got... we've got, no real need to work. Let's just move to somewhere sunny, away from my parents. Like Greece or Spain, and bring up the baby there together. My income from the Foundation is more than enough for us to live on.'

'Would you really do that?' I asked dubiously.

It was fine by me, but I sensed she would miss her friends and rivals at the Berlaymont more than she realised. And it was a dream I couldn't share with her. I had a major in the Ministry of State Security in Berlin and a Gaullist in Brussels with claims on me that couldn't be tossed aside.

'Maybe I would,' she said. 'Maybe one day. I don't know what being a parent is like.' I found her uncertainty disturbing.

'I have to make another call to Italy,' I said, excusing myself.

The phone at the hotel in Apulia rang for almost a minute before it was answered in a harassed voice by the proprietor's wife. Communication was difficult. I was reduced to saying Paola's name ever louder and '*Sono Thomas, sono compagno*' until her daughter took the receiver.

'*Ciao Paola! Sono Thomas.*'

'*Ciao Tommaso!*'

'Listen Paola, I'm dealing with a political emergency right now, one that affects Italy. I need to go to Rome on important Party business. Does your family know of a comrade there who can help me, someone prepared to use weapons, if necessary?'

'What's happening?'

There was a note of scepticism in her voice, struggling against the excitement that I could hear there too. I had nothing to lose by holding back from embellishing my story.

'When I was last in Italy, my German comrades and I uncovered a plot for a series of neo-fascist terror attacks across Europe. But no one here is taking it seriously. We need proof that we can only find in Italy. I need someone local in Rome that I can trust. Someone who can help me find things out and maybe have someone followed.'

'*Momento…*'

I could almost hear the cogs turning as she considered this, and I wondered if I'd gone too far with my own comic-opera. I really wished now that I'd given her the warning call I'd been weighing up last week.

'It has to be discreet,' I added whilst she thought. 'Don't tell anyone what I just said.'

Finally, she replied. 'My father knows a man from the war. I will find his address. But I don't have it now, you need to call again tomorrow. I know another comrade in Rome, someone I once met at a Festa dell'Unità in the North. You can speak with him too.'

I breathed an inward sigh of relief. I wasn't sure if she'd fully understood what I was asking of her, but I was right in what I'd said. I had nowhere else to go for help, not at this stage.

I thanked her, we agreed a time to speak the next day, and we rang off.

The irony was that in the past five minutes I'd been marginally more honest with her than I had been today with the woman I was meant to spending the rest of my life with.

The other irony was that no one else, apart from the communists whom America saw as a threat to the very existence of Italy, was prepared to actually do anything to save it when the chips were down.

Chapter Thirty-Six

In the half-light I saw her lying on her side, propped up on one elbow as she watched me finish packing and zip close the holdall. I'd planned to go yesterday, but she'd persuaded me to stay and leave before dawn for the long drive to Rome.

I hadn't taken much persuading. Whether because she knew I was going away to possible danger, or simply because of all the fresh air and exercise we'd been getting on the slopes, or even because we'd solemnised our marriage - for the past few days it was like she'd had some kind of permission to be more and more uninhibited in bed. After her grumpiness the day after the wedding, two nights ago she'd suddenly shown me the meaning of the word 'insatiable.' Then she'd had a good go at breaking her record last night too.

I wonder what she'd have thought, if she'd known about the package I'd received from Kramer a couple of days ago. Last night I'd taken it from the concierge who I'd paid to store it privately and stowed the Browning and the AK under the carpet of the Mercedes' boot. It wasn't a great hiding place, but until I got something made specially it would have to do.

'Who are you seeing in Italy first?' she asked, pulling her hair out of her eyes and round behind her neck.

And then the deliberate omissions, the half-answers, and the half-lies started again.

'Rizzo's father, to see if he can get me a meeting with Borghese.'

508

He was the first person I'd see in Italy, the first person that I already knew, that was. The very first place I was going to, as soon as I arrived in Rome, was the Casa del Popolo in the Centocelle quarter, to hunt down the PCI member whose name Paola had given me.

'As soon as you have a sense of what's happening you need to call Dirk.'

'Why?'

'Because that kind of information might be useful to him.'

It was too early in the morning for games.

'How exactly? For his investments?'

'He might have positions in Italian government bonds or in other holdings which a coup might affect.'

'Okay. If I have time I'll try.'

'No. You need to call him. Anytime, day or night.'

It was a bit late for her to be bringing this up now.

'Is he expecting me to call? He hasn't been particularly friendly so far.'

Her hair had slipped forward again. She wrapped the strands around her hand, pulling it away from her front to make sure I saw everything in the gloom.

'It's a small favour to my family. It can't hurt your standing with them. As soon as you know, one quick call.'

I dropped my wash kit next to four thick bundles of lire wrapped in brown paper.

'Why can't I call you, if I hear of anything definite?'

'I'll be skiing, like you said I should be.'

'I'm not happy about Dirk making any decisions involving your family's money based on my advice.'

The room was too dark to see everything properly, but I thought I saw her purse her lips.

'I'll see you in two days - or in two months, if a coup happens,' I said, before she had a chance to think of a new argument.

'You shouldn't joke. If a coup happens, you need to come straight back here,' she said, serious now.

I went over to kiss her one last time. 'I'll look after myself.'

At reception I asked for the Mercedes to be brought round to the front. While we waited, the concierge glanced down at the night book.

'There was another complaint made by the guests staying in the room next to yours last night, about the noise coming from your and Frau Lenkeit's room.'

'I can't help it if Nature takes its course,' I replied smugly. 'Anyway, I'm away for a couple of days. I need to attend to some business. Our neighbours will have a quieter night tonight.'

The concierge gave me a sceptical look as he nodded to the door of the hotel and the waiting car valet.

The drive to Rome took nearly ten hours and it was late afternoon by the time I eventually found the Casa del Popolo in the middle of a long row of municipal apartments on one of Rome's outer ring avenues. I parked the Mercedes a couple of blocks away and walked back to the PCI community centre. Compared to snowy Switzerland, fifteen degrees in Rome felt warm. The sun even made an appearance too. It wasn't the rich light of that fateful evening in Palermo, but it still cheered me up as I prepared for the delicate task of recruiting extra eyes and ears from the cadres of the PCI.

The Casa had a downstairs bar and cafe, with rooms off to the side for community activities. I went up to the counter and pushed across the piece of paper on which I'd written the name Paola had given me.

After much hesitation and feigned ignorance, the barman called over a comrade just leaving one of the classrooms. The new guy spoke English, a younger man with long hair and the Che Guevara look they all aspired to.

'Who are you looking for?' he asked in English.

'I was told I could find a Brichese here.'

'Who told you that?'

'A comrade from Bari.'

'Who?'

'Paola Amato.'

'You should have said. She arrived last night. She's staying upstairs.'

I raised my eyebrows at this news, touched by her dedication to have come all this way on the basis of a couple of phone calls. When I'd called back the following day for the addresses of the two contacts, she'd quizzed me some more and I'd told her when I was coming to Rome.

'Can you find her for me?' I asked. Helping these guys was going to be as hard work as I thought it might.

I ordered a beer and sat at a table where I could watch the staircase for her arriving. She was taking things more seriously than the intelligence agencies of both the East and the West. The ones that I knew of anyway.

After five minutes I heard a pitter-patter from up top and she came tripping down the steps, excited to see me. More excited than I was comfortable with.

'You came,' she said, leaning in for a kiss on the cheeks. My wedding ring was in my pocket. It had to be that way because Thomas Hofmann wasn't married, according to his passport.

'You came too,' I said, smiling encouragingly. This thing had to get done, no matter what. 'Did you tell anyone the reason why I called you?'

She havered for a moment. 'Not exactly. Not the party comrade who works here.'

'Who, Brichese?' I asked. 'Where's he now?'

She nodded over to the bar where Comrade Guevara was watching us from behind the counter. Maybe they were more switched on than they appeared.

'When we speak, let me explain to them why I'm here

in my own words,' I warned her. 'I need to find out for myself who I can trust. What I told you over the phone is true but it's not for everyone to know.'

The three of us went into one of the side rooms. There were a couple of posters up on walls. Innocuous stuff - combine harvesters in a field somewhere in the Soviet Union, Ukraine probably, and a photograph of a space rocket launch by night.

Innocuous, but then again not so much. Italians needed to stop looking to foreign countries for inspiration.

'Why did you call Paola a week ago? Why are you pestering us now? And who are you here on behalf of?' Brichese demanded.

She stiffened. I sensed an indignance on my behalf, but I was playing it cautiously for now. Johannes had dropped enough hints about how they might view Germans, of any flavour or party colour.

'I know Comrade Amato because I was on holiday in Bari earlier this summer and stayed at the pension run by her family. My everyday job is with the export department of East Germany's trade ministry.'

He raised his eyebrows at this.

'And you're here now, because…?'

'I've been sent to conduct some research into business opportunities in Italy and I'd like the advice of the Italian party on the reliability of certain individuals.'

'What sort of help, and what's in it for us?'

Well, that was my back-up story about a neo-fascist coup plot put on ice for a while.

'I need to have someone followed. I can pay you whatever the going rate is.'

Paola frowned, despite my warning - doubtless wondering if she was the one being tricked and if I was here for some straightforward underhand dealing after all. I flicked her a glance, trying to reinforce a sense of confidentiality between us.

'Where are your credentials?'

I slid across my East German passport and a business card which I'd had made up in a shop in Saint Moritz, copied from the one Schalck-Golodkowski had given me in Luxembourg.

Paola watched quietly for now. She'd seen the truck and my suntanned comrades in Bari and she knew something bigger was afoot.

Brichese flicked through my passport. 'You get around, don't you?'

'Can you help?'

'I'm not sure it's my responsibility. This sounds like something for one of the regional leaders.'

I pursed my lips. 'I'll pay you to find someone to watch for me, and to do it discreetly. Otherwise, I can pay your boss.'

It was Spinelli who'd told me to bribe someone.

Brichese looked at me with narrowed eyes. I wonder what the real Che Guevara would have been thinking just now.

Paola was looking at me thoughtfully too. I could see disappointment creeping into her face, and I gave her a quick smile.

'What does Paola get out of it?' Brichese asked.

Now she spoke up, but in rapid Italian. I really hoped she was telling him to come up with some names of people who could help watch the Villa Wanda and wasn't embellishing my story in her own way.

Finally, they were done.

'I might know of some people,' he admitted. 'They need the work right now. They won't ask questions. But they'll need to be paid well to keep them quiet.'

I got the message.

'I'll pay them through you, so you can decide what they should get out of it. But only if you keep this quiet. I also need somewhere to stay tonight.'

'We have rooms upstairs,' he replied.

Paola was too quiet for my liking at hearing this. Presumably separate male and female dormitories didn't pose too much of a problem to the determined. Then again, like most men, I was probably deluding myself in that regard.

We left the classroom and Brichese went off to rustle up the other comrades he'd mentioned.

I grabbed Paola by the elbow and pointed to the door with my other hand. 'Back inside. We need to talk.'

She didn't resist but stepped smartly, almost eagerly, back into the classroom. I launched into my speech before she got any other ideas.

'When can we see the man whom your father knew during the war. The one who might be prepared to fight?'

'Why didn't you tell Brichese what you told me over the phone. About the neo-fascists? Or are you not telling me the truth either?'

'Because this is more sensitive than you can imagine. It's even bigger than Berlin, it's a Moscow task.'

Her eyes widened.

'Don't you work for East Germany?'

'I'm a Russian, but I work with the Germans.'

Russian communists were definitely a cut above the *tedeschi*, for the light of admiration began to return to her eyes.

'We agreed to meet tomorrow morning. They don't have a phone. I wrote him a letter instead.'

'What did he do during the war exactly?'

'My father knows. But his friend was part of the armed wing of the PCI for a few years afterwards. Until the people who joined in peacetime eventually took over the party and made it soft.'

I guessed she was no particular fan of Brichese either.

'Do we have to use Brichese's people to watch my target? Does your father's friend know of people who could do it instead?'

But I was running out of time to arrange this if

something was happening tomorrow night.

I had no idea right now of what I'd do with the man she'd found. I'd no idea how long it had been since he last held a gun or planted a bomb. It didn't take an expert in counterinsurgency to know that sending rusty amateurs up against the remnants of the Decima Mas wouldn't be the smartest idea. Not if they were out for revenge, twenty-five years after the final defeat of the Salò Republic.

I parked in a tiny square, three or four blocks away from the address Caterina had given me for the Rizzos' apartment in Rome. I'd agreed to a time with her father when I'd gone down the mountain early one afternoon, telling Sophie she should try the runs on the upper slopes which were beyond my experience level.

As I got close, I realised the flat was on one of the streets leading away from the Pantheon. So much for her and Rizzo finding a cheap backstreets hotel to have sex in that day. He knew exactly where he was taking her. Or maybe it had been the other way around.

I rang and Rizzo's father invited me up. As I reached the top of the stairs, the apartment door opened and he stood there waiting with a half-sardonic, half-expectant expression.

'Come in.'

I followed him down the hall to a living room which overlooked the square. He sat himself down in a wide black leather sofa, arms stretched out to either side along the back. It was probably where his grandchild had been conceived, knowing how fast she got down to it.

'What exactly are you planning to do in Rome?' he asked.

'I need to speak to Borghese. Where can I find him, to speak to him in private?'

'You realise I'm just an observer right now? I've been told what's planned, but after what happened in Sicily I'm not expected, or needed, to take part in it.'

'That's convenient for you.'

'They knew not to ask me. But they also want to keep me close, to make sure I don't do the very thing I'm doing now - speaking to outsiders.'

'In June we'll be family.'

'In June I'll be family with the woman who's currently your wife, even though you're not wearing a wedding ring to prove it.'

He got up and went to a side cabinet to pour himself a vermouth. Without asking, he poured me one too.

'They've set up a command post for the operation down in Montesacro. At a boatyard owned by one of his supporters.'

'You need to get me in there,' I demanded.

'Not so fast. What is it that your people want to do anyway?'

'It's just a conversation. To see if we can persuade him to rethink. We've got no way to force him to stop.'

'Whatever it is that you want to say to him I'll be associated with it, as well as with you.'

'Then say I have a personal message for him from the Mafia, which you're not allowed to know. He'll take those guys seriously.'

'And do you have such a message?'

'Best if you don't know.'

We drove over to Montesacro, then down a dusty back road to a boatyard near to where a tributary joined the Tiber. Rizzo's father twisted and turned through the streets on the way there like he'd done this a few times already.

Borghese was dressed in an open-necked shirt and slacks, standing in an office at the back of the slipway, surrounded by the same aging commando types that Skorzeny had guarding him in Hamburg.

He looked up impatiently from a map spread out on the table as we arrived. Rizzo's father and he chattered in

Italian and he motioned for us both to come through and join him in a side office off the main one.

'What are you doing back here again? You only seem to bring bad news,' he said in English.

'What I have to say is for your ears alone, Comandante.'

He looked quizzically at Rizzo's father who shrugged and left us, closing the door tightly behind him.

I'd had enough. Everyone had encouraged this buffoon for too many years, with his far-right party presidencies and movements, his fascist-style 'Comandante' title and ambitions for even loftier ones than that: one-time pretender to the throne of Italy, according to Spinelli at our first meeting.

He almost made Skorzeny seem reasonable and sensible by comparison - or consistent at least.

'Comandante, I spoke with Di Luca two days ago. He confirmed something I had suspected. The organisation in Sicily will do nothing.'

'We've made other arrangements with the same type of people in Calabria.'

'It's more serious than a simple refusal. The Sicilians are reluctant to take part in something political where they risk going against their protectors within the CIA.'

'The CIA are on the side of anyone fighting against communism.'

'They're not convinced that the CIA are thinking as one in Italy right now.'

This was my shot in the dark. If the Stasi couldn't fully make their mind up about Italy, the same might also be true for other intelligence agencies. Especially if they were busy with more pressing problems, such as last-gasp coups in Chile. I only had to inject uncertainty into the discussion, not proof.

And if it was true what Johannes had claimed about the state of mind of James Angleton, Borghese's erstwhile and perhaps current CIA guardian angel, then who could be

517

certain of the Americans right now?

'You're going into this thing without the support of the one organisation that can really get things done in Italy,' I concluded.

Borghese smiled knowingly, slowly shaking his head.

'Signor Rizzo said you were an arrogant one. You don't know who really runs Italy, or anything about the CIA.'

'You're right. But I do know that the Mafia don't trust you. They think you're going to double-cross them, do a Mussolini and come into Sicily to shut them down if you take power.'

'What do you think?' he asked coldly.

'I don't believe that a patriotic Italian, saviour of Trieste, would stoop to the level of taking the Mafia's help, to be obliged to them. Not on a permanent basis, anyway. De Mauro did his best to undermine them for years with his journalism. But then they saw Signor Rizzo's arms deal go wrong and they began to wonder. You know how suspicious they are.'

While Borghese let me, I kept talking.

'I know Otto Skorzeny a little. We've met a couple of times.'

'Why is this relevant? How do you know him anyway?'

'All I can say is that there are certain sympathetic factions towards him within our own German intelligence services. Very discreet ones, for obvious reasons.'

He gave a slight shrug at this.

'But let me paint you another picture. When I saw Skorzeny last, two weeks ago in Hamburg, he was surrounded by bodyguards, fearful of the Mossad. But when I met him in Madrid at the height of the summer, we were able to go out alone for a drink at his local bar. A bar with pictures on the walls of Spanish troops who'd fought with us against the communists in Russia.'

'What are you trying to say?'

'If you decide that the time isn't right for an action now, if you're let down by your supporters here, you can always move to Spain to regroup. When I met Skorzeny in Hamburg we spoke about it. He'll use his connections with the regime there to smooth any arrangements that might need to be made.'

'And why would I turn my back on my country in its hour of need?'

He was nibbling, perhaps wanting to be convinced. I had nothing to lose so I played a card he would never have seen before, trusting that Rizzo's father had told him where I worked.

'Because the EEC will kill communism more surely than any Italian politician can. You just need to give the Commission time to work.'

He frowned as I gave him time to catch up.

'You've surely seen for yourself how many Italians have taken jobs in West Germany over the past few years.'

'What's your point?'

'Thanks to the EEC, employers can now much more easily break the left-wing trade unions by taking workers from the lowest wage nations. It was legalised two years ago – any worker in the EEC can travel to any other member state for employment. As I said, you need to give it time. And in other areas too. You want a strong, united European homeland without the Jews in charge? That's what the EEC will give us. All nations joined together, making sure Europeans keep at least one hand on the global reins of power.'

Skorzeny's lack of repentance in Hamburg had come in useful in the end. Inspiration for a fairy tale to be told to his fellow fascist.

'Are you done with your lecture?'

I nodded.

'You realise that for all the arguments for and against taking action, for all the advice that foreigners seem desperate to give us, one thing remains?'

'What is that, Comandante?'

He looked at me with narrowed eyes.

'Only Italians can help Italy. Only we can solve our problems. We've had a century and more of Germans and the other great powers telling us what to do. The tricolour belongs in our hands and in our hands only.'

He paused for breath. I'd tried reasoning with him, but I realised he was motivated by something which Germans were rapidly losing the ability to comprehend. The Russians and Poles had taken our lands, changed the names on the map, set the eastern half of the country against the western. He still had what we'd almost lost, what people like Sophie and the von Barten clique had already given up on, in the name of a myth called Europe - a love of people and place.

Although I knew better, although I knew what was the right and democratic thing to do, part of me wanted someone like Borghese to shake Italy up. So that someone else could perhaps start again and make the country all that it should be. To be all that the people on the outside of the DC's shadow state cabal, like Paola and her family, deserved it to be.

But none of this could I say to him.

'Yes Comandante, I'm done here. Signor Rizzo needs to take me back to the airport.'

'Here's my final word to you then. I don't know what you thought you'd achieve by coming here. But in the military, we obey orders and we stay true to our cause.'

I could have reminded him that he hadn't been in the military since nineteen forty-five. But he also reminded me that I was under orders of a kind myself. To a major, if only one in the secret police rather than the army. I needed to get out while the going was good.

'I wish you success Comandante. Europe's patriots are watching you. There are more of us than you know.'

Or in my case, many fewer allies than I cared for.

I emerged from the office to find Rizzo's father waiting.

'Well?'

'I told the Comandante I was returning to the airport.'

'Let's get moving then.'

On the way back to the centre, he quizzed me as to what Borghese had said.

'He talked about how the military didn't run, loyalty to his oath, that kind of thing.'

'What did you say to that?'

'Fifteen months as a conscript seven years ago doesn't qualify me to say anything. I've never been in a real war.'

'You did a neat job in Sicily.'

He insisted on driving me back to where I'd parked, not wanting me to hang around his apartment any more than he could help it, I reckoned.

'What will you do tomorrow night?' I asked as he pulled up behind the Mercedes, just before I got out of his car.

'I told you earlier, any meaningful involvement I had with Borghese finished when my son died. If you want to stop him in a way, such that nothing can be traced back to me, then I won't prevent you. I don't care either way.'

'Aren't you worried about being caught with him? Don't you have a lot to lose? Your military systems business?'

'You forgot what I told you the first day we met in Apulia. My company's products are essential for the defence of the West. Our latest blueprints are always held in a safe deposit box in Switzerland. If anyone here tries to threaten me, my lawyer in Geneva has instructions to send a letter to the Soviet consulate with the key.'

'I suppose you're the guy who owns a nuclear bunker in a valley outside Ragusa.'

'People like your new father-in-law and I aren't subject to the same rules as other men. Our agendas are much more ambitious than balding naval officers can imagine, let alone amateurs operating in the twilight zone between crime and espionage.'

I opened the passenger door a crack, about to step into the road.

He turned to look at me. 'You've done what you could by your own standards. Now you need to go back to your wife and look after my grandchild for me. Tell her to stop interfering and let the men take care of things. Her family knows I'm out and that I'm not taking part anymore.'

A cloud no bigger than a man's fist appeared on the horizon, as the old Bible prophet might once have said.

'What do you mean "stop interfering"? How is she still involved?' I asked uncertainly.

'She got put through to me at the boatyard, while you were closeted with Borghese. She said she'd received new information after you left Switzerland, that couldn't be relayed over the phone. She's coming to see him in person tomorrow morning.'

He frowned and put his head to one side. 'You don't know what she's talking about? Do you?'

I was immobile, one leg on the ground outside, hand frozen to the passenger door handle. My throat was dry and I could have sworn I smelt bile.

'Fuck me,' he said. 'I told you not to trust her and I was right, after all.'

I was still too stunned to say anything.

He carried on twisting the knife, and taking his time over it too.

'One last thing. Borghese met his old wartime friend from the CIA last night. Everyone's checking out his chances this weekend. There's no secrets left in Italy it seems these days.'

'Then keep this one for me,' I said finally, having just about mastered myself. 'I'm coming back to see you tomorrow, after she's been to see Borghese. What arrangement did she make?'

'There's a second command post up in Merici, not far from the boatyard. That's where we'll be from noon.'

'Did she give any hint to you? Of why she's coming to

see him?' I asked, a metallic taste in my mouth as I swallowed my pride.

'Why do I have no confidence that my grandchild is going to be looked after properly when this is all over?' he asked cynically, the irritation in his voice also plain to hear.

'You don't know what she's up to either?' I asked accusingly.

A mocking smile played round his lips for a moment. I began to wonder what he'd been like as a father to Rizzo, and to Caterina. Who knew what cruelties families inflicted on one another behind closed doors?

Before I really lost it, I growled '*arrivederci*,' got out, and slammed the door.

The drive back to the Casa took forty minutes and each one weighed as heavy as lead. When my choler had subsided enough for me to begin thinking again, too many questions crowded in.

Why was she coming? She knew I'd been sent to discourage a coup, so she must be trying to do the opposite, surely? And who was sending her, or was she acting on her own?

My mood darkened once more as I wondered if she'd suddenly turned on the taps in bed to get me to delay my trip to Rome until the last minute. I'd told her something was happening on the sixth and she'd made sure I didn't get away until that morning. Why, oh why, had she kept her own visit a secret from me?

But however we'd arrived at this point, the fact was, if we weren't working with one another, we were working against each other. And she was twelve or thirteen weeks pregnant with Rizzo's child too. No wonder his father had been annoyed. But it was nothing, not even close, compared to what I was feeling right now.

Paola was waiting for me when I got back to the Casa. We went back to the same classroom as earlier. I was still in the foulest of moods, scarcely listening to what she had to say.

'I went to the apartment of my father's friend from the war, to make sure he was there and could still see us tomorrow.'

'Did he tell you what he did back then?' I snapped, still trying to recover from having been poleaxed earlier.

'He was a sniper,' she replied defensively. 'He still has his gun.'

And there I had it, the decision was made for me. For if Licio Gelli was giving the orders to that fat fool, trying to relive the glory days of the Decima Mas, tricolour in hand, then Gelli would have to go. I no longer cared what happened to me. That traitorous bitch.

But where was it best to take him down? I had a home address, but he would have guards, alarms. And he might not show up there. He might not show up anywhere over the next two days.

One possibility was the Quirinale itself. After all, it had been De Lorenzo's meeting with the President which had kicked off the rumours around the supposed coup in 'sixty-four.

If you were holding all the puppet strings, would you send Borghese to the palace to make your demands, or go there yourself? Go there as a concerned citizen, to advise the President to call out the troops and round up the PCI. With a subtle suggestion of arrest or detention if he didn't. The answer, when you considered the bombastic Prince was obvious. Persuading presidents was delicate work, requiring the stiletto rather than the *manganello*.

It was all too neat and obvious. But what other option did I have? I wasn't so delusional as to believe there was any real chance of success, it was merely the best plan I could come up with on my own.

'Let's speak with Brichese again,' I told Paola.

She pouted, not making much of that idea.

'We have to, for Moscow's mission.'

I dragged up a smile and winked at her too, trying to remember how to charm the treacherous female sex. Not that it had ever worked for me much.

'You want access to a house overlooking the vehicle entrance to the Quirinale?' Brichese repeated, astounded.

'I need to watch who comes in and out for the next two nights.'

'This sounds political.'

'The man I asked your guys to watch is well-connected. That's why we're going to this effort to check him out.'

But by the look in Brichese's eyes I was teetering on the edge.

'I won't get involved in anything illegal.'

'I'm not asking you to. Just for the hire of an apartment.'

'You don't understand,' he replied. 'The PCI is the only effective opposition to the Italian Right. I won't be the one to jeopardise the position we've built up here over decades, not for any amount of money.'

Sure. When people said that, they generally meant something quite different.

I shrugged.

'Okay, I've had enough,' Brichese said. 'I need to take this to my boss here.'

'Go ahead,' I said. 'But we need a place with very special characteristics at short notice. Is he able to find something that expensive?'

In my head I went over the way back to the car through the streets around the Casa and wondered if I should wait in the atrium to make a quick getaway.

The irony was that I had a perfectly legitimate reason to be here and to ask for their help. I had to pretend to be a European fascist, if not an outright Nazi, to Borghese and Skorzeny. But when it came to being an agent of the Warsaw Pact, I ought to be able to be completely honest.

But now I began to sense why the PCI were out of

favour in Moscow and Berlin. I'd even said it myself, way back in the café that Sunday by the Cimetière d'Ixelles, speaking with Jan - my guess that the PCI had become institutionalised, captured by the very system they were meant to overthrow. If the DC took bribes for rezoning in the cities where they controlled the council, then why not the PCI in Red Emilia and elsewhere?

When I looked round the room at the posters of the Ukrainian wheat fields and Soyuz rockets, it suddenly felt very false. On the surface was the talk of revolution and workers to the barricades, but in the very same breath they criticised the Soviets for defending the socialist revolution in Czechoslovakia.

The real communists themselves were no better of course. They dressed up their regimes and pretended they were popular democracies, but when I listened to Spinelli's plans, did I have any confidence that the European federalists I worked for were any better?

And what of the von Barten family and their tricks? Again, why the hell was Sophie coming here? As I waited for Brichese to come back I calmed down some more and began to reflect.

If she was coming to Rome herself, why had she asked me to call Dirk, the family money man at any time of the day or night, as soon as I knew what was going on for certain?

Warning Dirk to get out of Italian bonds or whatever made sense on one level. But other odd comments from the recent past didn't. For instance, why had Rizzo's father said in Milan, when I came to tell him the news of the likely paternity of her child, that we Germans kept 'changing your mind' about Borghese? Or earlier, on the day of the funeral, that I didn't know 'what kind of people' I was dealing with?

But the thought slipped away for the moment because Brichese came back with a colleague. An older man with grey hair and the look of a real street fighter, unlike

Brichese's flowing-haired Guevara impression.

They barked at Paola to get out, then Brichese began.

'We don't have time to check you out properly, but you're not unknown to our Party comrade from Bari.'

I nodded at him solemnly.

'My colleague here knows of someone who cleans an apartment near the Quirinale which might do. The owners are away right now. But it's going to cost a lot.'

'Our Party funds aren't unlimited. I need to explain myself to my bosses too.'

There was a standoff for a few seconds as the strength of positions were assessed and risks weighed up.

'Tell me what you need,' I said. I didn't care. I was still spending Rizzo's father's money.

They told me, we haggled, and I paid them the full amount up front, for I wasn't planning to come back here after tomorrow.

'We're doing this to help a fellow communist. But don't take advantage of our hospitality. And don't ask our people to cross the line of criminality either. Otherwise we'll hand you into the Carabinieri ourselves.'

Whatever worked for them to justify to themselves. If this was the level of ardour for the Revolution, no wonder Paola was frustrated. And no wonder Jan's inspiration, Dutschke, had come up with a strategy of a creeping takeover of society's institutions. These sheep were no good for anything else.

'Don't take advantage of Comrade Amato, as you call her, tonight either,' was his farewell comment.

I had an interrogation to carry out in Switzerland before I could even begin to think about other women again.

Chapter Thirty-Seven

I had done what I could with Borghese. I hoped my words about not needing to go down the extra-parliamentary route would sink in, but if he really was a puppet then he'd be unable to make his own decisions anyway. Apart from self-preservation, perhaps.

I had no idea when today's fun would be over, so after an early breakfast at the Casa, I found a cheap hotel with parking and paid up front for a couple of nights. That was where the Mercedes was now, out of sight of everyone's eyes, especially my comrades.

Later that morning, Paola took me across the city to meet her father's friend. On the way she gave me a warning.

'I've told him you're Russian, like you said you were. I didn't say you're collaborating with Germans, so don't try to mention it, even though I'm translating.'

'I can guess why.'

'No you can't. You don't know what the Nazis did to his brother.'

Her father's friend lived in a high-rise apartment block which smelt of onions and poverty. Inside the apartment was just as shabby. There was a daughter or perhaps a daughter-in-law who came and went with squealing babies. I couldn't count them, because they all looked the same to me.

I thought of him as the Partisan, but I scarcely imagined he'd have been cast as one in a Soviet propaganda movie. Che Guevara he was not.

The Partisan at least lived up to the name I'd given him though. His gun was an old Wehrmacht Mauser carbine with a telescopic sight. Paola gave him a version of the story that she and I had agreed on the way over, and he seemed to understand what was needed.

In revenge for whatever reprisal his brother had been caught up in, going by the number of tiny parallel scratches on the stock of the gun, German mothers had paid a high price too. Thankfully for me, killing obviously hadn't bothered him during the war, and still didn't seem to now. The fistful of lire I showed him helped, I guessed, and he was happy enough to come along there and then. The Mauser was over a metre long and hard to conceal, but he'd dug out a canvas fishing rod case from a cupboard and that did the trick as we rattled back into the centre on the tram.

But now I was getting weary of the whole thing. I'd gone to a lot of effort for very little obvious benefit, to anyone. At least, not a benefit that anyone would ever recognise if this coup did fizzle out. Who ever saw the people behind the scenes, the people who worked to keep things just the way they were?

To be fair to Brichese, he had come through at short notice. He ought to have done after the amount of money I'd paid him. Paola had been given a set of keys – the cleaning lady's presumably - to an upper-floor apartment at the western end of the Quirinale, overlooking the two vehicle entrances on that side of the palace complex. The one furthest away was tiny, barely wide enough for a car, and I hoped it was closed at night, meaning we'd only have to cover the other.

But when I stood at the window to peer out past the shutters my heart sank. There little chance of a successful shot on a target at either entrance, in my estimation. The angle was very wide, meaning the Partisan would have to virtually lean out of the window to aim and fire.

I reckoned he might be willing to give it a go, maybe if Paola gave him a pep talk, but in my heart I knew it wouldn't really do.

I tried not to let my disappointment show to the others as we settled in for a long wait. There was a phone in the apartment and Paola had obtained a police radio scanner from somewhere. If the two guys I'd paid Brichese to watch the Gelli place saw something they were to call us from a phone booth. I just hoped they'd had the presence of mind to find a working one first, before starting their vigil.

Paola manned the phone and twiddled the dials of the scanner. I wasn't sure how useful the device was, but I appreciated her initiative in finding it. There was the odd tidbit, army trucks arriving from Rieti, a blockade to be set up on the road to Castel Gandolfo. But it was desperately thin stuff, any real signals were lost in the noise.

I waited until late afternoon and I was confident Sophie had seen Borghese and left, before making my way over to the plotters' other command post.

Rizzo's father came down and met me on the pavement outside.

'What did she want?'

'Are you sure you're connected to the BND?' he replied?

'Why?'

'Because she didn't drive here. She flew in by private jet this morning. That's the proper way to travel, if you work for a Western intelligence agency,' he said appraisingly.

It was all I could do to stop losing my temper again. And for another reason too. He would only have known that if he'd picked her up from Ciampino or if one of his men had.

'What did she say to him?'

'She claimed she had a report for his eyes only. She was carrying a document case on the plane.'

'The CAP report,' I said. 'To change the allocations in Italy's favour.'

'I don't know, I never saw it. I took her to Borghese, introduced them again, and left him with her.'

'What did she say she wanted to talk about?'

He licked his lips in anticipation.

'She claimed she had a promise of support to a new right-wing government, if the action for later tonight comes off, but I wasn't allowed to hear what it was.'

I lit myself a cigarette and drew fiercely on it.

'That would have been what the CAP report was about,' I said.

Rizzo's father shrugged.

'Did she sound convincing? Did she sound like she really wanted Borghese to go through with it?'

He frowned. 'Before I left them, she persuaded him to confirm tonight's date, that was for sure. He wasn't paying much attention to her story though. Then again, she wasn't wearing a wedding ring either.'

He grinned now.

'When the three of us talked that night on the lawn after the birthday dinner, Borghese spent almost the whole time trying to look down her cleavage.'

The image came into my head of her wearing a short skirt, standing next to him at a desk in the office at the back of the boatyard, bending down low over the report as she languorously traced out the new export subsidies on mozzarella with her finger. Or whatever.

I was utterly, insanely jealous. I surprised myself with my own rage.

'Walk with me,' I growled, barely getting the words out.

He shrugged again and tagged along behind. We went a couple of blocks in silence before I turned and cornered him.

'What did you and the von Bartens cook up together

back in the summer? You had a past during the war, but above all you're a pragmatist. Otherwise you wouldn't have built a nuclear shelter in the Sicilian hills but also be ready to offer industrial secrets to Soviets at the same time.'

'I'm not your oracle. Some things you need to work out for yourself. But I don't like the range of characters sniffing around the Comandante. There's far too many people involved now. Common sense should tell him to call it off.'

'We never found Licio Gelli, you know,' I said, hoping for a reaction.

'Then here's my final gift to you. Check at the Excelsior. He keeps a suite there permanently.'

'For a mistress?'

'I don't know if that's what you'd call the members of an unofficial masonic lodge who call on him here. The hotel people can tell you which room it is.'

My mind was still in a whirl. There were way too many balls in the air right now. Too many big decisions to make.

Rizzo's father looked at me more closely. Suddenly, he reached out and laid a hand on my shoulder.

'She gave you a shit deal. But ultimately, you've agreed to be my grandchild's father, even if no one expects it to be for very long. That means something to me. You also came to tell me that my son had died, when it was the duty of Di Luca to do so. That means even more.'

My shoulders slumped.

'One day you'll understand what's been going on,' he continued. 'When that happens, remember, it's not the fault of my son's child. If your marriage doesn't last, it will have a home with us in Apulia. I'll pay you to make that happen, if needs be. But I don't know if it's money that drives you.'

His hand was still on my shoulder.

'You have a strange way of motivating people,' I replied bitterly. We looked at each other for a second or two longer. I took another breath.

'All I ever wanted was a family.'

His hand dropped and he turned away. In that moment, I saw a flash of the same heart-aching regret that had been in Rizzo's eyes as he lay in the alleyway in Sicily, the golden evening sun beating down as his lifeblood flowed out onto the pavement.

Things began to hot up in the evening. Brichese's people had been watching the Excelsior since I gave them the word, and at eight Paola got a call to say Gelli had arrived.

I was sorely tempted to go down there. It was only a quarter of an hour away on foot. But I'd made my choice, I had to be where the likely moment of decision was to take place.

Maybe if he was at the hotel that meant nothing was happening tonight, after all. Whatever information Dirk might have been hoping for, he could get it from his sister. On the other hand, there was the temptation to call him with some false information and hopefully lose the family some money. Not that they would notice it, I was sure.

The hours passed and I had another cigarette, and then another one out of spite for my absent wife, who'd doubtless already landed back in Switzerland by now. Then I stopped. Petulance could wait until tomorrow.

Paola found pasta and cans of vegetables in the kitchen and made something for all of us while the Partisan watched the phone. We opened a bottle and shared that between us too. And then, at midnight, my time was up.

The phone rang. Paola answered, translating what they said line by line. 'He's on the move. If he's coming our way, he'll be with us in five minutes at most. He's in a black Mercedes.'

All the best people drove them, but even now I still wasn't exactly sure what to do. The angle to the entrances from the window hadn't narrowed any over the course of the afternoon.

She repeated the message in Italian for the Partisan's

benefit. He made his own mind up and got ready. He swung his rifle round to the left to point at the entrance to the side street and squinted down the scope, watching and waiting.

A hard rain started to fall, a sudden downpour masking the sounds of the city. Then he stiffened as he caught sight of movement, reporting with a few seconds delay as Paola translated.

'Here they come. They've stopped at the corner.'

This had to be it. It had to be. My unlikeliest of gambles had paid off, only because Gelli was doing exactly what had happened six years ago. But six years ago, the East German Stasi hadn't been waiting for the conspirators.

'Can he see the target to take a shot?' We hadn't given the Partisan the name of the man we wanted him to shoot, and he hadn't asked. But Paola knew who our quarry was.

She told me his answer.

'He says don't be stupid, look at the angle for yourself. If your target is there, he's sitting behind the driver.'

'*Ragazzi*, we have to stop him. By any means necessary. We can't guarantee a definite shot if they get moving and drive straight into the Quirinale. Won't the bullet pass through the driver and the seat at this range?' I demanded through Paola.

This was becoming a farce. It was no way to make rapid decisions.

'He's only doing it if he can make a clean shot and get away.'

I slammed my fists on the table.

'What's his problem? Our guy's sitting in a car over there by the corner. The palace guards will be hiding from the rain. We'll never have a better chance. If someone had done this to Mussolini fifty years ago…'

'Then it would have been Gabriele D'Annunzio who led the Blackshirts into Rome.' She replied for herself this time.

Whatever protestations I'd made to Kramer, about how he wanted me to operate in London were now long in the past. I knew I wasn't going to get away with it this time.

'I'm going down there myself.'

Paola chewed her lip, standing on the brink of her own moment of decision.

Who's with me? No one?' I asked the room.

This was it then. The final act. There would be no veterans from Africa with RPGs and an MG 42 this time. I'd come to Rome and all my hopes had died here.

With a contemptuous look at the others, I yanked the AK out of my bag. I inserted a full magazine, checked it was securely housed, and left the room. I didn't care if Paola and the Partisan were the last people I ever spoke to. I wondered if Borghese would have appreciated the irony of another German intervention in Italy.

I went out into the narrow street running along the high side of the Quirinale. It was in deep gloom, illuminated only by a couple of street lamps, several tens of metres apart.

The long walk down to the corner and the waiting car was the longest of my life, longer than when I walked unarmed up to Rizzo at the house in Sicily. But I was calm about it. I'd passed beyond the realm of caring for what happened to me next. I sensed the eyes of the comrades on my back from the house. Behind me, I even sensed the guards on the other side of the gate into the Quirinale.

And then I sensed something else. Glancing across the street, walking determinedly through a pool of light from one of the street lamps was Paola. She'd come downstairs after me and was heading for the car, eyes fixed firmly ahead, a small pistol in her hand that had appeared from somewhere about her person. If the occupants of the car were armed, the foolish girl was going to get herself shot before she could do any serious damage.

There was nothing for it, there never had been anyway. I picked up the pace, and as she saw my movement, so did she. It would be a race to the car to see who would shoot first, unless they were scared off and drove away.

I moved into the centre of the street and held the AK out to one side, stock folded up underneath, making sure as best I could that the distinctive banana-shaped magazine would be visible to the people in the car. Absurdly, Paola now started to jog and so did I, in an attempt to stay ahead of her.

Even though the light at the end of the street was stronger, I got to within fifteen metres of the car before the driver noticed me. I saw his mouth work in exclamation and then a jolt as if someone had thumped his seat from behind.

I brought the AK round to point at the windshield and gave the occupants a show of cocking the rifle and depressing the safety lever - continuous fire - not that they would be alive for long to notice once I pulled the trigger.

It was the worst preparation for an ambush that any Volksarmee instructor would ever have seen anywhere, thanks to Paola forcing my hand. But because it was the worst, the opposite of a stealthy approach and a sudden rattle of fire, it left the driver and his passengers in no doubt as to what was happening. Paola rushing up like a madwoman must have helped too.

The car engine revved momentarily, then the driver clashed the gears into reverse and shot off with a spin of wheels into the night. As they rounded the corner, I realised there had been two men in the back and a flash of spectacles from them both.

I returned to the house, Paola trotting along silently beside me. The Partisan was already packing up.

'You scared him off. I never got my chance,' he complained with a jerk of the hands and a frown. Paola didn't need to translate.

'What now?' asked Paola.

'Maybe that's all we needed to do. I know that I've done all that I can,' I said, and I meant it. Saved from disaster. Reprieved, as Rizzo hadn't been.

'I'm off to bed. I need to catch up on my sleep. Not had much the past week.'

It was the sun leaking in through the thin curtains which woke me. Not a shake on the shoulder from men with guns.

The radio news presenter was calm, no one was in the streets. I couldn't believe that everything was normal, like I'd woken from a dream. I even asked the waiter at breakfast what day it was. Tuesday.

I went back to my room, zipped up my bag with the AK inside it, and got into the car to resume my honeymoon.

But as I drove north, the sourness flooded back in. The kilometres unwound and I couldn't put off confronting the future forever. I still had several hours ahead of me to think and find a way out of this mess.

Where to start? Whatever the reason for Sophie and the von Bartens getting involved with Rizzo in the first place, it couldn't have been a favour to a friend in need, because she despised him. She must have done, to let him propose to her three times - and then to keep carrying on as if nothing had happened.

What was the other thing that Rizzo's father had said? Something along the lines of: 'At the start, it was just another discussion. Then it got more serious and became a speculative venture.'

What had he and Sophie talked about the day of the funeral? Had she been sounding him out, to see if he was still on board with some money-making plan? Why else apart from money would they have been in this thing together?

And then the latest claim that he'd made, only two days

ago? Of how his horizons were far more ambitious than even the leader of the Fronte Nazionale? How he wasn't subject to the same rules as other men? Not subject to the same limitations of imagination was what he really meant.

I drove on a couple of kilometres further, the needle on the speedometer creeping upwards. And then I thumped the steering wheel hard in frustration, causing the car to wobble off track for a second, roaring in anger at the lies.

People had been dropping hints all throughout this affair without me realising it. I was the expert at the half-truth and the half-lie, yet I'd been blind when they'd been used on me.

What was it that Sophie's father had said, back in the hunting lodge as the rain streamed down? 'We make sure we're protected if there's a swing in the markets.' Not just well protected - they'd been trying to control the timing of the swing themselves.

The slimy bastards. All of them, Italians and Germans. They'd heard about Borghese's plans and worked out a way they could use the situation for monetary gain. Including my wife.

Who knew? They might even have fanned the flames, nudged Borghese along the path, all for the prize of knowing or even controlling the timing of an event that could make them millions.

That couple of weeks after we'd first fucked and Rizzo had still been alive, I'd been well aware of how precarious my status with Sophie was, how I might one day be dumped like him for an even more exotic creature.

How the hell had we ended up married, then? Because she was quite happy, when it came to it, to pack me off from my honeymoon to go and try to argue against a coup. And then come down after me herself to make sure I failed. But that didn't make much sense either. The coup was already a dubious affair. The Mafia wasn't interested - the Sicilian one, at least. Rizzo's father had said only yesterday it should be stopped because there were too many people in the know. And at midnight last night I only had to wave my AK to frighten off Gelli and his bespectacled companion.

But did they even need to know which way it would have gone to speculate successfully? They'd just have bet both ways on Italian industrial stocks, or whatever it was that they did. Just as long as they knew the timing, when to close out the losing position and let the winning one run. That was why she'd jetted down to Rome and back up again. Because too much was at stake not to know. Maybe she'd had to. Maybe carrying on with helping her father until the conclusion of Borghese's attempt had been the price of him changing the prenuptial contract.

Now the shame washed over me, as I remembered the scepticism of my friends, the horror of Kramer, and above all, the quiet disappointment of my mother at what I'd done in signing my life away to Sophie.

I reached Milan and came to a fork in the autostrada. One way showed the signs for Nizza, the other for Switzerland. 'Nizza' - Nice in France, where doubtless I could find a twenty-four-hour recruitment office for the Foreign Legion. Change my name and sign on for five years. Or even stay as 'Thomas Hofmann.' I wouldn't have been the first German to do so in recent times, I'd met one myself last year.

Even Kramer couldn't find me there in the Legion's tender embrace. Nor could Sophie and Rizzo's… would it be a bastard after all?

But that was a fantastical, childish way to think. A coward's way out. Sophie hadn't taken that path when faced with her own decision. She had taken me though, '*bis der Tod Euch scheidet*' the vows said.

But if Rizzo hadn't bled out under the golden Sicilian sun, and instead had returned to Brussels to accuse me of murdering Ernst von Barten, there would have been no way she could have married me in front of her family. And I wouldn't have stood in Rizzo's way, either. In that version of my life, I would have gone to the Legion and let him be father to his child. For I knew how desperately I wanted to know something of mine, whoever he was.

Whatever the circumstances I now found myself in, one thing was certain. No matter the hurt I felt, no matter the sense of betrayal, I had to forgive her. Just as I was forgiven. And I was forgiven every day, for every day I had to ask for it. The things I did demanded it.

How much of this had come about from me not being straight with her? But even if I had, would she have been with me? Or was this the last time she'd deceive me. A special circumstance, a business affair that had started before we were married.

The junction slipped by, but I'd already made one choice.

As I drove on up over the Alps, I thought one last time about whether to come clean and tell her about my work with the Stasi and, I suspected, the French SDECE.

I still hadn't decided when Lake Saint Moritz came into view.

Epilogue

My flight got into Brussels at three, but I didn't go straight to the hospital. Instead, I got the taxi driver to drop me off at the Porte de Hal and I wandered into the neighbouring gardens.

I sat for a while on a bench under the trees, chain smoking three or four cigarettes.

With a sigh, I got to my feet and crossed the Boulevard de Waterloo, walking slower and slower as I neared the entrance to the Saint Pierre.

Mechanically, I asked for her private room and climbed the stairs, each tread another step closer to my fate. To my future self.

I knocked at the door and entered. Sophie watched me with sombre, exhausted eyes as I approached the bed. I looked down at the bundle in her arms and gently unwrapped it.

My daughter searched for the light with screwed-up eyes. The baby's skin was jaundice-yellow, but her tight, dark curls were just like those of her father.

I waited too long before reaching out to take the child. Sophie saw my hesitation, and I saw the hurt in her eyes.

It didn't excuse me, but then she hadn't seen and done the things I had in London.

Afterword

Just after midnight on December 8th, 1970, Junio Valerio Borghese, sometime *Capitano di fregata* in the Royal Italian Navy, received a phone call at the 'political' command post of the plotters, an office on the Via di Sant' Angela Merici in Rome, cancelling the coup which had been about to start imminently.

Borghese and whoever called him are now both dead, so we are unlikely at this remove of time to ever know the other person's identity, although there are any number of candidates. General Vito Miceli, head of Italy's espionage agency, the SID and possible member of the P2 Masonic Lodge is one. Others are Lieutenant-Colonel Spiazzi, the artillery officer who claimed he warned Borghese of a double-cross and Licio Gelli, secretary of P2, who also made the same claim.

A deeper mystery is why the operation was cancelled at that point in time. To his dying day, all that Borghese would say on the matter was that when he turned away from the phone to announce that 'external support' would not be forthcoming, he was following orders from a higher authority.

Jeffrey Bale, in his 2017 book, *'The Darkest Sides of Politics (Vol. I)'*, describes the movements on the night in detail and sets out the different parties and factions involved in the run up to it - and there were a lot of them. This summary is mainly drawn from his work.

There is even debate as to whether Borghese's coup was ever meant to have been followed through or had always been intended to be pulled at the last minute. But at the operational level the evidence is that a real action had been planned: one with stolen guns and neo-fascist groups, armed Italian State Forest Rangers and even part of an artillery regiment of the army.

Borghese's frantic attempts that night to find reverse gear worked - the plotters dispersed, the armed units returned to barracks and no one was any the wiser for the next three months until the story broke in the press, as these things always seem to do in Italy.

This comment has a bearing on the story, for the whole thing was arguably a leaky ship from the start. The natural propensity of Italians to talk and their love of conversation was part of the reason why the training of the Decima Mas (10th Motorboat Attack Squadron) during the war took place on an isolated estate several kilometres outside the main naval base at La Spezia. In Borghese's 1954 autobiography he claimed it was easier 'to get an Italian to lay down his life than to make the sacrifice of holding his tongue.'

In fact, when it comes to unravelling the intent behind the so-called Golpe Borghese ('Borgia Coup'), one challenge is the sheer number of accounts from the participants as they tried to justify their actions, cover them up or simply smear their rivals over the next 13 years of investigations and subsequent inconclusive trials.

The disinformation campaign in the aftermath started early. The right-wing press dismissed the coup as merely the final fling of a fantasist veteran from what was effectively for Italians, the 1943-45 civil war. A parody film was made in 1975 by the director Mario Monicelli called *'Vogliamo i colonnelli'* - 'We Want the Colonels.' The title of Monicelli's movie was a reference to the 1967 military coup in Greece, which had been backed by the CIA.

The movie was released in March 1973, but six months later there were even more parallels between the Golpe Borghese and events outside Italy. In September of that year the CIA successfully concluded its three-year campaign to remove Salvador Allende from office as president of Chile. Allende was Latin America's first elected Marxist leader, who had come to power in November 1970 after a protracted run-off process.

To give a sense of the American reaction to this, even before Allende was named president the CIA had tried to provoke the Chilean armed forces into a pre-emptive coup using local right-wing proxies. One of their moves was a kidnap attempt by mutinous officers on the head of the Chilean Army, General Schneider, who was seen as a moderate and against any interference by the Army in the democratic process. The kidnap was bungled, leading to the General's death and a wave of revulsion against the mutineers which ultimately underpinned Allende's support. Thus, a mere month before the Golpe Borghese, the US had seen the effect of an extra-parliamentary action gone wrong, perhaps giving them pause for thought elsewhere. And while Italy had its concerned supporters within the US security community, the country was nowhere near at the same dangerous tipping point as the Chilean domino had been. Logically, risks needed to be balanced with rewards.

But history is the history of personalities. Since June 1969 the US ambassador to Italy had been Graham Martin, a protégé of Nixon. Martin came to Italy most recently from Thailand where he had been ambassador between 1963 and '67. He ensured crucial Thai support for the Vietnam war - the Royal Thai Navy's U-Tapao air base became one of the most important strategic air assets in South East Asia, from where the first B-52 strikes ('Arc Light' missions) were launched in 1965. Martin was to return to the region in 1973 to become the last US ambassador to South Vietnam. He was no soft touch for communism and had lost a family member in the war in Vietnam back in 1965.

So when Martin arrived in Italy in the middle of the 'Hot Autumn' of industrial unrest he shut down the local

CIA station's approaches to the moderate wing of the PCI. Instead, he reinvigorated the embassy's links with the Italian far right using unofficial channels, mirroring the working style of his ultimate boss, the US president.

Richard Nixon tended to de Gaulle's view of what a president should be and accordingly sought to concentrate power in his own hands through a semi-official network of his supporters. The appointment of Henry Kissinger as National Security Adviser, effectively bypassing the State Department (Foreign Ministry), reflected this approach, a path which ultimately took Nixon to Watergate in 1972.

In the autumn of 1970 Nixon embarked on a 9-day European tour, visiting the UK and Ireland, Franco's Spain, Tito's Yugoslavia and Italy, giving him the opportunity to meet Ambassador Martin and take the temperature of the country for himself.

In Italy, Nixon had another inside man, too - Hugh Fenwich, an expatriate who worked for the Italian defence electronics firm Selenia and confidante of Borghese's right-hand man, Remo Orlandini. Fenwich's exact status within the security community remains unclear. He was potentially an unofficial CIA sleeper in Italy, but to the plotters at least, he claimed he had direct, personal access to Nixon himself.

Although Nixon's 1968 election pledge to end the war in Vietnam carried with it the implication that the South Vietnamese domino might one day fall, it would have been inconceivable to allow Italy, one of NATO's staunchest allies in Europe, to go the same way. After all, thanks to American involvement, the April 1948 Italian general election victory of the Democrazia Cristiana ('DC') party over the Communist Party (PCI) had represented the first ebbing of the red tide in Europe - only two months previously Czechoslovakia had fallen to a Soviet-backed coup.

It is not implausible that Nixon and his advisers,

perhaps supported by certain factions within the CIA, watched the recovery of the Italian left in the late '60s and were amenable to local suggestions to strike first before the West had a real geopolitical problem on its hands. To do so, America might have well turned to one of the CIA's longest-standing 'go to' Italians, Borghese himself.

At the end of the Second World War, Borghese's path crossed with that of the future CIA's paranoid counter-intelligence chief, James Jesus Angleton. Angleton was one of the key personalities of the Cold War CIA and paranoid seems hardly too strong a word to describe him. From 1964 onwards he had become increasingly convinced that the agency was deeply penetrated by the Soviets, based on his debriefing of two senior defectors from the KGB to the CIA. After all, he'd seen what the Allies had done to the German Abwehr during the war and how the KGB had already devastated the reputation of MI6 with the Cambridge Five (coincidentally, the first James Bond novel appeared in 1952, the year after the initial defections of the traitors - perhaps it was intended as a PR exercise for damage limitation). Angleton was the person who believed the China-USSR split was a simulation by the KGB to trick America. He believed that Kissinger was being manipulated by the KGB and that two Canadian prime ministers, the West German chancellor Willy Brandt and Britain's Harold Wilson were passing secrets to the USSR (although in the case of Brandt, his secretary, the Stasi agent Günter Guillaume, was).

Angleton had grown up in Mussolini's Italy as a teenager (like Fenwich, his father was another American expatriate in the technology sector, who ran the local franchise to distribute NCR cash registers - the Microsoft of its day). The end of the Second World War saw Angleton back in Italy with the CIA's predecessor, the OSS, disguising Borghese in an American uniform and whisking him out of the northern zone to avoid reprisals by the Resistance.

The US interest in Borghese seems to have been as much in his late-war irregular warfare activities against communist partisans, as his technical knowledge of the underwater sabotage operations which the Decima Mas had carried out in the early part of the war. Decima Mas agents in the Salò Republic, such as Mauro De Mauro, had infiltrated the Resistance and the unit's Vega Battalion operated behind Yugoslav lines. The West was a newcomer to fighting the Soviets and NATO's own stay-behind resistance organisation, Gladio, was only formally established in 1956.

After Angleton was done with him, Borghese was turned over to the new post-war Italian authorities and tried for aiding the enemy and for war crimes. The trial was arranged to take place in Rome, where he would have the chance of facing more lenient judges than in a court in the North, the Decima Mas' area of operations.

Indeed, Borghese's twelve-year sentence in 1949 for collaboration was later reduced to eight and then in mid-1949 he was released by the Court of Appeal, his four years in prison since 1945 having been counted toward his sentence. Initially, a life sentence had been expected, which he escaped because of lack of evidence directly connecting him to the atrocities perpetrated by the Decima Mas on the Resistance.

Once Borghese was back in circulation, his name came up again as a useful person to know. Notwithstanding the victory of the DC in the 1948 election, the PCI took almost a third of the popular vote. Now a caucus of representatives from the US Embassy, Vatican, Italian employers' federation and harder-right elements within the DC sought to reinforce the pro-NATO consensus in the country and guard against the growth of the left. As part of his assistance in shoring-up Italy, the head of the CIA assigned two of his most trusted subordinates, one of whom was Angleton, to the task.

The caucus' strategy had two elements: to reinforce the

parliamentary right, making sure they stayed loyal to NATO and, secondly, to prepare for the worst with an extra-parliamentary insurance plan. This was where Gladio later played a role - ostensibly as a genuine stay-behind organisation, but its secrecy, access to facilities and arms also allowed its members to potentially be used for pre-emptive political 'counterinsurgency' interventions.

As part of the parliamentary strategy there were discussions on drawing the neo-fascist MSI and the Monarchist Party together, which is where the idea of a King Junio Borghese came in for the briefest of moments. Another attempt to control the fringe right, according to Bale, was a proposal allegedly made by the CIA to Borghese that he should sponsor a 'national front' political movement and build up a coalition of veterans' organisations.

This proposal caused consternation among the MSI, who recognised it as a threat to themselves. In response, in 1951 they approached Borghese with the offer of the post of honorary president, which he took - possibly with the agreement of Angleton. Once appointed, he did reinforce the Atlanticist pro-democracy wing over the national socialist-leaning anti-American 'Evolan' wing - for a time. Because the danger with any agent sent into an organisation to play a role, is that once embedded, their loyalties may shift over time - a variation on Stockholm Syndrome as they get close to the personalities they are meant to be spying on. It appears in fact that Borghese became more extreme and anti-parliamentary the longer he stayed in the MSI, a stay which extended until 1954 when he eventually resigned and dropped out of sight politically for the next 12 years. But the MSI didn't fade away after Borghese left, they continued to consistently take around 5% of the national vote, right up to the party's demise in the early '90s.

After America's scare in Italy in the late '40s and '50s,

things seemed to be under control for a time. In 1948 the communists had secured a 31% share of the national vote, collapsing to 22% in 1953. But after a ten-year hiatus their share was starting to slowly but steadily grow again, from 25% in 1963 to 27% in 1972 (they peaked at 34% in 1976). Despite American support to its opponents, the PCI was the biggest political party in Western Europe, in a country which was the geographical key to NATO's so-called 'southern flank'.

The scale of America's ongoing support to Italy reflected this status. In the general election year of 1972, the US budget to support the centrist parties was $8 million (around $50 million in 2020 values) - of which 10% was covertly paid to General Miceli, who as mentioned earlier, was head of the SID at the time.

This was the context in which right-wing factions in Italy began to dust off the earlier 1964 De Lorenzo plan and turn their thoughts again to halting the gradual long-term recovery of the PCI.

The communists' rise was partly a protest by Italian voters against the increasingly moribund *'partitocrazia'*, the merry-go-round of short-lived governments which supposedly ran Italy. Back in the '50s, this had unintentionally resulted in industrial policy which defaulted to a relatively laissez-faire position, which in turn led to economic boom. Italy's income per head more than doubled over 1950 to 1970, from 46% of UK income in 1950 to 82% in 1970.

But despite the boom, or in part, because of its results, all was not well underneath. The weak governments of the '60s didn't respond rapidly to the demands of internal migration and the rising expectations of standards of living which fuelled the protracted period of worker unrest of 1968-73.

Urban planning or the lack of it was also a feature of the rapid growth of the economy and internal population movement. Almost half a million homes were built in 1964 but of total investment in housing between 1948 and 1963, only 16% was made by the public sector. By 1970 one in six homes in Rome had been built without a proper building permit and shoddy construction without earthquake proofing resulted in collapsed building and deaths. The echoes of this were still being seen in 2018 with the collapse of the Ponte Morandi autostrada bridge in Genoa. The bridge had been completed in 1967 but was subject to continuous remedial work from the '70s onwards.

By 1970, workplace tensions had been mounting since at least 1962 and Italy's student protests started in November 1967, peaking in May 1968, the month when de Gaulle fled France for a few hours to a French Army base in West Germany. In March 1968 there was a national general strike which set the scene for the so-called 'Hot Autumn' in 1969 which saw strikes mutate into factory occupations, kidnapping of managers and running street battles with the riot police. It was a golden era for the unions.

In autumn 1969 1.5 million workers took part in strikes and in 1970-71 these had increasingly spread to white collar workers and the public sector too. Membership of the two principal trade union federations (the CGIL and CISL) grew from 4 million to 5.4 million over 1968-72 in response.

In all of this, the PCI seems to have been caught flatfooted. Within the younger cohort of voters, the student protestors were sometimes as anti-communist as anti-capitalist, dismissing the PCI as having been captured by the establishment. The Party's youth wing, the FGCI, made little impact on campus. Even the communist-affiliated trade union federation, the CGIL, refused to take orders from the Party as it sought to avoid being outflanked to the left.

Within the Italian right, different strands of opinion emerged as on what to do. Bale described one of these strands as 'presidentialist', looking to de Gaulle's example when he took power in 1958 and established a strong executive to counterbalance parliament and the uncertainty of parliamentary debate. Nixon tried to do the same during his term in office. The 'presidentialists' in Italy were tired of endless coalition governments - the curse of the proportional representation voting system. They saw how during de Gaulle's eleven years in power, he had successfully steered France away from civil war over Algeria and then again during the protests of '68 and thought Italy could benefit from the same style of government.

The other key strand, which Bale calls 'establishment manipulators', were always on the lookout for ways to play the existing system and turn national political turmoil to their own personal advantage - judiciously investing political capital for a return in the form of new obligations owed to them and an expanded network of patronage.

Public servants are drawn from the society they serve, and the security agencies of the time reflected the overlapping personal networks and factionalism seen in the parliamentary parties. Italy possesses two national police forces, the Carabiniere (like the Gendarmes in other European countries, part of the Defence Ministry) and the Pubblica Sicurezza, part of the Ministry of the Interior. In 1970 both the Defence Ministry and Interior Ministry possessed their own intelligence agencies, the SID and the UAR respectively. There were factions within the agencies, and even allegations of a 'shadow SID', hidden within the official spy agency.

From the start, the 1970 coup attempt was the child of many fathers. There may have been no particular trigger for its genesis, but instead a sequence of events which took on a life of their own and were manipulated by various interested parties along the way.

One of these way-stations was the agitation by the

German-speaking majority in the former Habsburg province of Alto Adige (South Tyrol) in the '60s for a return to Austria. In 1966 this triggered a counter movement by Italian nationalists, the 'Tricolour Committee.' It also triggered a return to politics by Borghese as one of the leaders of the Committee and as a public speaker at their rallies.

Before we get to the events of mid-1970 onwards, another thread to Borghese's story needs mentioning. Sometime after his departure from the MSI in 1954, Borghese was given a sinecure as President of the Bank of Commercial & Industrial Credit. This episode didn't turn out well - the bank later collapsed, and Borghese and his business associates were tried for fraud (Borghese got a slap on the wrist from the authorities). More interesting is the person who eased him into the position - Michele Sindona, owner of the same Illinois bank used by the CIA to transfer $4 million to the Greek Colonels in 1967.

Sindona was a smart Sicilian lawyer who moved to northern Italy in the '50s, became a money launderer for the Mafia, and developed other connections too. In Milan he made friends with Cardinal Montini, who in 1963 became Pope Paul VI. In 1969 Sindona was made an adviser to the Vatican Bank, the Institute for the Works of Religion ('IOR').

In 1972 he bought another US bank, in Long Island, perhaps to service the operators of the East Coast end of the transatlantic drugs trade - the American Mafia. However, his financial empire began to unravel only two years later thanks to the global stock market crash in the wake of the Oil Crisis. Another web Sindona was caught up in was P2, the Masonic lodge in Rome where he was a member, which linked him to Licio Gelli.

Gelli was a former Fascist intelligence officer who decided to enhance his network of connections by joining the Freemasons in 1963. His abilities were recognised in 1967 by the Grand Master of Italy who asked him to take over P2 and rejuvenate the failing lodge. According to different sources Gelli was officially made secretary in either 1970 or 1971.

Back again to Borghese - the Tricolour Committee of 1966 was the overture to his founding of the Fronte Nazionale ('FN') in 1968 which built on the organisation set up for the South Tyrol campaign.

In the aftermath of the coup, the counterintelligence division of the SID, Office 'D', suggested that the FN had been sponsored by rogue elements in the Italian secret services for that purpose right from the start. However, as Bale notes, intelligence agency support doesn't preclude the idea that Borghese was also working to his own agenda of starting a mass movement along Gaullist lines. In a journalist interview four days before the coup, Borghese noted with approval the million people who had come to Paris to support de Gaulle in a May '68 counter protest.

In 1969 political turmoil in Italy went up a notch. The 'Hot Autumn' of strikes has been referred to already. In December of that year a false-flag bombing attack in Milan's Piazza Fontana attributed to anarchists killed 17 people and the so-called 'Years of Lead' (*'Anni di piombo'*) of left- and right-wing terrorism got underway in earnest. The following year saw a violent revolt in Reggio Calabria over the proposed location of the new regional capital, with the far right and Calabrian 'Mafia' (the 'Ndrangheta), keeping the pot stirring. The unrest included other 'spectaculars' such as the July 1970 bombing of the Freccia del Sud ('Southern Arrow') train which resulted in six deaths.

Over 1969-70, Borghese continued to make plans and the FN recruited senior officers in the armed forces (or they were encouraged to join by Borghese's intelligence agency sponsors). Finally, by late 1970, everything was in place. A key piece of the jigsaw for the plotters was the confirmation of General Miceli, as head of the SID in

October 1970 - he would later be arrested in 1974 for his part in the coup attempt. With Miceli in place, the coup was finally set in motion for 7th December - deliberately chosen as the anniversary of the Japanese attack on Pearl Harbor with the plotters using the same 'Tora' codeword which launched the attack.

Their movements that night are described at length in Bale's book, but a couple of points are worth repeating.

While Borghese was ex-navy and on the side of the Japanese in WW2, fifty years on, references to Pearl Harbor still seem a clumsy choice for someone potentially hoping for US support. According to Borghese's FN lieutenant, Orlandini, the chain of events leading up to the cancellation at midnight that night which included communications sent to the NATO naval base in Malta which were meant to have been relayed to Nixon in the US but instead were 'blocked' by persons unknown, meaning Nixon's supposed authorisation never came.

A more likely explanation is that General Miceli called it off when he realised that the plotters had been discovered by a rival faction in either the UAR or SID, a few hours too early to guarantee success that night. After all, the right had managed to successfully threaten a coup in 1964 (the De Lorenzo Affair) and they could always try again later, if extreme action was still required. Indeed, the impression of a temporary delay was what Borghese conveyed to some of the waiting plotters when he put the phone down.

Another claim was made by the artillery officer, Lieutenant-Colonel Spiazzi, who had been leading a column of trucks from his regiment into Rome, ostensibly on a counterinsurgency exercise. He said he was the one to make the call because he'd learned during the course of the evening that Borghese was to be double-crossed by the coup's political sponsors.

A further claim was made by Licio Gelli himself. According to his account, his task that night was to arrest

President Saragat. As late as 1998, access by an investigative unit of the Carabinieri to examine the guest list of the 7th December 1970 for the Quirinale was being denied by presidential order - another of the imponderables of that night. One last mystery movement is that of Angleton himself. According to a 1976 newspaper report, he was in Rome before the attempted coup and left shortly afterwards.

But even if at the time Borghese accepted the cancellation as a temporary check, in the end, that particular set of plotters weren't to get the chance to try again.

The first arrests took place in March 1971 and General Miceli was forced into retirement in 1974. The real problem was that everyone knew something of what was going on or was somehow connected: the CIA, Gladio, P2, Carabinieri, senior Air Force officers, Army, UAR, SID (and the shadow SID organisation inside the SID). And that's even before you get to the plethora of neo-fascist 'ultra' groups and assorted regional Mafias. The Sicilian Mafia belongs on this list too. According to certain state witnesses ('*pentiti*'), one of the first deliberations of the newly reconstituted Mafia Regional Commission in 1970 was whether to take part in Borghese's coup. According to another witness, Francesco Di Carlo, the journalist Mauro De Mauro, childhood friend of Borghese was killed because he'd discovered the coup.

There are any number of possible points of failure, but whatever it was, fundamentally, from within Borghese's own resources and allies there was insufficient chance of success and they recognised this, albeit late in the day.

All of the above sounds akin to the script of a Dan Brown novel (Bale's account also mentions Opus Dei and the Knights of Malta lurking in the background for good measure too) and quite foreign to a northern European reader. Given that complex tapestry, as a final thought, ponder the mountain that the EU still has to climb to erase national differences in people's minds and create the new European state that Spinelli dreamed of.

And the Mafia? Quite likely they did make it to Brussels in one way or another. The head of the Agricultural Directorate's tobacco subsidy division fell from an EU office building on the Rue de la Loi in 1993 whilst under investigation for fraud. The fraud investigation was closed after his death and the Commission withheld the report into his death from MEPs.

The Greek and Italian tobacco growers must have lamented his passing, though, given that he managed to quadruple the subsidies paid to them between 1980 and 1991.

Enough said.

Miscellany

Firstly, my heartfelt thanks to Francesco Lari for his encouragement and his advice on the cultural context in several areas. *Grazie mille!*

If the plotters had gained control of the TV station, the proclamation below was intended to be read out by Borghese himself:

'Italians! The hoped-for political shift, the long-awaited coup d'état has taken place. The political formula that has reigned for twenty-five years and has carried Italy to the brink of economic and moral collapse, has ceased to exist. In the next few hours, in successive bulletins, the most immediate and opportune steps to deal with the current disequilibrium of the nation will be indicated. The armed forces, the forces of order, the men most able and representative of the nation are with us; on the other hand, we can assure you that the most dangerous adversaries, those who want to subjugate the country to a foreigner, have been rendered powerless. Italians! The state that we will create together will be an Italy without distinctions or political colouration. It will have only one flag, our glorious tricolour. Soldiers of the Army, Navy, and Air Force, forces of order, to you we will entrust the defence of the homeland and the reestablishment of internal order. We will not promulgate special laws or institute special tribunals. We ask only that the existing laws be respected. From this moment on, no one will be able to laugh at you, offend you, wound your body or spirit, or kill you with impunity. In placing the glorious tricolour in your hands again, we invite you to raise your voices in our overwhelming chorus of love: Italy! Italy! Viva Italy'

A couple of points are worth bringing out. *'Subjugate the country to a foreigner'* refers to the 'foreign' anti-Catholic ideology of communism. *'Soldiers ... to you we will entrust the defence of the homeland and the reestablishment of internal order'* was an invitation to the armed forces to take control of the coup. Borghese was not to be a Mussolini figure in this drama.

'We will not promulgate special laws or institute special tribunals' was disingenuous, though - different teams of plotters were supplied with handcuffs and tasked with the arrests of opponents. A Gladio base near Alghero in Sardinia was to have been used to hold prisoners in secret. By way of example elsewhere, in Chile in 1973 Allende shot himself rather than be taken alive by Pinochet's forces.

After the coup, Borghese fled to Spain where he died in August 1974 aged 68, his death subject to many rumours from arsenic poisoning to overexertion in bed with a Romanian princess.

Incidentally, Skorzeny also died in Spain, in April 1975, but in his case definitely from lung cancer. His trip to Hamburg in November 1970 was for the removal of two tumours on his spine, leaving him paralysed until he taught himself to walk again the following year.

The other mystery of late 1970 is: who ordered the abduction of Mauro De Mauro? As he was abducted, rather than simply gunned down in the street outright, two possibilities suggest themselves - ransom or the extraction of information. De Mauro was no saint, a deputy commander of the Fascist police in Rome, later a member of the Decima Mas intelligence branch along with his wife. He infiltrated the Resistance as a spy and was implicated in the Ardeatine Caves massacre when 335 Italians were shot in the head on 24th March 1944 to avenge the deaths of 28 SS men (from South Tyrol) killed by partisans the previous day.

He reinvented himself as a left-wing anti-Mafia journalist after the war and there are any number of theories as to his disappearance. Several are centred around his investigation into the plane crash of Enrico Mattei, CEO of ENI, in October 1962. Lots of powerful people had good reason to stop Mattei's geopolitical games and presumably would have wanted to find out from De Mauro just how much he'd discovered of who was behind the bombing.

For the Mafia, De Mauro was a dead man walking anyway, because of his earlier investigations. Killing him would have invited retribution from the state, so perhaps they had to wait until friendly factions within the government wanted rid of him as well.

By 'friendly factions', this principally means the DC, but doesn't mean they were friendly per se. Their link man to the Mafia, Salvatore Lima, was mayor of Palermo and local representative of Giulio Andreotti, seven times Prime Minister of Italy. Andreotti was a real charmer, the same person who in 1976 refused to negotiate with the Red Brigade kidnappers of his DC political rival Aldo Moro, a kidnap which ended in Moro's murder.

But ultimately, De Mauro already knew too much, without the *pentiti* Francesco Di Carlo needing to suggest the journalist was about to reveal his former wartime commander's plans.

Staying with the Mafia, echoes of the 1974 collapse of Sindona's Franklin National Bank, when the Vatican's IOR bank lost an estimated $30 million were heard again in 1982 when another P2 lodge member, Roberto Calvi, was found hanging under Blackfriars Bridge in London. Calvi was chairman of the Banco Ambrosiano and two weeks before its collapse he'd warned the Pope about the impending failure in a letter. The Vatican was implicated as the IOR had been used as a vehicle to siphon off funds from the stricken bank and they later paid out $224 million in a settlement to its creditors.

In the novel, the use of the term 'tradition' to refer to the Mafia (*Cosa Nostra* - 'Our Thing') by the Adviser comes from the phrase 'men of our tradition' used by the crime boss Joe Bonanno in his 1983 autobiography. He allegedly retired from business in 1968 to Nevada but Douglas Valentine's account of the US Bureau of Narcotics and Dangerous Drugs (the predecessor agency to the DEA), *'The Strength of the Pack'*, suggests he was active afterwards.

East Germany supplied training teams to armies and security ministries throughout the Third World. The Democratic Republic had a presence in Sudan between 1969 and 1971, until President Nimeiry took a firmer grip on power and realigned his regime away from the Soviet bloc, initially towards China.

East Germany's Sudanese involvement came almost at the end of the country's first civil war between North and South. In what is today the independent country of South Sudan, the Anyanya rebels received various degrees of outside support. This assistance included training by the notorious West German mercenary, Rolf Steiner, who had previously fought for the Biafrans against Nigeria.

Markus Wolf, head of the Stasi's HVA foreign intelligence service relates in his autobiography how East Germany agreed with Sudan and Libya to help capture Steiner. The Ministry's attempts to locate the soldier of fortune were successful and they advised the Sudanese on his interrogation after capture, too. Wolf's account barely scratches the surface - there are surely plenty more stories of Africa and the Stasi out there to be told one day.

Gabriele D'Annunzio was one of the original leaders of the *squadristi*, the black-shirted street fighters armed with *manganelli* (truncheons) who brought Mussolini to power. D'Annunzio's colourful career requires a book of its own, but it effectively ended in 1922 when he fell from an open window while he was high on cocaine, importuning the sister of his mistress.

The steel wedding bands worn by Rizzo's grandparents were replacement rings awarded by the state on 18th December 1935, the 'Giornata della Fede'. As many as 70% of married adults in Rome publicly gave up their gold wedding rings to help pay for the war in Ethiopia.

Religion was on its way out in Italy in 1970. According to Paul Ginsborg's book, *'A History of Contemporary Italy: 1943-80'*, a 1956 survey showed 69% of Italians regularly attending Mass, but by 1966 another study returned a figure of 40% with only 6% classified as '*devoti*'. 1969 saw a national referendum approving the legalisation of divorce.

Abortion has always taken place, but whereas it had been legalised in the UK in 1967, in many countries in 1970 this was not the case. East Germany legalized it 1972 and West Germany in 1974. In the US, the 'Roe vs Wade' Supreme Court decision was handed down in 1973, where the right to abortion was 'observed' in the penumbra of a woman's privacy rights (but not the right to life for the child growing inside the same woman). Belgium didn't legalise abortion until 1990 when King Baudouin abdicated for a day rather than give royal asset to a law against his conscience.

According to the historian Antony Beevor 1.4 million women were raped by the Red Army in Germany's Eastern Territories. Abortion rates and hospital admissions were used to estimate 100,000 victims in Berlin. The wife of the West German chancellor at the time of Reunification, Hannelore Kohl, was one of these - at the age of twelve. There is sufficient detail in the public domain already without needing to repeat it here. It suffices to say that the psychological damage was real too, and the first three books in the series try to capture some of that.

What is unconscionable, is that sexual abuse of this

nature should have been perpetrated and covered up in a European country not subject to invasion. But that is a story still to come.

Short Bibliography

Christopher Booker & Richard North, 2005 & 2016: *The Great Deception: The Secret History of the European Union*

Jeffrey Bale, 2017: *The Darkest Sides of Politics, Vol I*

Maud Bracke, 2013: *Which Socialism, Whose Détente?*

Nigel Cawthorne, 2009: *The Mammoth Book of the Mafia*

Christopher Duggan, 2013: *Fascist Voices: An Intimate History of Mussolini's Italy*

Alfred McCoy, 1972, 2003: *The Politics of Heroin*

Jack Greene & Alessandro Massignani, 2009: *The Black Prince and The Sea Devils*

Paul Ginsborg, 1990: *A History of Contemporary Italy: 1943-80*

David Hannay, 2000: *Britain's Entry into the European Community*

James Holland, 2008: *Italy's Sorrow*

Stuart Smith, 2018: Otto Skorzeny: *The Devil's Disciple*

Altiero Spinelli & Ernesto Rossi, 1941: *For a Free and United Europe*

Douglas Valentine, 2019: *The Strength of the Pack*

Stefan Wolle, 2019: *The Ideal World of Dictatorship*

Markus Wolf, 1998: *Memoirs of a Spymaster*

Printed in Great Britain
by Amazon